Praise for the novels of Elizabeth Heiter

"A terrific, gripping, page-turning debut by a talented new voice in suspense!"
—*New York Times* bestselling author Allison Brennan on *Hunted*

"This is a really excellent thriller—fast-paced and exciting!"
—*New York Times* bestselling author Suzanne Brockmann on *Hunted*

"*Hunted* is a nonstop, thrilling read that will leave you breathless, and Evelyn Baine is a sharp and gutsy heroine you'll want to follow for many books to come."
—*New York Times* bestselling author Tess Gerritsen

"Want to read a top-rate thriller? *Vanished* had me turning page after page. Wow. When you talk about our most-promising new thriller writers, put Elizabeth Heiter on the list!"
—R. L. Stine

"Elizabeth Heiter does her research, and it shows in this superb FBI thriller. With a ripped-from-the-headlines plot and excellent characterization, *Seized* is a true winner. Don't miss it."
—*New York Times* bestselling author J.T. Ellison

"The riveting and virtually impossible to put down *Seized* establishes Heiter in the upper tier of thriller writers."
—*The Providence Journal*

"*Seized*...is a taut thriller that could be torn from tomorrow's newspaper headlines.... Heiter's latest is a thought-provoking thriller by a rising star in contemporary crime fiction."
—*The Lansing State Journal*

Also by Elizabeth Heiter

HUNTED
VANISHED
SEIZED

Look for Elizabeth Heiter's next novel
available soon from MIRA Books.

ELIZABETH HEITER

STALKED

MIRA

ISBN-13: 978-0-7783-1974-0

Recycling programs
for this product may
not exist in your area.

Stalked

For questions and comments about the quality of this book, please contact us at CustomerService@Harlequin.com.

www.MIRABooks.com

Printed in U.S.A.

This book is for Paula Eykelhof,
an incredible editor and an even more incredible person.
I am a far better writer for having worked with you.

Dear Reader,

Welcome to the world of The Profiler! If you've already read the first three books in the series, thank you for returning. In this book, a teenager disappears, leaving behind a note foretelling her own death, and FBI profiler Evelyn Baine must unravel the girl's secrets...before one of those secrets leads to her own death.

If this is your first visit to the series, Evelyn's story began in *Hunted*, in which she tracked down a deadly serial killer known as the Bakersville Burier and learned just how deadly it can be to get inside the head of a killer. In the sequel, *Vanished*, Evelyn tackled the case she'd waited most of her life to investigate—the disappearance of her best friend—when the Nursery Rhyme Killer resurfaced after eighteen years of silence. After *Vanished*, the short story "Avenged" (free through my website) takes Evelyn Baine and her new boyfriend, HRT agent Kyle McKenzie, on an island trip together...but their vacation is interrupted when bodies begin washing ashore. And in the third book of the series, *Seized*, Evelyn tackles what looks like a routine investigation—until it lands her on the wrong side of a hostage situation and in the middle of an emerging terrorist threat.

Stalked marks new challenges for Evelyn and former HRT agent Kyle McKenzie, who's now in a new role...with a partner you might remember from *Hunted*. I hope you enjoy following Evelyn and Kyle as they navigate their newly revealed relationship and two very different cases that may have a deadly connection.

After *Stalked*, I'll be back with three more books in my romantic suspense series, The Lawmen! You can keep up with me and all the books, as well as get extras and join my newsletter, on my website at www.elizabethheiter.com. You can also find me on Facebook at Facebook.com/elizabeth.heiter.author and Twitter as @ElizabethHeiter. I love to hear from readers.

As always, my heartfelt thanks for reading!

Elizabeth Heiter

FBI Terms and Acronyms

BAU—Behavioral Analysis Unit. The BAU is where FBI "profilers" (the official name is Criminal Investigative Analysts) work. BAU is part of CIRG (Critical Incident Response Group) and is located at Aquia. BAU agents provide behavioral-based support to the FBI, as well as other federal, state, local and international law enforcement agencies, including profiles of unknown subjects (UNSUBs).

CIRG—Critical Incident Response Group. CIRG provides rapid response for crisis situations around the country and integrates tactical, negotiations, behavioral analysis and crisis management resources. BAU (Behavioral Analysis Unit) and HRT (Hostage Rescue Team) are part of CIRG.

ERT—Evidence Response Team. ERT agents are specially trained FBI agents who collect evidence at crime scenes. Being on ERT is a secondary position, so these agents also work regular Special Agent duties.

HRT—Hostage Rescue Team. Under CIRG (the Critical Incident Response Group), HRT is part of the FBI's tactical response for crises. Unlike SWAT, their members work full-time as HRT agents and respond to incidents involving hostage rescue, barricaded subjects and high-risk arrests. Their motto is *Servare Vitas* (To Save Lives).

SA—Special Agent. Special Agents investigate violations of federal laws and assist state and local law enforcement. There are more than thirteen thousand Special Agents (as part of more than thirty-five thousand FBI employees).

SSA—Supervisory Special Agent. SSAs run squads. Each field office of the FBI has numerous squads, broken up by type of investigation—white collar, intelligence, civil rights, counterterror, violent crime, etc.

SWAT—Special Weapons and Tactics. All the FBI field offices have SWAT teams, and Special Agents who are SWAT members do so as an ancillary duty—in addition to work on a regular squad. SWAT agents handle high-risk tactical operations. Some police departments also have their own SWAT teams.

UNSUB—Unknown Subject. UNSUBs are targets of investigations where the person who committed the crime is not known by name.

WFO—Washington Field Office. The FBI has fifty-six field offices across the US and Puerto Rico, as well as approximately 380 Resident Agencies (smaller offices). The WFO and its connected Resident Agency have jurisdiction in Washington, DC, and northern Virginia.

STALKED

Prologue

"You've got to stop this."

Her husband's voice reached her slowly, as if from a great distance, even though she knew he was standing at the doorway to her daughter's room. Instead of turning, Linda Varner continued methodically pulling things out from underneath Haley's unmade bed.

A red-and-white cheerleading pom-pom. A bright pink sweatshirt Haley wore over everything. A stack of glossy magazines, dedicated to the things a teenage girl worried about, like how to know if a boy had a crush on her.

Linda suppressed a sob before it passed her lips. Still, she felt her body shudder and knew her husband had seen it.

"This won't bring her home," Pete said softly, in the kind of careful, muted tone usually reserved for funeral homes and grave sites.

Linda squeezed her eyes tight, bringing the sweatshirt up to her nose. She inhaled, hoping to breathe in some of the too-sweet vanilla scent her daughter loved to wear, but there was only a slight musty smell.

How could Haley's perfume have faded so quickly?

Linda sat there, the sweatshirt crumpled against her

nose, her body hunched protectively, until she heard her husband sigh and walk away. Only then did she open her eyes and look around Haley's room. Everything seemed so *untouched*. The police had been careful not to disturb anything, wearing their sterile gloves and their solemn expressions as they'd searched for some hint of where Haley could be.

Linda glanced back at the doorway. It was empty.

Pete would be back later. They did this routine every night. He'd give her another hour, then he'd coax her to bed. Some days she'd stand and follow him willingly; when she felt glued to the floor, he'd carry her. Then he'd hand her a glass of water and those pills her doctor had prescribed and she'd dutifully swallow two, let the blackness consume her.

Pete had stood by her. She knew it hadn't been easy—that *she* hadn't been easy to live with lately. But he could only share so much of the loss. He loved his stepdaughter, but he'd only been in her life for a few years.

"Where are you, Haley?" Linda whispered into the stillness.

Today marked exactly a month since her daughter had gone missing. Since Haley's boyfriend, Jordan, had dropped her off at school for cheerleading practice. Since her best friend, Marissa, had waved to her from the field on that unusually warm day, watched her walk into the school, presumably to change before joining Marissa at practice.

She'd never walked out again.

When she hadn't reappeared, Marissa had been sent to the locker room to get her. Only she hadn't been there. A search of the school hadn't turned her up. Now, thirty days later, they still hadn't found her.

How did a teenage girl go missing from *inside* her high school? No one could answer that for Linda. As time went by, the cops seemed to have fewer answers and more questions.

But Linda *knew*. She knew with some deep part of her she could only explain as mother's intuition that Haley was out there somewhere. And not buried in an unmarked grave, as she'd overheard two cops speculating when day after day passed with no more clues. Haley was still alive. Linda knew it. She was alive, and just waiting for someone to bring her home.

So every day, Linda forced herself out of bed, dressed in her most professional clothes and a heavy layer of makeup to hide the haggard signs of grief and went to the police station for an update. When she finished there, she talked to the news channels, begged them to do another feature or even a small mention of Haley, so she wouldn't be forgotten. So people would keep searching for her.

Then she moved on to social media, the places her daughter had visited and which she'd never had any interest in until now. Each day, she posted two new messages. One requesting any information about her daughter's whereabouts, which was shared thousands of times because of all the press. And one directly to her daughter, letting Haley know she'd never give up, never stop looking.

Only at night, after she'd shown the world how strong she could be, did she come here, and indulge her weakness. Her fears.

Why wasn't there more information? Why hadn't anyone spotted her and come forward? How could a seventeen-year-old girl just disappear?

Linda clutched the sweatshirt tighter, feeling the sobs

well up again. She fell against Haley's bed, trying to hold them in, and the mattress slid away from her, hard enough to move the box spring.

Linda slipped, too. Swearing, she sat up, then froze as the edge of a tiny black notebook caught her attention.

The book was jammed between the box spring and the bed frame. The cops must have missed it, because she'd seen them peer underneath Haley's mattress when they'd looked through the room, assessing her daughter's things so matter-of-factly.

Linda's pulse skyrocketed as she yanked it out. She didn't recognize the notebook, but when she opened the cover, there was no mistaking her daughter's girlie handwriting. And the words...

She dropped the notebook, practically flung it away from her in her desire to get rid of it, to un-see it. She didn't realize she'd started screaming until her husband ran into the room and wrapped his arms around her.

"What? What is it?" he kept asking, but all she could do was sob and point a shaking hand at the notebook, lying open to the first page, and Haley's distinctive scrawl.

If you're reading this, I'm already dead.

1

Kyle McKenzie leaned across the table in the tiny Italian restaurant with the dim, romantic lighting, and said in a too-calm voice, "I start my new job at the Washington Field Office tomorrow."

Evelyn Baine felt the same surge of regret she always felt when this topic came up. "I'm glad they had a spot open up for you there."

They both worked for the FBI, her as a profiler in the Behavioral Analysis Unit, and Kyle, up until a month ago, as an operator for the Hostage Rescue Team. He'd been off work since taking a bullet on a mission. She'd known how risky the mission was and couldn't help but think she hadn't pushed hard enough to stop HRT from going in. Now here they were. Kyle pretending he was okay with leaving the job he'd loved. And her pretending she didn't feel guilty as hell over it.

He shrugged his good shoulder, the one that hadn't been torn up by a bullet. "Yeah. I'm surprised I got it, but I wanted to stay close. To you, of course, and…"

He trailed off, but she knew the rest, anyway. He wanted to be close to his old team. The FBI's Washington Field Office was only a forty-five minute drive—with a siren—from Quantico, where HRT was located.

Evelyn worked in Aquia, the town right beside Quantico, herself. The entire time she'd been at the BAU, she'd gotten used to Kyle making the eight and a half-mile drive to see her at her office. He'd pretended he wasn't coming to see her. But everyone around him had seen through it. Eventually, so had she, and she'd decided to act on it. Now, they'd been dating for six months, and even though she saw him more often, she'd missed seeing him at work, missed their old office banter, over the past month.

He missed the team. She knew it, even if he wasn't saying it out loud. As an HRT agent, he got sent out on critical missions—everything from stopping a prison riot to rescuing hostages from inside a survivalist compound to assisting with overseas rescues in war zones. The rest of the time was spent training for those missions. It was completely different from being a regular Special Agent.

She wasn't sure if he'd be able to return to that life. She couldn't imagine doing it herself, even though she'd worked in a Violent Crimes Major Offenders squad for six years before coming over to the BAU.

She stared across the candlelit table at him now, seeing the tension he was trying to hide. Maybe he could go back to HRT someday. But more likely, his career was going to head in a different direction.

She fiddled with her napkin, reflexively looking at the door of the near-empty restaurant as it opened. Until very recently, she and Kyle had hidden their relationship. It felt strange to be out in public, in Virginia, where someone from the FBI might see them.

Ironically, they'd only been able to officially tell the FBI because he no longer worked in the Critical Incident Response Group, which included both the BAU and HRT. He'd wanted to announce it from the start. She'd been sure that would mean reassignment for one of them. And she didn't have quite two years in at the BAU—where she hoped to stay until mandatory retirement, which was still twenty-seven years away.

She gave him an embarrassed smile when she realized it was just another patron that had drawn her attention to the door. Some habits were hard to break. "This feels weird."

He smiled back at her, making crinkles fan out from his ocean-blue eyes, and the slightest hint of dimples dent his cheeks. "Maybe you enjoy your secrets a little too much."

Maybe he was right. She'd always been a private person, and in an office full of profilers, keeping anything to yourself wasn't easy. It was ingrained in them the same way it was in her: assess everyone you meet, try to see through the mask to what was underneath. Dig up those secrets.

She tried to relax, unbuttoning the loose-fitting suit jacket she'd worn straight from the office. It hid the SIG Sauer she always kept strapped to her hip, but didn't exactly scream "date clothes."

When the restaurant door squeaked open again, and she instantly looked over, Kyle twined his fingers through hers across the table, and the light contact brought her attention back to him.

"What do you say we get dinner to go?"

His big, calloused hand seemed even paler wrapped around her tiny, darker one. So different, just like their personalities—but somehow they worked.

She nodded, but before she could add, "Let's go," her phone buzzed from her pocket.

She pulled it out, but the instant she saw Dan Moore's

name pop up, she regretted grabbing it. Her boss calling her at nine at night meant a new case had come in, one that couldn't wait.

Six months ago, she'd been his go-to agent for urgent cases, because she didn't mind the late-night calls. Hell, she lived for the job.

But right now? With Kyle McKenzie's deep blue eyes staring back at her? "This better be good," she muttered before answering, "Dan? What's up?"

"Remember the case file that made the rounds in the office last month?" Dan replied without preamble. "The missing teenager?"

"Right," she said slowly. She'd been through fifty cases since then, but that one stuck out.

A seventeen-year-old girl last seen walking into her high school had gone missing, no signs of foul play. The BAU had passed the police file around the room, but there hadn't been enough to go on to give a solid profile, and they hadn't been able to spare a profiler for more in-depth involvement.

"Did they find her?" Evelyn asked.

"Would I be calling you if they had?" Dan snapped, then said, "Sorry. Look, we told the police department this was probably a stranger abduction since no body had turned up, and the noncustodial parent hadn't run. But now they have a note, suggesting the kidnapper was someone in the girl's life, after all."

"Okay," Evelyn said slowly as Kyle unthreaded his hand from hers and walked over to the waiter. Undoubtedly he was ordering food to go, knowing their evening had just ended.

"So, if it's someone in her life, shouldn't—"

"Yeah, normally that would make it more of a straightforward police matter. But we can spare a profiler for a week or so, and the note was disturbing. The girl left it herself. She predicted her own death."

Evelyn let the words sink in. "They have a body?"

"No. Still no sign of the girl. But the mom is hysterical, and she's gotten close with the local news stations. The police need help getting in front of this."

"If she predicted her death, there's more to the case than it seemed."

"You got it," Dan agreed. "Detective Sophia Lopez is expecting you." He hung up, as details of Haley Cooke's missing-persons case came back to Evelyn.

"Nice talking to you, too," Evelyn muttered. Her boss was usually terse—at least with her—but lately he'd been abrupt with everyone. She tucked her phone into her jacket as Kyle returned with to-go bags of food.

"Duty calls?" Kyle guessed, glancing around the still-empty restaurant. "I guess our big debut night on the town will have to wait."

She nodded ruefully. Apparently they weren't the only ones who had been hiding something from the people around them.

So had Haley Cooke, the seventeen-year-old girl whose background had revealed a popular, straight-A student whose most dangerous pastime seemed to be standing on top of a cheerleading pyramid.

What had she gotten involved in that she thought would get her killed?

The Neville, Virginia, police station looked interchangeable with hundreds of other stations Evelyn had been to in her BAU tenure. But the detective standing in front of her in figure-hugging blue jeans and an elbow-length red blazer better suited to an afternoon luncheon than hiding the Glock at her hip definitely didn't resemble the average police officer.

"Detective Sophia Lopez." The woman held out her hand, complete with deep red polish, and stared expectantly at Evelyn. She was already tall—topping Evelyn's petite five-foot-two by at least eight inches—but a pair of high-heeled boots gave her an extra boost. Her long, dark hair dangled in a loose ponytail that seemed impractical for crime scenes, and her bright red lipstick looked out of place in a police station. But her intense stare was 100 percent cop.

"Special Agent Evelyn Baine," she replied, shaking firmly.

To the mostly male officers around them, they probably seemed to have a lot in common. Two women in law enforcement—one biracial and the other Latina—giving the typical first-impression handshake. Hard, so the other person would know they weren't to be messed with. Matched with solid eye contact, projecting seriousness.

But if Sophia's clothes were similar to a clerk at a trendy boutique, Evelyn dressed more like the male officers, in a baggy, solid-black pantsuit. Her heels were always under two inches; enough to give her a little extra height, but not so high she couldn't run in them. While Sophia seemed to want to stand out, Evelyn liked to blend in—hide in the background where she could watch and analyze everyone.

She studied the detective in charge of the Haley Cooke case, taking in the incongruities, trying to decipher her from just a greeting.

She didn't just profile the predators, although that was in her official job description. To do it well, she also had to figure out the personalities of the other law enforcement officials on the case. Figuring them out fast made for an easier working relationship, usually a better reception to her profiles. Especially since the head detective wasn't always the one requesting her presence. Often, that pressure came from above, such as a police chief or a mayor, and usually because of media attention.

As Evelyn tried to work an instant profile, Sophia's steady stare broke, a wide grin stretching across her face and making all of her uneven features seem to come together. "All right. That's enough posturing. We're both hard-asses and we both know it. Come on. I'll show you what we've got on the Haley Cooke case."

She spun, striding down the hallway at a pace that had Evelyn jogging to keep up.

At the end of the hallway, Sophia shoved open a door and ushered Evelyn into a room the size of a janitor's closet. It smelled like a janitor's closet, too, as though it had been used to store cleaning products until very recently. The scent of bleach made Evelyn's eyes water, and she blinked it away before taking in the pictures and timelines tacked to every available wall space.

Sophia pushed back a pair of chairs and a small folding table that took up most of the room. "I know. It's a pathetic amount of space to devote to the investigation of a missing teenager. But it's what I've got. So I work with it."

Evelyn nodded, not saying this was more space than she'd expected, given that the case was a month old and the leads were nonexistent. Then again, Neville, Virginia—home to approximately ten thousand people in the summers and thirty thousand when the local university was in session—probably didn't see very many missing-persons cases.

The BAU, on the other hand, was inundated with countless missing-persons investigations. Rarely did Evelyn consult on a case with only one victim. But every so often, one would come along where the investigation was getting nowhere, and if the perpetrator was a stranger, a profiler could change everything. A regular investigation would struggle to find a kidnapper who had no connection to the victim's life, but a profiler could do it.

"You want me to put that in our fridge?" Sophia asked.

Evelyn glanced down at the Styrofoam take-out container still clutched in her hand, dinner she hadn't had a chance to eat. "Thanks," she said, handing it over as her stomach growled.

After Sophia left the room, Evelyn spun in a slow circle, studying the images thumbtacked right into the drywall. At the center of most of them was Haley Cooke. Seventeen years old, a junior at Neville High School. The media loved to refer to her as "all-American."

Blonde, blue-eyed, with a smile on her face in every picture Evelyn had seen. People probably couldn't help returning that smile.

Evelyn had a sudden flashback to another blond-haired girl, one who'd never had the chance to grow up. Cassie, her best friend, whose disappearance had sent Evelyn into profiling. Was this how she might have looked if she'd made it to seventeen?

Evelyn pushed the bittersweet thought aside and focused on Haley. Her routines, her relationships, her personality—they would all contribute to Evelyn's victim profile. That would help her figure out who could have grabbed her.

"Loved by everyone" was another thing the media

constantly repeated about Haley. Whether it was because her mother had cozied up to all the local news stations or because the complete lack of clues had captivated the country's interest, Haley's face had become very well-known.

Which made it even more unusual that no one had seen her since she'd walked into that high school a month ago. Unless she'd never come out because she'd been killed there. But if that was true, surely they'd have found a body by now.

The case was bizarre. Although the BAU specialized in bizarre, this one had given Evelyn a bad feeling from the moment she'd seen the case file. A beautiful young teenage girl goes missing without a trace. The ending wasn't usually positive.

From the limited information in the case file a month ago, there'd been no way to give a solid profile, but her gut had screamed "stranger abduction." Since Haley had predicted her own death, though, it seemed her gut had been wrong.

"Here," Sophia said, and Evelyn turned to find the detective holding out a flimsy cup. The smell of overcooked coffee filled the small room.

Instead of telling Sophia she didn't drink coffee, Evelyn smiled her thanks and took the scalding-hot cup. "Why don't you give me the highlights? And let's look at the note the mother found. Can we confirm Haley wrote it?"

"Haley's mom says it's her daughter's handwriting." Sophia perched on top of the folding table, making it creak loudly underneath her. "Most of what we know you've probably already seen on the news. It's as though someone plucked her out of thin air. Poof. Gone. Forensics is giving us nothing at the scene."

"Who else was around?"

"Her boyfriend drove away after he dropped her off, and the cheerleaders on the field saw him leave. Otherwise, there was a coach on the field, and some students in the library with a teacher. None of them saw her inside, and no one saw her leave the school, but when her friends went inside, they couldn't find her."

"What about other exits?"

"Yeah, there are others, but the way the school is situated, it's not likely she could have left without being seen. You've basically got the front entrance—where Haley was dropped off—near the main road. On the right side, you've got the field where the cheerleaders were practicing. They can see the front entrance from there. Then, on the left, you've got another open field the school uses for soccer and other sports. That one butts up against a neighborhood. Some wooded area in between, but not much. Then the back—faculty parking, service entrance. Probably the least visible, but that leads out to a side street. No one saw Haley leave that way, either, though they might not have. Still, it happened fast for an abduction."

When Sophia took a breath, Evelyn cut in. "How far were the locker rooms where she was supposed to be from the back entrance?"

"Not close. Someone would have had to know exactly where she was, gone in and grabbed her and then subdued her fast, without making noise. The library *is* fairly close to the locker rooms, at least close enough that they surely would have heard if Haley screamed. Then…this person would have needed to carry Haley out without anyone seeing. Doable? Maybe. But unlikely."

"Either someone was prepared to take that kind of

risk, or Haley went willingly, at least at first," Evelyn said. "What do you make of the note?"

"Ah, the note." Sophia swiveled on the table and pulled the evidence list out of the box. "One sentence."

Evelyn took the list and looked at the description for the last item, the notebook. The matter-of-fact words sent pinpricks down her spine. "'If you're reading this, I'm already dead.'"

"Yeah. Ominous."

"And there was nothing else in the notebook? No other information?"

"None. We even checked for indentations in case she'd written more and then torn the pages out, but there's no indication of that."

"Did you run the note for prints?"

"Yep. We found Haley's prints. And Linda's—Haley's mom. That's it."

"And the mom just found it today?"

"Yes. Between the box spring and the bed frame."

"So, you guys missed it when you checked the room?"

Sophia frowned.

"What I'm asking," Evelyn clarified, "is could it have been put there *after* Haley went missing? Could it have been planted?" For a case this high profile, a month was a long time for such a key piece of evidence to go unnoticed.

"I don't know. We checked under the mattress. Could we have missed it? Yes. I mean, it was jammed in an odd location. And we were there to learn more about Haley. We were looking for any hints of what could have happened, get a sense of her personality, her secrets. We weren't taking everything apart—we were trying to be sensitive to the family. Could the note have been put there after we searched the room? That's also possible. But if someone planted the note, then why?"

"Attention," Evelyn suggested. She'd seen it before, sometimes a misguided attempt to get more manpower on a case, and sometimes just to get the victim's family back in the limelight. "The girl's mom has been on the news—"

"Exactly," Sophia agreed. "Linda Varner doesn't need a stunt to get more attention for her daughter's case. The woman quit her job. She does nothing but try to get resources for this. But it's all about finding Haley. She wouldn't plant evidence that might lead us in the wrong direction."

"You sure?"

"You're the profiler," Sophia said. "But speaking as a cop—and a mother myself? Linda Varner appears to be the devastated mother of a missing child. Do they sometimes do things they shouldn't, trying to make sense of what they're going through? Sure. But I don't think that's what's happening here. Linda knows I'm working the case. I talk to her every day."

"Every day?" Evelyn interrupted.

"Yep. Every single day, she shows up here, regardless of how many times I tell her I'll call if I have anything new. We might as well have a standing appointment. And anyway, Linda confirmed the note was written in the daughter's handwriting."

"The mom—"

"It's not Linda's writing," Sophia broke in. "Could she have gotten someone else to write it? I guess so, but then we're looking at a conspiracy."

Evelyn nodded. Conspiracies were relatively rare. The simplest explanations were most often the real ones.

"So, even if we think someone else put it there, Haley still wrote it."

"Which leaves us at the same place."

"Right." Sophia's shoulders slumped, and Evelyn suddenly saw the dark circles underneath the detective's heavy-handed concealer.

The dark circles weren't all from this case, either, and Evelyn realized Sophia was older than she'd initially thought—probably nearing forty.

"She was into something she shouldn't have been," Sophia said, ticking off possibilities on her fingers. "Or she knew something she shouldn't have known, saw something she shouldn't have seen. Or she was a victim who'd decided to finally tell, and someone wanted to shut her up." Sophia shrugged. "Whatever it is…"

"She almost certainly knew who grabbed her," Evelyn finished.

"And if Haley's note is right," Sophia said softly, "that person has already killed her."

2

Early the next morning, the door to the broom-closet-cum-office burst open, and Evelyn looked up from the Haley Cooke case file. She'd left late last night and returned early enough that she might as well have just slept at the station. She'd barely had time to swing by the BAU office first, squeezing in a quick chat with Kyle on her hands-free while she drove to the station and he headed to his physical therapy appointment.

Standing in the doorway now was Quincy Palmer, the grizzled, veteran detective Sophia had introduced her to last night. He made up for having no hair on the top of his head with a thick salt-and-pepper beard, wore his detective's shield dangling around his neck even inside the police station and didn't seem capable of cracking a smile. She'd also learned he had poor boundaries when it came to other people's food in the police fridge. Her 2:00 a.m. dinner had been a candy bar from the vending machine after he'd eaten her pasta.

"You're not going to be happy about this," Quincy announced.

"What?" Sophia asked, barely looking up from the report she was reading.

"Morning news." He turned and headed back the way he'd come, offering no more information.

"Shit." Sophia dropped the report on the table and followed.

Evelyn trailed behind them, not even trying to keep up. They turned into the break room—it smelled of gunpowder and body odor—on the other side of the station. There were a handful of patrol cops inside, drinking coffee and chatting before their early morning shift started. A small TV was on in the corner, the sound low.

Quincy turned it up loud enough that the other cops scowled at him and left the room. Sophia and Quincy ignored them. Evelyn gave them rueful nods and stepped out of the way.

There, standing in front of a big white colonial in well-tailored dress pants and a bright blue sweater, was a middle-aged woman with dark blond hair and sad blue eyes. Microphones were pointed at her from all directions, as though she'd called a news conference.

"Linda Varner," Sophia said unnecessarily. Haley's name had been a staple on the morning news for a month, but it had been a while since Evelyn had seen her mom in front of a camera.

"Where's the husband?" Evelyn wondered. The first few days after Haley's disappearance, she'd gotten used to seeing Linda Varner speaking into the microphones, with Pete Varner standing slightly behind her, silently holding her hand. Always playing the part of the dutiful husband, and yet Evelyn had gotten the feeling it was for show. "What's going on? Do they still camp out at her house or did she call them?"

Sophia shook her head, but it seemed to be at the TV rather than any response to Evelyn's question. "Don't do it, Linda."

"My daughter left behind a note," Linda said, her voice strong and clear.

"Damn it," Sophia snapped. "What the hell is she thinking?"

"She must have called the press," Evelyn said softly. What a disaster.

"What did the note say?" one reporter asked.

"When did you get it?" another called.

"I found the note last night," Haley's mother said in the same steady, even voice, almost as if she was reading from a script. "It said…" Her voice suddenly broke, and her chin dropped to her chest before she tipped her head back, looking determined. "It said she feared for her life."

"Well, not exactly," Sophia noted. "I can't believe she's doing this. She knows better."

"It said she knew someone was coming after her." Suddenly, Linda was staring directly, unnervingly, into the camera. The shot zoomed in close on her face. "My daughter suspected someone was stalking her. That person grabbed her. But I know she's still out there. I know she wants to come home. So, whoever you are, know that we won't stop looking. We're going to find my daughter, and unless you let her go, that means we'll find you, too."

The camera was so close that when she stopped speaking, Evelyn could see Linda swallow, could see the shallowness of her breathing despite her calm demeanor. From a distance, she looked put together. Up close, the cracks were showing.

When Linda didn't say any more, the reporters started yelling over one another with questions.

"That's all I have to say." Linda stepped back, opened the door and disappeared into her house.

Sophia lifted the remote and stabbed at a button. The TV went dark. "Unbelievable."

"Have you talked to her about the press and—"

"Hell, yes," Sophia said as Evelyn glanced at Quincy, who stood silently in the center of the room, arms crossed over his barrel chest, watching them.

She wondered about his role. In the short time she'd been involved, he seemed to show up a lot, and stick around for the details. "Are you involved in the investigation?"

He grunted at her. "Nope. This is a small station. Sophia and I are the only experienced detectives. Sophia's handling this case close to full-time, and she's a single mom with two kids at home."

"That's irrelevant," Sophia snapped. "I'm not the only cop with kids."

"Yeah, well, you're the only detective here working all night long, while a babysitter watches your kids. Believe me, that can't lead to anything good. When's the last time your good-for-nothing ex…" He trailed off as Sophia's lips tightened and she jammed her hands on her hips. "Anyway, it means I'm getting called in on nearly everything else. Just consider me an interested party."

"We had a lot of department turnover last year," Sophia told her, dropping her arms to her sides.

She still looked annoyed with Quincy, but Evelyn got the impression they were friends, and she seemed to shake it off fast.

"We've got some new detectives, but they're not fully up to speed yet," Sophia added.

From the loaded gaze Quincy was sending Sophia, Evelyn had a feeling there was a story there, but instead of asking, she said, "Should we talk to Haley's mom again? At this point, the damage may already be done, but—"

"I'll handle it," Sophia cut her off. "Fact is, I can't stop Linda from talking to the press. She's doing anything she can to keep Haley's story in the news. And honestly, if I were her, I'd probably be doing the same thing. Maybe it will even help. If she's still alive, someone must have seen her."

"Sure, but put too much pressure on her kidnapper and if she's alive—"

"I know." Sophia grimaced. "She won't be for long. So, let's get down to it. You've looked through the files. What do you think? *Is* she still alive?"

"I need to get a closer look at all the players before I can answer that," Evelyn hedged, because although she was ready to give Sophia a *victim* profile, she had too little to go on to give a helpful *perpetrator* profile. "But why would Linda think the note meant her daughter had a stalker? Did anything turn up about a stalker?"

Sophia sighed, pouring herself a cup of coffee from the break room carafe as she shook her head. "No. But Linda's convinced Haley was grabbed by a stranger. She's thought that since the beginning. She's talked herself into thinking a stalker set his sights on Haley the week before Haley went missing, when Linda was away at a work conference. She can't bring herself to believe it's someone she knows."

"But it makes no sense for Haley to leave some cryptic note if she thought a stranger was stalking her. She'd tell someone."

"Agreed," Sophia said.

"Why would she leave the note at all?" Quincy spoke up. "If it was a stranger, why not tell someone she was scared right away? And if it *wasn't* a stranger, and she really feared for her life—if she really believed that if anyone ever found the note, it would be too late for her—then why not write down his name? Or at least give us some details so we can figure it out. I mean, by then, if she's right, that person can't hurt her anymore."

"That's a damn good point, Quincy," Sophia said, and looked at Evelyn. "You have a take on that? You think the whole thing could be some kind of hoax, could be planted?"

"I really doubt it," Evelyn said. "But you're right. It's an odd note. We should consider the possibility that Haley had an entirely different intent, that she didn't name anyone because there was no one to name."

"Meaning?" Quincy asked.

"Meaning, maybe she ran away, and she left the note behind to send everyone in the wrong direction."

"That's what Haley's dad is claiming."

"Linda's husband?" Evelyn asked, surprised.

"No. Haley's biological dad. Bill Cooke. He went to the press, too, not long after Haley went missing. It didn't get as much airtime because he doesn't have Linda Varner's presence or persistence and he isn't the custodial parent. But he claimed Haley ran away from home because of abuse."

Evelyn gaped at Sophia. "I didn't see anything about that in the case file. Did you investigate that possibility?"

Sophia dumped her coffee down the sink, muttering under her breath, then said, louder, "Of course. And it is in the file. You probably haven't gotten to Bill Cooke's interview yet. But I haven't found anything to substantiate his claim. If anything, I'm seeing signs *Bill* was abusive and that's why the parents divorced."

"How long ago?"

"The divorce? About three years. Right before Haley started high school."

"Okay. What about the stepfather? Any possibility of abuse there?"

"Well, technically, Bill was blaming Pete all along," Sophia said. "But we looked into Linda, too. And we didn't find anything at all. Although quite frankly, I'm not so impressed with Linda's husband. He's—" Sophia seemed to be searching for a word, then finally settled on "—cagey. I'm not seeing evidence of abuse. Doesn't mean there isn't any, as I'm sure you know. But as far as Bill's claims go, they seem to be intended to hurt Linda more than help Haley."

Evelyn got ready to ask more, but Sophia preempted her. "Look, the divorce was ugly. Really ugly. There was a custody battle and Bill lost big-time. Haley was old enough to have a say, and she wanted nothing to do with him. Haley never went as far as to say there was abuse, at least not in the court documents I dug up, but Linda got primary custody. Bill got a few weekends a year. From what I can tell, his time was usually cut short."

"By who?" Evelyn pressed.

"According to Linda, that was Haley's choice. But given the animosity there…" She shrugged.

"So, this could be a custody issue," Evelyn suggested. "Maybe *Bill* grabbed Haley, and he's claiming abuse by the mother's new husband to deflect attention."

"It's a possibility," Sophia said. "But if he grabbed her, where is she? We've interviewed Bill Cooke, several times. He lives in a little brownstone in DC. He won't let us in, but he's got almost no yard. The houses there are close together. I've talked to his neighbors, and they can tell me what he watches on TV at night. It would be pretty hard to hide a seventeen-year-old in there, especially one who's been on the news as much as Haley, and particularly if she didn't want to be there. If he took her, wouldn't he have gone into hiding?"

"Maybe he's waiting for the search to die down before he moves her," Evelyn said.

"That might work with a four-year-old," Quincy spoke up.

His deep voice startled Evelyn. Even though he'd planted his large frame in the middle of the room, he'd been so quiet she'd nearly forgotten he was there.

"But hiding a seventeen-year-old is a little trickier," he continued. "I agree—he'd have a hard time keeping her there if she didn't want to stay."

"I know it's a long shot," Evelyn said. "But we need to look into it, especially in a case where there was a hostile dispute over custody. And with Haley turning eighteen in less than a year, maybe Bill Cooke figured this was his last chance, especially if Haley was threatening to cut him out of her life entirely."

Sophia nodded slowly. "Yeah, that's true. I don't really like Bill Cooke for this, but honestly, I don't really *like* Bill Cooke at all. I wouldn't be surprised that if we do discover there was any abuse happening, he's at the center of it."

"Okay," Evelyn said. "Let me finish reading through the case files. Because all I can give you now is about Haley."

"A victim profile?" Sophia asked. "Tell me."

"Well, the key thing here is that Haley is very high risk for whoever took her. And the location and timing was high risk, too. He—or she—had to be certain he could pull it off."

Sophia nodded. "Someone close to her."

"Someone Haley trusted," Evelyn said. "Because

either she walked out of that school with her abductor, or she let him get close enough to subdue her without screaming."

"Maybe she expected the person," Quincy suggested. "Or there was more than one of them and they overpowered her."

"Both are possible," Evelyn agreed, "but remember, no one heard her yell for help, or any kind of struggle. So as soon as I finish reading this case file, I want to meet all the people in Haley's life. Anyone who could have grabbed her, or might have insight into why she thought her life was in danger."

"Bill Cooke?"

The man scowling at her from behind a screen door might have had a strong resemblance to his daughter at one time. Blond hair, now receding back to the middle of his head, faded blue eyes, heavy lines alongside his mouth that suggested once he'd had reason to smile a lot. Now, from the top of his balding head to the bottom of his muddied boots, everything about him screamed "angry."

"Yeah." Bill glanced from Evelyn to Sophia as they stood cramped together on the small stoop in front of his house. "What now? You haven't found her, have you?"

"Don't you want us to?" Evelyn asked, surprised by the tone of the question.

Bill stepped back, held the door open. "Maybe she's better off if you don't. I'm telling you, Haley ran away. Linda's looking for attention, but my daughter was just trying to escape."

"You think she ran away?" Evelyn prompted as she slid sideways past Bill and stepped through the doorway, taking in the tidy entryway tracked through with fresh mud.

They didn't have any snow, but the ground was still near frozen. Where had Bill Cooke gone to get mud all over his boots?

"Yeah, and I've told that to Detective Lopez here a hundred times. Who are you? New to the police force? Don't you people share your notes? No wonder you can't find Haley."

Ignoring the dig, Evelyn held out a hand as Bill stepped farther back. Sophia joined them inside, closing the heavier door behind them and shutting out the fierce wind. It may have been unusually warm over the past month, but it was still January.

"Special Agent Evelyn Baine. I'm consulting from the FBI on your daughter's case."

Instead of shaking her hand, Bill wrapped two work-roughened hands around hers and squeezed; she tried to remember what he did for a living.

"I appreciate the thought, Agent Baine. But my daughter is fine."

"Have you heard from her?" Sophia asked, stepping forward slowly, and making Bill drop Evelyn's hand and move back. Instinct when someone stepped into your personal space, and a smart way for Sophia to get farther into the house.

She'd told Evelyn that he'd never invited her inside before, instead always insisting on meeting at the police station. Evelyn had wanted to do this interview spontaneously, hoping it would change things, but she was still surprised he'd invited them in so easily. If he'd ever had Haley hidden here, it suggested he didn't now.

"No, I haven't heard from my daughter. And I doubt I will. At least not until she's eighteen and she can fi-

nally be free of her mother and Linda's new husband."
He spat out "husband" as if it was a dirty word.

Sophia stepped forward again, but this time, Bill
didn't move, just crossed his arms and stared back at
her. The aggression in his eyes was barely concealed
by the exasperation.

"Why are you so convinced she ran away?"

"We've been through this. Haley hated living in that
house. Linda's new husband is a real jerk. He resents
having to deal with a teenager, treated Haley like crap."

"How so?" Evelyn asked, hoping he'd be more willing to go through the details again if she was the one
asking, instead of Sophia.

He studied her, and she could see him cataloging the
details: long, dark hair, carefully knotted into a bun;
light green eyes from her mother that always stood
out against light brown skin, which had come from
her father; prim black suit, cut too large to conceal her
weapon, that made her look even smaller than she already was.

She suspected he'd be like a lot of suspects and trans-
late "small" into "not a threat." If he was responsible
for Haley's disappearance, though, she vowed to make
him regret it.

"Haley never told me any specifics. But she made
all these offhand remarks about Pete Varner that made
me think…" He shuffled his feet, drawing Evelyn's attention back to the mud on his boots, an odd contrast
to the clean, tidy house.

At least what she could see of the house. The three of
them were jammed into the entryway, just far enough
back that Evelyn could peer into a small living room.
Everything looked dust and knickknack free, but nothing had much personality. Just a dark, matched set of

furniture and a big-screen TV, probably purchased after the divorce.

She wondered how much of Bill's animosity had justification, and how much was just resentment toward his family for moving on. Then again, all she knew about Linda's new husband, Pete Varner, was what was in the background checks Sophia had completed. Nothing had stood out, other than his job installing vending machines. A job that took him to a lot of high schools, including Haley's. Maybe he'd seen the daughter before he'd married the mother.

"You think there was sexual abuse?" Evelyn cut straight to the point, watching Bill carefully.

His head jerked backward at the question, and he shook his head. "No, not… No. I don't think so."

"So what kind of abuse? Does Pete hit her?" Evelyn pressed.

"I—I don't know. Maybe." Bill fidgeted. "What I know is she was unhappy. What I know is she hated it there. She ran away." He yanked his wrist up, stared at his watch, then said, "I've got to be somewhere soon. Call next time and I'll come to the station."

"This could help us locate Haley," Evelyn started.

"You're not asking me anything I haven't already told Detective Lopez," Bill responded. "And here's the thing—I *know* Haley ran away. I'm not going to help you bring her back to her crazy mother and that asshole she married."

"What if she didn't run away?" Evelyn pushed, even as Bill got in her personal space, practically herding her out the door. "What if you're wrong?"

She didn't move, just tilted her head back so she could look up at Bill, who had almost a foot on her. Sophia stayed right beside her.

"I'm sure—"

"You haven't heard from her," Evelyn reminded him. "Which means there's a chance someone took her. Even if there's only a small possibility she's in trouble, don't you want to make sure she's okay?"

Something shifted in Bill's eyes, but Evelyn couldn't be certain what she'd seen before he blinked and it was gone.

"That didn't happen," Bill insisted, and this time, he actually put his hand on her arm, pushing her backward. "I want you to leave."

Evelyn pulled free of his grasp, and planted her feet farther apart. "Okay." She peeled off a card and handed it to him. "But the FBI doesn't usually waste their time chasing runaways. Call me if you think of anything that might help."

She turned and headed for the door, but not before she saw him frown down at her card.

Once they were back in Sophia's police car, Evelyn asked, "What does Bill Cooke do for a living?"

"He's a construction foreman. Why?"

Evelyn nodded. That might explain the mud on his boots, although she still found it odd that he'd track mud through his ultraclean house to answer the door for them. Especially since he hadn't wanted them there. But maybe he hadn't looked through the peephole before he'd opened the door. Or he'd been so anxious to deal with them and then get rid of them he wasn't worried about the mud. "Just curious."

Sophia jabbed her keys into the ignition, but didn't start it up. "Okay, I have a question, too. What do you think? Is Bill Cooke lying to us? Did he take Haley?"

Evelyn frowned at the house as they sat in the driveway. She could see the curtain move at the front of the house, as though Bill was watching them. "He's lying. I'm not sure what about—maybe the abuse claims. But he seemed genuinely surprised—and worried—when I mentioned sexual abuse. So, it's hard to say. I don't think he would have let us in the house if he had Haley in there. But does he know where she is?"

She sighed, wishing there was an easy answer. "Maybe. He was quick to insist he hadn't heard from her, but when I asked if he was positive she was okay, he looked like he *wasn't* sure. Still, it is odd he's not more worried about her condition or where she might be, who she could have run off with. That could be a sign he's not concerned because he knows the answer. His behavior was a little contradictory."

Sophia tapped her hands on the wheel in a frustrated *thump-thump-thump*, and then started up the engine. "What do we need to do so you can point us in a solid direction? I'm running in circles with this case. And if Haley's out there somewhere, I want to bring her home."

As she pulled out of the driveway and Evelyn watched the curtain flutter back into place in Bill's front window, Sophia added, "And if Bill's abuse claims are legit, I want to deal with that, too."

"Let's talk to Linda and Pete, then," Evelyn said. "Profiling isn't a Magic 8 Ball. I can't just talk to someone for ten minutes and tell you if he did it. But once I get a better handle on all the players, I should be able to help you narrow your search."

Sophia's phone rang, cutting off any reply she'd been about to make. She pressed the phone to her ear as she turned onto the street. "Lopez."

There was a pause, and although Evelyn couldn't hear whatever was being said on the other end of the call, Sophia's suddenly furious expression told her it was bad news.

"You've got to be kidding me," Sophia said into the phone, then gave a heavy sigh and said, "Yeah, I'll deal with it."

She ended the call and tossed her phone onto the console, muttering, "Un-fucking-believable."

"What is it?"

"You wanted to meet Haley's mom?" Sophia gunned the engine. "Let's do that now. I've got some things I want to say to her myself."

"What was the call about?" Evelyn asked, bracing her elbow against the door as Sophia took the turns out of Bill Cooke's neighborhood too fast.

"As if that TV interview wasn't enough, someone just posted a picture of Haley's note online."

"What?" Evelyn gaped at her.

"You heard me," Sophia said. "Now the whole world knows that Haley predicted someone was going to kill her. Which means all the wackos who weren't *already* calling our tip line claiming to have seen her are going to start now, claiming to have killed her."

"And it tells everyone with an internet connection that the person who grabbed Haley Cooke is probably someone she knows," Evelyn said.

"Yep," Sophia agreed. "Which means whoever did it knows we could be on to him. That person could be destroying evidence as we speak. And if Haley was wrong, and someone had been keeping her alive before…"

"He might worry we're going to start focusing on people Haley knows, and that could make him act."

"Yeah. If Haley didn't predict her own death before, whoever leaked that note might have just caused it."

3

"He's lying." Linda Varner stood in the doorway of her house, arms crossed over her chest. Her husband stood behind her, peering over her shoulder.

While Linda was an odd mixture of pissed off and frayed nerves, Pete Varner just glared suspiciously. Evelyn pegged Linda as being in her midfifties, but Pete had to be a decade younger. He had a weight lifter's build, and his long, thin face seemed mismatched to his body. He stuck close to Linda, as though he was trying to protect her.

Still, he seemed oddly at ease. After less than thirty seconds in Linda's presence, Evelyn felt the woman's twitchy nerves transferring to her, but Pete was calm.

Sophia visibly tensed and Evelyn could tell she was working hard to stay composed. "Who's lying?"

"My ex-husband," Linda said. "He called here, made a big fuss about you visiting him. He obviously thought we sent you, which—"

"We know what that bastard said," Pete Varner interrupted his wife.

"He's been claiming from the start that Haley ran away from home." Linda opened the door wide for them. "If you'd believed his lies about Haley running away and he'd prevented the police from investigating, I would have killed him."

"I'm not sure you want to say that to a police detective," Sophia muttered, stepping inside and adding, "This is FBI profiler Evelyn Baine. She's consulting on your daughter's case."

Linda's wide eyes darted to Evelyn and she gripped Evelyn's outstretched hand with both of hers. In contrast to Bill Cooke's rough, strong grip, Linda's freezing-cold hands felt desperate and shaky.

Evelyn studied her closely, taking in the bloodshot eyes Linda had tried to disguise with heavy coats of mascara.

Pete wrapped his arms around his wife from behind, making Linda drop Evelyn's hand.

The move was somehow both protective and aggressive, and Evelyn hid a frown. Could there be merit to Bill Cooke's claim? Was Pete just watching out for a wife who'd been thrust into the spotlight after personal tragedy? Or was he keeping her within sight at all times to make sure she didn't spill a secret he wanted to keep hidden?

"Did you find something?" Linda asked frantically, bringing Evelyn's attention back to her. She clutched her husband's arm, her fingernails biting into his skin. "Did you make a profile we can see? Of the person who took her?"

"Actually," Sophia said, "we're here to talk about how one or both of you is hindering our investigation, and could be hurting our chances of bringing Haley safely home."

Evelyn tried not to grimace at the harsh tactic, especially since Haley could already be dead, but she knew how badly media leaks could damage a case.

"Wh-what?" Linda stuttered, leaning backward, even though there was nowhere to go, with her husband pressed against her back.

"*Someone* released a picture of the note from Haley's notebook onto the web this afternoon," Sophia continued, moving closer until she was practically in Linda's face. "Between that and your little stunt on the news, you're putting our investigation—and possibly your daughter—at risk."

"I—I…" Linda's face went so pale that Evelyn actually stepped forward to catch her if she fell.

Not that it would be necessary, since her husband practically had a death grip around her shoulders. He was glaring at them, but there was something else in his eyes that gave Evelyn chills.

Recognition made her breathe faster and her fists clench. She knew that look. The look of someone who felt sure he held all the power. Someone who thrived on control, usually at the expense of others.

A memory flashed through her mind, of a man who looked nothing like Pete Varner. A man who'd dated her mother, but who'd stared at ten-year-old Evelyn with a predatory intensity. A man she'd known instantly to try to avoid.

She'd done her best, which was difficult with a mother prone to passing out on the couch, surrounded by the stink of stale vodka. She'd escaped a very bad fate through pure luck and a little desperate ingenuity. If the flimsy lock she'd latched on the bathroom door hadn't held long enough for her to climb out the window…

Evelyn's attention shifted to Linda and she noticed the glaze over the woman's eyes. Had she started taking medication to numb the pain of her daughter's disappearance or had she been on painkillers before?

Anger flooded, and she knew it was directed more toward her own mother than at Linda Varner.

It must have shown on her face, because Pete suddenly snapped, "Leave her alone," bringing Evelyn's focus back to the conversation. "We had nothing to do with leaking the note."

"Since you two are the only ones who had access to it before it landed in a police evidence room, I highly doubt that." Sophia's dark eyes filled with her own fury.

She was so angry it made Evelyn wonder if Sophia had a similar tragedy in her own past. Or maybe she'd just taken this case too much to heart, since she had young children. Either way, Evelyn and Sophia were probably both projecting too much. And it might shut Linda and Pete down, prevent them from cooperating.

"Maybe one of your cops leaked the note," Pete said, sounding smug instead of outraged.

Evelyn put a hand on Sophia's elbow. This wasn't getting them anywhere. The damage was done, and Linda looked ready to faint. Besides, Evelyn had a feeling they'd get a lot more out of her if they could separate her from Pete, which she didn't think would be happening today.

The detective glanced at her, gave her a small nod even as fury still radiated from her clenched jaw and flared nostrils, and stepped back.

"Look," Evelyn said, trying to hide her own animosity as she addressed Linda instead of looking up at Pete. "What's done is done. But we want you to understand there's a reason we were keeping the note out of the media. It's best for your daughter that we *don't* share certain parts of the investigation. Going forward, you should talk to us before the media."

"Okay," Linda said, her voice small and quiet, tears in her eyes. "Pete just thought—"

"We thought it would help put pressure on whoever grabbed her," Pete interrupted. "Get him to think the police were closing in on him, so he'd let her go. The media is starting to lose interest. And we've got to keep Haley's face in front of people, so they keep watching for her, so someone comes forward if they see her."

So, it had been Pete's idea for Linda to go on the news. Evelyn wondered why he hadn't stood beside her, the way he had for other news conferences.

Then again, if Pete didn't want Haley coming home because *he* was hiding a secret, leaking the note wouldn't really help him if she'd run away. And if a stranger had grabbed her, but the note had been about Pete, would leaking it cause her abductor to panic? Maybe not, but Evelyn didn't have the luxury of assuming anything.

"If someone has your daughter," Sophia said slowly and deliberately, "we don't want that person to panic."

Evelyn glanced up, past Linda's wide-eyed horror, expecting to see smugness on Pete's face, but it was wiped clean. Instead, he seemed genuinely shaken.

"Oh, my God," he whispered. "I never thought—"

"We're already running damage control," Sophia said, holding out a hand that Linda gripped so hard Evelyn could actually see her cutting off blood flow, turning Sophia's fingertips an unnatural white.

Sophia glanced questioningly at Evelyn, and she nodded at the detective. Linda was clearly too distraught to answer a lot of questions, and this trip had answered a few things for Evelyn already.

It told her that whatever mistakes Linda might have made, Sophia was right about one thing. Linda was desperate to get her daughter back, but she hadn't planted the note.

Pete still looked horrified, a little pale underneath a tan that had to be from a spray bottle. But was it an act?

Beneath the distress in his eyes was something shrewd and slimy. But it didn't mean he had anything to do with Haley's disappearance.

From the outside, to the media, Haley was the perfect, all-American teenager and her family the new normal: divorced, one parent remarried, visitation rights for the other. To the world, family and friends were grieving and searching as hard as they could for Haley.

But up close, there was a strange dynamic in this household. And there was clear animosity between the Varners and Bill. Where did Haley fit in? How many secrets did this family have?

"We should go." Evelyn nodded at Linda, who reluctantly released Sophia's hand.

It was time to dig as deep as they could into the people closest to Haley, and see what they could unearth.

How the hell had his life come to this?

Quincy Palmer stared into the cracked mirror in the station's dingy bathroom, and didn't like what stared back at him. Sure, he looked pretty much the same on the outside. Same grooves alongside his mouth and across his forehead that had worn deeper and deeper with age. Same thick beard, just more white in it now. It was his eyes that bothered him.

He'd stopped meeting his own gaze in the mirror three months ago.

No one else seemed to have noticed the change in him. It probably said a lot about the strength of his personal relationships, and he tried to see it as a positive. If no one else could see the difference, no one would wonder what had caused it.

The bathroom door opened behind him, and Quincy looked up, nodded into the mirror at one of the newbie officers and walked out the door. Back into the buzz of the station.

Things were crazy with news of the Haley Cooke note being released to the media. What had the parents been thinking?

And what the hell had happened to Haley? The case was weird enough on its surface, but he was the only one here who knew how hard it should have been to grab Haley Cooke.

Because he'd had his eye on her for three months. He'd been watching her closely—stalking her, by the legal definition. It had been his job to make sure she didn't do anything out of the ordinary, and if she did— say, if she showed up at the police station—it was his job to take her statement. Then to make sure that statement disappeared.

Twenty years on the job, and he'd never taken a payoff. Never taken a bribe. Never looked the other way.

And then this mess. They'd found his one weak spot, the one thing that would make him throw away twenty years of dedicated service to a job he believed in so much he'd given everything for it. Given his marriage, given his relationship with his son, given all his free time. It had become his life.

If this came out, though, it wouldn't matter that he'd had nothing to do with Haley's disappearance. And it really wouldn't matter that he'd done his damnedest to find her.

Because he knew they'd make him take the fall.

* * *

"That family is hiding something," Evelyn told Sophia as they walked into the police station.

Sophia had fumed the whole drive back, but now she just seemed dejected. "*Everyone* in this case is hiding something."

"What happened? What did you learn?"

The deep voice made Evelyn jump, and when she turned, she saw Quincy Palmer rushing toward them. His pale face was flushed, blotchy red above his heavy beard.

"I don't know," she told Quincy, wondering if his own cases ever took him out of the station. "But my guess would be some kind of abuse. Either the father or the stepfather."

"Really?" Sophia stopped walking, and turned to face her.

Evelyn nodded. "But honestly, with this much scrutiny on the case, with this much media attention, I doubt a seventeen-year-old girl could stay under the radar if she had just run away. I think someone made her disappear. Maybe it started with her going willingly, maybe not. Either way, at this point, chances are, we're not looking for Haley." At Quincy's deep frown, she said apologetically, "You know the statistics."

Sophia nodded, her shoulders slumping. "We're looking for her body. I know. But I've learned all about this girl. Everyone I talk to loved her—her classmates, her teachers, her neighbors. They all say the same thing. Haley was nice to everyone she met. This is a sweet kid, with a bright future. I want her to beat the odds."

"So do I," Evelyn said. "Maybe she will." She tried to sound upbeat, but the fact was, she'd handled too many missing-persons cases.

More than half a million people were reported missing every year in the US alone. The first twenty-four hours were crucial, the first forty-eight the most likely time to make a live recovery. After a month, the chances were practically nonexistent. Especially when the victim was a beautiful teenage girl.

It wore her down, being asked to provide profiles on case after case where the victims would probably never come home. Sometimes, all she could hope for was to bring some closure to the family left behind. Maybe this time would be different. Maybe they could really find Haley, give her back that bright future.

No matter the outcome, she vowed to help find the answers Sophia had been so desperately searching for over the past month. She didn't care how many secrets she had to expose to do it.

Sophia and Quincy looked back at her, both solemn and serious.

"What's next?" Sophia finally asked, her upbeat tone sounding forced.

Before Evelyn could answer, a plainclothes officer raced down the hall, her eyes bright with excitement as she skidded to a stop in front of them.

"Detective Lopez," she panted. "We just got a note."

When she took a breath, Sophia asked, "What sort of note? Someone else claiming to have knowledge of Haley's—"

"No. Not a whack-job letter. This one matches the handwriting from the note you brought in yesterday."

"What?" Quincy barked. "The note Haley left in her bedroom? That means—"

"This is from Haley. She's still alive."

4

Of all the agents in the Washington Field Office, what were the chances he'd be paired with Jimmy Drescott? Kyle wondered as the Supervisory Special Agent in charge of the Civil Rights squad introduced them.

Kyle had spent the morning filling out paperwork, before finally making his way into the WFO's bullpen. It looked a lot like the field office in New York where he'd started his FBI career in counterterror, years before joining the HRT. Really, it resembled any other office building in the DC area. Only this particular office happened to be populated by men and women carrying Glock pistols.

"Mac," Jimmy said, using the nickname Kyle had been given by the HRT. Jimmy stood slowly as the squad supervisor glanced back and forth between them, having just brought Kyle over to introduce him to his new team.

Apparently he'd just missed the rest of the group—two were testifying in court and the other four were out on a case. So, just Jimmy Drescott waited in the Civil Rights squad's little corner of the bullpen.

"You two know each other?"

"We've met," Kyle said, holding out his hand. The last time he'd seen Jimmy, the man had been lying under a big fir tree in Evelyn's front yard, a near-fatal knife wound slicing through his neck.

"You moved out of Violent Crimes?" Kyle asked. That was where Jimmy had been assigned the last time they'd met, working a case that Evelyn had consulted on nine months ago.

Kyle was actually a little surprised Jimmy had stayed in the FBI. He'd lost his partner that night, and he'd almost lost his life.

But here he was, standing in the WFO, a neatly groomed beard covering the ugly scar Kyle knew had to be underneath. Otherwise, he looked pretty much the same, resembling a TV version of an FBI agent with overgelled hair, a nicer suit than most agents could afford on a government salary and his jacket open to display his gun.

"Yep," Jimmy replied, shaking his hand vigorously, as if they were old friends.

Maybe because the last time they'd seen each other, Kyle had helped save his life.

"I needed a change of pace. I figured a new challenge would be good for me." He grinned widely, showing off straight, white teeth.

Same old Jimmy apparently. Except maybe amplified, if that was possible.

This was going to be interesting, Kyle thought, but what he said was, "Good to see you."

"Great," his new supervisor said, looking frazzled as she glanced at her watch. "Because I have a meeting with the Director in twenty minutes. Since you guys are already friends, Jimmy can get you up to speed on the squad's open cases."

She nodded at Jimmy on her way out, and he winked back.

Kyle might have thought they were involved, except he remembered how Jimmy had incessantly flirted with Evelyn when she'd consulted on a case with the young agent. It was pretty nervy to hit on the head of the squad, but he'd never pegged Jimmy as shy or subtle.

"You want to talk me through the details?" Kyle asked, rolling his new desk chair over. It had been nearly four years since he'd worked in a bullpen. Half a day at the WFO and he already felt hemmed in. Already missed the rush of adrenaline as he wrapped his hands around a thick rope dangling out of a hovering helicopter and glided to the ground at Quantico. It's what his old partner would be doing right now, as practice for future missions.

He could get used to the routines of regular casework again, that standard blend of 90 percent hard work and frustration for the 10 percent payoff when you finally got the excitement of closing a case. He could get used to the jacket and tie instead of the cargoes and T-shirts, staring at a computer screen all day instead of carrying sixty pounds of tactical gear. Or so he'd been telling himself ever since he found out he'd lost his spot on the HRT because of his injury. Maybe one of these days, those words would ring true.

"Don't get too comfortable, Mac." Jimmy's voice interrupted his thoughts.

Kyle glanced up, wondering if Jimmy knew about his own near-death experience, and saw Jimmy was hanging up his phone. "What?"

"We're heading to the hospital." Jimmy scooped a pair of car keys off his desk and double-timed it for the door. "Possible human trafficking case."

Kyle stood and followed a little more slowly. Nine months ago, Jimmy had been bubbling over with rookie enthusiasm. Apparently having a serial killer try to slice through his carotid artery hadn't dimmed it at all.

"Come on," Jimmy called after him, and Kyle picked up his pace, shaking his head and wishing he could tone down his new partner's excitement—or borrow some.

"We're heading to the Neville University Hospital," Jimmy said as he got into his FBI-issued sedan and floored it out of the underground lot before Kyle had even buckled in. "The victim is a student there. Cop on the scene said they're going to move her soon—she's in bad shape, and they're not really equipped to handle it—but she was insistent."

"Insistent about what?"

"She wanted to talk to the FBI. The cop tried to take her statement, but the girl knows her stuff. She told him she was reporting a federal crime and wanted a fed on the case."

"Is she pre-law?"

"At Neville University?" Jimmy snorted. "Maybe, but they don't have a law school, so I doubt it. You know what the locals call that place, right?"

"I can guess," Kyle said as Jimmy spoke over him, his voice keeping pace with the speed of his sedan.

"Nepotism U. It's a good degree, don't get me wrong, but if you're local, getting in there has as much to do with your last name as it does your grade point average."

"Jeez. Watch where you're going," Kyle snapped as Jimmy jumped a curb, then raced onto an on-ramp for the I-395 freeway.

"Come on, man, what good is the siren if you don't get to use it every once in a while?"

"I don't think taking a victim statement warrants a siren," Kyle said, even as Jimmy rolled down the window and slapped it onto his roof.

"Doctors want to move her to a new hospital. I want to get her statement."

"Next time, I'm driving," Kyle muttered, then asked, "What about a victim specialist? If we've got a possible human trafficking victim—"

"You're right." Jimmy tossed his phone over. "Pull up Aliyah Aman. She's good. Have her meet us there."

"Sure thing, boss," Kyle said as he dialed, but Jimmy must have missed his sarcasm, because he didn't even glance over, just punched down harder on the gas.

Faster than Kyle had expected, even with Jimmy's racetrack speeds, they were on campus, winding through the cobblestone roads at just above the posted limit. Students started to cross at random spots instead of crosswalks, and jumped back as their sedan didn't slow. They passed frat houses that resembled castles and an administration building that boasted the kind of intricate architecture that spoke of old money.

"Here we go," Jimmy said, sliding into a parking spot in front of a more modern building. "The Neville University Hospital. Let's find out what we've got."

Kyle grabbed his arm before Jimmy could get out of the car. "The victim specialist is still twenty minutes out."

"Fine. Let's at least see if the cop is even right or if we've got a totally different situation. If we need to wait to question her, we'll wait."

He couldn't argue with that logic. Dropping Jimmy's arm, Kyle followed him inside.

The smell hit him first, that antiseptic scent mixed with stale air and sickness. It took him instantly back to a month earlier, when he'd woken up in a hospital in California, pain in his shoulder and numbness in his arm. As the room had come into focus, he'd seen Evelyn first, looking panicked in the chair at his bedside. Then he'd seen his partner on the other side, and the expression on Gabe's face had told him instantly. He was hurt badly enough to put his whole career in question.

Pushing the memory aside, he glanced around the much smaller hospital he was standing in now. The emergency department was bustling, but most of the people in the waiting room looked bored rather than in distress. Staff behind the counter gossiped as he and Jimmy approached and showed their credentials.

"We're here to speak with Tonya Klein," Jimmy said, flashing a big smile at the college-age student behind the desk.

"Is that a real badge?" the girl replied, her eyes widening as she glanced from Jimmy to Kyle.

"It is," Kyle said. "Can you take us to Tonya? We need to speak with her."

"Of course, sure," the girl replied, flustered as she led them down the hall, through a few doorways and toward a room with a police officer sitting on a chair outside.

The officer looked little older than the students he was supposed to protect. He stood slowly as they approached, scowling enough to make the girl back up as she gestured to the room, telling them, "That's Tonya's room. The doctor thinks she might need to go to the Inova Fairfax Hospital. She's real beat up."

She continued backing away as the officer thrust out a hand, which Jimmy shook.

"I'm with campus police," the officer said. "I took the call. I tried to take her statement, but all she'd do was demand you guys." His face flushed an angry red as he continued, "Didn't matter how much I explained the law to her. She thought she knew better, little bi—"

"She said she was the victim of human trafficking?" Jimmy pulled his hand free, which seemed to take real effort.

The officer huffed an ugly sound through his nose. "Yeah, but it's pretty obvious what's really going on."

"And that would be…" Kyle stepped forward, getting in the guy's personal space a little, pissed off by his attitude.

The officer's attention shifted to him, and Kyle could actually see him trying to decide which of them would win in a fight. He figured he'd won when the guy stepped back and muttered, "She's just a prostitute. Probably got beat up by her pimp."

"You get much prostitution at Neville?" Jimmy asked.

The officer's scowl returned. "On campus? No. But there are slums close by. She could have wandered in."

"I thought she was a student at Neville?" Kyle asked.

"Yeah, well, maybe tuition was a little much for her. I'll let you guys take it from here," he said, animosity pouring from him as he strode away.

"Now there's a guy I'd hire to protect a campus full of college students," Jimmy said, rolling his eyes as he pushed the door open to the hospital room.

Kyle almost walked into his back as Jimmy stopped short right inside the doorway.

Jimmy's mocking tone was gone, replaced with a softer, more subdued voice as he said, "Tonya Klein? I'm Special Agent Jimmy Drescott with the FBI's Civil Rights squad." He moved over a little and added, "This is my partner, Kyle McKenzie."

The woman staring back at him could only do so through one pale blue eye, webbed with red from a burst blood vessel. The other was swollen completely shut, and dark purple. Her cheek was swollen, too, and covered with a bandage. Blood still caked her hairline, where her long dark hair had been shaved so a doctor could sew up the kind of cut that might have come from a broken bottle. Her hands, resting on the stark white sheet, were bloody and bruised, a few fingers splinted. Defensive wounds.

Whoever had attacked her, one thing was certain: Tonya Klein had fought back hard.

Good for you, Kyle thought. Regardless of what her story was—whether she was truly a human trafficking victim or if she'd been pulled into prostitution some other way—both pimps and traffickers knew how to make it hard for anyone to get out. Most of them gave up, learned to take the beatings and other abuse, just to survive.

"Thanks for coming," she croaked in a tone that had Kyle looking at her neck.

As she lifted her head, he saw it. More bruising, this time on her neck, and it explained not only her voice but also the damage to her eye. Strangulation victims often showed hemorrhaging to the eyes. And he could actually see the darker spots in the bruises above her collarbone where fingers had pressed in.

This hadn't been the kind of beating meant to teach a lesson. Someone had wanted Tonya Klein dead.

He caught Jimmy's eye and the younger agent nodded, then told Tonya, "We have a specialist on the way. Her job is to make sure you have all the resources you need. We can wait for her to get here before we start—"

"No," Tonya barked, and Kyle tried not to cringe at the cracks in her voice.

It was painful to listen to her talk. He couldn't imagine how badly it hurt to do it.

"Do you want us to wait for a family member to come and sit with you?" Jimmy asked.

"No. They're all back in Alabama. It's too hard for them to get up here."

"Do you want to try to write it down?" Kyle asked.

"No. I just want to tell you, before…" She cut herself off, then began again, keeping her attention firmly on the sheet as she spoke, her voice flat and emotionless. "I was trying to get out. They'd warned me about what would happen, but I couldn't take it anymore. I tried to go to the police. But they came after me and…" Her hands fluttered into the air, revealing more bruises snaking up her arms. "They said there was only one way out. And that was a body bag."

Her voice was flat as she said it, as though she'd heard similar threats often enough that it hadn't surprised her. Or—a cynical agent who'd heard it all before might think—as though she couldn't generate real emotion because she was making that part up.

"Okay." Kyle eased himself into a seat next to the bed, careful to keep his distance as he took out a notepad. "Is it all right if I sit here?"

She gave a small nod.

This was an intense reentry to regular casework. When he'd worked counterterror, he'd seen some human trafficking—it was a common way to fund terrorist operations—but he'd never been the one sitting in a hospital room, taking victim statements.

Jimmy pulled up a seat on the other side of her bed as he asked, "Do you know who attacked you?"

She shook her head, cringing and clutching her side with her splinted fingers.

"How many people attacked you?" Kyle asked. "Would you be able to describe them?"

"They wore ski masks. There were two of them, but I don't know who they were."

"Okay. Could you tell if they were male or—"

"Yeah, they were men," Tonya interrupted. "Not even all that big, either, but they could hit."

"Did they say anything to you?" Jimmy asked.

She shrugged, a short jerk of her shoulders that made pain flash in her eye. "Just what I told you. About how there was no getting out."

"Do you remember the exact words?"

"He said, 'We warned you about trying to leave. There's only one way out, and that's a body bag.' And then they started punching. I swore to myself that it didn't matter what it took, that I was finished. But I knew they were going to kill me in that alley and..." Her voice broke. "I told them I'd come back—I *begged*—and they said it was too late. And then one of them hit me with a bottle that was lying in the alley. I passed out after that. I'm not sure what happened, if they just thought they'd killed me or—"

"Two students saw you. They scared off your attackers and called 911," Jimmy said.

"Now what?" Tonya asked. "Because I read where sex trafficking victims can be protected, that the FBI will go after whoever is behind it."

"That's right," Kyle said slowly, glancing at Jimmy across the bed. He could see the skepticism in Jimmy's face, and he tried to keep an open mind. Nothing about this suggested human trafficking yet, but colleges were the new recruiting grounds, so he wasn't ruling anything out.

"Let's backtrack a little bit," Jimmy said. "To before today's attack. What can you tell us about your situation, about the people threatening you?"

"I…" She shook her head, her hand tightening against her side as she looked at the bed instead of them. "I don't know who they are. I got an email at first." She flushed, then said, more quickly, "There was a video attached. A video of me and it was…"

When she didn't finish, Jimmy asked, "A sex video?"

"Yeah. But I didn't take it. I never would have slept with the guy if I knew he was taping it. The email said it would go out to everyone I knew if I didn't show up at this warehouse outside of town. I didn't know what to do. I thought about going to the police, but I didn't want anyone to see the video. But I was thinking about it, anyway, when I realized the email was gone. I don't know what happened to it. I didn't delete it, but it just wasn't there anymore."

"There are programs that can delete an email after it's been viewed," Jimmy said, frowning as he jotted notes.

"So I had nothing, no proof, and I figured the police wouldn't believe me if I just went to them and said the email had disappeared. But they still had the video, so I went to the meeting. I thought they were going to ask for money—not that I had any—but they didn't. There were a couple of guys there and they made me…" She trailed off, then whispered, "It might have been the same two who attacked me today—their voices were familiar, but I can't be sure. Anyway, when I got back to my dorm, there was an envelope under my door. There were pictures of my family inside, from when they came with me to orientation and the special scholarship luncheon—I'm a scholarship student. I can't afford this place. Even with the scholarship, I had two jobs. Anyway, after that, I just did what they told me."

"Were there threats against your family?" Kyle asked.

"Not specifically," Tonya said. "But they didn't need to say it. They knew who my family was! I wasn't going to risk it."

"Did you try to go to the police before now?" Jimmy asked.

"No. I quit my jobs—the other thing in the envelope was instructions. They told me to stop working, and there was some money to cover my next tuition payment, so I did. I wasn't supposed to tell anyone. They said they were watching all the time."

"Do you still have the envelope?" Kyle asked.

She shook her head, looking up at him for the first time since she'd started telling her story. "No. They said to destroy it, and I was scared they'd know if I didn't."

"Okay," Kyle said, subtly glancing at his watch and wondering where the victim specialist was. "Can you tell me who you were sleeping with in the tape? And how long ago did this happen?"

"It was—" She cut herself off, suddenly lurching forward, clutching harder at her side.

"Are you all right?" Jimmy asked. "Do you want me to get a doc—"

"No, I'm okay," Tonya said, leaning back against the pillow. But just as fast, she jerked forward again and her heart monitor went off.

It took so long for anyone to respond that Kyle almost ran out to get them, but finally a pair of nurses came in, and pushed him and Jimmy out of the room.

As they stood in the hallway waiting, Jimmy asked, "What do you think?"

"I don't know," Kyle admitted. "It's pretty obvious someone tried to kill her. But as for why? Her story could be true."

"Or she could be looking for federal protection for

some other reason," Jimmy said. "She admitted looking up information about the FBI providing resources for human trafficking victims." Before Kyle could agree, he added, "Or she could be a prostitute who wants to get out, but doesn't want to admit she was ever breaking the law, so she makes up a claim of being forced into it."

"That's possible, too," Kyle said, but the petite college student didn't seem like a typical prostitute. Still, if her story was true, blackmail was an unusual recruitment method. "We should get more specifics on the warehouse she mentioned," he said just as a pair of doctors came racing down the hall and into Tonya's room.

One of the nurses walked out a minute later and told them, "You might want to come back tomorrow. She's got to go into surgery."

"What for?" Jimmy asked.

"We suspect she has internal bleeding." The nurse started to head past them, still jotting notes on her clipboard, and when they didn't follow, she snapped, "Come on. You're going to need to move. They're about to take her up to the surgical floor."

"All right." Jimmy pressed his card into her hand. "Have someone give us a call when she's out of surgery."

Kyle followed him out of the hospital, Jimmy texting away on his phone. "Aliyah got caught in traffic. I told her to head back and we'd call her when we can come for another interview, but that I think it's a no-go," he said.

"You think she's lying?"

"Not entirely. But it sounds way too amateurish to be a human trafficking setup. Not that it couldn't work, but there are a lot of potential holes. Not to mention that whoever took the sex tape used to blackmail her had to be involved, meaning there's a personal connection. If you ask me, this is some kind of revenge scenario. Definitely needs follow-up, but this is probably a case for the local police." He tucked his phone away and picked up his pace. "Come on. Let's see if anything else came in while we were here."

"Sure," Kyle replied. "But toss me your keys."

"What for?"

"I'm driving back. And we're not dropping this so easily. I want to talk to the two students who called 911, and get their side of the story. Whether or not we're talking about human trafficking, someone tried to kill this girl. And I want to know why."

5

"Haley's still alive," Sophia repeated, staring slack-jawed at the note that had appeared at the station.

"Let's not get ahead of ourselves," Evelyn said. "We don't know when this note was written. And we don't know if Haley was coerced."

"If it's legit," Sophia said grimly as she finally looked up from the note, "then we've got a whole different case to investigate."

"Are we sure someone didn't just copy Haley's hand-writing?" Quincy asked from over Evelyn's shoulder.

The three of them were crowded around the note, no one touching it because they didn't want to add prints—or smear any. Other cops stood at a distance, necks craned as they tried to get a look.

"We can have a handwriting expert at the FBI take a look," Evelyn said. "They should be able to tell us if it's Haley's writing or an imitation. They might even be able to identify signs of coercion, although with a note this short, I don't know."

"Really? They can tell coercion from this?" Quincy sounded skeptical as he read the note aloud. "'Stop look-ing for me. I'm safe, but I won't come home for another beating from Stepdaddy. Let me go.'"

"Maybe," Evelyn replied, then turned to face Sophia. "You know the case best. Does this sound like Haley's voice to you? Is this how she'd talk? Is that what she called Pete?"

"It is," Sophia said slowly. "Her friends all referred to him that way, said it's what Haley called him, in kind of a mocking way. They didn't get along, but none of her friends thought he was abusive, at least not that they were willing to tell me. But what about the last part? *'Let me go'?* Am I the only one creeped out by that? Shouldn't it be just 'leave me alone'? Why 'let me go'? This is the kind of language people use when they're waiting to die."

Her phone beeped and Sophia pulled it out of her pocket, then swore. "Well, let's push coercion right up the list," she said, then turned her phone toward them and pushed Play on a video attached to an email that went by too quickly for Evelyn to read.

Bill Cooke's craggy face filled the screen, pressed close to what was obviously a camera on a home computer. He looked furious, and he was wearing the same clothes he'd been in when they'd stopped by his house earlier in the day.

"My name is Bill Cooke. My daughter, Haley, ran away from home to escape abuse from her stepfather. This bullshit about a stranger stalking her is just that— bullshit. She's out there somewhere, and I want her to know I understand, and I support her decision." He'd been staring down during most of the talk, but he suddenly looked up and stared directly, intently, into the camera. "Haley, you do what you need to do, honey."

The video went black and Quincy stared at Sophia. "That's it?"

"Isn't that enough?" Her lips curled upward with

restrained fury. "Just what this case needs. The parents fighting on a public stage, distracting from the real problem."

"Maybe it will help us," Evelyn said. "Where was this posted? And what time did it go up?"

"On Bill's social media. The video was posted pretty soon after we left his house today, but it's already been shared a thousand times." Sophia shoved her phone back into her pocket. "You'd think her parents don't want Haley to come home, with all the shit they've started pulling. I don't know where this is coming from. Maybe Bill wasn't the easiest guy to deal with, and Linda was a bit hysterical, but none of them fucking *impeded* the investigation before now."

"So, what?" Quincy broke in. "Bill made the video three hours ago, and we already have a note from Haley? That's fast for coercion. It would mean—"

"If the note is really from her, then someone is holding her nearby, to be able to see the video, tell Haley what to write, then deliver it to the station this quickly," Sophia finished.

"And if not, the person who sent this is still nearby, somewhere close, so hopefully it won't take long to nail his ass," Quincy said.

"It could be Bill himself," Sophia said. "Whether he has her or not. I'm sure he has samples of her handwriting he could copy."

"You have cameras, right?" Evelyn asked.

"We sure as hell do." Sophia headed for the front desk, even as she barked at another officer who'd come over. "Bag the note. Get it logged into Evidence now."

"Someone just got sloppy," Quincy said, keeping pace with Sophia. "Maybe this will be the break we need."

"Wait," the officer who'd told them about the note called, running after them. She was young, probably not long out of high school herself, and bursting with newbie enthusiasm. "It came in with the mail. I took the stack of mail from the carrier myself."

The young officer took a step back as both Quincy and Sophia stopped in their tracks, spinning toward her. Evelyn hurried to catch up, wishing she had a longer stride.

"The normal carrier?" Sophia demanded. "How did it come so fast, then, if it went through the postal system? Unless Bill's video was a coincidence. Or he sent the letter himself, before he posted the video."

"Why did you get the mail?" Quincy asked.

"I—" She glanced from one detective to the other. "Sergeant Jett stepped out, so no one was at the desk out front. I was there. I took the stack. Yes, the normal carrier brought it. I dumped the stack on the desk and was going to leave, but I noticed this letter had no postage. I was going to ask the carrier, but she'd left and—"

"You sure she gave it to you?" Sophia said. "No one dropped it in the pile?"

"I'm sure."

"Shit," Sophia said. "Okay, we'll talk to the carrier. Let's take a ride."

Sophia was already racing for the door, but Evelyn snagged her elbow before she could get far. "Hang on. Let's look at the cameras first."

"But if—"

"How would a piece of mail with no postage get into a mail stack coming into a police station?"

Sophia frowned back at her, then nodded slowly. "It must have happened nearby. Otherwise, the person couldn't be sure it would get delivered. It might end up being sent back, since there was no postage."

"Except the envelope had the station as the return address, too," Quincy called out. "It would have ended up here either way."

"But not in the stack. They would have asked for the postage, right?" Evelyn asked.

"I guess so. All right, let's pull the tapes." Sophia turned, heading back toward the front desk, where the sergeant who usually sat there was returning. "We need the footage from around the station for the last few minutes, Amber," Sophia told her.

Amber stood, frowning as she set down the sandwich she'd just started eating, and gave an exaggerated sigh. "All right. Come on."

She moved to the side, letting Sophia behind the desk. As Sophia's raised an eyebrow, Evelyn joined them in the tight space.

"Here we go," Amber said, picking up a remote and rewinding on the tiny screen mounted beneath the desk.

Evelyn glanced at Sophia, who nodded.

"We have live picture surrounding the station. Amber can go back and look at anything that's happened in the last twenty-four hours. After that, it automatically backs up. It's a good system." She leaned closer to the screen. "Stop!"

Evelyn leaned forward, too, as the mail carrier suddenly pitched forward at the edge of the camera, and a hand darted out and steadied her.

"There!" Sophia shouted, making other officers glance their way.

"What?" Evelyn asked as Sophia rewound once more, then hit Pause and pointed.

"He bumped her on purpose, then grabbed her arm

to steady her while he slipped an envelope in the stack with his other hand. Sneaky bastard. Not quite pickpocket good, but that was pretty ingenious."

"He?" Evelyn pressed. "All I see is an arm, in a dark sweatshirt. Do we have another angle on this?"

Sophia glanced back at Amber, who frowned and shook her head. "This is at the far side of the station. We have cameras mounted on all sides of the station, but not just out on the street. And the person who did this was standing in the alley. Probably waiting for the mail carrier to come by. There aren't cameras there, not even from other businesses."

"Are you sure?" Sophia pressed. "Maybe the bank has an angle that we can—"

"I'm positive," Amber insisted. "We had a couple of muggings there a year ago. The station took a lot of heat because it was so close and it took us a long time to identify the person."

"I remember," Sophia said. "But I also remember you pushing to get cameras in there."

"That's a battle I lost," Amber said. "We barely have the budget for this." She gestured to the screen still on pause below the desk. "Sorry."

Sophia handed over the remote and leaned against the wall. "We can't catch a break. And this can't be dumb luck, the guy being so perfectly positioned."

"If whoever took Haley is from around here, he'd probably know about the muggings," Evelyn said. "If the police took heat for not having cameras there, I'm guessing it was in the press?"

"You'd be guessing right," Sophia said. "Amber, I want you to get a hold of our mail carrier. Get her in here and ask her to describe this person as soon as you can find her." She looked at Evelyn. "And since we already think Haley's abductor is someone she knows, let me introduce you to a guy who wears a lot of sweatshirts."

Evelyn followed as she headed for the door, glancing back to see Quincy step behind the desk. "Who?"

"His name is Jordan Biltmore."

"Haley's boyfriend? The one everyone saw drive away after he dropped her off at school?"

"That's the guy," Sophia replied, not slowing down as she left the station and got into her car, parked in front. "Let's go for a ride."

"School is in session," Sophia said unnecessarily as she drove onto the Neville University campus.

They'd driven across a ridiculously ornate bridge over a man-made pond to enter campus. Students' tuition money at work apparently, because Sophia told her the university had put it in at a cost of several million. It made for a hell of an entryway, but the whole thing seemed a little ridiculous to Evelyn, who'd never before been on the relatively small Neville campus.

Now, they were moving at ten miles an hour as they wove down narrow cobblestone streets lined with hickory and maple trees. Students darted out in front of the car in laughing groups as they chatted and hurried to their next classes.

"Aren't any of them worried about getting hit by a car?" Evelyn muttered.

"At Neville U? Probably not. On campus, pedestrians think they have the right of way no matter where they are. You've got to be careful driving through here, especially at night."

"So, tell me more about Jordan Biltmore," Evelyn

said as they drove along at a maddeningly slow pace, deeper and deeper into the small college campus.

All Evelyn knew about Neville U was its reputation as being the go-to college for kids from wealthy Virginia families with decent-enough grades. To balance out the rich kids, there was a hefty scholarship fund that brought in out-of-state students with fantastic grades and not-so-fantastic funds. A degree from Neville wasn't quite Ivy League level, but that didn't matter for top-level job hunting if you had the right last name.

And Jordan Biltmore, a sophomore and Haley Cooke's boyfriend, had the right last name. The son of billionaire CEO Franklin Biltmore, Jordan probably could have gotten into Neville with grades bordering on dismal. But according to the brief stats she'd seen on Jordan, he was actually close to a straight-A student.

"Jordan and Haley had been dating for about six months when she went missing. Apparently they met when Haley went to a party on the college campus," Sophia said, making a slow turn into the parking lot of a building way nicer than any frat house Evelyn had ever seen.

"Haley's friends seem to like him—or seem to be jealous that she's dating a billionaire's son who's in college. Her mom seems lukewarm, but isn't so crazy about the idea of her high school junior dating a college kid."

"What about Bill? And Pete? What do they think of Jordan?" Evelyn asked as Sophia squeezed her sedan into a parking spot meant for a coupe.

"Pete grunts about the age difference and what college boys are really after when you ask him, but otherwise, he doesn't seem to have anything bad to say about Jordan specifically. Bill—as far as I could tell—had never met Jordan. To be honest, I'm not sure he even knew Haley was dating this kid until she went missing and Jordan's name was in the news."

"Hmm," Evelyn mused. "That says a lot about his relationship with Haley if she'd been dating Jordan for six months. And yet, he's acting pretty damn certain that she wasn't abducted. Kind of strange for someone who doesn't seem to know as much as he should about her life in general."

"Yep," Sophia agreed, shutting off the engine. "I can't be sure he didn't know. Bill acts as though he was aware they were dating, but just hadn't met Jordan. But the impression I got? He was lying. He wanted me to think he was a more involved father, especially with the news attention. But today, I'd love *your* take on Jordan. He's been extremely cooperative, and honestly, since a squad full of cheerleaders saw him drop her off and then drive away that day, I'm not sure how he could have done it. But he's just—" her lips pursed, and finally she settled on "—too smooth."

Evelyn shifted to face her. "What do you mean?"

"Maybe it's just the rich-kid, son-of-a-CEO thing, but the vibe I'm getting is someone who's happy to help, because he's sure we'll never catch him."

"Huh. All right."

"I mean, his alibi is solid. But he just bothers me. Have you ever gotten that feeling about someone in a case?"

"Oh, yeah." Plenty of times, with her job.

"What happened when you got the vibe?" Sophia asked.

"Sometimes you get that feeling for the obvious reason—because they did it. Other times there's some other thing they're guilty of, related to the case or not. And sometimes it's just a person who's using what happened to get in the limelight. The bad feeling we get is because they feel guilty they're enjoying their fifteen minutes of fame—which they wouldn't have gotten if a person they loved wasn't missing or dead. Let's go chat with Jordan and see why you're getting that impression from him."

She followed Sophia up a well-groomed pathway to the front door. When Sophia knocked on the door, it swung open by itself, revealing an interior as ornate as the outside. Except that there were brightly colored bras hanging off the enormous crystal chandelier in the entryway, empty pizza boxes piled on the antique table in the living room and a pair of frat boys curled up asleep, one on each end of the dirty but obviously expensive couch.

"Here we go," Sophia said. "Neville's most notorious frat house."

"What are they notorious for?"

"Being awesome, mostly," someone said from much closer behind her than anyone should have been able to get without Evelyn sensing a presence.

She spun around and craned her neck up at the college student giving her an "aren't I charming" grin. His dark blond hair was perfectly groomed, his low-slung jeans and Neville U sweatshirt just a tiny bit rumpled and his dimples were on full display. He held a cup of coffee in one hand and tucked a pair of keys with an Audi key chain into his pocket with the other.

As Sophia spun around, the flirtatious grin dropped off his face, replaced by sudden worry. "Detective Lopez. Do you have news? Did you find Haley? Is she okay?"

"We don't have anything new," Sophia said.

"Jordan Biltmore?" Evelyn guessed.

Disappointment—or maybe relief—slumped his shoulders, then he studied her again, as if he was assessing her role or importance, and he stuck out a hand. He gave her the kind of handshake more appropriate for a business meeting than standing on the threshold of a frat house that stunk of old beer and dirty socks. "That's right. And you are?"

"Special Agent Evelyn Baine, from the FBI."

Her title should have made an impression on a kid his age, either concern about the FBI's involvement if he was involved, hope for more resources on his girlfriend's case if he wasn't or just plain awe if nothing else. But he simply nodded at her, the strength of his handshake revealing power in his lanky frame.

"If there's nothing new, what's going on?" he asked Sophia.

"Let's find a place to sit and chat."

"Sure." Jordan angled his head around them and yelled, "Brent! Jim! Get lost."

The pair of students sleeping on the couch jolted awake. One looked ready to snap back at Jordan, but at the sight of Sophia—who held up her detective's shield—they both shuffled off into the cavernous house.

Evelyn glanced around as they walked in, seeing a kitchen off to her right, fully stocked with gleaming stainless appliances she doubted the frat boys used. There was even a pair of vending machines neatly lined up next to the fridge. She assumed the bedrooms were off the hall to her left and up the giant staircase beside the entryway.

"Take a seat," Jordan said, gesturing to the couch.

As soon as they were seated, instead of doing the same, he planted his free hand on his hip and stared down at them. "You must have news if you're back here." Before they could answer, he added, "If it's about that crazy video her dad released, let me tell you, Haley didn't run away."

Evelyn looked up at him, wondering about his background besides the wealth and the important father. For a nineteen-year-old, he had a lot of confidence to usher two law enforcement officers into seats and then stand in a symbolic position of power himself. Was he doing it on purpose or subconsciously?

"Why do you say that?" Evelyn asked, staying comfortably seated. Let him believe he was in charge.

"About her dad? Because how would he know what happened to her? Believe me, unless he actually did it, he has no clue. He just wants the attention, because his family left him and he's miserable."

"Do you have reason to suspect Haley's dad kidnapped her?" Sophia asked.

Jordan shrugged, setting his coffee on the table between them. He finally sprawled on one of the plush leather chairs across from the couch, his long legs stretched out in front of him. "No, but the guy is an asshole who used to smack her and her mom around."

"Haley told you she was abused?" Sophia demanded, leaning forward as though this was news to her.

"Nah. Haley was too sweet to actually say it. She always gave everyone the benefit of the doubt, always had excuses when someone did bad shit or treated her wrong. But I can read between the lines."

"Give me some examples," Sophia insisted. "What did she say to make you think that?"

"She usually clammed up when anything to do with her dad came up. But she told me once that she was glad they'd divorced, him and her mom. That she couldn't take living with him anymore."

"Did she ever mention running away?" Evelyn asked.

Furrows lined his forehead and he sat forward, crossed his arms over his chest. "Well, look, yeah, she might have mentioned that a few times, but it was a while ago. And she never actually would have done it. Besides, her dad was out of the picture. I mean, sure, he had some sort of partial custody. She had to visit every once in a while, but it wasn't like he was around all the time." He stared hard at Sophia. "If there's one thing I know for sure, it's that if Haley *had* decided to run away, she wouldn't do it this way. She'd never let her mom worry. *Never.*"

Sophia nodded, her expression telling Evelyn that everything she'd learned about Haley in her investigation meshed with what Jordan was telling them.

"What about her stepdad?" Evelyn asked.

"Pete?" Jordan rolled his eyes. "She thought he was kind of an ass-hat, that's for sure. She definitely avoided him."

"Did she ever talk about him being a threat?"

"No. She wasn't his biggest fan, but he's sort of a weirdo, so that's no surprise. You've asked me all this before."

Sophia glanced at Evelyn, giving a small shrug, and Evelyn jumped in.

"Jordan, I want to go over what happened when you dropped Haley off at school. Everything you can remember."

"Sure." He glanced between them. "But I haven't thought of anything new."

"That's okay. I just want to hear it from you instead of a police report." Sometimes, even with witnesses who were telling the truth, repeating the details raised inconsistencies, gaps in memory or brand-new information.

Jordan's whole body tensed. "It was a pretty typical day. Haley's school day was over, and I'd been to my morning classes. I picked her up after she finished for the day and we just drove around a bit. We got some ice cream because, for December, it was crazy warm. It's probably why her team was practicing on the field instead of in the gym. The cheerleaders," he clarified.

When Evelyn nodded, his focus went back to some spot on the wall, as though he was searching his memory for details that might matter. "She acted happy. Nothing seemed wrong, like I told Detective Lopez before." He shook his head, but he still wasn't looking at them. "I didn't see anyone weird hanging around. I watched her walk toward the school when I dropped her off. She turned back and waved at me. It's the last thing I remember before I drove away."

He stared at Evelyn again, a sad, desperate look in his eyes. "I should have waited, seen her go inside. But I assumed she'd be safe there."

"So you didn't actually see her go inside?"

"No. But didn't her friends? I thought the cheerleaders saw her go in. And besides, where else would she go? The whole reason I dropped her off was for her cheerleading practice."

"And she didn't tell you anything about meeting someone later?"

He shook his head. "No. She was going to grab a ride home from practice with Marissa."

"Marissa Anderson," Sophia interjected. "Haley's best friend. They were on the cheerleading squad together."

"And she never spoke of anyone she was afraid of? No one who was hassling her?"

"Other than her dad?" Jordan shook his head.

"How were things going in your relationship?" If they'd only been dating for six months, as Sophia had said, that meant they'd met while Jordan was at Neville U and Haley was still in high school. It wasn't a huge age difference, but the experience difference between a high school junior still living at home with her mom and a college student, living in a frat house, could be huge.

"Fine." Jordan shrugged. "Good."

"No arguments? Neither of you were seeing anyone else?"

"We weren't exclusive, I guess. I mean, we hadn't really talked about it. But no, neither of us was seeing other people."

"Are you sure?"

"Yeah."

"No jealous exes, then?"

Jordan gave a short laugh. "Haley didn't have any exes. And no, not on my end."

"So no one you can think of who might want to hurt her?"

"No! Everyone loved Haley. She was sweet, innocent. No one would want to hurt her." He sounded offended by the idea. "I heard about that note her mom talked about on the news—some kind of stalker—but I can't believe she wouldn't have told me." He visibly puffed up. "I would have protected her."

"She never mentioned thinking that someone might be following her around?"

"No."

Evelyn nodded, not surprised. She stood, and Sophia slowly did the same.

Jordan stayed in his seat, staring up at them. "That's it? Why haven't you found her? It's been a month, and you're back here questioning me about the same old things?"

"Sometimes people remember new details if they go through it again," Evelyn said calmly. Most of the time, she consulted from a case file and not directly on a scene, but when she did talk to families and friends, she was used to the frustration and anger and fear. And Jordan's seemed genuine.

"We'll be in touch," Sophia said.

As they headed for the door, the high-pitched whine of a young woman reached them. "Seriously? You went out and got yourself a coffee and didn't bother to get me one?"

Evelyn glanced back and saw a blond college student in tight yoga pants and a T-shirt that swallowed her, ultrared lips pursed in a pout as she stared down at Jordan. Her hair was a mess, and she'd clearly just climbed out of bed, thrown on some clothes, swiped on some lipstick and went looking for Jordan.

He darted a look over his shoulder and flushed when he caught Evelyn's eye.

Instead of lingering, Evelyn walked out the door.

"So much for the worried boyfriend act," Sophia muttered.

Evelyn frowned, pausing to glance backward. Jordan's reaction when he'd first spotted Sophia hadn't seemed faked. Sure, he might have had nothing to do with Haley's disappearance, and still be sleeping with someone else, but he'd said he wasn't seeing anyone besides Haley. Was he just too embarrassed to tell them he'd already moved on? Or was it all a lie?

As the girl stomped out of the frat house, looking annoyed, Sophia stopped her. "How long have you been dating Jordan Biltmore?"

"Dating?" the girl scoffed. She flipped her hair over her shoulder. "Met him at the frat party last night. I should have gone home with one of the other guys hitting on me. Asshole didn't even share his coffee." With that, she headed past them, toward the center of campus.

Sophia stared after her a minute, then stomped toward the car, looking pissed off on Haley's behalf. "I'll tell you one thing. I don't care whether he's found himself a new girlfriend, or he's just sleeping around. It's been a month since Haley disappeared. That's pretty damn fast to move on in any way, if he really cared about her. Jordan Biltmore just hit the top of my suspect list."

6

"I don't know how he did it, but it's got to be him, right?" Sophia demanded as they sat in her sedan in the parking lot of the frat house. The sun beat down on them, making the car feel like a sauna despite the mid-forty-degree temperatures.

Sophia made no move to turn on the car, just shifted to face Evelyn, her face wrinkled with distaste. "I mean, his girlfriend disappears off the face of the earth, and he's out boinking sorority girls? Isn't that classic behavior for someone who killed their partner? I've seen that in the news a ton. Shit, I can name a whole bunch off the top of my head. It's practically a bad joke."

"Maybe," Evelyn said, unbuttoning her suit jacket, glad she'd left her winter coat in the stuffy police station. "But we usually see that with married couples, one spouse killing another to be with a mistress. This is a little different. Jordan could have just as easily broken up with her—it's not as if they've got marital property or kids together. If he's involved, I doubt it's his way of breaking up with her. I've seen stranger things, but behaviorally, that'd be pretty odd. Still, we have to take into account that he's nineteen and he could just be immature."

"Immaturity is the least of his personality flaws."

Evelyn nodded thoughtfully. "But he has Haley up on a bit of a pedestal. He views himself as her protector, and I think he's getting an ego boost from the fact that a girl like her would date him."

"She's a high school student," Sophia countered. "Is that really brag-worthy to a college guy?"

"He referred to her as 'sweet and innocent.' Things he obviously thinks he isn't. She's the ideal he thinks he wants, but he's still chasing after other women when she's not around."

Sophia snorted angrily. "Or he's just a jerk. You see what I mean about the smug bullshit, right? Seriously, this kid thinks he owns the world. And maybe Haley, too."

"He's definitely an entitled rich kid. That doesn't mean he killed Haley, though. If he's going to be a legitimate suspect, we need to figure out how he could have dropped her off and driven away and then come back to grab her."

"Maybe he circled back," Sophia said stubbornly. "Look, at this point, you've met all the key players in Haley's life. If it was someone close to her, chances are it's one of the people we talked to today. So, which one is it? You said you'd have a better sense once we talked to them. So, lay it on me. If you think it's someone other than Jordan, fine. But I want to focus this investigation."

Evelyn held in her frustration that Sophia wanted her to hand over some magic solution. At least Sophia wanted her help, unlike a lot of officers who dismissed profiling out of hand. "The problem with a case where there's only one victim is that we don't have patterns of behavior to analyze. It's the patterns that give us some of the most useful information for profiling. And we don't really have a crime scene, either. We have a last known location, but we can't say for certain she was grabbed there, or if she snuck out on her own. Which means we have to work off the events of the day, from witnesses, and I have to profile the players. Unfortunately, it's a process."

"Okay," Sophia said, her voice quivering with restrained frustration. "So, what can you tell me? Can we narrow it down?"

"I think you're right about Haley's mom not having anything to do with the abduction," Evelyn said. "I don't think she has any idea what happened to her daughter. Her reactions don't seem faked, and I doubt she's that good of an actor."

When Sophia looked ready to agree, Evelyn added, "But that doesn't totally get her off the hook. I'm pretty sure she's medicating, which is part of the reason I don't think she'd be able to successfully hide her reactions. It's logical that a doctor would prescribe her something in this situation, but we shouldn't make assumptions. We should consider whether the medicating is new, or if she might have been abusing prescriptions—or something else—beforehand. It's not alcohol—" Evelyn knew the smell and look of that too well to be fooled "—but illegal drugs could be a possibility."

"Illegal drugs?" Sophia scoffed. "Seriously? Linda Varner?"

"Let's just look into it. If she's been abusing drugs for a while, maybe she missed what was happening right under her nose."

"So your bet is Pete Varner? You think, what?" Her tone turned sour. "That he was sexually abusing her?"

"I get a weird feeling from him. I want to take a closer look at him and Bill Cooke. The timing of that new note was suspicious—especially if we can confirm it's Haley's handwriting."

"It happened really fast after Bill's little video," Sophia agreed.

"Which could mean that Bill walked down into his basement and made Haley write it as soon as we left. Or he faked it, because he knows her writing, and she's not around to do it herself. And quite frankly, he's strangely calm, just going about his usual business, for someone whose only daughter has been missing for a month. Everyone reacts differently to tragedy, and it's possible his calm response is denial or repression. But it could also be that he killed her, either because she didn't want anything to do with him, the way her mom and Jordan are claiming, or because he wanted to try to make Linda look bad."

"You think he might have been trying to set Linda up? That he'd kill his own *kid* to do it?"

"Unfortunately, it's not unprecedented. For someone who seems to have spent no time with search parties or hanging out at the police station waiting for updates, Bill sure hasn't wasted an opportunity to point fingers. Which to me says one of two things. He doesn't need updates on the search because he's involved and he already knows what happened to Haley, or he cares more about sticking it to his ex than whether his daughter is okay."

Sophia nodded, not looking entirely convinced, and Evelyn added, "And I agree with you about Jordan. He might be telling the truth about Haley, but if he could lie so straight-faced about not seeing anyone else when there was a woman literally in his bed, we need to see what else he might be lying about."

Sophia let out a heavy sigh and finally turned on the ignition, getting some air circulation in the car. "So, we're not really any further along, are we? It's the dad, the stepdad or the boyfriend. And both Pete and Jordan *did* take part in the search parties, in those early days. Bill's the only one who didn't. Does that mean he's our prime suspect?"

"Unfortunately, it's not that easy. The others could be taking part in the search parties and calling for updates to *seem* innocent, and to hear where we are in the investigation."

"Okay, that's not helpful. So, what now?"

"Two things. When we get back to the station, let's try to get Haley's medical records."

"To look for signs of abuse." Sophia nodded, but the set of her jaw was grim. "I already reviewed them and there's nothing there. And I asked both Linda and Haley's best friend about the week before Haley went missing, when her mom was out of town and Haley was alone with Pete. She didn't say anything about abuse to either of them. But we both know that doesn't mean there wasn't any."

Evelyn nodded, Pete Varner's demeanor still nagging at her. Quick flashes of a face in the semidarkness came to mind, a man with no name, when she was ten years old. That same predatory aura.

Little needles crept up her spine and she forced the memory back, trying to stay objective.

"All right," Sophia said, her eyes narrowing, letting Evelyn know her detective instincts were buzzing, seeing that Evelyn was thinking more than she was saying. "What's the second thing?"

"I want to meet this best friend. The last person to see Haley before she went missing."

"Did you find Haley?"

The girl staring hopefully at them in the doorway of her house with the dark curly bob and the wide blue eyes wore the clothing of a twenty-five-year-old, but the expression of a five-year-old. Hopeful and afraid, all at once.

"We haven't found her," Sophia told Marissa Anderson, Haley's best friend.

The girl's shoulders instantly slumped and the hope in her eyes shifted into wary concern. "So why are you here?"

"Can we come in?" Sophia asked. "I want you to go over that day with Evelyn Baine here. She's a profiler with the FBI."

Marissa studied her, looking intrigued. "Like on that TV show?"

"Except I don't get a private jet," Evelyn joked.

It must have fallen flat, because Marissa just frowned. "All right. Come on in."

She held the door open, letting Sophia and Evelyn into the bright blue entryway. With three of them, it was crowded, especially next to a bench overflowing with cheerleading pom-poms, a pile of colorful hoodies and a big stack of toy cars and airplanes.

"Let's go upstairs, where my brothers will leave us alone."

"We can talk to you with a parent—" Sophia started, but a woman peered around a doorway from what must have been the kitchen and called, "No need, Detective Lopez!"

She walked into the front hallway, wiping her hands on a dish towel, as Evelyn and Sophia came in. "You said you didn't find Haley, right? That's what I heard?"

"That's right," Sophia told the woman who must have been an exact replica of her daughter back in high school. Now, gray roots peeked through her dark hair, and her blue eyes were ringed with dark circles and bracketed by lines.

She held out a hand. "Jan Anderson. You're a pro-filer?"

Evelyn shook the proffered hand, surprised at how calm Jan was about the police questioning her daughter. Then again, maybe she was just used to it after a month-long investigation. "That's right."

Before she could properly introduce herself, Jan continued, "If Detective Lopez called in the FBI, it must mean some wacko grabbed Haley?"

"No," Sophia said.

Marissa wrapped her arms around herself as if she was trying to ward off bad news.

"It's a complicated case," Evelyn said. "We're trying to look at it from every angle."

"All right." Jan put a hand on her daughter's shoulder and Marissa shook it off. "Call down if you need me, honey."

"Mom," Marissa groaned, her cheeks tinged with pink. "I'm fine." She turned and led them up a wide staircase lined with family pictures.

Evelyn stared at them as she walked up, to avoid looking straight ahead as Marissa led them upstairs in her too-short skirt and hoodie.

She was a little surprised Jan Anderson let her daughter walk around in clothing so revealing, but then again, all the signs of teenage rebellion were there.

"Here," Marissa said, leading them into a room that practically exploded with pink, and had clothes draped over every available surface. She scooted a pile off a desk chair in one corner and spun it around for Sophia, who took a seat.

"I can get another from my brother's room."

"I'm fine," Evelyn said, glancing around again, noticing how different this room looked from Haley's. "How long have you and Haley been best friends?" she started, wondering what they had in common apart from cheerleading. Haley had been a straight-A student, but from what Evelyn had gleaned from the notes on Marissa, she was closer to C+/B- grades. They were both cheerleaders, and seemed to spend a lot of time together, but Haley took art classes and volunteered, while Marissa acted in school plays and had a retail job after school.

"Since we were kids," Marissa said, and Evelyn tried not to crack a smile.

They were still kids, at least in her mind. Focused on all the normal concerns of a high school student, she assumed. Then again, at seventeen, Evelyn had been dealing with the sudden return of her alcoholic mother after seven long years away. She'd been getting her grandma settled in her first nursing home after her stroke, and making the tough decision to go to college early so she wouldn't have to live with her mother.

She forced herself to listen closely, and not take anything about Marissa—or Haley—for granted. Assumptions could derail an investigation.

"How'd you meet?"

Marissa flopped down on the bed, resting her chin in her hands. "We lived in the same neighborhood. Before Haley's parents split up, she lived down the street. A whole bunch of kids from our elementary school lived here actually, and we all used to play together. But Haley and I got tight. We've pretty much done everything together ever since."

"Like cheerleading?" Evelyn asked, acting on a hunch. "Did she join for you?"

"Yeah." Marissa tugged at a lock of hair, twisting it around and around her finger. "How'd you know?" Not waiting for an answer, she continued, "Haley did gymnastics when she was little, so I knew she'd be good at it. I had to convince her to try out for the squad, but once she joined, she loved it. Cheerleading is the best way to get guys to notice you."

"And did they?"

"Of course. I mean, Haley didn't need it after she met Jordan, but it's still nice to be noticed."

Marissa's voice changed at the mention of Jordan, and Evelyn wondered why. "What do you think of Jordan?"

Marissa stopped her hair twirling. "He's super nice. He drops her off for practice and takes her out for dinner all the time. He'd do anything for her."

Jealousy, Evelyn realized. That's what she'd heard in Marissa's voice. But was it because Haley was dating a college boy, or specifically because of Jordan?

"What about the day Haley went missing?" Sophia jumped in, her thoughts obviously taking a different track than Evelyn. "You saw him drop her off and then drive away when Haley walked into the school?"

"Yeah," Marissa said. "Well…" She frowned. "I saw him drop her off and drive away. I guess I didn't actually *see* her go inside, but she must have. She was walking toward the school and I watched Jordan leave, and then when I looked back, she wasn't there. But there's nowhere else she could have gone."

"How'd Haley meet Jordan?" Evelyn jumped in. She watched the girl closely, certain she'd stumbled onto a different secret. Because instead of watching her best friend walk into the school, Marissa had been watching Haley's boyfriend drive away.

Marissa sighed. "Six months back, I begged her to go with me to this party I heard about at Neville U. I had a friend who went there, and he said I couldn't miss it. The party was at Jordan's frat, and that was where we met him. Practically the next week, he and Haley were official."

"Officially dating?" Sophia asked.

Marissa rolled her eyes. "Yeah. It's like if he'd given her his class ring or pin, or whatever you used to do back in the day."

A smile quivered on Sophia's lips. "Okay."

Evelyn frowned, wondering at the inconsistency. Jordan had said they weren't exclusive, but it sounded like Haley had thought they were. Had Jordan been lying to her? "Were they sleeping together?" Evelyn asked, and Sophia's eyebrows rose.

Marissa fidgeted on the bed and she flushed. "Nah. Haley was waiting. Seemed crazy to me. I mean, Jordan was a catch! She should have done it, hooked him even more." Her lips pursed. "Though he sure seemed crazy about her, anyway."

"And since then, you haven't seen Jordan with anyone else?" Sophia asked. "They were exclusive?"

"Jordan?" Marissa scoffed, and just when Evelyn thought she was going to say he dated around and Haley had no idea, she finished, "That guy *adores* Haley. He was exclusive."

"Are you sure—" Sophia started, but Evelyn cut her off.

"What about Haley?"

Marissa fidgeted, went back to the hair twirling, but this time she brought the hair up to cover her mouth. "She was crazy about Jordan, too. I mean, look, she's my best friend."

"But she was cheating on him?" Evelyn persisted, even as Sophia gave her a "what the hell" look.

"She never said—"

"But you suspected it?" Evelyn interrupted.

Marissa frowned down at her lap. "I didn't want to rat her out or anything."

"This could help us find her," Evelyn said softly.

Marissa cringed. "I'm sure it has nothing to do with that, but yeah, she was seeing someone else. I don't know what she was thinking. She had *Jordan* and he wasn't enough for her?"

"Do you know who else she was dating?"

"She never told me," Marissa said, a hint of petulance in her tone. "I don't know why she kept it from me. I wouldn't have ratted her out to Jordan. But I could tell. I've known Haley since we were little. I always knew when she was keeping things from me."

"You never talked to her about it?" Sophia asked, skepticism in her voice.

"No." Marissa sat straighter, sounding defensive. "And I didn't say anything before, because what does it matter? I didn't want to spill her secrets, not when they have nothing to do with someone grabbing her."

Evelyn didn't have to glance at Sophia to sense her frustration. She wondered if they were thinking the same thing. What if Haley's secret had nothing to do with her cheating on Jordan? What if that was just wishful thinking on Marissa's part because she wanted him for herself? "Are you sure the thing Haley was hiding was that she was seeing someone besides Jordan?"

Marissa fidgeted, not meeting their eyes. "Yeah, I'm sure."

"Marissa," Sophia said in the sort of stern, listen-to-me tone Evelyn imagined she probably used on her own kids. "We need to know every detail, no matter how small it might seem. It could help us find Haley."

Marissa frowned, tugging at the bottom of her skirt. She was silent for so long Evelyn almost broke in, but finally Marissa said, "I'm pretty sure that's why she was being secretive."

"Okay," Sophia said, pen poised over her little notebook. "What about not seeing Haley actually go inside?

Are you sure? You didn't look back? When was the last moment you remember actually *seeing* Haley?"

"I watched her walk up the walkway toward the school's door. She was carrying a bag—her cheerleading stuff—and she turned back to wave at Jordan. That's when I looked back, too. He waved at her and then drove away. I watched his car go around the bend, and when I looked back, Haley wasn't there. But she must have gone inside, right?" Marissa glanced back and forth between them, looking a little panicked.

"Probably," Sophia agreed, standing and looking pointedly at Evelyn. Signaling that she was ready to go.

But Evelyn didn't want to give up on the other line of questioning, so she took one last stab at it. "Marissa, if you had to guess who Haley was seeing besides Jordan, who would it be?"

Marissa bit her lip, her eyebrows dipping down as she stared up at Evelyn, suddenly resembling a little kid and not the grown-up she was trying so desperately to be.

"I don't know his last name," Marissa said so softly Evelyn had to lean closer. "But I saw him and Haley together once and they seemed…too friendly. At first, I thought they were trying to get to know each other, because of Jordan, but then…the way he was looking at her…"

"Who is it?" Sophia asked.

"Nate," Marissa replied. "Jordan's best friend."

7

"The girl is dead."

"What?" Kyle McKenzie looked up from his computer screen, rubbing the top of his injured shoulder, which was throbbing. He'd overdone it in PT last night and he was paying for it today. If his physical therapist was to be believed, there was only so far PT was going to take him—and it wouldn't be far enough. But he refused to believe that.

Hunching over a computer all morning wasn't helping, though. Day two in the WFO and he felt as if he'd been locked inside the three gray walls of a cubicle for weeks already. Like an industrial-colored tomb. "Who's dead?"

"Tonya Klein. A couple of hours ago."

Kyle sat straighter, his fists tightening reactively. She'd fought so hard to survive the attack in that alley, and still she'd died from her injuries. "What happened? I thought she made it through the surgery okay."

"She did." Jimmy peered at Kyle over the top of their shared cubicle wall. "I didn't quite understand all the medical jargon, but apparently her internal injuries were worse than they thought. She had some kind of blood clot, and it traveled to her brain. They just notified her family. And her roommate, to get next of kin information."

"Damn it," Kyle muttered, picturing the bruises and splints on her hands that had proven she'd fought hard for her life, and the dead stare in her eyes that showed she'd long since stopped believing she had anything to live for.

He opened his desk drawer and strapped on his hand-cuffs and his Glock pistol—a far cry from the multi-tude of weapons he was used to carrying with the HRT.

"Where are we going?" Jimmy asked, coming around the cubicle with his own weapon already on his hip and looping his handcuffs through his belt.

"I want to go back to that campus. Talk to her room-mate. I want to know what got Tonya Klein killed."

"She came to us claiming she was trafficked, so we can make an argument for jurisdiction," Jimmy said, following as Kyle headed for the door. "But I'm not sure there's anything there."

"Maybe not," Kyle agreed. Maybe his desperation to be back in the field had him itching to solve this case. Or maybe he just needed to be useful, instead of sitting in the office doing paperwork. But most of all, Kyle admitted to himself, it was the way Tonya had looked when she'd told her story. The bruising on her neck re-minded him of an injury he'd seen on Evelyn the same night Jimmy had almost died. Ever since then, strangu-lation cases had particularly pissed him off.

"I'll drive," Kyle said, pulling out the FBI-issued keys he'd hung on to the day before.

"Come on, Mac," Jimmy muttered. "They gave us the siren for a reason."

But in the parking garage, Jimmy climbed into the passenger seat without comment, flipping on the heat, since the temperature had finally returned to normal. Tiny snowflakes were even drifting slowly onto the windshield as Kyle pulled into the street and headed back toward the Neville campus.

"I did some digging yesterday after we got back," he told Jimmy as he wound through the surface streets toward the freeway. "The university confirmed that about three months ago Tonya quit her two campus jobs. But she paid her midyear tuition payment on time and in full. The man I talked to at the bursar's office sounded surprised about that. He said Tonya came in on a partial scholarship, that she was from a very low-income family and even with her jobs they knew making her tuition would be a struggle."

"Well, that matches what Tonya told us about them paying for enough of her tuition so she could quit her jobs," Jimmy said. "But why the hell would human traffickers pay that? Why wouldn't they let her fail out, pull her deeper into their network? Otherwise, they'd be giving away a big chunk of their profit right from the start. I know girls in these situations can be earning upward of a thousand dollars a night, but tuition at Neville— even for a semester—is costly. They'd be losing a lot of money first. It doesn't add up."

Kyle nodded as he hit the gas and merged onto the freeway. "Yeah, but neither does a standard pimp paying for her tuition."

"No, so maybe it's neither," Jimmy said. "Maybe that first tape really was about revenge, and her being attacked is connected to it somehow. I've seen stranger things. But I've got to tell you, I've been on a few human trafficking cases since I moved over to Civil Rights and this is pretty strange."

Before Kyle could agree, Jimmy began ticking off

reasons on his fingers. "The whole point of human trafficking is to make money. How can they do that if they're paying the college tuition that this girl struggled to pay with multiple jobs? The setup is also weird. She's still living in the dorms, and going to classes, and then what? She goes out in the evenings for the sex trafficking, by herself? How does she know where to go, who to meet? And how are they going to keep control of her that way? Short term, sure, the threat she talked about would probably work, but long term?"

"Well, long term she came to us," Kyle pointed out.

"Not really. She got beaten up trying to get away and *then* called us. Who knows if she would have called us if she'd made it out without getting hurt."

Kyle frowned, whipping around slower cars and getting into the left lane. Jeez, maybe Jimmy was right about the siren—he could use the adrenaline rush. "She said she tried to go to the police and that's why they beat her up."

Jimmy pulled out his notebook and flipped back through some pages. "You're right. But we don't know if she just mentioned that she was going to the police and these guys heard about it, or if she actually did report it and they didn't believe her. Or, obviously, if her story is just unreliable."

"We need to see if there's an incident report with the campus police or the locals."

"Yeah," Jimmy agreed. "We can make some calls when we get back to the office. I don't want to stand around a police station all day waiting for someone to dig that up."

"I want to talk to the roommate," Kyle said half an hour later as he pulled off the freeway and drove into Neville's pristine campus. With the snow coming down on the tree-lined cobblestone streets, students carrying books and walking in pairs, it looked picture-perfect. The kind of place any parent would want to send their child. But was there a dark side to the idyllic little college campus?

"This is it," he said, pulling up in front of a building that didn't even remotely resemble the college dorms where he'd lived so many years ago. He remembered big, block buildings jammed full of tiny, utilitarian rooms. This place could have been a billionaire's home.

"You know Tonya's roommate's name?" Jimmy asked as they got out of the Bureau car.

"Janelle Cooper. Also a freshman. They were paired by the school, didn't know each other before they started at Neville."

Jimmy glanced back at him. "You already did some checking up on this case, huh?"

"It doesn't sit right with me." He picked up his pace and caught up with Jimmy as he reached the dorm entrance. "I agree with you that it doesn't outwardly resemble human trafficking. But it's ringing all my warning bells."

Jimmy nodded, grabbing the door as someone opened it from inside, then flashing his badge—and a big grin—at her when she looked concerned. "FBI. Can you tell me Janelle Cooper's room number?"

"Third floor," the girl replied, juggling a stack of books and sliding past Jimmy without another glance. "Room 309."

"Well, I guess that answers my question about dorm security," Kyle said as they skipped the elevator and started up the first flight of stairs. He took them two at a time, grateful for the chance to get a little exercise.

"I showed her my badge," Jimmy protested.

"Yeah, and she didn't even look at it." He hurried up the rest of the stairs, hearing Jimmy huff behind him, trying to keep up.

He only had to knock once before Janelle opened the door. She wore ripped jeans and a sweatshirt that swallowed her, but her makeup was perfectly applied, her eyes neither red nor puffy.

Jimmy said she'd been told about her roommate's death. So they probably hadn't been close.

"Janelle Cooper?" When she nodded, Kyle held up his credentials. "I'm Kyle McKenzie, with the FBI, and this is my partner, Jimmy Drescott." The words felt odd on his lips. Normally, when he announced himself as FBI, it was at a much higher volume, and spoken while holding an MP-5 submachine gun.

"This is about Tonya?" When he nodded, Janelle stepped back inside, slipping her bag off her shoulder and onto the floor. "We shared a room, but I barely knew her, so I can't tell you a whole lot. And I've got class in twenty minutes. I hope you don't have a lot of questions."

Kyle tried not to let his distaste show. "Do you know about Tonya?" he asked gently, just in case he was wrong and no one had notified her.

"That she died today? Yeah, I got a call." She sighed and sank onto the bottom bed of a messy bunk. "Look, I don't mean to be insensitive. It's horrible what happened to her, but let's get real here. She should have seen it coming."

Kyle frowned at the anger in Janelle's tone, wondering if she was blaming the victim because it was easier than dealing with what had happened to Tonya.

"Why's that?" Jimmy asked, stepping into the room and closing the door behind them.

* * *

'I'm not really back into the swing of things,"
Evelyn as they drove away from the BAU offic
uia, where she'd finally checked in after two da
istered in the tiny Neville police station.

It had been strange going back to Aquia. In her sho
me at Neville, she'd gotten used to Sophia's constan
ergy, to the frequent interruptions from Quincy an
e curiosity of the other officers in the small station
he near silence in the BAU office had struck her today
a way it never had before.

The stack of cases waiting on her desk had prompte
nusual anxiety, reminding her that she couldn't spen
orever on the Haley Cooke case. And although she'
ade progress—she knew the players a little bette
hich was the first step in creating a profile—she wa
ar from solving Haley's disappearance. It had been tw
ays since she'd been handed the case. She didn't kno
ow much longer she'd need—or how much time Da
ould give her before she'd have to move on.

She could tell Kyle was facing his own frustration
e'd picked her up after work looking pensive, his typ
al state since he'd left the HRT. She twined her fin
ers with his over the gearshift. "This job at the WF
only temporary, anyway. You'll get back to the HRT
he forced herself to sound certain, because if anyon
uld do it, it was Kyle. Pure determination had gotte
m back to work sooner than expected, and she kne
applied that never-give-up attitude to everything.

"Yeah, maybe," he replied, his attention on the road
tone more unsure than she'd ever heard it.

It would be a challenge—they couldn't hold a sp
him, and places on the HRT were highly compe
, with rare openings. But he'd gotten in once, a

Janelle flushed. "You know what she was doing, right?"

"We were hoping to get your take on that," Kyle told her.

"We weren't close, so she didn't talk to me, but it was obvious what was going on. I mean, she didn't bring guys back here, thank God. But she came home later and later every night, looking like…" Janelle's lip curled. "It began really quickly after school started. The first two months, I thought she was pretty normal. But then it started and, wow, that girl barely slept. She's from Alabama, did you know that? I don't know how she got into it so fast."

"What was she into?" Kyle asked, not wanting to lead her anywhere.

"At first, I thought she was just—you know—sleeping around. But it happened too much. And then she quit her jobs, which I know she needed to pay her tuition. But her bills got paid, anyway." Janelle glanced at her phone, and her words sped up. "She was getting paid for it."

"Do you know if she was working for someone?" Jimmy asked.

"What, you mean a pimp?" Janelle shrugged. "If she was, I never saw him, but I guess it would explain how she found all these guys willing to pay her."

"Was she suddenly spending a lot more money?" Kyle spoke up.

"Tonya?" Janelle snorted. "No way. I guess she wasn't charging enough, because I loaned her money for dinner last week."

"Did you ever get the feeling she was being threatened, or that someone was coercing her?"

Janelle's forehead creased. "You mean, forcing her

to do it? No. She seemed different, definitely, but not scared. More, I don't know, depressed?"

"What about anyone hanging around more than usual? Watching her? Or did she ever mention anyone that scared her?"

"Not that I saw. We didn't really hang out, especially after she started all her 'jobs.' Honestly, I was trying to get a room reassignment. I mean, over the last month or so, she was better. She seemed to be taking a break, but I doubt it was going to last. And anyway, how could someone force her to do that?"

Instead of trying to explain it to her, Kyle asked, "She wasn't going out as much the past month?"

"No. But she kept obsessively checking her phone as if she was expecting calls. Maybe these guys got tired of paying. I don't know, but I didn't want any part of it."

Kyle glanced at Jimmy. They hadn't recovered Tonya's cell phone. He wondered if her attackers in the alley had taken it. "Is there anything else that seemed unusual in the past few months? Anything else you can tell us about Tonya's routines that changed?"

Janelle looked at her phone again and jumped to her feet. "No. Like I said, we didn't hang out, especially once she started this. She was hardly ever here, but honestly, the whole situation made me nervous. She wasn't bringing guys back here, but what if she decided to start? The truth is, what she was doing scared me. I tried to stay as far away from her as I could. And I've gotta go. I'm not going to make it to my class unless I leave now, and the professor grades on attendance."

"What about other friends we could talk to?" Kyle persisted.

Janelle tossed her bag over her shoulder. "Until she

started staying out all night, she kept to classes and her jobs, really."

"So no one she was seeing or hanging fore three months ago?" Kyle persisted as sh foot, holding open the door. Because what said before made sense—if she'd initially b ened because of a sex tape, then someone personally was probably involved.

"No. Not that I ever saw, and definitely no brought back here."

"All right," Jimmy said, following her out and handing her his card. "Give us a call if yo of anything else, anything at all."

"Yeah, sure," she replied, dropping it into he where she'd probably never find it again and lock the door behind them.

As she disappeared into the elevator, Jimmy l back at Kyle. "I hate to say it, but I think this is for the locals."

"I'm not sure," Kyle disagreed.

"Come on, man," Jimmy said, amusement in h "We'll get a real case. Just be patient. This isn't th You can't be a hero every single time."

He headed for the stairs, and Kyle follow slowly, a sour feeling in his stomach. Was Jimm Did he just want there to be a case here be needed some purpose outside of the HRT? V ally that rusty at regular casework?

It was possible, he admitted silently. But h shake the feeling that there was more going o Tonya's death wasn't as straightforward as i

And the one thing he sure as hell hadn his time as a regular special agent was his He wasn't giving up on this case yet.

she knew his team valued him. She'd thought he was just discouraged when they'd talked about it before, but now she wondered. Was there more to it?

Before she could figure out the best way to broach it, he said, "It's this case we've got at the WFO. Jimmy thinks there's nothing here, and he could be right. Nothing we're learning stacks up with human trafficking."

"Human trafficking?" Evelyn heard the surprise in her voice. Trading in other human beings was one of the fastest growing criminal enterprises, but investigations were complicated, with the traffickers notoriously difficult to locate and prosecute. "Out of where? And did you say Jimmy? It's not Jimmy—"

"Drescott?" Kyle glanced at her. "Yep. He switched to Civil Rights. I guess I didn't mention that, did I?"

"No, I definitely would have remembered if you'd told me Jimmy Drescott was your new partner." She hadn't worked with Jimmy for very long, but she'd spent most of her conversations with him resisting rolling her eyes. He wasn't a bad agent, just a huge flirt, with more confidence than experience or common sense.

She remembered the way he'd looked the last time she'd seen him, at the hospital after having his neck stitched up. "How's he doing?"

"Same old Jimmy."

"Huh." She was surprised the experience hadn't changed him, but maybe he was good at hiding it. "Sorry—what were you saying about the case?"

"Well, it's out of Neville U, which is the other reason it seems implausible, but I just—"

"Neville University?" Evelyn broke in.

"Yeah. Why?"

She twisted to face him. "Haley was dating a kid

who goes there. So, really? Trafficking at Neville?" She hadn't heard anything about that from Sophia.

"Honestly, it's a long shot that it's a legitimate trafficking operation. But if it is, then the girl was probably targeted because she was far from family, had no immediate support system and had limited means. As far as we know, we've only got one victim, and from the afternoon I spent on the phone with the Neville police station and the campus police, there are no incident reports involving this girl. And no similar assault reports at Neville University, either. If there is a trafficking ring at Neville, it's pretty far under the radar."

"Then why do you think that's what's happening?" she asked, knowing sometimes an agent's gut instinct, even when it went against all the evidence, could be right. She relied on hers more than she'd ever admit, because although profiling was about psychology and behavioral evidence and statistics, it was also about instinct. And every Special Agent, whether they knew it or not, had a little bit of a profiler in them.

Kyle's forehead creased, as though he was trying to figure it out himself. "It's the girl's story. She might have been lying, but sitting there in her hospital room, I believed her. If it wasn't a trafficking ring, I think she believed it was. I think she was being threatened. The details don't line up, but they're also too specific to be completely made up. Not to mention, someone tried damn hard to kill her. There's a case here. I'm just not completely sure what it is—and if trafficking is happening, my guess would be amateurs."

"Well, that's possible," Evelyn said slowly, even though Neville University seemed an unlikely spot for sex trafficking recruiters. On the whole, the students were too well-off, had too many resources easily at their disposal, to be lured in by the hope of a high-paying modeling job or some other easy-money promise that traffickers often used. But maybe it wasn't about money. At the college level, a lot of the trafficking was actually a vulnerability game—a "Romeo" who swept in and over time manipulated the victim into the sex trade. "Are you looking at some kind of boyfriend scenario?"

"Nope, not a romancing at all. This is straight-up threats," Kyle said, picking up speed as he hopped on the freeway and headed toward her house. "It's definitely an odd setup. It could be a one-off sort of situation. The victim died, so we don't have anywhere near the amount of details we need."

"So is the squad taking the case on?"

"I don't know about the squad," Kyle said. "But I am."

Since her conversation with Kyle the night before, Evelyn hadn't been able to get the human trafficking angle out of her head. Nothing about Haley's behavior suggested she'd been pulled into a trafficking ring— she had no unexplained injuries, no sudden depression, no drop in her grades. But if Kyle's theory had merit, she couldn't let go of the coincidence that there was a major criminal enterprise at the same university where Haley's boyfriend attended school.

So, instead of going to the BAU office or the Neville police station that morning, Evelyn had gone directly back to Marissa Anderson's house. She stood on the stoop now, shifting back and forth until Marissa opened the door.

In deference to the light snow that had begun falling yesterday and hadn't stopped, Marissa was wearing leggings underneath another tiny skirt, and a Sherpa-lined hoodie. "Hi." The single word was loaded with surprise.

"Evelyn Baine. I'm the profiler—"

"I remember. What's happening? Did you find her?" She peered around Evelyn, as though she was looking for Sophia. Or maybe hoping Haley herself would be standing in the driveway.

"No. I'm sorry. I just have a question about Haley's schedule, and I thought you would know best."

Marissa nodded, stepping back to let Evelyn inside. "Sure. Come on in. Mom and Dad just took the boys to church."

"Do you want to wait—"

"It's fine." Marissa led her straight back, into a cheery yellow kitchen with rooster items on every available surface. Evelyn must have looked perplexed, because Marissa rolled her eyes and said, "My mom is obsessed with them. You wouldn't believe how many things you can buy in the shape of a rooster. Anyway. What did you need to know?"

Evelyn sat at the scarred wood table and shifted to face Marissa, who was leaning against the counter, looking anxious to help.

"How often was Haley at Neville University?"

"On campus?"

Evelyn nodded.

"Hardly ever. I mean, that's where she met Jordan, of course, when I took her to that party. But her mom wasn't crazy about Haley going to a college campus. Actually, she was pissed off when she found out Haley and I went to the party. Haley was grounded for a week. And her mom didn't like Haley dating a college guy, either, but she kind of came around on Jordan. He's pretty charming. It's hard not to get along with him.

Anyway," she said quickly when Evelyn was about to speak, "mostly he came to her."

"Are you sure?" Evelyn asked. "I'm not looking to get her in trouble or tell her mom. But I need to evaluate who Haley knew, who she hung out with, who might have seen her. To do that, I need to know where she spent her time."

Marissa frowned down at her feet.

"What is it?" Evelyn pressed. Could there be a connection? But how in the hell would Haley Cooke have gotten mixed up with a sex trafficking ring?

"I'm not lying about the campus thing." Marissa stared at Evelyn straight-on, her expression earnest. "Look, I would have loved if Haley would go there more." Her lips twisted self-consciously. "I wanted her to introduce me to Jordan's friends, and I tried to get her to go to more of the parties. But they weren't really Haley's thing. Plus, Jordan knew Haley's mom was nervous about her dating him, and I think he was trying to get on her good side. So he always drove to her house or got her from school or whatever. I think she'd been on campus maybe two or three times."

"So, what aren't you telling me?" Evelyn asked, leaning forward. "I promise, whatever it is, I'll keep it to myself if I can. But anything you can tell me might help. Sometimes, the smallest things, the most inconsequential things, are what break a case."

"Okay, okay," Marissa said, dropping into the seat next to her. "Remember what I said before about Haley cheating on Jordan with his best friend?"

"Yes."

"Jordan's best friend goes to Neville University, too. So, even though Haley never went to campus with me, and hardly ever with Jordan, she might have gone there to meet Nate."

"How sure are you about this?" Evelyn asked, sensing there was more to it than simple suspicion on Marissa's part. Was it just more of Marissa's desire to have Jordan for herself?

"I'm positive. I didn't want to tell on her, but I saw her and Nate together. Besides, yesterday I could tell you and Detective Lopez really wanted to know about Jordan. Detective Lopez doesn't like him, but if you ask me, it's Nate you should be looking at. That guy... he was just creepy."

"Okay," Evelyn said, getting to her feet. "Are you sure you don't remember his last name?"

"No. Wait! It was Smokes. Or Stoker. Or... Stokes! Nate Stokes!"

"Thanks," Evelyn said. "This could really help."

Marissa grinned, a huge smile that caused her blue eyes to sparkle and made her seem like a typical teenager, not the best friend of a girl who'd been missing for a month. "Maybe I could be a detective someday."

Then her smile fell, and those pleading blue eyes locked on Evelyn. "You're going to find her, right?"

In that instant, Evelyn saw herself in Marissa. Her own best friend had gone missing when she was twelve, not seventeen, but she remembered feeling the same desperation she saw in Marissa now. Remembered trying to act normal, pretending not to hear the whispers all around her about whether or not Cassie would ever be found, about all the horrible things that might have happened to her.

She put her hand on Marissa's arm and squeezed. "I'm going to do everything I can. I promise you I won't give up."

Her own words echoed in her head the entire drive over to Neville University. She didn't make promises she couldn't keep, especially not to friends and families of victims. And the fact was, her days on this case were limited. There were too many profiles that came into the BAU every single day and too few profilers to handle them. She needed to work faster.

That anxiety pushed her as she hurried into the administration building at Neville University, flashed her credentials and asked to speak with someone about a student.

They got her settled in back with the heat blasting on high and air so dry that she needed a bottle of water as soon as she sat down. She waited ten minutes, her feet tapping and checking her watch, thinking about all the bad luck they'd had in this case. She'd woken this morning to a call from Sophia, telling her the mail carrier who'd brought the note from Haley couldn't give them anything. She remembered someone bumping into her, but she'd grumbled that she dealt with people all day long and couldn't describe them all.

They needed a break badly. And Evelyn hoped the tall, cadaverously thin man who walked in and held out a bony hand could give her one.

"I understand you have a question about a student."

"That's right. It's about—"

"I'm familiar with the Haley Cooke case. And I'm sure you're familiar with privacy laws."

"All I need—"

"But given the gravity of the situation, you tell me what you need, and I'll do my best to accommodate you."

Evelyn tried not to snap at the constant interruptions. "I need information about a student named Nate

Stokes. I just need to know where I can find him to ask him some questions."

"Nate Stokes?"

"That's right." She waited for him to start digging in the shiny new file cabinet behind him or tapping away on the state-of-the-art laptop on his desk, but instead he just leaned toward her across the desk.

His bony hands locked together on top of the desk. "Why do you need to talk to Nate?"

"It's connected to Haley's case."

"Someone kidnapped Nate, too?" he squeaked.

"Excuse me?"

He let out a breath. "Excuse *me*," he said, sounding embarrassed. "But I also need to speak with Nate Stokes. This is a pretty small campus. I'm the head of Administration and I run a tight ship. Every semester, I can tell you the names of anyone who missed a tuition payment or who's on academic suspension."

"Is Nate on suspension?"

"No. Nate missed a tuition payment. And he stopped showing up to classes. We tried to get ahold of family, but Nate's parents died while he was a minor. He has a trust fund and his uncle technically got custody, but apparently the reality was that Nate was pretty much on his own. He was…unreliable, I guess is the best way to put it. We figured this was more of the same."

"What do you mean? Did he leave school? When did this happen?"

"He left school, yes. He disappeared, really."

"Disappeared?" Evelyn shifted closer and tried not to let disbelief or anger into her voice. In a town as small as Neville—even if the campus was in some ways separate—she couldn't believe no one had mentioned a second missing kid. Of course, technically, Nate Stokes was an adult. There were a whole different set of rules there than when a child disappeared. "Did you file a police report?"

"The campus police looked into it. They couldn't find him. But again, Nate has a history of this kind of thing. This isn't the first time he's taken off, missed a bunch of classes with no word to anyone and then came back acting as if nothing happened. We figured he'd turn up. But now that you're saying he's connected to Haley…" He leaned back in his chair, frowning.

"What?"

"Nate went missing the week before Haley."

8

"How the hell did I not know about this?" Sophia railed. "How is it that no one found this relevant enough to file a missing-persons report? And why did no one mention it in the past *month* while we tried to track down Haley? How could Jordan not have mentioned it?" She smacked the wall with an open-faced palm, hard enough to make the board of Haley's pictures shake.

"I don't know," Evelyn said, sitting calmly at the folding table, even though she shared Sophia's frustration. "But we need to take a look, see if there's any chance it's connected. I know Bill, Pete and Jordan were at the top of our suspect list, but I think we need to pause and look into Nate. If the Admin guy is right, the timing is awfully coincidental."

"Yeah, or the whole thing is connected, and I've been running in circles for no good reason," Sophia snapped, then took a calming breath. "Okay. You're right. Let's go back to the university and see what's happening. Because I've never heard the name Nate Stokes before now, and if this guy was Jordan's best friend, why the hell didn't he mention someone *else* he knew had recently gone missing?"

"He might have thought Nate just took off and it had

nothing to do with Haley. Marissa's theory is that Nate and Haley were seeing each other behind Jordan's back, and that Jordan's and Haley's families didn't know anything about it. Teenagers keep secrets."

Sophia frowned. "Maybe. But his name didn't turn up in Haley's room, either. And given everything I know about Haley, I'd be surprised if she was cheating on her boyfriend with his best friend."

Evelyn was about to make an argument for how often people acted in ways that would surprise everyone around them, but Sophia spoke first.

"I'll tell you what—if you drive this time, then I'll play bad cop with Jordan when we get there."

"Sounds good," Evelyn said, getting to her feet just as her cell phone rang. She took a peek, saw her grandma's number and frowned. "Hang on a sec. I need to take this."

She stepped out of the tiny war room for Haley's case and into the mild chaos of the police station. Ducking into a quiet corner, Evelyn answered the phone. "Grandma?" Her grandmother, Mabel, lived in an old-age home near Evelyn's house. It had been just her and her grandparents since Evelyn was ten years old and they'd rescued her from the hellish existence that was living with her mother. After her grandpa's death when she was fifteen and her grandma's stroke when Evelyn was seventeen, it had been her turn to become the caretaker. But Evelyn visited and called regularly; Mabel didn't usually call her, especially not in the early afternoon.

"Evelyn?" Her grandma's voice was confused.

Evelyn closed her eyes and took a calming breath. Mabel's dementia had been getting worse for years. Some days she was still perfectly coherent; other times, she didn't know who Evelyn was. Most often, she recognized Evelyn, but thought it was a long time ago, when her husband was still alive, and Evelyn was just a little girl.

"Yep, it's me, Grandma. How are you doing?"

"I'm ready to go home now. I think we should head home."

"You are home, Grandma."

"No, home to Rose Bay."

Something twisted in Evelyn's chest. Mabel hadn't been back to Rose Bay since Evelyn had left for college, thirteen years ago. But Mabel still thought of it as home, the house they'd brought Evelyn to live in. It was the place that held some of the best and worst memories of Evelyn's life. Both the joy of living with people who loved and cared for her, and the trauma of her best friend going missing. The case that had driven her into the FBI.

"We've got to stay here right now, Grandma, okay?"

"Okay, but Lily wants to go home."

Lillian Baine. Evelyn's mother, and Mabel's only daughter, whom neither of them had seen in thirteen years.

Evelyn knew trying to explain it to her grandmother was pointless, and would only upset her. Instead, she said, "We'll go home soon, Grandma. Just get some rest now, okay?"

"Okay, Evelyn, honey. Come see me soon."

She hung up before Evelyn could say goodbye, and Evelyn tucked the phone into her pocket, longing for the days when her grandma's mind was still strong and sharp. But she knew those days weren't coming back, and she needed to be grateful for what she still had.

"You ready?"

Evelyn started, her head still in the conversation, and spun around to find Sophia standing behind her, a laptop in one hand and a cell phone in the other, looking impatient.

"What?"

"Let's find out what happened to Nate Stokes." Without waiting for a reply, Sophia headed for the front of the station. Other officers stepped aside as she plowed through with her typical long stride and swinging arms.

Evelyn followed in her wake, trying to shake off the worry about her grandma. This was normal. But it didn't matter how many times it happened, she still had trouble accepting her grandmother's mental decline.

"Let's go!" Sophia called when Evelyn stepped outside, shivering.

The snow had finally stopped, but it had left behind a crisp midforties temperature that made Evelyn wish she'd paused to grab her coat.

"Coming, coming," Evelyn muttered, putting her focus back where it belonged as she unlocked her car and climbed into the driver's seat.

As she pulled out of the parking lot, she told Sophia about the human trafficking investigation Kyle was running that might be centered at Neville University. "Have you heard of any rumors about that? Has the Neville police station received any reports of crimes that might be connected? Sex crimes in particular?"

Sophia looked up from where she'd been typing away on her phone to shoot her a look of disbelief. "Human trafficking? Out of *Neville University*? Not a chance. I mean, look, their campus police takes more calls about things that happen on campus than we do, but the things we see coming out of Neville are pretty much what you'd expect for a college town. Theft, vandalism, assault—usually parties that get out of hand and a couple of kids getting into a fight."

"What about sexual assault?"

"It's a college campus," Sophia repeated. "You know those stats. Neville is pretty typical."

Pretty typical meant about one in five women at Neville were sexually assaulted. "Is there a chance any of those have been connected to human trafficking?"

"I seriously doubt it. I mean, we get acquaintance rape. We've seen a handful of victims who were drugged, and a very small number of stranger attacks. But I've never heard of anything systematic coming from Neville. And certainly not anything organized, the way you'd expect with human trafficking."

"What about location?" Evelyn asked. If there *was* human trafficking happening, they would probably have one—or a handful—of specific locations where the interactions with customers happened.

There was silence, and Evelyn glanced over to see Sophia looking pensive, her phone held as though she was mid-text. Finally she shook her head. "I don't think so. Nothing that stands out as a place with high traffic for reports. But when we get back to the station, we can ask Quincy. He has a pretty good rapport with the campus police. He might have a better sense if anything seems unusual."

"Okay," Evelyn said as she slowed for Neville University's cobblestone roads.

"You're not suggesting Haley was trafficked, are you? Because there was nothing to suggest she'd fallen in with a strange crowd, or that someone new had come into her life, which would be standard warning signs, I'd think. And Haley had no decline in grades, no depression, no unexplained injuries leading up to her disappearance."

"Hmm," Evelyn said. Those were also warning signs

for other kinds of sexual assault. Haley having none would suggest Pete wasn't threatening her, either. Of course, some victims hid it better than others.

"We'll leave the trafficking case to the Civil Rights squad and focus on Haley," Evelyn said when Sophia looked ready to continue. She pulled into the parking lot at Jordan's fraternity house.

"Well, let's focus on this case," Sophia said, stepping out of the sedan. "Let's go talk to Mr. Smug."

"We should consider the possibility that Nate and Haley ran off together," Evelyn said as she hopped out of the car and hurried to catch up with Sophia, who was heading for the frat house.

"No way."

"I know there was a week in between, but maybe that was to throw off suspicion."

"Come on—"

"I've seen similar cases, especially with kids Haley's age. Impressionable, easily convinced that they don't have options by an older, charming guy."

"You're suggesting, what? That Nate told Haley they needed to run away to be together, just because Haley was dating Jordan? Doesn't that seem a little dramatic?"

"Maybe. Or maybe either Pete or Bill was abusing her and Haley confided in Nate, then he convinced her this was her best option."

"But why Nate?" Sophia argued. "And not Jordan? Plus, even if they did run away together, a lot has happened since then. So, what? They drove far away, to stay holed up in a motel and ignore the massive media focus on Haley? Is it really probable that no one has recognized her in a month?"

"Or something bad happened to both of them."

Sophia frowned. "I liked it better when you thought

Haley was a kidnap victim," she said, and knocked on the frat house door.

A full minute passed before anyone answered, but when the door finally opened, a droopy-eyed kid stared back at them, his hair sticking up at odd angles and the stench of old beer seeping from his pores.

The odor made Evelyn long to take a step back. She associated the smell of old beer with her childhood. With her mother and her mother's boyfriends. With angry slaps and one attack that had changed her entire life. She resisted the urge to move away and instead stepped a little closer and peered into the house.

Behind him, there were red plastic cups everywhere. One of the chairs in the front room was overturned, there was a fist-sized hole in the wall and a long chain of clothing dangled from the chandelier all the way to the ground, like a bizarre ladder to nowhere. Apparently Saturday night at the frat house had been wild, and everyone was still recovering well into Sunday afternoon.

"Big party last night?" Sophia asked at a volume obviously intended to make the kid's head hurt.

"Shit," he said, backing up and clamping a hand over one ear. "Stop yelling. I'll get Jordan." He stumbled off, muttering curses not quite under his breath.

Sophia walked inside, looking around, and Evelyn followed. The frat house looked as if it had been in the path of a hurricane, and it smelled as if someone had dumped an entire keg of beer on the floor.

"Disgusting," Sophia muttered as Evelyn wondered how it had looked so clean last time if this was the way they partied.

Somehow, she couldn't imagine Jordan Biltmore— or any of his frat buddies—holding a mop.

"Detective," Jordan said, sauntering into the room,

dressed in jeans and a sweatshirt, a pair of shades over his eyes. "Agent Baine," he added with a nod in her direction. "I'm guessing it would have been all over the news if you'd found Haley, so what can I help you with this time?"

"You can take off the sunglasses and sit down," Sophia said in a stern cop's tone.

He gave her a half smile and removed his sunglasses. His eyes were a little bloodshot, but he didn't look or smell hungover. "What's with the attitude?"

"What's with the secrets?" Sophia fired back, more animosity than Evelyn had expected in her voice.

Jordan's smile dropped. "What do you mean?"

"Where's your best friend?"

"Nate?" He sounded surprised, and confused.

"Yes, Nate. We heard from the school that he's been missing for over a month."

Jordan let out a short, genuine-sounding burst of laughter. "Nate's not missing."

"Where is he?" Evelyn asked, stepping a little closer, wanting to look at micromovements Jordan made, any small twitches or involuntary actions that might suggest he knew more than he was telling them.

"Who the hell knows? But that's Nate." They must have looked dubious, because Jordan continued. "Look, we grew up together. He's always this way. Best guess is that he took his dad's plane—well, I guess technically it's Nate's plane since his parents died, but I always think of it as Old Man Stokes's plane—and flew himself to some beach because he was sick of the cold. Wouldn't be the first time."

Sophia gave him a look full of disbelief. "And he didn't tell anyone?"

"Nah. He never does. He's my best friend, but he's

not exactly what you'd call reliable. He does whatever he wants. Always has."

"What about family?" Evelyn asked. "Would they be able to tell us—"

"I doubt it," Jordan cut her off. "He wasn't close to any of them before, but after his parents died and he hit eighteen, he lost touch with the rest of the family. But Nate's had his pilot's license for years, got it on his seventeenth birthday. He did the exact same thing last year about this time. Just got sick of the cold and flew off to Florida. Stayed there six weeks, didn't tell any of us. I actually covered his midyear tuition so they didn't kick him out of his classes. The dumbass still hasn't paid me back. But he came home with a great tan, a stupid new tattoo and some crazy stories."

"So you're not concerned that he took off right before Haley went missing?" Sophia persisted.

Jordan frowned. "Nate going to chase beach bunnies for a couple of months has nothing to do with Haley disappearing. Nate does this all the time. Doesn't matter how many times you tell him it's not cool to bail on stuff—we had an English Lit class together this semester, and he was going to tutor me, 'cause he's great at English, but did he think about that? Of course not. He just had ti—uh, girls—on his mind."

"What about Haley?" Evelyn asked. "Did she and Nate get along?"

Jordan snorted. "They barely knew each other. I mean, they'd met, but I wouldn't have ever made her and Nate hang out. He would have liked her fine, but she'd have hated him." He flung his arms out, gesturing to the mess around him. "This? Totally not her thing. Haley wasn't a partyer. She's not a stick in the mud or anything, but she's not wild. And, I mean, I live at a frat house, right? Some crazy shit happens here, but honestly, it's not really my scene, either. I got this stuff out of my system a long time ago."

Evelyn tried not to let her skepticism show. He was a sophomore. How long ago could he have gotten frat life out of his system?

Sophia didn't hold back. "If this isn't your scene," she snapped, "then why do you live here?"

He plopped onto the couch, spreading his arms wide over the back of it. "Legacy. My dad belonged to this frat, too. Besides, it's a lot nicer than the dorms. And Nate rents one of the only decent houses on campus anywhere near the action. This place is pretty cool." He looked around him at the pool of beer on the coffee table and a pair of someone's boxers hanging from the end of the chair that was still upright. "Or it will be once the maids come by. Despite the crazy parties, these are a good group of guys."

"Tell me about Marissa," Evelyn said, changing the subject and getting a questioning look from Sophia.

"Marissa Anderson?" Jordan rolled his eyes. "Wannabe."

"Wannabe what?" Sophia asked.

"Haley," Jordan said simply. When they both stared at him, he sighed and continued, "It's no secret she was jealous of Haley. Haley's prettier, smarter and she's got me."

Sophia must have given him a look, because Jordan laughed and added, "Hey, you know what? I'm a pretty decent catch. But that's not what I mean. Just that Marissa wanted to date a college guy, too. She wanted Haley to introduce her. Hell, she wanted *me* to introduce her. But Haley's mature. Marissa *acts* like a high school kid."

"Did Nate know Marissa?" Evelyn asked, wondering how Marissa could have caught Haley and Nate together if neither of them came to campus much, which seemed to be the party line. But then again, maybe Nate came to Haley, the way Jordan had. Though that still didn't really explain how they would have gotten into a secret relationship to begin with, if they barely knew each other.

"Nah." His lips pursed. "Well, you know, Marissa and Nate might have met at that first party, the one where I met Haley. Nate was there. I think that's the only time he and Haley met actually. Marissa could have been introduced to Nate that night, too. I don't really remember, 'cause that's when *I* met Haley." He smiled, much softer than his typical smug grins. "She made it hard to focus on anything else."

"Okay," Evelyn said.

Jordan suddenly seemed to snap out of his reverie and leaned forward, staring at her questioningly. "Why are you asking about all this? What's going on?"

"Your friend went missing a week before Haley. We need to look into that."

"Nate's not missing," Jordan insisted.

"Until we can locate him, as far as we're concerned, he's missing," Sophia said firmly.

Jordan got to his feet, his fists clenching. "I don't want you wasting your time on my dumbass friend. He'll show up next month with bleached hair and great stories about all the girls he fu—met on the beach. Focus on Haley. She's your concern." He took two fast steps forward, aggressively enough that Sophia shifted her stance, angling the hip that held her weapon away from him.

Jordan's gaze shifted from Sophia's angry expression

down to the hand hovering over her gun and held his palms up in a submissive gesture. "I'll call him, okay?"

He took two steps back and tapped his phone, waited a minute, then cursed. "Nate, it's me. Call me as soon as you get this, asshole. I'm serious. Haley's missing and I need you, man." He hung up and told them, "I'll call as soon as I hear from him. Just please don't take time away from Haley's case for Nate. He's fine."

"What if him running off is connected to Haley going missing?" Sophia asked softly.

"How?"

The response was so instant, so bewildered, that Evelyn didn't believe he was faking. He either truly believed Nate and Haley had no connection or he was one of the best liars she'd ever met.

She gave Sophia a subtle nod. Time to move on.

"I don't know," Sophia said. "But the timing is close together. Do you know the name Tonya Klein?"

Jordan jerked backward. "The girl who died yesterday?" When Sophia just stared at him, he said quickly, "Yeah, well, I heard about it around campus. But people said she was a prostitute. She got killed by her pimp? What does that have to do with Nate? Or Haley?"

"Maybe nothing," Sophia said.

"Thanks for your help," Evelyn added. "Give us a call as soon as you hear from Nate. Better yet, ask him to call the station."

She turned to leave, Sophia on her heels, and Jordan ran after them.

"Wait! *What* is going on? Where the hell is my girlfriend?"

"Believe me, Jordan," Sophia said, "I wish I knew."

9

"I don't know about this," Linda Varner said.

"They promised not to air anything without the permission of the police," Pete reminded her.

"But after what happened before—"

"This is different," Pete assured her. "I got it in writing from the reporter. She won't air the special until she gets permission. But this is your chance to get the focus totally on Haley. If that profiler can't find her, this could be what we need to bring her home. Someone must have seen her. We need more public awareness."

Linda nodded, knowing in her heart that he was right. It had been thirty-four days, and still nothing. They needed a miracle. And Ginger Tippens might have been the least seasoned reporter at their local news station, but she was also their most dogged. If she was willing to do all of this on her own time, put together a full hour episode that just focused on Haley, maybe they could use it to bring Linda's daughter home.

"Okay. Let them in."

Pete nodded, kissed her cheek and opened the front door.

Linda always figured reporters were less perfect in person, but Ginger Tippens looked exactly the same as she did on TV. A short blond bob, serious brown eyes behind cat-eye glasses, a snug gray skirt suit and three-inch heels.

Ginger held out a tiny hand, but shook with confidence, her eye contact firm. "Thanks for giving me this opportunity, Mrs. Varner."

She gestured to the dark-haired man hunched behind her, a heavy-looking camera perched on his shoulder. "This is Eric. He suggested this approach today and I think it's going to help. He'll be doing the filming. Don't worry—we've worked together before and he's going to do a great job for you."

Linda started to hold out her hand to Eric, but Ginger stepped forward and kept talking. "We want to give viewers a closer look at who Haley is. Get them invested in bringing her home. Make sure every single person out there who owns a TV or a computer would recognize Haley, and knows how badly her family wants her to come home."

Linda felt herself tearing up, the antianxiety medicine she'd downed this morning beginning to wear off. Her husband's strong arms wrapped around her waist as she nodded.

"And we have your word that none of this will air until we get the police's approval?" Pete stressed.

"Absolutely," Ginger promised. She looked back at her cameraman. "Where should we start?"

"Haley's room," he said in a soft, shy voice, probably used to being invisible behind that big camera. "Let's show where she spends her time, what's important to her. Remind viewers she's just a teenager. Show them her personality while you two talk about her."

"Yes," Ginger enthused. "He's right. It pulls at their heartstrings. This is how the big shows always do it.

Okay?" When Linda nodded, she headed toward the stairs, taking them two at a time.

Linda glanced questioningly at Pete as the cameraman followed silently on her heels.

"Remember Regina James?" Pete whispered. "The woman whose daughter went missing a few years ago on vacation overseas? She did this, and I bet you can still picture her daughter, right?"

Linda shivered and she felt an overwhelming need for another pill. Pete was right. She *did* remember exactly what Regina James's daughter looked like; she'd probably never forget.

But despite the massive amount of press coverage, Regina's daughter had never been found.

"I don't know what we're doing here," Jimmy groaned. "Campus police said they've seen no signs of trafficking."

Kyle didn't mince words. "Neville's campus police are incompetent."

Jimmy nodded as they walked into the Neville city police station. "Yeah, you're right. But even they can't be stupid enough to miss obvious signs of trafficking."

"The campus police are fine for handling bike thefts and bar fights, but I'm sorry, they're not going to spot a human trafficking ring if it set up shop alongside their campus."

"None of the warehouses we visited seemed designed to traffic in sex," Jimmy reminded him.

"Sure, not anymore they don't," Kyle argued, heading for the front desk. "Maybe someone cleaned up shop—or moved it—once Tonya made it to the hospital. They didn't expect her to live long enough to tell anyone what had happened."

"Hopefully they don't know she did," Jimmy said.

They'd tried to keep that part out of the news, letting media know only that she'd died during treatment. As far as Kyle could tell, reports that she'd asked for the FBI hadn't leaked.

"What about these guys who called the ambulance for Tonya?" Jimmy persisted. "Where the hell are they?"

"That's what I want to know," Kyle said. They'd made the 911 call from a campus safety phone, but hadn't given their names, just reported an attack and then hung up. At least they'd interrupted the assault, saved Tonya's life long enough for her to file a report.

But there were no traffic or security cameras near that phone, so they didn't have high hopes for finding the callers unless they came in on their own.

"This whole situation is just off," Jimmy said.

Silently, Kyle agreed, which was part of why he couldn't let it go, even though they still had nothing to substantiate Tonya's claims. The crime scene hadn't given them anything, other than bottle shards they were having tested for DNA or prints. By the time they'd visited the scene after leaving Tonya's hospital room, it had already been trampled by curious students. The first sign of the incompetence of the campus police, but not the last.

"Can I help you?" the sergeant at the front desk at the city station asked, tapping her fingers against the fake wood.

Jimmy flashed his credentials and a toothy grin. "FBI."

The officer just stared back at him, a bored expression on her face. "Good for you, hon. You want to tell me what you're here for?"

Kyle hid a grin as Jimmy fumbled to put his creds back in his pocket. "We need to talk to one of the detectives."

"Detective Lopez and that other FBI agent who set

up shop here are out. You can talk to Detective Palmer." She came out from behind the front desk, slid her key-card into a door and held it open for them, ushering them into the back of the station. Instead of following, she pointed out a tall, heavyset man with a bald head and a thick dark beard streaked with white. "That's Quincy Palmer."

Kyle hurried through the bullpen with Jimmy at his heels. It was pretty calm by FBI standards, with a few plainclothes officers in discussion, some support staff on computers and a pair of uniformed officers on their way back out to patrol.

Before he and Jimmy were halfway across the room, Quincy set down the bagel he'd been eating and crossed his arms over his chest, scowling. "More feds?" he asked before Jimmy could pull out the creds he was reaching for in his jacket.

Kyle held out a hand. "Kyle McKenzie, from the Washington Field Office. This is my partner, Jimmy Drescott."

"DC," Quincy said, sounding surprised. "Not more profilers?" Not giving them time to reply, he said, "Come on," then grabbed his bagel and coffee off the credenza along the back wall and headed for an office.

The room he ushered them into was barely large enough for the three of them to stand comfortably in-side. It reminded Kyle of being crammed inside indus-trial ductwork—which he'd once had to do for an HRT mission. Every spare vertical surface in the room was covered in pictures and timelines and suspect infor-mation.

Kyle took a step closer to one of the walls with the most pictures tacked to it, instantly recognizing Haley Cooke from the news coverage. This was the case that had Evelyn obsessed and running in circles. And visiting Neville University.

Getting right to business, Kyle said, "We're following up on a death at Neville University that happened yesterday."

Quincy raised a pair of bushy, white-streaked eyebrows. "The Klein girl? I assumed you were here about Haley." He frowned, taking a big gulp of coffee and suddenly seeming a lot less interested.

"That's right," Jimmy said. "Tonya Klein. She claimed she was being trafficked out of Neville U."

"Trafficked?" Quincy said, stepping backward and bumping the wall. He shook his head and moved forward again, setting down his coffee and half-eaten bagel on the drooping folding table that took up most of the room. Then he focused on straightening the pictures he'd knocked askew. "No way."

"Why do you say that?" Kyle asked.

Quincy turned back toward them. "Well, who would be trafficking her? Everyone there is wealthy enough to buy and sell that whole damn place. Why bother with some small-scale trafficking ring?"

Kyle nodded, understanding the sentiment, erroneous as it was. Trafficking was one of the fastest-growing criminal enterprises because it made money. And just because someone had tons of money, didn't mean they wouldn't want more. Still… "Who said it was small-scale?"

"Well, if it was large-scale, don't you think we'd already be investigating?" Quincy demanded.

"They can be hard to spot," Jimmy said, giving Quincy no sign of what Kyle knew: that he didn't believe it himself.

"Okay, then what are you here for?" Quincy demanded. "If you think we'd have missed it, anyway?"

"We want to know if you've seen any other signs?" Kyle said, trying to keep his tone even. Quincy had leaped fast into annoyed and uninterested. Either he wasn't a fan of working with the FBI in general or he'd had a bad day. "Anything from unusual reports—either from the victims themselves or from witnesses—to signs of money laundering at the university or unusual activity at supposedly empty locations, maybe the warehouses you've got on the outskirts of the university?"

"Nah," Quincy said. "Neville U gets some crime, but mostly minor stuff. I mean, the biggest issue we see there is kids speeding in their Ferraris."

"What about Haley?" Kyle asked.

"What *about* Haley?" Quincy parroted, crossing his arms over his chest. "The girl was grabbed at her high school, not at the university."

Kyle didn't really think she was connected, either, but he hadn't lasted in the FBI by being sloppy. "What—"

"What the hell happened to that girl?" Quincy continued. "I thought your profiler unit was supposed to be the best. But we're no further along than we were the day Haley went missing."

"The BAU *is* the best," Kyle said, pissed at the implication Evelyn wasn't doing her job. Trying not to get sidetracked, he got back to why he was there. "What about Tonya? Did she ever file *any* kind of report here?"

"Nope."

"Don't you need to check?" Jimmy asked.

"I don't have to." He cleared his throat. "I checked yesterday, after I heard. Figured we didn't have anything, but I wanted to confirm it. You know, in case we had any names in a report we could follow up on. Grievances, that kind of thing."

"And there was nothing at all?" Kyle asked, trying to keep a poker face.

"No."

"All right," Jimmy said with a sigh. He shook Quincy's hand. "Thanks for your time."

Kyle kept quiet as they walked back through the bull-pen, said goodbye to the sergeant at the desk who still seemed unimpressed by them and headed to Jimmy's car. Only once Jimmy had pulled out of the station did Kyle say what he'd been thinking. "There's something odd happening at that station."

"What do you mean? With Quincy?" When Kyle nodded, Jimmy shrugged. "He seemed a little territorial. Maybe he just doesn't want anyone to think he was sleeping on the job—doesn't want to believe a sex trafficking ring could have come in without him noticing it."

"Maybe," Kyle said, unconvinced. "But for someone tight-lipped about everything except Haley Cooke's disappearance, that was a lot of explanation for how he looked into past reports involving Tonya."

"What are you suggesting?" Jimmy asked. "You think he destroyed incident reports?"

"No, I'm wondering if he took a call and didn't report it."

Jimmy looked skeptical. "He's a detective. He's not going to be first to the scene, Mac."

"Not unless someone calls and requests a detective, and there's no reason for a patrol call. Think about it. When Tonya got to the hospital, she asked for the FBI. I thought it was because she was looking for federal-level protection, but maybe that's not it."

Jimmy scowled. "You think she couldn't trust the police?"

"I think we should take a closer look at how the Neville police station operates."

"Let's take a walk."

"Where do you want to go?" Evelyn asked as Sophia marched out of the frat house.

"Nate's place is pretty close to here. I messaged the head of campus police on the way over and he gave me the address. He said he'd meet us there, and I want to take a look. See if there's any sign of a struggle, or any indication he packed up for a trip to the beach."

"Or if he packed up to run off with Haley," Evelyn said softly, glancing back to see Jordan standing near the window, staring after them, looking frustrated.

"What do you think?"

"He didn't seem to be lying about Nate."

"Yeah, well, did you think he was lying about being all broken up about Haley until that girl came out of his bedroom?" Sophia asked, walking down the long pathway from the frat house at a speed that had Evelyn jogging to keep up.

"Point taken. But although it might be distasteful, Jordan could legitimately be upset about Haley and still be sleeping around. Being a jerk doesn't make him guilty of hurting Haley. He might not have appeared to be lying about seeing anyone else because he didn't think he was."

When Sophia started to argue, Evelyn cut her off. "He might have been faithful before she went missing. It's about his perception, not reality. But if he thought it wasn't lying because that girl didn't count, he wouldn't need to try to hide signs of deception. But this thing with Nate is different."

"How?" Sophia asked, still not sounding convinced.

"Either Nate does this a lot and Jordan legitimately doesn't know where he is and doesn't think he's in danger, or Jordan's flat-out lying. And if he's lying, he's good."

"Well, maybe he's an entitled little sociopath," Sophia said as they moved through campus. Students bundled in coats glanced at her furious expression and got out of the way.

"Maybe," Evelyn agreed. "I know you don't like him, and I hear you on that. But I want to look into these coincidences. First the letter from Haley right after we visit Bill and then finding out Nate went missing a week before Haley."

"People and their fucking secrets," Sophia muttered. "Makes me want to sit my kids down and administer a couple of polygraphs."

A burst of laughter escaped Evelyn's lips and Sophia scowled. "I don't have teenagers yet, but when they get a little older, I'm totally serious. I might steal one from the station."

"How old are your kids?"

"Eight and ten. It's not easy on them, their mom being a cop in a small town. Their mom being a single woman in a small town. But they're good kids." She grinned, then nodded at the small house up ahead of them. "Most of the time. That's the place."

"That's where Nate lives?"

"That's where Nate rents." Sophia looked around, then zipped her jacket higher up her neck. "Damn. The guy from campus police isn't here yet. He was going to let us in."

Evelyn raised her eyebrows. "We have the authority to go in? Does Nate have a roommate?"

"No, but Nate has a landlord. And the campus police thought he'd be happy to hand over a key. Wellness check. The university says Nate hasn't shown up in five weeks and hasn't paid his tuition."

Sophia checked her phone and frowned, then asked Evelyn, "What did you think about Jordan's reaction when we asked about Tonya?"

"I don't know," Evelyn admitted. "It's possible he was surprised we brought it up, because he didn't think there was any reason it would be connected to Haley. Then again…"

"He reacted when we said the name," Sophia said. When Evelyn nodded, she said, "Let me just ask Marissa. See what she has to say, if she knows Tonya." She scrolled through her contacts, then called Marissa.

"Marissa? It's Detective Lopez. Sorry to bother you on your weekend." There was a pause, then Sophia laughed. "Good. Look, I just called to see if you know the name Tonya Klein?" Another pause. "You sure?… No, that's it. Thanks."

She tucked her phone away and shook her head at Evelyn, then called out, "There you are! It's cold out here."

Evelyn turned to see a heavyset cop climbing out of a campus police car. He grumbled unintelligibly under his breath, then took his time walking past her and Sophia to unlock the door to the house in front of them. "Lock up when you're done."

He turned to leave and Evelyn grabbed his arm. "I've got a couple of questions, if you don't mind."

"I do mind," he mumbled, but instead of heading back to his car, he followed Sophia inside Nate's rental house.

"No immediate sign of struggle," Sophia stated the obvious as they walked into the living room.

The room was sparsely furnished, sparsely decorated.

Really, everything about it was sparse. It barely looked as though anyone lived there.

"What's Nate's financial situation?" Sophia asked. "From what Jordan said about the private plane, I expected…" She looked around again, seeming perplexed. "More stuff."

"Maybe he spent it all on the rent," the police officer said dryly.

"You know Nate Stokes?" Evelyn asked.

"No, but I know living here, next to frat row, in a single home by himself? It ain't cheap."

"Still," Evelyn said, walking through the near-empty living room, which boasted nothing but a dark brown leather couch with a hideous checkered throw over it. "This is odd. Maybe Jordan is wrong. Maybe he did clear out."

"Or maybe he just isn't the nesting type," Sophia said.

"Maybe." She headed into the kitchen and glanced around, repulsed by the pungent scent in there.

"Ick," Sophia said as she peered into the trash can. "Well, either he didn't plan to come back and didn't care if his whole house stank of rotten food, or he didn't know he was leaving for a long time."

"Or he expected a maid to come by," Evelyn said.

"Maybe, but then why didn't one come by?"

"I don't know." Evelyn opened the fridge, finding it stocked with boxes of pizza, packs of beer and energy drinks. "Let's check the rest of the house."

She glanced back at the campus police officer, who was following reluctantly behind them. "Have you had any reports of gang rape in the past year?"

He jerked to a stop. "No, of course not."

"Two or more assailants?" Evelyn persisted, because all she knew from her discussion with Kyle was that

Tonya had claimed *men* had assaulted her at a warehouse after blackmailing her.

"Not that I've heard of," he said, sounding offended that she'd ask.

She squinted at him, wondering how reliable he was. "What about warehouses in the area?"

"Warehouses?" He shook his head. "Not on campus."

"Near campus?"

"Sure. Some, but that's not my area."

"Not your jurisdiction, you mean?"

"Right. Not my problem."

"Okay. Thanks. That's all I need." She wasn't going to get anything useful from him. She headed down the hall toward the bedrooms and heard him moving in the other direction, back toward the front door.

"Well, this looks more lived in," Evelyn said as she peered into the first bedroom, which Nate had turned into a gaming room. Four low-slung armchairs took up the center of the room, and they all faced a big-screen TV hooked up to every game console imaginable.

She kept going, glancing briefly into a second bedroom that Nate had set up as a study. There was a stack of textbooks on the desk, alongside two laptops, but it was ultraneat, like Nate didn't spend a lot of time there.

She walked into the bedroom. Unlike the nearly empty living room, stuff was everywhere. Clothes on the floor, a bunch of electronic toys on a dresser and a surfboard up against one wall.

"I wonder how many surfboards he owns?" Sophia said.

Evelyn spun around to find her standing in the doorway. "Jordan mentioned Nate going to the beach."

"I don't see car keys anywhere," Evelyn said. "For that matter, there was no vehicle in the driveway, either."

"We're not exactly going to be able to tell if he packed a suitcase," Sophia said. "But this seems to be the mess of a nineteen-year-old boy, not the scene of an abduction."

"I agree." Evelyn sighed and glanced around once more. "I don't think we're going to learn much here. And the landlord can let us in, but I don't want to go through anything not in plain sight without a warrant. Not for a wellness check."

Sophia headed back the way they'd come, calling after her, "Once we get back to the station, I'll start making some calls. See if I can find out if Nate filed a flight plan five weeks ago."

"And if so, how many people were on that flight plan," Evelyn added, hurrying to catch up.

As soon as she got back into her sedan at the frat house, Evelyn turned the heater way up.

"I'm going to give a few of Haley's other girlfriends a call," Sophia said, fiddling with her phone as Evelyn drove across the dramatic bridge leading out over the huge man-made pond at the main entrance to the campus.

"Ask them if they've heard anything about Haley and Nate," Evelyn said, marveling at a university that would spend money on a pond this enormous, and a bridge to go over it, instead of just a regular road.

"That's the plan," Sophia replied. "But I'm telling you—ahhh!"

Sophia's words turned to a yell as a loud pop sounded from the back of the vehicle, which suddenly fishtailed. Evelyn struggled to whip the wheel right, but it still skidded left, across the other lane and straight toward the low concrete wall separating them from the expanse of water twenty feet below.

10

"Shit!" Sophia screeched beside her as Evelyn wrestled with the wheel, her heart beating a panicked *thud-thud, thud-thud* against her rib cage. She hit the brake, and the now-flattened right rear tire made a horrible, high-pitched metal-on-concrete sound like a warning siren.

She jammed her foot down harder, fighting to keep the wheel from spinning underneath her painfully tight grip. The low concrete divider came closer and closer as she warned Sophia, "I can't stop! Hang on!"

The impact made her head whip forward, as a horrible crunching sound filled her eardrums and something exploded in her face, filling her eyes with grit. Pain hit from her face to her chest, but still she kept her foot pressed down hard on the brake, even as her hands were wrenched back and away from the steering wheel.

She heard Sophia let out a brief, pained scream and then the car stopped moving. At least, she thought it did. She couldn't seem to blink her eyes clear, and she struggled to take a full breath. The ground felt stable, but for all she knew, the front end of the car was dangling over the bridge.

"You okay?" she croaked to Sophia, realizing the

white gunk in her eyes and the pressure against her chest was from the air bag deploying.

Punching it down out of her face so she could look out the windshield and take stock, she discovered the front of her car had crumpled in toward her, and they *had* hit the divider hard enough to break through it. There was a gaping hole in front of her, a clear view to the ground twenty feet below.

Panicked, she tried to crane her neck to see better, without shifting her weight and the pain intensified. But she was fairly sure all four wheels were still on the bridge, and she realized her foot was still jammed down hard on the brake.

She shifted the car into Park, and tried to throw the parking brake for good measure, but it wouldn't budge. "Get out very slowly," she warned Sophia.

When the detective didn't respond, Evelyn blinked more to clear her vision and peered through the swirling white powder toward Sophia. The detective was fumbling to get her seat belt off, and she looked a little shaken up, but Evelyn didn't see any serious injuries.

"You okay?" Evelyn asked again.

"Yeah, if I can get this belt off and get out of the car," Sophia replied, yanking on the seat belt to no avail.

Evelyn tried hers and it came off without a problem. She leaned over, trying to help Sophia without shifting her weight too much since she didn't know how stable the car was, when a flash of red from behind the detective caught her eye.

Another car, coming toward them way too fast.

"Stop!" Evelyn yelled, even though her windows were still up. The windshield had cracked and splintered, but hadn't broken. She slammed her fist down where the horn should have been, but either she wasn't hitting it through the deflated air bag or the air bag's deployment had ruined it. The motion made the car rock forward a bit, and dread bounced in the pit of Evelyn's stomach.

Sophia looked through the windshield, and then fumbled harder with the seat belt. "Get out, get out!" Sophia shouted when Evelyn reached toward her, trying to help.

No matter how hard they both yanked, the seat belt was stuck. And the harder they pulled, the more the car rocked back and forth, sliding forward inch by inch toward the edge of the bridge. Evelyn glanced up, afraid of how far over the edge they'd gone, and discovered the crumpled front was definitely hanging off the bridge now. The wheels were still sliding. She glanced the other way, to see how close the other vehicle would be, wondering how the driver could have missed her on such a perfectly clear day.

The red vehicle was stopped a few feet away and someone was climbing leisurely out of the driver's seat.

"Help!" Evelyn called out.

She stared out the spiderwebbed windshield again, at the crumpled front of the car, and felt it slide forward another inch as Sophia's door was suddenly wrenched open and then someone bent low in the doorway.

"Jordan," Sophia said, surprise and suspicion mingled with the panic in her voice.

"What happened? Are you two all right?"

"We're fine," Evelyn said. "But Detective Lopez is stuck. And this car is going over. We need to get her out."

"No worries," Jordan replied, frustratingly calm. "Hang on." He dug around in his pocket until he pulled out a pocket knife.

"Shit!" Sophia leaned toward the center of the car, making it rock again.

"Relax," Jordan said, amusement in his tone as he knelt down and brought the knife closer. "Don't move, either of you, or you're going to make the car slide forward."

Evelyn pushed the rest of the air bag back and fumbled with her door until she got it open, carefully, as slowly as she dared. Was Jordan right? If she jumped out, would the car move again, send Sophia over the bridge? If she didn't, would Jordan hurt Sophia? She didn't think he would stab her in broad daylight, but he was still a suspect, he had a knife and Sophia couldn't go anywhere.

Then there was a rasping sound, and a big tear, and Jordan folded up the knife and tucked it away, holding out a hand to Sophia.

"Wait," Evelyn warned. "Let's get out at the same time. I don't want to mess with the weight distribution. On three?"

Sophia nodded, and Jordan counted down.

On three, Evelyn heaved herself out of the car so quickly she hit the concrete hard. The car let out a loud groan, rocking back and forth, back and forth, until it slid forward a fast foot.

Evelyn scooted backward, away from it, as her FBI-issued sedan suddenly pitched again, shooting over the edge and down to the ground below with a huge *boom*.

Smoke billowed up toward her, and Evelyn leaped to her feet. She swayed, then steadied, and peered through the smoke, trying to make sure Sophia had made it out. Finally she saw the detective, on the ground beside Jordan, who looked a little surprised himself, as if he hadn't actually expected the car to go over despite his warnings.

"Holy shit," he breathed as he got to his feet and

stared over the edge. "Whoever built this bridge did a crappy job." He glanced at her. "Or maybe you're a damn reckless driver?"

Evelyn scowled back and he let out a shaky laugh, then reached a hand down for Sophia, who took it and let him pull her to her feet.

She was swaying a little, too, as she said, "Thanks."

"Lucky I happened to come this way," Jordan said. "Most of the students drive around, instead of using the bridge. It's longer, but usually faster."

Sophia's eyes narrowed.

"Very lucky," Evelyn said, because she didn't want Sophia giving away her suspicion any more than she already had. They'd left the car at Jordan's frat long enough for him to have caused the flat tire, but why would he? Just to scare them? If he'd put a nail under it, he might expect them to get a flat, but a blowout this fast was bad luck. Plus, there was no way he'd have been able to time it so they'd lose control on the bridge. And what were the chances they'd hit so hard the car would go over?

Besides, if he'd wanted them dead, he could have left them here. Instead, he'd pulled Sophia out.

And although he was definitely on the list, he wasn't their prime suspect—or at least he wasn't Evelyn's prime suspect. She knew Sophia had a negative opinion of him, but the fact was, Evelyn couldn't figure out a solid motive for him to want to hurt Haley. And they were *far* from bringing any charges against him. So why throw suspicion on himself by trying to hurt them in a car crash?

It was probably a fluke, an accident. Except Jordan being on the bridge was a hell of a coincidence.

There'd been way too many coincidences in this case, and she didn't like it at all.

In the distance, she heard sirens approaching.

As the police car cruised to a stop, Evelyn stared at the smoke still surging up from her destroyed sedan, wondering.

Where was Haley Cooke? Where was Nate Stokes? What had really happened to Tonya Klein? Was it all connected?

And was someone sending her and Sophia a warning to back off?

"The consensus seems to be that Marissa was spreading rumors about Haley and Nate, trying to break her and Jordan up."

Evelyn looked up from her spot at the corner of the tiny folding table in the war room for Haley's case. She and Sophia had been cloistered in here for hours, since they'd hitched a ride back to the station from a campus police officer.

The Bureau was having someone drop her off a new vehicle, and she'd be filling out a lot of paperwork later. This was the second car she'd destroyed in the past year. But at least the EMT at the scene had declared her to be fine medically.

"You talked to more of Haley's friends?"

Sophia pressed her fingers to a bruise high on her cheekbone from the air bag. "Yeah. It was no secret Marissa had a crush on Jordan."

Evelyn set down her pen and stared up at Sophia, who had stood and was shifting her weight back and forth, seemingly unable to sit still, despite her soreness from the crash.

Evelyn was feeling the effects, too. Hours later, her

ribs still ached. They weren't cracked—she knew from experience that felt a lot worse. But most of her body was stiff, and she suspected when she got home, she'd discover a lot of bruises.

"What do you think?" Evelyn asked. "I mean, I hear you on Marissa's jealousy, and maybe even spreading rumors among their mutual friends. But would she give *us* information she knew was false? No matter her feelings for Haley's boyfriend, she and Haley have known each other a long time. She seems to be honestly concerned about Haley, and to want her found."

"I'm not sure," Sophia admitted. "Unless she hopes she's got a shot with Jordan and the rumors about Haley and Nate are to make her feel better about trying to steal her best friend's boyfriend while Haley is missing?"

Evelyn considered. "Maybe. Except as far as I can tell, Jordan hasn't seen Marissa since Haley went missing."

"The most I got from one of Haley's other friends was that Nate had a crush on Haley, too. She was at the party the night they met Jordan. But she didn't think Haley had hung out with him since that night. Even if Nate was interested, supposedly he backed off once Jordan and Haley got together after the party. And no one but Marissa seems to think Haley had any interest in return."

She tapped the wall behind her, where she'd added one picture of Nate Stokes and one of Tonya Klein next to the dozens of Haley. "Too many things have happened in the past month for none of it to be connected. Marissa spreads rumors about Nate and Haley and then they both go missing?"

"Maybe the wrong person believed those rumors."

"You mean Jordan," Sophia said, and it wasn't a question. She shuddered a little. "I've got to be honest. When he came toward me with that knife in his hand…

the look on his face? He wanted to scare me. Make me think I had to pick between being stabbed or crashing over the bridge in that car. It's not going to surprise me if we find out he did something horrible to both of them." She plopped back down in the other folding chair. "But I hope for Haley's sake that's not the case."

"I hear you."

"I'm also not totally convinced Jordan didn't cause that flat tire."

"Maybe." She wasn't sure of Jordan's innocence in the situation, but there were too many variables for him to have predicted what had happened. He'd definitely seemed surprised on that bridge when the car had flown over.

And if his intent had just been to give them a flat, to make them think he could hurt them if they came after him? That seemed a little far-fetched even for someone with his swagger.

Sophia rubbed the back of her neck, then glanced at her watch. "I've only got the sitter for another hour. I'm going to have to wrap this up soon. But I did check to see if Nate filed a flight plan. I'm not finding anything. The hangar where he usually keeps his plane said it wasn't there now, but I'm not sure that means much, since for all we know he just left it at another hangar. Apparently he's done it before. How'd your search go?"

"Abuse is hard to find."

"And even harder to prove," Sophia agreed. "You see any warning signs?"

"With Pete? Nothing really stands out. If he has any signs of sexual misconduct or questionable behavior around minors, I haven't been able to dig it up. That doesn't mean it isn't there, but if it is, no one has ever suspected. He married Linda about a year ago. They'd been dating since pretty close to the time she and Bill separated."

"Right." Sophia nodded, already up to date on Linda and Pete's basic details.

"Sorry. Anyway, I checked back a bit to see if I could find anything in Pete's past. Given the age difference between him and Linda and how fast he showed up in the picture after her divorce from Bill—"

"Yeah, I'm pretty sure Linda was seeing Pete before she and Bill separated. Maybe not truly dating yet, but they'd met. Family and friends thought things were heading in that direction. I think they saw the end coming before Bill did."

"So Bill could have some animosity even then? Maybe he thought Haley also knew about it? Or maybe he's one of those guys who'd rather have Haley dead than see another man take over his role as father figure?"

"It's possible," Sophia said.

"I've definitely seen that sort of pathology before, with spouses and kids. And Bill has a history of violence, if not abuse."

Sophia's forehead crumpled. "What do you mean? I know we talked about the possibility Bill was abusive, but I didn't find anything."

"This guy has serious problems with anger and aggression. I didn't find anything in terms of his family— no unusual hospital visits or unexplained injuries as far as friends or relatives knew of—but at the workplace he's been written up for acts of aggression."

Sophia leaned closer. "What exactly?"

"Aggression toward the only female contractor on a job site, punching a wall at a construction site, taking a baseball bat to a coworker's car. There's probably more, but those are the ones bad enough to have been documented. They should have filed a police report on at least the car incident, but they didn't, just cited him."

"Wow." Sophia leaned back, frowning. "How'd you find this?"

"I finally got a hold of his supervisor, who seems to be a personal friend of Bill's. Took me a while to get it out of him—I think he was worried about being in trouble for not letting Bill go—but eventually he told me."

"Damn it," Sophia snapped. "When I talked to his coworkers, they mostly looked down and mumbled that he was fine. I got the impression he didn't have a lot of friends there, but not that he was violent."

"Maybe no one wanted to get on his bad side."

"That's definitely possible." Sophia scowled. "But I'm investigating a missing seventeen-year-old. You'd think people would be more forthcoming."

"Secrets," Evelyn replied. "They can seriously derail any case."

"Yeah," Sophia agreed. "How many are we going to have to dig up before we find Haley?"

Evelyn's tense shoulders finally came down as she walked into the senior living center where her grandma lived. The familiar mix of antiseptic and floral scents filled the air and the usual sounds of nurses and staff bustling through the halls and laughter coming from the game and lounge room off to her left made her smile.

After a hard day, there was nothing quite like visiting her grandma.

It didn't even matter that she hadn't stopped for dinner yet, so her stomach was growling. Or that she'd definitely gotten a pinched nerve from the car crash, and probably a little whiplash. Her arms were tense, as though she was still using every bit of her strength to grip that steering wheel. But it was all a little less noticeable now.

"Hi, Melanie," she said to the woman at the front desk as she approached.

"Evelyn, hi!" Melanie looked up from a stack of patient charts. "I just got in, so I can't tell you how she's doing, but I can grab one of the nurses and ask."

"That's okay," Evelyn said. "I'll just head back."

"Sure. You know the way."

Usually, she appreciated a little warning, just in case her grandma's dementia had a particularly strong grip on her. Knowing ahead of time generally made it easier to pretend nothing was wrong. Because her grandma's mind might be slipping, but not how well she knew her granddaughter. She could generally still tell if Evelyn was upset.

Today, though, Evelyn didn't want to waste time. She just wanted to see her grandma, whose familiar crooked smile and soothing voice reminded Evelyn of everything that was good about her childhood.

Heading down the hall toward her grandma's room, Evelyn's pace quickened. She already had a smile on her face when she pulled open the door.

But her grandma wasn't alone. Standing next to the rocking chair where her grandma sat was Lillian Baine.

Dread filled her gut as she blinked back sudden tears, determined not to let her mother see them.

What the *hell* was her mother doing here? How had she even known where Mabel lived?

"Evelyn!" Lily said, a smile plastered on her face as she opened her arms and stepped forward.

Evelyn instinctively jerked backward, bumping the door. She hadn't seen Lily since she was seventeen years old. And even then, it had been brief. Her mother had shown up in Rose Bay when her grandma got sick, expecting to slide back into their lives as if she'd never been gone.

Evelyn hadn't let it happen then, and she wouldn't let it happen now.

"Evelyn," her grandma said, staring up at her with a mixture of confusion, disapproval and hurt. "Your mom has come home."

Lily frowned down at her mom, clearly not understanding what was happening, since Virginia had never been Lily's home, and resentment hit Evelyn so hard she could feel it tingling on her skin.

Of course Lily didn't realize Mabel Baine was confused because of the dementia. Lily hadn't bothered to look after anyone but herself most of her life. And even at that, she'd failed miserably, drinking herself into oblivion most of Evelyn's childhood, until at ten her grandparents had taken Evelyn away.

And yet, somehow, Lily had aged well, none of the pain she'd caused others showing on her face. It seemed unfair. The years had added a little droop to her cheeks and a few lines near her eyes, but she'd had Evelyn young and she still looked young herself. The same blondish-brown hair, only a few errant streaks of gray now. The same pale English-Irish skin, smooth and unlined as though she looked after herself. And as Lily turned back to Evelyn, she saw her mother's moss-green eyes, still sharp and strong.

They were the same eyes Evelyn saw in the mirror every morning. She hated the reminder of how identical they were to Lily's eyes.

"Don't look at me that way," Lily whispered. "I'm clean now. I've changed. I want another chance. Another chance to…to be in your lives."

"Bullshit" formed on Evelyn's lips, but she held it

in for her grandma's sake and instead forced herself to say tightly, "Let's go into the hall."

Lily looked ready to object, so Evelyn gave her best profiler's glare, the one she used on serial killer suspects she absolutely knew were guilty.

Lowering her chin, Lily walked into the hallway.

Evelyn blinked the don't-mess-with-me expression clear and bent to kiss her grandma's forehead. Softly, she said, "Grandma, I'll be back in just a minute, okay?"

"Sure, honey," Mabel said, looking from the empty doorway to Evelyn. "Don't scare her off," she whispered as Evelyn headed for the door.

Evelyn stumbled a little, pain clamping down on top of the anger. She didn't want her grandma upset, didn't want Mabel getting her hopes up after all this time. Because it didn't matter what Lillian Baine claimed. Evelyn didn't believe for a second that she'd changed.

Stepping into the hallway, Evelyn closed the door behind her. She'd half expected Lily to already be gone, but she was standing there, nervously pulling at her shirt hem.

"Evelyn," Lily started. "I know—"

"I don't want you here," Evelyn said, pushing aside that tiny part of her that longed to have her mother's best self back, the woman she'd known when she was just a little girl.

It was so long ago Evelyn barely remembered, the time before her father died when she was five. But she knew somewhere inside Lily was a different woman, the mother she'd been before she'd lost Evelyn's father and turned to cheap liquor and dangerous men.

"I understand why you feel that way, but—"

Evelyn cut her off again. It didn't matter that Lily's

eyes looked clear, that she didn't reek of liquor the way Evelyn remembered. "No."

She wasn't going to let Lily worm her way back into her life, and she certainly wasn't going to let her mess with her grandma's mind. Give her hope that her daughter was back, that her daughter was different. Because if there was one thing Evelyn had learned in those horrible years between five and ten, it was that Lily Baine might have moments of change, but they never lasted. The only thing that did was the hurt she left in her wake.

Evelyn took an aggressive step forward, the way she'd do if she was in an interrogation room with a subject who thought he could push her around. "I won't let you give her false hope. I want you out of here. And I don't want you coming back, not ever."

"Evelyn," Lily protested, lifting her hands, palms up. "Things are different now. You'll see."

"I won't see." She got right up in Lily's face. "You leave now and don't come back, or I'm going to do whatever it takes to make you stay away."

Lily stepped back, her placating, hopeful expression turning wary. "You can't—"

"I'm not a scared ten-year-old hoping your newest boyfriend won't hit me or try to rape me," Evelyn said, realizing her voice was getting louder and starting to attract attention, but unable to quiet down.

Lily went pale and swayed on her feet, shaking her head.

"Don't pretend you didn't know." Evelyn jutted her finger toward the entrance. "Get out! Now!"

Tears glistened in Lily's eyes, but she spun and ran out so quickly she almost tripped as she disappeared from the nursing home.

11

The next morning, Evelyn sat in her cubicle at the BAU office in Aquia, her head pounding as if she was the one who drank until she passed out. But unlike her mother, Evelyn had never touched the stuff. Instead, she'd spent the night plagued by memories, until she'd finally given up on sleep and driven into work early in the new sedan the FBI had issued her.

They'd pulled her old one out of the man-made lake last night and discovered a nail in the tire. If it had been an attempt to kill her and Sophia, it had relied heavily on luck. She'd been thinking about it on and off all morning, finally forcing herself to push it out of her mind. Without more to go on, they had to focus on other leads.

She already knew her email was full of flagged items, cases Dan wanted her to evaluate, and a blinking light on her phone told her follow-ups were needed on other cases.

As much as she might want to be, she wasn't assigned to Haley's case full-time. There were other subjects to profile, other victims missing or dead who needed her to search for their justice, too.

Usually, she got one chance. One review of the case

file, a brief amount of time to send back a profile, to hope the case officers knew how to use it. Quite often, she never found out the outcome. But certain cases were different; when the time or media pressure was especially intense, she had the chance to get heavily involved, in person and on-site. In some ways, they were the best cases, because she generally got to see them all the way through to the end. In other ways, they were the worst, because she wound up knowing the victims so much better. And most of them didn't get a happy ending.

She'd been trying to work through the stack of other cases. But all morning, she'd been plagued by thoughts of Haley. The longer she'd spent locked in that war room in Neville, the more she'd seen in seventeen-year-old Haley what her childhood best friend, Cassie, might have become if she'd lived to be a teenager. Both blond and blue-eyed, both nice to everyone they met, both stolen away from the lives they were supposed to lead.

At least, Evelyn was still assuming Haley had been abducted. But she couldn't eliminate the possibility she'd run away. She and Sophia were going around and around: Bill had a violent past and a grudge. Pete had no warning signs on paper, but in person, he made both her and Sophia's investigative instincts ping. And Jordan was too smug, too sure of himself, even amid his girlfriend's disappearance and the police's constant visits.

Evelyn's job was to profile each of the players, and lead Sophia in the right direction. It was frustrating as hell to only be able to say that she thought the perpetrator was someone close to Haley, someone they'd definitely interviewed in the course of the case.

She wasn't sure how much more she could contribute. She should go to Dan and tell him it was time to move on. Her profile of Haley's abductor was sketchy at best, and she wasn't sure more time would change that. Possibly only more details would, and that was an investigator's task.

But Dan had been unusually distracted lately, and unusually lenient with her time and talent. So, she was staying as far below his radar as she could, for as long as she could. Because she couldn't shake the feeling that she was close, that the pieces were about to come together, and she needed to be there to see it through.

"Evelyn."

Greg's voice startled her and she spun her chair to find her closest friend at the BAU—and the agent who'd trained her—standing outside her cubicle. From the way he was leaning up against the cubicle wall, she suspected he'd been there a few minutes.

She smiled at him, even though she knew it wouldn't matter. He'd known something was off from the moment she'd walked into the office this morning. He'd asked about it, but she'd broken her rule about trying to be more open with people and said she was just tired from yesterday's accident.

This was Greg—the guy who knew her better than anyone here, the guy who had a solid nine years of profiling experience behind him. No question, he knew she was lying. But he'd let it go, at least for the moment.

So had Kyle, last night on the phone, when he'd immediately asked what was wrong after she'd answered. She'd told him about the car crash, told him she just needed some sleep when he'd offered to come over. Somehow, he'd known there was more to it. She'd used her minor bruises and aches as an excuse to ring off, but she knew he'd be asking again. And she didn't want to talk about her mom's visit yet, not even with Kyle, who knew her history.

Or with Greg, who was such a good friend that he'd become practically family over the years. He stared at her now, his lips pursed and his fawn-brown eyes narrowed, as though he was trying to read her mind. He'd shed his jacket hours ago, rolled up the sleeves on his perpetually coffee-stained button-down and even loosened the wild paisley tie Evelyn was pretty sure his daughter had chosen for him.

"I'm meeting Gabe for lunch. Want to join us?"

Gabe was Greg's cousin, a taller, blonder, younger version of Greg with more easy jokes and less case experience. In the not-quite two years Evelyn had been at the BAU, he'd become her friend. He'd also been Kyle's partner on the HRT.

Nostalgia hit, for the easy banter Gabe and Kyle used to bring to the BAU office when they'd run over after a training session at Quantico. It would inevitably piss Dan off, and half the time he'd give either her or Greg the evil eye.

At the beginning, she'd resented the distractions, and been flustered by the attention. Then she'd developed a friendship with both of them. She hadn't seen Gabe in a while, but it felt somehow wrong to go to lunch with him and Greg without Kyle.

Evelyn shook her head. "Not today. I need to get through some of these other cases so Dan doesn't pull me from the Haley Cooke disappearance."

Greg frowned, but he nodded. "I know how badly you want to solve that one. But I've got to tell you, I looked at the initial case file, too, and there's not a hell of a lot to go on profile-wise."

"I know." But she had to believe she could help, had

to believe if she just kept looking she'd find the one missing piece that would tell her what had really happened to Haley.

Greg pushed himself away from the cubicle wall, making it shake. "And one of these days, you're going to have to accept that Mac isn't running over here with Gabe anymore. You're not being disloyal by coming out with us. Mac would want you to go."

Evelyn flushed, suddenly missing the way everyone here called Kyle "Mac." She mumbled a weak "Okay," and watched Greg head for the door. He was right. Greg was always right.

It scared Evelyn that he didn't think Haley's case had enough to go on, either. But somewhere out there, a seventeen-year-old girl—if she was still alive—was praying she'd make it back home to her family.

Evelyn couldn't fail her.

"Mac!"

Kyle jerked in his seat as his name echoed over the sound of all the other agents talking. He stood up in his drab gray cubicle, still devoid of any personal touches, and saw Jimmy rushing toward him.

"We've got a lead. Finally!" Jimmy announced before Kyle could ask what was going on, or the agents around them could do more than glare at Jimmy's loud tone.

"What is it?" Kyle rolled out his bad shoulder, not overly excited. Jimmy got worked up easily, and of the dozen active cases the squad had, all of them seemed far from the big break they needed.

"Cyber crimes did a great job with Tonya's computer."

"Seriously?" Kyle's pulse picked up. This was the

case keeping him up at night, the one he knew had more to it than anyone else was willing or able to see. Tonya was also the first victim he'd seen in his new role at the WFO, the first victim to personally ask him for help. And it didn't matter that she hadn't lived to see it—he still planned to get her whatever justice he could.

Jimmy waved a flash drive he was clutching. "Apparently the sex tape is real."

"You recovered it?"

"Yep. Our guys—and gal," he added with a grin, since there was one woman on the WFO's cyber squad, "were able to pull it off Tonya's laptop." He raised his voice a little. "Let that be a lesson to everyone that nothing ever really gets deleted."

Another agent on their squad rolled her chair out just long enough to give Jimmy a look Kyle interpreted to mean "you're an idiot," then rolled back to her desk and the case she was working.

Kyle's enthusiasm dimmed a little; he'd been hoping for more. He hadn't ever doubted the sex tape as leverage. The real question was whether it was a simple revenge scenario or if there was really a human trafficking ring behind it. And if they could prove it. "Could they tell where it came from? Could they identify the guy in the tape with Tonya?"

"They're still working on the trail. The email came from one of those anonymous sites, and it's been shut down recently. Not the site, the email address. Anyway, apparently the video is of Tonya and some guy. The cyber agents couldn't identify him, but maybe we can. Let's take a look."

Kyle grimaced, not particularly wanting to watch a sex tape Tonya hadn't even realized was being made. In that moment, he was very thankful he hadn't landed on the cyber squad, which dealt with reviewing child pornography online. He knew the importance of shutting that crap down, but he couldn't imagine sorting through those images, hunting for the people who'd taken or shared them. Talk about a job that would keep you up at night—the burnout rate from that squad was one of the highest in the Bureau.

"All right," Kyle said, following Jimmy to his cubicle. "Let's see what we've got."

Jimmy started the flash drive and a video popped up on his screen. Just an empty room initially, pretty unremarkable, with a brown leather couch in the center of the frame, an ugly blanket tossed over the back of it. No windows that might give a hint to location. No personal items that might indicate whose house or dorm or building it was. And no people.

"That's not Tonya's place," Jimmy stated the obvious. Tonya's dorm wasn't that spacious, and it wasn't that empty.

"No. But now we know the other person in the tape was almost certainly involved in threatening Tonya—or providing the tape to whoever did. There was a chance someone might have set up a camera in her dorm and just hoped they'd get something—meaning, whoever else was in the tape wouldn't necessarily be privy to it. But if they're bringing her to a location that already has one?"

"A definite setup," Jimmy agreed. He fast-forwarded a bit, then pressed Play when Tonya and a lanky, tow-headed guy came into the frame.

The man—kid, really, Kyle decided, pegging him close to Tonya's age—backed Tonya toward the couch until they both fell onto it. Tonya looked a little uncertain, but didn't protest as the guy—wearing jeans and a Neville University sweatshirt—kissed her with a lot of enthusiasm but not much finesse.

Kyle squinted at the tape, trying to figure out what was bothering him. "Do you recognize this kid?"

"I haven't gotten a good look at his face. Mostly just the back of his head. But we saw that same sweatshirt all over campus. Pretty good chance he's a student. Why? Do you know who he is?"

"He looks familiar."

"Someone in Tonya's life?" Jimmy offered. "One of the friends we talked to, you think?" He leaned a little closer to the screen, as if that would help him see the guy's face better. "I don't think any of them had hair that light. This kid spends a lot of time outside, or he gets his hair streaked at the salon." He shook his head as the kid fumbled with Tonya's top, getting nowhere. "I wish we'd had time to ask Tonya who else was on this tape."

Jimmy turned up the volume a little on his laptop. "Maybe we'll get lucky and she'll say a name. Even a first name would help."

"Maybe," Kyle agreed, not particularly hopeful. The only sounds coming from the speakers were grunting and moaning.

Then they traded places so the guy could get a better angle to take Tonya's shirt off, and Kyle told Jimmy, "Pause it!"

His partner jabbed the pause button and stared at him. "What? You recognize him?"

The boy was glancing directly at the camera now, a smug glint in his eyes and a smirk on his face that Kyle wished he could smack off. Soon, he promised himself as he tried to wiggle a name free from his memory.

"Where have I seen him?" Kyle muttered, taking in

the hazel eyes, the angular cheekbones, the oddly full lips. It was the nasty smirk, Kyle realized. He'd seen it somewhere, but not in person. In a photo.

"I don't know," Jimmy said, as if Kyle had been asking him. "But we can take a screenshot and show it to Tonya's roommate or go back around—"

"Son of a bitch," Kyle said as he remembered the picture. It wasn't from his case at all. It was from the wall in the room where Evelyn had been working at the Neville police station. "This is the kid who went missing from Neville right before Haley Cooke."

Jimmy looked perplexed. "Who?"

"His name is Nate Stokes."

12

"Well, if it isn't Evelyn Baine."

Jimmy Drescott gave her a big smile—the kind he certainly thought was charming—as he and Kyle approached the table she'd snagged in a coffee shop just off the Neville University campus. He wove around the shop's erratically placed tables, his booming voice making the few patrons look up from their mugs. When he finally reached her, he leaned down and gave her an enthusiastic, too-tight hug.

She awkwardly patted his arm, always uncomfortable with hugs. But after the case they'd worked together nine months ago, there was a bond between them that would never be broken. They'd both been targeted to die by a man who'd claimed a lot of victims—including Jimmy's first partner.

As Jimmy settled into the seat next to her, Kyle gave her a smaller, knowing smile and a wink. "You've already got your tea?"

When she nodded, he said, "I'm going to grab a coffee. Jimmy?"

"Same."

When Kyle walked over to the counter, Jimmy studied her with unnerving intensity. "So that's why I never got anywhere with you, huh?" He gave an exaggerated sigh while Evelyn tried not to flush or fidget.

While Jimmy wouldn't have gotten anywhere with her, anyway—he wasn't her type—having him know about her relationship with Kyle made her uneasy and she wasn't entirely sure why. Maybe she preferred to keep her personal life just that: personal.

It wasn't a secret anymore, she reminded herself. She and Kyle had officially filed paperwork with the FBI. She needed to get used to people knowing.

She glanced at Kyle, standing at the counter in a dark blue suit, jacket buttoned to cover his weapon. With his broad shoulders and muscular build from years of training on the HRT—which was essentially the FBI's version of Special Operations—he looked more natural in the casual clothes she was used to seeing him in at Quantico. But she could get accustomed to the suit.

Jimmy laughed at her. "I guess the secret's really out, huh?"

Realizing she'd just been caught ogling her boyfriend, she got her head in the game. "So, Nate Stokes," she said as Kyle rejoined them, setting coffee in front of himself and Jimmy.

"Thanks, man," Jimmy said, then shifted to face her. "Yeah, so, like your boyfriend told you on the phone, we've got him in a sex tape with Tonya Klein."

"What happened with her autopsy?"

Kyle frowned, looking frustrated. "Internal bleeding. She had a clot travel up to her brain, which is what killed her. The autopsy revealed a number of old injuries consistent with rape, but it wasn't conclusive. We're talking about old tears that didn't heal properly. It doesn't look like she got medical treatment."

"And we haven't been able to identify the perpetrators of her attack," Jimmy chimed in. "Tonya said two big guys, maybe the same men who assaulted her when she went to the meeting about the blackmail, but beyond that? The scene was wrecked. No forensics. Well, really, too much forensics—there was no way to separate everyone who trampled it from the perpetrators. We took the bottle used to hit her, but all we got were smudges, no usable prints."

"And you haven't been able to find anything on the human trafficking angle? Other than the possible evidence of sexual assault?"

"If there is a human trafficking angle, it's well buried," Jimmy said.

"Which is strange, considering the setup," Kyle added. "Because what Tonya described? It sounds amateur in the execution. I mean, abandoned warehouses for deals? Sex tapes for leverage? There are less risky ways to do this. Plus, the payoff to Tonya with her tuition seems pretty unusual for a human trafficking ring."

"Very," Evelyn agreed. "Well, maybe it *is* amateur, some kind of independent operation. Otherwise, we'd be seeing more of a strategic setup, probably where the girls operate out of a semilegitimate business. One that pays taxes on the other side of the business and uses it to funnel funds and people."

"Right," Jimmy said, reminding Evelyn that he had just as much experience as she did with human trafficking. Maybe more so, since it was one of his primary focuses on the Civil Rights squad.

"We see it often with massage parlors and strip clubs," Jimmy continued. "Or even cleaning services, especially for the labor-based trafficking."

"Well, an amateur setup might make sense, especially if we're talking about some college kids who think they're entrepreneurs," Kyle suggested.

Evelyn nodded slowly. "You think Nate Stokes was part of the trafficking ring."

"It makes sense," Jimmy agreed, tossing a still photo from the video of Nate and Tonya on the brown couch onto the table. "He set up the sex tape. It was clearly planned."

"That's Nate's apartment," Evelyn said. "I recognize that couch. And the ugly plaid blanket. It's all he had in his living room. And you know, it might explain the way his house looked."

Kyle leaned forward. "What do you mean?"

"His living room was—well, just what you see. Oddly empty. The rest of his house was more of what you'd expect for a college kid. Plus, he lives alone, in an area where you'd have a lot of drunk women walking by, because he's right near frat row."

"You think he chose Tonya as a target after a frat party?" Jimmy asked. "Because Tonya told us the pictures of her family that were sent to her were from some kind of scholarship welcome event."

"Not necessarily, about the targeting. But after he decides on a target, he might try to pick her up at one. You know, pretend he just ran into her. It's an easy spot to strike up a conversation with someone you don't know. And it's also a little strange that he lives by himself. Obviously he can afford it, but his best friend lives in a frat house, so why not Nate?"

"He wants privacy for the filming. My guess is this wasn't his only blackmail attempt. Maybe Nate is trying to run the whole thing himself. It would explain the lack of leaks, if there's no one to talk." Jimmy looked over at Kyle.

"But this isn't a one-man operation," Kyle reminded him. "We've got at least three, because the two guys who beat Tonya up did it after Nate had been missing for five weeks."

"Well, the obvious choice is Nate's best friend," Jimmy said. "Maybe him living in the frat is a way to get access to these girls."

"Maybe." Evelyn heard skepticism in her voice, but it wasn't necessarily about Jordan being involved. She knew his smug confidence had bothered Sophia from the start. That smugness could have come from this blackmail or trafficking operation, rather than Haley's disappearance. Or maybe he was guilty of all of it.

She thought back to their last meeting with him on the bridge. Sociopaths would have the kind of twisted desire to do that: give someone a flat tire, scare the hell out of them and then show up pretending to help while hoping their appearance caused even more fear.

Still, his concern over Haley felt real to her. And he was young to be able to master that kind of facade.

"Maybe?" Jimmy pressed when she went silent. "What do you think about Jordan being involved?"

"He's certainly got to be at the top of the suspect list. He's just connected in too many ways. First, his best friend goes missing, then his girlfriend goes missing, and now the missing best friend is tied to some kind of sex coercion at minimum and possibly human trafficking? The problem is Jordan's alibi for Haley's disappearance is pretty solid. It's possible he swung back around after he dropped her off at school, but he ran a high risk of someone spotting him. The cheerleaders would all recognize his car, because they'd just seen him drop Haley off."

"Maybe he went around the back?" Jimmy asked.

"Maybe. But then why not establish a better alibi? Not drop her off at all that day, not appear to be anywhere near the school when she was grabbed."

"Maybe he had someone else grab her," Jimmy suggested.

"But who? Nate was already missing at that point."

"We know there's someone else involved in the trafficking ring," Kyle reminded her. "It could have been the third guy who grabbed Haley."

"I know it's the most obvious answer," Evelyn said. "But let's say Jordan and Nate are trafficking women and Haley finds out, so they decide to make her disappear. Why did Nate disappear first?"

"What if Nate suggested Haley needed to go, Jordan disagreed and took out his friend, but then realized Haley really was a liability and got rid of her, after all?" Jimmy said, his voice gaining volume with excitement.

"It's a possibility," Evelyn agreed. "But if that's the case, Jordan is a hell of a liar."

"Or maybe Nate did it, and Nate's not really missing. Maybe Haley was at the wrong place at the wrong time, and saw what they were doing. He *knows* he has to get rid of her, and he takes off to avoid Jordan, then comes back to town to grab Haley?"

"That's possible, too," Evelyn said. "But if he took off around the same time he grabbed Haley, it makes it more likely we'd suspect a connection, even if he disappeared first. Would he risk law enforcement looking for him by doing that? Would he fear Jordan's wrath that much?"

"Or our third player is the ringleader and *that person* actually killed Nate, then grabbed Haley," Kyle suggested. "Then this guy and Jordan continued cleaning house and they beat up Tonya in that alley."

Evelyn nodded slowly. "That's our most probable scenario, I guess."

"You don't sound convinced," Kyle said.

"I saw Jordan the same day you came to campus to talk to Tonya," Evelyn reminded him. "He had no evidence of any injuries. And you said Tonya's knuckles showed she'd fought back hard. Jordan was wearing a sweatshirt, but he should have had bruises on his knuckles at the very least if he'd just beaten a girl up. Not to mention that when I saw him, he'd just gotten back from picking up coffee."

"So he could have—"

Evelyn interrupted. "I doubt he'd been gone long, because there'd been a girl waiting for him in his bed. I'm pretty sure when we dig into this we're going to find Jordan has an alibi."

"This kid has an alibi for everything," Kyle mused.

"Which either means he's really smart or really lucky," Evelyn said.

Kyle nodded grimly. "Or we're looking in the wrong place completely."

"Jordan is connected," Sophia said the next morning once Evelyn told her about her visit with Kyle and Jimmy. Linda Varner had just left the station after her daily check-in. "No question."

"I agree," Evelyn said. "But maybe not in the way we've been thinking. Even if he managed to slip away from the girl at the frat house while she was sleeping, how did he make it back without any blood on him, without any scratches or bruises? Kyle said Tonya had clearly fought hard."

"Maybe he made the other guy do all the hard work,"

Sophia suggested. "That sounds like an entitled little rich boy."

"Any thought on who that might be?"

"I don't know. Jordan seems to have a lot of friends, but not a lot of close friends other than Nate. But it would explain Haley's note. She learned about Jordan's criminal dealings and thought because she'd found out that he was going to kill her." Sophia tapped her fingers on the desk, faster and faster. "It's the motive we've been struggling over for so long. This has got to be it!"

"We're a long way from an arrest warrant," Evelyn reminded her. "We basically have a theory. Kyle and Jimmy haven't been able to find a warehouse in the area used for the scheme, and they haven't come up with any other evidence of trafficking. All we can conclusively say at this point is that Nate taped himself and Tonya having sex. We presume he used it to coerce her into sex with other people as part of his and Jordan's illegal business, but we have no concrete evidence of that, either."

"And that someone paid her tuition," Sophia reminded her. "We should get into Jordan's and Nate's finances."

"What if we bring Jordan in for official questioning?" Evelyn proposed. "See if we can get him to give us access in order to rule him out. Phrase it as though we wonder if Haley's kidnapping was a for-hire thing. Maybe grilling him at the police station will make him more uncomfortable."

"Nothing seems to make that kid uncomfortable."

"Except Haley being missing," Evelyn reminded her.

"He's faking," Sophia insisted.

"I don't know." Sociopaths were hard to read. She'd been fooled by them before. But her gut was still telling her Jordan was genuinely worried about Haley, which made no sense if he knew what had happened to her.

"Maybe her abduction was connected to the trafficking, but it wasn't ordered by Jordan. We need to figure out who's in charge."

"Let's get the kid in here. Hang on while I talk to my chief for a second." Sophia pulled open the door and was about to head through it when she stopped suddenly. "Quincy. What's up?"

The other detective was standing at the doorway as though he'd been about to knock. Or he'd been eavesdropping.

Evelyn squinted at him, remembering what Kyle had told her the other night about getting an odd feeling about Quincy. He'd wondered if the Neville police station was hiding reports that could connect Neville U to human trafficking.

Nerves bundled up in her stomach remembering all the times Quincy just seemed to be nearby. Did he suspect Haley's disappearance was connected to a trafficking operation that he was helping to hide?

"Just wondering how the case is going," Quincy said.

"We're looking into a new lead…" Sophia started.

Evelyn stood up and moved closer so she could see Quincy's reaction to the question she was about to ask. "Have you ever taken a report at Neville University by yourself because someone called and specifically asked to speak to a detective?"

Quincy blinked a few times, but his expression didn't change. "No. Why?"

"If something like that happened, the call would still get logged, right?"

He frowned at her, fists clenching at his sides before relaxing. "Why would you ask me that?"

"You tell me," Evelyn said as Sophia's head swiveled back and forth between them.

"Whoa," Sophia said as Quincy demanded, "What exactly are you accusing me of here?"

Evelyn kept her face impassive. "Have you heard anything about human trafficking happening at Neville University?"

His lips curled. "This is the second time the FBI has asked about that. You have any evidence there was trafficking happening? Anything at all? Do you people actually look at the evidence or do you just make up theories and hope you can force the facts to fit them?"

He shook his head and then stormed out before she could reply.

Sophia turned toward her, eyes wide. "What the *hell* was that?" She pushed the door shut so no one in the bullpen would overhear any more. "You suspect Quincy? He's been here twenty years. He's a hell of a cop and he's a good guy. He trained me. I trust him enough to let him take my *kids* places—and for me, that's saying a lot. He'd never hide that kind of report. No way."

"He reacted when I asked," Evelyn said quietly.

"Of course he did! I'd react if you asked me that, too!"

"We need to look at the records of calls that came in over the past nine months."

"Seriously? You know how much time that would take? We have Haley's case to solve."

"It could be connected."

"Bullshit," Sophia snapped. "I know Quincy Palmer. This job has been his life for years. His son is grown, his wife is gone, and this is what keeps him going. He would never toss a report. Never. And besides, if he did, don't you think the person would have called again?"

"Not if she was dead," Evelyn said softly.

"I don't believe for one second that Quincy took a

report from Tonya and then tossed it. And I'm not going to investigate another detective," Sophia said. "I don't even have the authority to do that. We'd have to get the chief involved—and Internal Affairs. And quite frankly, if there *was* a report that got tossed, it wouldn't be Quincy to blame. It would be one of the detectives let go this past year."

Evelyn frowned. "Who was let go? And why?"

"We used to have two other detectives. It's why Quincy and I have been so swamped since Haley's disappearance. They were partnered up, and I guess there were allegations of inappropriate behavior at a crime scene. I don't know all the details—the higher-ups tried to keep it under wraps—but they're gone now."

Evelyn glanced at the closed door, wondering if she'd been wrong about Quincy. Two recently fired detectives were better suspects for impropriety than a twenty-year veteran with a supposedly spotless record. But Quincy's unusual interest in Haley's case bothered her.

"We good here?" Sophia pressed, anger still lacing her voice. "If I go talk to the chief about bringing in the son of a billionaire CEO, you're not going to go harass our most decorated detective, right?"

"What does this billionaire CEO father do?" Evelyn asked.

Sophia rolled her eyes. "Biltmore? Jordan's the son of Franklin Biltmore." When Evelyn didn't respond, Sophia raised her eyebrows. "Biltmore Gaming? The video game company?"

Evelyn shrugged. "I don't play video games."

Sophia laughed. "Okay, fair enough. I have two sons. But I don't let them play anything from Biltmore Gaming. Their most popular games are virtual world adventure games, except we're not talking about dungeons-and-dragons type stuff. This guy's idea of an adventure is collecting points by slaying opposing armies, and collecting treasure by pilfering the spoils of war. The avatars are all men, any women in the game are scantily dressed and standing on the sidelines and it's actually part of the games to 'pillage and rape' when you win a battle."

Evelyn felt her lips curl in disgust. "And people buy this?"

"It made Franklin Biltmore a billionaire." She opened the door. "There's no accounting for taste," she added as she headed through the bullpen toward her chief's office.

As Evelyn watched Sophia go, she saw Quincy staring at her from the other side of the bullpen, a furious expression on his face, and she wondered if she'd been totally off base. Or if she'd showed her hand too soon.

If he had taken a report and hidden it, had she just given him the time to make the evidence disappear completely?

Damn that FBI profiler.

Quincy Palmer could see her staring at him now, from across the bullpen, assessing him, trying to uncover his secrets. He glared back, pissed off at her for seeing what no one else had noticed and pissed at himself for becoming the kind of cop who had that kind of secret.

Except that she was wrong. He knew exactly what she'd been getting at. She thought he'd taken a call from the suspected human trafficking victim, that he'd told the traffickers about it and caused the victim to get beaten up. Caused her death. And that the next thing he'd done was fail to write up a report, adding injustice to the crime.

It flat out wasn't true. He'd never met Tonya Klein, never set eyes on her before he'd seen the picture Sophia had tacked onto Haley's war room walls. He'd never taken a report from anyone that he'd failed to write up.

But Evelyn Baine was right about him, too, damn her. Because he'd agreed to hide one report *if* it ever came in. Haley's report.

For three months, he'd been trying to figure out what Haley knew that had caused someone to threaten his family. Trying to figure out what crime he was going to help cover up to protect someone who was probably beyond saving.

Now, he suspected that crime was human trafficking. It made him sick, even though he'd never hidden anything, because Haley had never come forward with any report. And even though he'd heard no hint of that happening at Neville University, it suddenly made perfect sense.

But he'd never suspected. He'd agonized over his decision ever since he'd made it, but what choice did he have?

He'd gone along with it, followed Haley around to get a sense of her schedule, to try to figure out what she might know. But for the most part, she'd acted like a normal high school kid. Not someone who was afraid for her life, not someone who knew a secret that could get her killed.

But when he'd seen Haley with Jordan, the kid had given him a wonky feeling. His cop radar had started beeping and wouldn't stop.

He'd suspected for a month now that it had been Jordan who'd blackmailed him. But he couldn't be sure. And although he had been careful, he must have gotten rusty at tailing suspects, because lately he'd begun to think Jordan knew Quincy was following him.

He turned away from Evelyn, wishing he could tell her what he knew about Jordan. Wishing he could help Haley. But he couldn't do it. Not at the cost of his son. And he hated himself for it.

So he headed back to his desk and kept the truth to himself: there was no way Jordan Biltmore had swung back around to the school and grabbed Haley Cooke. Because Quincy had trailed Haley to the school that day, but he hadn't stayed. He'd followed Jordan around for the rest of the afternoon.

Whoever had grabbed Haley, it wasn't Sophia and Evelyn's prime suspect.

13

"Jordan Biltmore has lawyered up," Sophia said a few hours later, as soon as Evelyn walked into the Haley Cooke war room.

She'd gone to the BAU office for a few hours, hoping to get marginally caught up while Sophia put the pieces in place to bring Jordan into the station. Meanwhile, Sophia had gotten her chief on board, put together a compelling "we just need your help" story for Jordan. And apparently all for nothing.

"Seriously? After you called and told him we just had a few more questions that could help us find Haley?"

"Yep. Initially, he made all kind of noises like, 'Oh, sure, I'll be in to the station in a few hours. Happy to help,' all that BS. But Jordan's attorney showed up with him. Said he's representing Jordan and all conversations should go through him from here on out." Sophia slammed her hand against one of the chairs, sending it crashing into the other chair and knocking them both to the ground, almost taking the folding table with them.

She squeezed her eyes shut for a minute, then let out a heavy breath and picked the chairs up. "Way to make himself look guilty, huh?"

Evelyn frowned, staying clear of the table until Sophia got it together. "That's kind of odd. Until now, he's been willing to help. Or, at least, he's been giving the appearance of being helpful."

"Yeah, well, I guess he's worried we're closing in on him."

"Maybe."

Sophia stuck her hands on her hips. "Why do you sound unconvinced?"

"From my perspective, either Jordan had nothing to do with Haley's abduction and he's genuinely worried." When Sophia looked ready to argue, Evelyn continued, "*Or* he's guilty as hell, and he's an amazing liar. The thing is, if he's that good, and that sure of himself, why all of a sudden is he scared to talk? What changed?"

"Hmm." Sophia's arms dropped to her sides. "I don't know. Did your FBI friends talk to him?"

"No, not yet. They are digging into him, though. He's the only person with a strong, obvious connection to Nate, and since they ID'd Nate in that blackmail video, Jordan's probably involved in the trafficking. But he wasn't in it alone."

"You think Nate was the ringleader? Or Jordan? Maybe they cooked up the plan together?"

"I doubt either of them was the ringleader," Evelyn said. "We know there's at least three people involved, so I'd guess the third person is pulling the strings. He might have been the one who grabbed Haley if he thought she suspected what Jordan was into."

Sophia nodded thoughtfully. "You're thinking someone older, I assume? Maybe someone who's done this before?"

"That would be my guess. Mostly because even though some aspects of this seem very amateurish, obviously there's some real skill here at keeping it hidden. Because if the trafficking *is* happening, Kyle and Jimmy are having a hell of time proving it."

"Well, let's see what we can do." Sophia grabbed two thick file folders with big, block lettering on the front of each. One said Haley Cooke. The other read Tonya Klein. She tucked the Tonya Klein one underneath and strode purposefully for the door.

"Where are we going?" Evelyn asked, following.

"To Interrogation. I don't care how many lawyers Jordan tries to get between him and our investigation. I'm still going after that bastard."

"He's here?"

"Yeah. Waiting in Interrogation with his lawyer. But if he hurt Haley, a lawyer won't help him. I'm going to make him pay for it for the rest of his sorry life."

"I can't argue with that," Evelyn said. "But do you have everything we talked about set up?" They'd discussed the best way to get Jordan to slip up if they brought him to the station. They hadn't counted on a lawyer, though, and Evelyn had a feeling Jordan had access to good ones.

"Absolutely. Let's do this."

Evelyn tracked her through the bullpen, ignoring the dirty looks she got from a few of the officers—probably from her loud conversation with Quincy earlier—and to the other side of the station.

"Here we go." Sophia pulled open the door to an unmarked room and led Evelyn inside.

Jordan was already sitting at the short conference table, slouched in his seat, hands tucked behind his head. He didn't move when she and Sophia walked in, but the man next to him wearing an expensive suit and perfectly groomed hair stood and held out a hand.

"Declan Lorimer, JD," he said, giving stiff, hard

handshakes to both of them before he sat back down and gave Jordan a pointed look.

Jordan's hands dropped to the table and he straightened in his seat.

Sophia took a seat across from the pair, but Evelyn remained standing, just to Sophia's left.

Jordan seemed to know his lawyer, the way he responded to Lorimer's nonverbal cues. A family friend, maybe? Or perhaps legal counsel for his father's company?

Sophia gave no indication she was concerned about the unexpected addition of a lawyer as she dropped the stack of files in front of her, loudly, drawing attention to them. The Haley Cooke file was on top, completely covering the Tonya Klein file. "I'm Detective Sophia Lopez. We appreciate you coming in. We just have a few questions about Haley—"

"I want to remind you that Mr. Biltmore is here of his own volition," the attorney interjected.

"Jordan isn't under arrest," Sophia reminded him.

"Is he a suspect?"

"Everyone is a suspect," Evelyn said flatly before Sophia could reply.

Lorimer's attention focused in on her. "And you are?"

"Special Agent Evelyn Baine, from the FBI."

He seemed to have already known the answer, and Evelyn got the impression he was just trying to control the conversation.

Sophia started out slow. "Haley was wearing her cheerleading uniform when you dropped her off at school the day she went missing?"

Jordan shook his head. "No. Like I told you before, she brought it with her. Her outfit and the pom-poms. She had a million of them—pom-poms, I mean. She always had a big gym bag with her when she had cheer-leading practice."

"Can you tell me what was in that bag the day you dropped her off?"

"All I know is she said she had her cheerleading stuff. I didn't look in her bag or anything." He glanced from Sophia up to Evelyn and then back again. "Why?"

"Just making sure we have all the details right," Sophia said blandly, tapping her fingers on the file and drawing Jordan's attention there. "The two of you went out for ice cream beforehand."

There was a pause, as though Jordan was waiting for a question, then finally he said, "Yeah. I've told you this before. We went for ice cream, I dropped her off, then I went back to campus. Why are we going over this again? Where the hell is my girlfriend?"

His voice rose at the end and his lawyer gave him a pointed glance, making Jordan scowl, then clamp his lips closed.

"We're looking for her," Sophia said, her voice still calm, almost monotone.

Evelyn knew she was doing it on purpose, to piss Jordan off, but they hadn't gotten to the real questions yet.

"Was anyone else with you at the ice-cream shop?" Sophia asked, tapping the file again, louder this time.

"No."

"Did you see anyone you knew there?"

"Jeez, I don't know. There were kids from school there, I think, but this happened a month ago! I don't remember who."

"Your school or Haley's?"

"Both, I think."

"Nate?"

"Nate what?"

"Was Nate there?" Sophia clarified.

"No. He was—well, hell if I know where he was. By then, he'd gone off to wherever Nate goes."

"Have you heard from him?" Sophia continued as Evelyn watched Jordan's face for any minute ticks. "Since you left that message, I mean?"

"No," he said, despair and anger in his tone.

But still no worry, Evelyn noticed with interest as the lawyer's shrewd gaze drifted up to her face, studying her as closely as she was watching Jordan. Probably wondering what she saw in his client.

"I doubt he's even checking his phone," Jordan said. "Best guess is he's spending every second on the beach, not worrying about any damn thing but himself."

This time, there was a hint of uncertainty in his tone.

"What's this all about?" the lawyer interjected, pulling his attention off Evelyn and directing the question at Sophia. "If you want to talk to Nate, why don't you call him?"

"We've tried," Sophia said. "We're getting no answer. And Jordan is Nate's closest friend."

"Why do you care what Nate's up to, anyway?" Jordan demanded, then his lawyer put a hand on his arm and Jordan snapped his mouth closed.

"We've explained to you that Nate went missing a week before Haley," Sophia said, still in her patient, emotionless tone.

"And I've explained to you that Nate isn't missing!" Jordan yelled, leaning toward her across the table.

Evelyn gave Sophia a quick tap on the shoulder and Sophia pulled the Tonya Klein file out from underneath Haley's, sliding it on top.

Jordan's Adam's apple bobbed once before his narrowed eyes lifted to Sophia's. "What the hell is this about?"

"We're finished here," the lawyer said, standing up.

"I want you to find Haley," Jordan barked. "This has nothing to do with Nate or this dead prostitute. This—"

"Let's go," the lawyer said, gripping Jordan's arm. To Sophia he said, "I don't know what you're trying to pull."

"I'm not trying to pull anything," Sophia said. "I want Jordan to tell me how Nate knew Tonya."

Jordan yanked his arm free of his lawyer's grip. "Nate *didn't* know Tonya."

Sophia slipped the picture from the top of the Tonya Klein file—which was mostly blank paper, since it wasn't actually their case. But Kyle had faxed over a copy of a still shot from the video that clearly showed Nate looking up at the camera, a smirk on his face, while Tonya sat on his lap.

Jordan glanced at it, then at Sophia, then at Evelyn. His lawyer grabbed his sleeve again, trying to drag him out the door, but Jordan resisted. "Okay, I guess Nate did know her. I didn't know. But let's be honest. If this girl had a reputation for sleeping around, Nate would be all over that. But he has nothing to do with Haley."

He glanced over at Evelyn once more, betrayal on his face as he let his lawyer lead him out of the station. But betrayal toward Nate for doing something he didn't know about or toward them for trying to trick him? Evelyn wasn't sure, but she was certain about one thing.

The look of betrayal had been genuine, unforced. But the expression that had been missing from his face when he'd looked at that photo? Surprise.

There was no question in her mind. Whether or not he'd been involved in setting it up, he'd already seen the video.

* * *

This was her least favorite time of year.

It was only five o' clock, but after digging as deeply into Jordan Biltmore and Nate Stokes as they could, she and Sophia had called it a day. Sophia had to get home to her kids, and Evelyn needed a night away from the office. Away from *any* office.

She shivered as she stepped out of her car and into the sad light of the flickering bulb overhead at the gas station closest to the Neville police station. Only five o'clock and it was already dark and dreary. They were just halfway through January and Evelyn was desperate for spring, especially now that last month's unusual warm spell had ended.

She dug into her pocket for her credit card with one hand while buttoning her wool coat even higher with the other. The gas station was empty, no long wait like she would have certainly found closer to Aquia. And she wanted to hurry.

She was early for a change. She had a good hour before dinner plans with Kyle, but she was rushing, because she had to drop her brand-new Bureau-issued sedan off in Aquia first. She wasn't allowed to drive that on nonwork business. After Aquia, she had to go home, not straight to the restaurant. Kyle was picking her up there.

Evelyn was slipping her credit card into the machine when she saw movement reflected in the side-view mirror on her car. She whipped around, her right hand darting down to her weapon even as her left one came up to protect her face.

Someone in a black jacket and a black ski mask covering everything but his eyes and lips rushed toward her fast, a baseball bat swinging.

Evelyn ducked, feeling the *whoosh* of air over her head. Her palms hit the cold concrete to brace herself as her heart thudded, filling with panic and disbelief. She'd gotten distracted. She hadn't heard this guy approach until he was too close.

He let out a sound of angry frustration and she glimpsed the bat rising again. He was going for another hit, this one on the top of her head.

Dropping onto her butt while angling her whole body sideways, she swung her legs toward him, catching him at the knees with all her strength.

The bat clattered, bouncing on the concrete, the handle slamming onto her arm hard enough to make it buckle. He went down, too, hard and fast, with a surprised grunt of pain.

Before he could get up, she shoved herself to her feet and took a step back, reaching for her weapon. But as she moved backward, she bumped into someone. A big someone, much taller than her, with a broad chest.

Panic set in fast. She was trapped, with the gas pump on one side, her car on the other, one man behind her and another in front of her.

Protect your weapon. The words drilled into her at the FBI Academy roared in her head as she angled her holster away from the guy behind her, simultaneously slamming her head backward.

She hit him in the chest, and only pushed him back a step. She heard him moving forward again, and the guy in front of her was getting to his feet, so she acted fast. Trying to clear her gun from its holster with two assailants this close wasn't going to happen, so she did the next best thing.

She ran forward, leaping over the guy still half on

the ground, and screamed as loud as she could. Hoping someone would hear her and call the local police.

The guy behind her got ahold of the back of her coat as she jumped, and tried to yank her back. They both went down, him slipping on the bat and landing half on his accomplice.

Evelyn scrambled to her feet and spun, fumbling for the SIG Sauer nestled at her hip, as the second guy got his footing. Leaving his own bat on the ground where he'd dropped it, he ran at her.

He slammed into her like a linebacker, even as she pulled her weapon free and slipped her finger under the trigger guard. They went down together, him heavy on top of her with limbs flailing. The ground came up to meet her painfully fast, even as she saw the second assailant moving toward them both.

Then the blast of a gunshot made her flinch and warm blood rushed over her hands.

Kyle glanced at his watch and frowned as he rang the bell at Evelyn's house again. Admittedly, he was early and she was often running late—especially when she was coming from work—but he had a bad feeling.

He wasn't sure why. When she'd called earlier in the day and asked him to fax over a picture from the sex video, he'd gotten the impression she was getting somewhere on Haley Cooke's case.

And he was finally—finally!—getting somewhere on Tonya Klein's case. Based on the tape showing Nate, and Tonya's claim that the tape had been used to blackmail her into sex for money, he'd gotten a warrant for Nate Stokes's home and finances. The judge had given him a little leeway because Tonya had died and he wasn't able to get any more information from her.

So far, their white-collar squad hadn't been able to pull anything useful from Nate's finances, though they'd said with the amount of money the kid had, it could take a while. Kyle was hoping eventually they'd turn up a trail that would lead them to Nate himself.

If Nate had filed a flight plan in the last two months, they couldn't find that, either. But after searching in Nate's house all afternoon, they'd found a hidden compartment in his desk.

Jimmy had discovered it, and Kyle had been impressed. They'd come away from the scene with a book of what seemed to be names and numbers. They were in some kind of code, but Kyle was sure this was the key.

He was betting the book was used to manage the finances of a small human trafficking ring operating out of the college. Now, he just had to prove it.

Kyle walked quickly back to his SUV, parked in Evelyn's driveway and got ready to call Evelyn's cell when his other phone rang. His work cell phone.

He debated ignoring it, but a quick peek showed the Neville police station as the caller. The tension in his shoulders eased. Evelyn had probably gotten caught up in the case and lost track of time.

"It's Mac," he answered. "I'm at your house."

"What?" The voice on the line wasn't Evelyn. "Uh, this is Detective Sophia Lopez, from the Neville police station. I'm looking for Special Agent McKenzie?"

The worry kicked back in, instantly doubling. "This is Agent McKenzie. Sorry. I thought you were Evelyn. What's going on? Is Evelyn still there?"

"Um, no, she's not. I tried calling her first, but I couldn't reach her. Look, I just got some news I think you're both going to want to hear."

"What is it?" he asked, even as his mind was on a different question: Where the hell was Evelyn?

"I'm on my way to the hospital. I don't think our cases are connected, after all. I thought you'd want to know as soon as possible."

"What?" The word *hospital* stopped him in his tracks, and he tried to disconnect it from his worry about Evelyn. She was probably fine; traffic was bad at this time of night and she almost certainly hadn't left on time.

"A victim just showed up in Head Waters and they took her to Augusta Health. She's in bad shape, but she's talking, and she's saying she was abducted by a stranger."

Kyle frowned at the increasing speed of Sophia's words, trying to piece together what any of this had to do with him. "Was it Haley?"

"No, but she claims she saw Haley Cooke. It looks like Haley's disappearance has nothing to do with trafficking. It was probably a stranger abduction, after all. Because this girl says they were being held together, that Haley Cooke was abducted by the same person."

14

Someone was screaming. Something was ringing. And the world underneath her was vibrating to the beat of pounding footsteps.

Suddenly realizing her eyes were closed, that she must have blacked out, Evelyn jerked, blinking and trying to move. Then she became aware of the heavy weight keeping her from taking a full breath, of the sticky wetness on her hands and stomach. Blood.

Hers? His? Both? It was hard to tell.

She gasped for air and lifted her head, which was all she seemed able to move. The guy who'd come at her was lying on top of her, the way they'd fallen. He was still, his arms dangling loosely on either side of her, like a macabre hug.

Past him, she could see a dark figure running away. The other attacker, she realized. She must have only blacked out for a few seconds.

Relief settled briefly over her that the second attacker was leaving, because it wasn't going to be easy maneuvering into a fighting position. The weight on top of her was making it hard to breathe, hard to tell if she was injured, too.

When she turned her head toward the source of the

screaming, she realized someone was standing next to her. A teenager, so pale he looked ready to fall down next to her. How he was managing to scream while breathing that rapidly was kind of amazing.

"It's okay," Evelyn said, her voice weak under the weight of her attacker, who must have had fifty pounds on her.

She slid her finger carefully out from underneath the trigger guard, and repositioned it underneath the trigger itself, so she couldn't accidentally snag it on anything and pull it again. Then she shifted, trying to shimmy out from underneath her attacker, who was either out cold or dead.

"I'm FBI," she told the kid, whom she assumed must have come out of the gas station. "I'm with the FBI," she repeated until he stopped screaming. "I need you to call the cops. Tell them an FBI agent was attacked at your gas station."

"I hit the alarm," the kid managed, staring at her with comically wide eyes as she finally managed to slide out from underneath the masked man.

"I was in the back. I didn't hear what was happening at first. I wasn't supposed to be back there, but I was just having a smoke. A cigarette!" the kid added, shifting his weight back and forth as she suddenly noticed the smell of marijuana in the air.

"It's okay," she told him, attempting to calm him down as she got to her knees and tucked her weapon back in its holster. Then, trying to ignore the blood on her coat and her skin that made her itch with the desperate need to clean it off, she pressed two shaky fingers to her assailant's neck. When she removed them, she left behind two perfect fingerprints, made in blood.

"Dead." She sat back on her heels, trying to regain

her equilibrium as the sound of a siren came closer and she realized the ringing she'd heard earlier was the phone in her pocket. It started up again just as a Neville city police car raced into the lot and slammed to a stop.

"Dead?" the kid squeaked, backing away from them as two young officers leaped out of the police car.

"Stop there!" one of the officers barked, weapon out, and Evelyn put her hands slowly in the air.

"I'm with the FBI," Evelyn said calmly. "Special Agent Evelyn Baine."

"Agent Baine?" the officer repeated, coming closer and squinting at her in the poor lighting. Then he seemed to recognize her and refocused his gun on the kid still backing away.

"He's okay," Evelyn said. "The other assailant ran."

The officer lowered his weapon and called to his partner, "We're all good."

"What happened here?" the second officer asked, putting her gun back in its holster.

Evelyn tried to come up with names for the officers, but even though she vaguely recognized them from her six days at the station, she couldn't. "Two masked men attacked me at the gas pump."

When the first officer bent to check the man bleeding out on the concrete, Evelyn said, "He's dead. I shot him during the attack." She didn't mention that she hadn't fully intended to shoot; she'd been preparing to when he'd slammed into her, and the impact had jarred her finger into the trigger.

Thank God the impact hadn't also jarred the gun, redirecting it back toward her.

"Okay," the officer said, calling the situation in over his radio. As the second officer pulled the kid off to the side to ask him questions, the first one said to her, "Do you know what this was about? Was it random or were they after you?"

Evelyn shook her head, replaying the moment she'd seen movement in her car mirror. "I have to assume it wasn't random, but I'm not really sure what it's about." Her best guess was the Haley Cooke case, but why?

She longed to pull the ski mask off her assailant, but she didn't want to touch anything until the FBI's Evidence Response Team agents arrived. "Let me call in the FBI to handle the crime scene," she told the officer. The attack on her made it a federal issue, and the FBI probably had better—and certainly faster—evidence response capabilities than the tiny Neville police station.

She wiped her bloody hands off as best she could on the sides of her wool coat, which was going in an evidence bag, anyway. Then she pulled out her cell phone and dialed Kyle's number with shaky hands, her adrenaline still pumping.

"Evelyn?" Kyle answered, concern in his voice after just one ring.

"It's me. I'm still in Neville."

"Did Sophia get ahold of you?"

"Sophia? No. Why?"

"Why are you still in Neville? Are you heading to Fisherville? Is everything okay?"

"What's in Fisherville? And yeah, I'm fine, but we're going to need to cancel dinner. I just got attacked heading out of Neville. I want you guys to handle the crime scene."

The FBI higher-ups probably wouldn't be thrilled that she'd essentially handed her boyfriend a crime scene, but it made sense. There was a potential connection between their cases, so they were already informally working together. This would just make it official.

YOUR PARTICIPATION IS REQUESTED!

Dear Reader,

Since you are a lover of our books – we would like to get to know you!

Inside you will find a short Reader's Survey. Sharing your answers with us will help our editorial staff understand who you are and what activities you enjoy.

To thank you for your participation, we would like to send you 2 books and 2 gifts – **ABSOLUTELY FREE!**

Enjoy your gifts with our appreciation,

Pam Powers

SEE INSIDE FOR READER'S SURVEY

For Your Reading Pleasure...

YOUR READER'S SURVEY
"THANK YOU" FREE GIFTS INCLUDE:

▶ **2 FREE books**

▶ **2 lovely surprise gifts**

PLEASE FILL IN THE CIRCLES COMPLETELY TO RESPOND

1) What type of fiction books do you enjoy reading? (Check all that apply)
- ○ Suspense/Thrillers
- ○ Action/Adventure
- ○ Modern-day Romances
- ○ Historical Romance
- ○ Humour
- ○ Paranormal Romance

2) What attracted you most to the last fiction book you purchased on impulse?
- ○ The Title
- ○ The Cover
- ○ The Author
- ○ The Story

3) What is usually the greatest influencer when you <u>plan</u> to buy a book?
- ○ Advertising
- ○ Referral
- ○ Book Review

4) How often do you access the internet?
- ○ Daily
- ○ Weekly
- ○ Monthly
- ○ Rarely or never.

5) How many NEW paperback fiction novels have you purchased in the past 3 months?
- ○ 0 - 2
- ○ 3 - 6
- ○ 7 or more

YES! I have completed the Reader's Survey. Please send me the 2 FREE books and 2 FREE gifts (gifts are worth about $10) for which I qualify. I understand that I am under no obligation to purchase any books, as explained on the back of this card.

194 MDL GJ23/394 MDL GJ24

FIRST NAME	LAST NAME

ADDRESS

APT.#	CITY

STATE/PROV.	ZIP/POSTAL CODE

SUS-216-SUR16

READER SERVICE—Here's how it works:

Evelyn heard him muttering curses, then the sound of a car started up. "I'm coming. Where are you?"

"At a tiny gas station close to the Neville police station." She glanced up at the sign. "Fillers."

"Are you sure you're okay?"

"Yeah, I'm fine. One of the guys got away, and the other one is down."

"Do you recognize him?"

"I don't know yet. He was wearing a ski mask. I didn't want to touch it until the ERT got here."

"A ski mask?" Kyle's voice picked up speed. "Describe it."

"Just a typical ski mask. Black, just eye and mouth holes. Standard-issue asshole gear."

"That's what the men who attacked Tonya Klein wore."

Evelyn felt a shudder rip through her, residual fear creeping in. What he meant was the men who'd *killed* Tonya Klein.

She glanced back at the man lying dead, facedown on the pavement, and into the distance, the dark night suddenly ominous. "I brought up Nate's sex tape to Jordan Biltmore at the station this afternoon."

"Damn it," Kyle muttered. "You think he'd have the nerve—and the stupidity—to attack a federal agent near a police station?"

She stared hard at the body on the ground. "The one I killed isn't Jordan, that's for sure." He was too tall, too massive. "The other one?" She tried to remember his body type, but all she could think of was the moment she'd smacked his legs, how he'd come down hard. He'd been a little shorter than this guy, but still strong. "I'm not sure."

"Did you injure him?"

"Probably bruised his legs. Otherwise, I don't know. He hit the ground hard."

"Okay. After we clear the crime scene, Jimmy and I will pay Jordan Biltmore a visit, see if he's got any bruises."

"Are you close?" Evelyn asked as the cops blocked off the street entrance to the gas station and pulled out some portable lights for the scene.

"I was at your house. I'll be there in thirty."

Which meant he was speeding like a lunatic. "Okay, I'll be here." She got ready to let him go, so they could both make the other necessary calls, when she remembered, "What did you say about Fisherville?"

"Oh, yeah. Detective Lopez called me a few minutes ago. Someone showed up in Head Waters, claiming she'd been abducted and escaped. They took her to Augusta Health Hospital. She also claimed Haley Cooke was there. Detective Lopez wants you at the hospital as soon as possible."

Three hours later, once the FBI had cleared her to go after the incident, Evelyn's helicopter landed on the roof of the hospital in Fisherville, Virginia. They'd gotten special clearance to land there, so she could arrive as soon as possible after she'd answered everyone's questions and could finally leave the crime scene in Neville.

She hopped out and stayed low, keeping clear of the blades and the wind, waving to the agent who'd come back into work in the middle of a family movie night to fly her. Kyle could have done it, except he was still working the scene at Neville.

He'd arrived pissed off and determined, and Jimmy hadn't been far behind him. They'd unmasked her attacker, and neither she nor Kyle or Jimmy had recognized him. The guy was young, probably in his early twenties. He'd had no ID on him, no cell phone, nothing identifiable. The Medical Examiner would fingerprint him, so she hoped they'd get a name soon.

She wondered if someone was missing him tonight, if he had a family who had no idea he'd gone out and tried to kill a federal agent with a baseball bat. And she wondered who'd asked him to do it.

Between this attack and the flat tire that was looking less like an accident, all the signs were pointing straight at Jordan Biltmore. But was he cocky enough to be that obvious? And if he *had* been behind it, why not just let their car go over the bridge? Why help them? Or was someone setting him up to take the fall?

And for what? Haley's disappearance? The trafficking? Both? And if there really was human trafficking happening at Neville University, where were the other victims? No one else had come forward, and as hard as Kyle was pushing, they still had no arrests.

Putting the questions aside for now, Evelyn ran to the hospital door, her movements awkward and clunky with Kyle's too-big coat wrapped around her. Her own jacket was sealed in an evidence bag back in Neville.

A hospital security guard met her at the elevator and took her down to the floor where they had Gillian Murray. Evelyn had spoken to Sophia on the ride over and discovered that the girl had only just been medically cleared to talk to the police. Sophia was waiting for her, probably impatiently.

"Here you go." The security guard pointed down the hall to the room on the end, but Gillian's room was obvious. There was a police officer standing guard outside the door, looking serious, and Sophia was pacing back and forth nearby.

As soon as she saw Evelyn, Sophia jogged over, meeting her in the middle of the hallway.

"What's the story?" Evelyn asked.

"You tell me. Are you all right?"

Sophia looked her over, probably searching for injuries, but other than the slight headache and residual shakiness after the adrenaline faded, she was fine.

"Yeah. Kyle and Jimmy are investigating. They'll call if anything breaks."

"It has to be connected, right?"

"Probably. You should be careful, too," she warned Sophia. "I got one of them, but the second guy ran. And I'm honestly not sure what we're close to that's got someone spooked, because we're nowhere near an arrest."

"Well, maybe the guy you shot will give us a lead. He's got to have connections your friends can follow. Maybe one of them will lead straight back to a suspect."

"Let's hope so."

"All right, then let me share what I know about Gillian Murray." Sophia spoke softly, leaning close so they wouldn't be overheard. "She showed up at a truck stop along US250 in Head Waters. Guy who found her thought she'd crawled there, she was so covered in dirt and grass and branches. He said she was freezing and confused. Couldn't say where she'd come from, panicked if anyone came near her. The trucker called the police and they brought her here. That's when she told a nurse she'd been abducted. Said she didn't know the guy who'd grabbed her, but that she did recognize the person in the basement with her, from all the news reports."

"Haley," Evelyn said.

"Yeah."

"How reliable is she?"

"I don't know. I was waiting for you to talk to her, remember? But the doctor tells me her injuries aren't for show. So, whether or not she was right about Haley, she's not lying about being a victim." Sophia let out a heavy sigh. "Evelyn, this girl had hypothermia. I'm guessing there was also sexual assault, but the doctor says she just shakes her head when they ask about that. They won't know for sure without an exam, and she'd have to consent to that—which so far she hasn't. And one thing we *can* confirm? She's seventeen, same as Haley. She went missing a week ago out of a little town about thirty miles south of here."

"Between here and Neville," Evelyn said grimly.

"Yeah. Apparently the girl has a known stalker that the police were leaning on pretty hard, so no one thought to call us in Neville. Everyone was so sure this guy did it, but it looks like they were wrong. And her disappearance only made local news, so I never heard about it." Sophia shook her head. "Fucking jurisdiction."

It was a problem Evelyn was all too familiar with, and one that, being in the FBI, she could sometimes help bridge. "Okay, let's go talk to her."

Sophia hesitated. "Have you done this before? Interviewed a victim who's been through such an awful experience? I mean, I've investigated rape cases and even a kidnapping, but this kind of captivity? If she's right about Haley, this guy has had her for a *month*. And what little I know so far? I don't think Gillian saw daylight the entire time, so Haley hasn't, either. How do we get the information we need about Haley, while still being sensitive about whatever Gillian suffered this past week? And how do I ask a seventeen-year-old girl what she endured locked up in some sicko's basement?"

"I can take the lead," Evelyn said, trying to mentally

prepare herself. Unfortunately, long-term victims of captivity weren't anything new for her. But they were some of the most difficult cases emotionally.

It was hard enough when she had to try to reconstruct how a victim had died or been tortured, but when that torture had gone on for days or weeks or even years? Imagining the kidnapped women feeling the hope drain away a little more each day, thinking their terror was never going to end?

Sometimes they were so broken down they never recovered. In other cases, they bonded emotionally with their abductor through systematic brainwashing or just to survive. Even the strongest victims of this sort of captivity came out forever altered.

She hated this kind of case.

Victim interviews weren't particularly common for her, and they were definitely outside her comfort zone. Her partner, Greg, was much better at them; he always knew the right balance between being careful with the victim and helping the case. That had never come as naturally to Evelyn. But this could be their chance to find Haley before it was too late.

Still, talking to a seventeen-year-old girl who'd been kidnapped and brutalized? Evelyn tried to push back her anger and focus on what she needed to do. Gillian telling them her story, being part of finding the person who'd done this, could help her heal.

"Let's go," Evelyn said, heading for the door, with Sophia a little slower than usual on her heels.

At her knock, a faint voice called, "Come in."

The girl in the center of the big white room stared wide-eyed as Evelyn and Sophia entered. Evelyn recognized the look immediately—some in law enforcement called it the thousand-yard stare. Characteristic of shell shock from trauma.

She was bundled up under piles of stark white hospital blankets, gauze around the wrists peeking up to clutch the top of the covers. Her short, dark hair looked matted and dirty, and there were dark circles under her bloodshot eyes, and a bruise high on one pale cheek. She was hooked up to monitors and an IV bag and all the wires and tubes looked overwhelming attached to such a small girl.

She was Haley's age, but physically they were very different. Where Haley was slim but muscular, Gillian was just petite, her wrists nothing but skin and bone. But apparently she'd run track, and it had served her well today.

The police officer who'd picked Gillian up had confirmed there was nothing for miles around the truck stop where she'd been found, and the girl seemed to have been running for quite a while. She'd done it all in temperatures hovering around freezing and wearing loose pajama pants, a T-shirt and bare feet. The office had tried to ask her where she'd come from, what had happened, but she hadn't spoken a word until she'd gotten to the hospital.

Somehow, she'd found the strength to escape, then went as far and as fast as she could, until she found help. Now, with the adrenaline faded, she was struggling to stay awake, but she was probably afraid of reliving her captivity in nightmares. Or maybe just afraid that if she closed her eyes, the escape would turn out to be a dream and she'd be back in whatever hell she'd endured.

"I'm Evelyn Baine, from the FBI, and this is Sophia Lopez, from the Neville police department. Would it be okay if we asked you a few questions?"

The girl blinked, her eyes shifting slowly as she nodded, and Evelyn knew she'd already been asked if she was comfortable talking to the police. Evelyn also knew her parents were down the hall, taking a break at her request while she told her story.

A strong girl, Evelyn recognized immediately. Not just physically but emotionally. Most seventeen-year-old kids would want a parent with them. Gillian obviously wanted to spare hers the details of what had happened to her.

Evelyn pulled up a chair near the bed and nodded for Sophia to do the same. "If there's anything you're not comfortable talking about, we can just skip over it for now, okay? Our first focus is making sure that you're okay, and our next one is catching the person who did this. Until then, I want you to know that there's going to be an officer at your door around the clock, okay?"

She gave another quick nod, and Evelyn could tell Gillian felt nowhere close to safe. Evelyn also knew, from too many other abduction cases, that it would take her a long time to get there. Maybe years. In some cases, never.

Because Evelyn had no idea how much Gillian would be ready to talk about now, she started with the details she needed fastest. There was always the possibility that Gillian's escape would prompt her abductor to act, which meant time was crucial. They didn't know if the abductor was going to run and take Haley with him to a new location. Or if he would just eliminate Haley.

"Do you know the person who took you?"

Gillian shook her head.

"Okay. You didn't recognize him at all?"

A brief pause, then another head shake.

"Are you sure you didn't know him? Not even someone you might have just seen before?"

"Maybe," Gillian croaked, her words slow and pained. "He seemed a little…familiar. But I definitely didn't *know him* know him. I might have just seen him…somewhere."

He'd stalked her first, Evelyn figured. It made sense, if he'd grabbed first Haley out of Neville, and then Gillian from another small town two hours north. Gillian might have spotted him one day, vaguely remembered him because her internal warning system had gone off.

"What about Haley?" Sophia interjected. "Did she know him?"

Gillian frowned, then shook her head.

"Are you sure?" Sophia pushed.

"I don't think so," Gillian rasped. "I guess I never asked. But she never said she knew him, so I assumed she didn't."

"Was it just one person?" Evelyn asked, wanting to be thorough. "One man?"

"Yes," Gillian said. "Except…"

"Except what?"

"I got out because of someone else. Another man. I'd never seen him before. I barely even saw him then, because the basement was dark, and the lights… He opened the basement door. He told us to run."

Evelyn's heart rate picked up. "And you ran?"

"Yes."

"You did really good. Really good. Do you know how far you ran?"

Gillian took a heavy breath, loud enough that Evelyn could hear it, then she shook her head. "It felt like forever. I just kept going and going and going. Hours, I think."

"When you came out of the basement, were you in a house?"

"Yeah."

"Okay. And when you came out of the house, were you in a neighborhood?"

Gillian shook her head, her whole body twitching. "No. I saw another house, but way off in the distance. And it looked—I don't know—maybe abandoned, so I ran the other way. And then there was nothing for so long. Just trees. I ran through them as fast as I could, but I was sure he could see me, that he was chasing me, and I thought I was going to fall and—"

"It's okay," Evelyn interrupted as Gillian's voice picked up speed until she was panting. "You made it."

"I did." Gillian squeezed her eyes shut a second, then opened them wide again. "I did."

"And what about Haley?"

Gillian looked blank.

"How did you know it was her?" Sophia interjected.

"I recognized her. From the news. And we were down there together, so we talked. We weren't really sure what he wanted, or what would make him mad, so mostly we did it when he let us turn on this old TV. We'd turn the volume up and whisper. But she told me her name."

"What else did she tell you?" Sophia asked.

"That he was never going to let us leave." Gillian sucked in another fast breath, her hands shaking despite how tightly she was clutching the blankets.

"What happened when you ran?" Evelyn prompted, wanting to remind her that she'd made it, that she was safe now. "When the man told you to run, and you got to safety, what did Haley do?"

She could almost feel Sophia holding her breath as Gillian frowned, staring down at her lap.

"She ran, too. I don't know which way she went, but we ran to the door together. She was right behind me. She got away, too."

15

"Still nothing." Sophia sighed, dropping her cell phone into the cup holder between them in her unmarked police car.

She and Evelyn were driving back from the hospital in Fisherville after talking to Gillian Murray. Not long after the girl had dropped her bombshell about Haley escaping with her, doctors had checked her monitors and pushed them out, telling them to come back later.

If Gillian was right, hopefully Haley would show up somewhere, too, alive and looking for help. There were patrol officers combing the area all around the truck stop where Gillian had appeared. But so far, no one had spotted Haley.

And the area Gillian had described—rural and not very populated—matched a lot of Highland County, which was near Head Waters and one of the least densely populated counties in the United States. They'd probed for more specifics about the house or the area, but Gillian's focus had just been running as fast as she could. Information she could give about the area was sketchy.

So, for now, responders were searching the lands, but not knocking on doors. Gillian's description was too vague for a search warrant, and too much pressure on a kidnapper who'd have no legal requirement to let officers into the house could prompt him to run. Or—if he'd caught up to Haley—to make her disappear for good.

Hopefully, they'd get more from Gillian later, once the immediate stress of her escape and the confusion and mental fogginess from her hypothermia wore off. But after her experience, they also had to be careful not to push too hard too fast or they could lose her help altogether.

They drove in silence for a few minutes before Sophia said, "The things she said about Haley were pretty detailed."

"Yeah." Evelyn rubbed a hand over her eyes, exhausted and fighting sleep. "She's either telling the truth about Haley being there or she watched a lot of coverage on the case."

Sophia gave her a confused glance, then returned her attention to the road, nearly empty at almost two in the morning. "Why would she lie about that?"

"It happens for a lot of reasons. But sometimes victims also get confused."

"You mean, someone else was there and she just thought it was Haley?"

"Right. Because she was abducted a week ago, she'd probably have seen all the news on Haley. So, when she was there, she could have made the assumption. Or even made up that she wasn't alone, because she needed someone to talk to, and to help her cope. It's a possibility, but I think we should proceed assuming Haley was really at that house."

"If only we knew where it was," Sophia said.

"If she got away, a lot of police officers are out looking for her."

"Yeah, but what if this guy caught her again?"

Evelyn glanced over at Sophia in the dark car.

Many times, when Evelyn got involved, the victims were already dead. She remembered clearly the first case she'd worked with the possibility that the victim could come home alive. She'd thought it would get easier the longer she did the job. In some ways, it did. She knew what to expect now: the long hours, the tremendous highs and lows, the fear and the hope.

But in other ways, it always felt like the very first case. Every victim was unique, every perpetrator a puzzle she had to piece together. And most of the time, trying to unravel what had happened sent her deep into the country's most depraved minds. And into the minds and hearts of the people they hurt.

"For now, we have to operate on what Gillian told us," Evelyn said. "It's cold out there. If Haley was dressed the way Gillian was, we need to find her before exposure gets her. We have to hope she made it away from that house, too."

"Yeah," Sophia said, her voice heavy with the knowledge that no one had spotted Haley yet, and it had been almost nine hours since a truck driver had called 911 after seeing Gillian.

They drove in silence for a few more minutes and then Sophia asked, "What do you make of Gillian never having been to Neville?"

"We should check with Haley's parents, see if Haley was ever in Gillian's hometown. But honestly, both the fact that Gillian's abductor was a stranger and the fact that she didn't recognize the photos of anyone from our case? Haley's abduction probably has nothing to do with realizing someone she knew was running a human trafficking ring. And it probably has nothing to do with *anyone* we've been investigating."

Evelyn tried to keep the frustration out of her voice, but knew she was failing. When she'd looked at the Haley Cooke case a month ago, her gut had screamed *stranger abduction*. Haley's note had changed everything.

Now the question was, how was the note connected? Gillian said Haley hadn't known her abductor, but was she right? Could it have been someone on the periphery of her life that they hadn't even considered? Or someone Haley didn't want to admit to Gillian she'd misjudged so badly?

Sophia took a long sip from her takeout coffee, which had to be cold by now. "This is not good. If Haley doesn't just show up somewhere, and Gillian can't identify her kidnapper, we're back to square one. Worse than square one, really, because now we don't even have any suspects."

"Haley didn't make it."

Evelyn looked up from what had become her normal working spot over the past seven days, the cramped folding table in Haley's war room. She blinked, realizing she'd been staring so intently at what she'd been writing that her eyes had gone blurry.

Evelyn glanced at her watch and frowned. Noon. "We don't know that. We can't think that way."

Sophia sank onto the chair beside her and gave her a halfhearted smile. "Come on, Evelyn. It's been nineteen hours since 911 got the call about Gillian. If Haley ran, either she's dead from exposure or he caught her—and maybe killed her. And since no concerned neighbors called the police about two teenagers being chased by someone, we can assume no one saw it."

"Someone saw it," Evelyn disagreed. "The guy who helped Gillian escape."

"Yeah, fat lot of good that does us."

Evelyn tapped her pen against the paper she'd been furiously writing on since she'd arrived at the Neville police station an hour ago. After coming back from Fisherville, she'd gone home and slept a solid six hours, then driven back to Neville, praying she'd be greeted with good news about Haley. In case she wasn't, she already had the next step in mind.

"The thing about Haley's case before is that we didn't have a useful crime scene, and we didn't have a pattern because her abduction didn't seem to be part of a series. Before, it was tough to profile the offender, because we had to rely on profiling the people in Haley's life. There were too many variables, making it hard to narrow down."

"No kidding," Sophia said, lowering her head into her hands.

She looked exhausted, like she'd never gone home after she'd dropped Evelyn off. Knowing Sophia's dedication to the case, that wouldn't surprise Evelyn at all. Except she knew Sophia was a single mom with two young boys at home. So, she'd probably gone home long enough to look in on her kids and get everything ready for their day today, then came back to the station.

"That's all different now," Evelyn said.

Sophia lifted her head. "Yeah?"

"Now we have a second victim, a pattern, and we have two unknown subjects—the abductor and the Good Samaritan."

"Not much of a Good Samaritan," Sophia muttered, "Or he would have turned this guy in right from the start."

"You're assuming he knew what was happening right from the start."

"And you think he didn't?"

"I think we can't assume either way. But now that we have more information—a single scenario instead of a variety of possibilities—I can give you a profile. More than just the most likely suspects. Or less, depending how you look at it, since we don't have names this time around. But I can tell you what kind of person he is."

Sophia nodded slowly. "Things like what kind of job he probably holds and where he might live?"

"Exactly. I'll know a lot more once we have another chance to talk to Gillian, but I can at least get us headed in the right direction. The details she can give us about how this guy acted, the things he said and did? That will tell us a lot more, and I'll be able to tweak my profile once we talk to her about that."

Sophia nodded. "I'm going to call the hospital in a few hours, see how she's doing. Check if we can drive back up there and ask her more questions." Sophia peered over her arm at the paper Evelyn had been scribbling on for the past hour. "Is that the profile you started? Can I have it?"

"I'll tell you what I think. I'd recommend against putting it in the police file."

"Because then it's discoverable if we get a suspect to trial," Sophia said immediately. "Got it."

Making a profile part of the official case file was sometimes useful, but the problem was after they made an arrest, the profile could be used in the trial. And criminal personality profiles weren't magic. They pinpointed the most likely attributes of a suspect given the information at hand, but if anything didn't match—and chances were, something wouldn't, because profiles were more about the total picture than the individual pieces—then the defense would jump on it as "proof" they had the wrong person.

Most police detectives weren't familiar enough with profiles to know the negatives, and Evelyn's surprise at Sophia's comment must have shown, because she said, "I did my research before I requested the BAU's help."

"I guess so." Evelyn smiled. "Okay, so I'm basing my profile on what we already know about Haley—who she is, her routines, all of that—and on the new information from Gillian. My profile relies pretty heavily on Gillian's story, so besides just getting *more* details, we need to confirm some of the things she's already told us. We talked to her immediately after her escape, so details could become clearer when she doesn't have pure survival at the forefront of her mind."

"Okay," Sophia agreed. "I'll take the profile with a grain of salt."

"Profiles," Evelyn stressed. "Both the perpetrator and the guy who helped Gillian get away."

Sophia nodded slowly. "That guy might actually be the key."

"I agree. He's the weaker link. He helped Gillian get away. He tried to help both of them. Obviously he's got strong ties to the abductor, but enough of a moral compass to act independently. If we give him the right motivation, he might turn in the perpetrator."

"And what do you think is the right motivation?"

"I'll get there. Let me give you the specifics on the people I think we're looking for here."

"I'm ready," Sophia said, looking anxious as she settled on the corner of the table, hands clasped tightly in her lap.

"Some of the details may change once we confirm

whether or not Gillian was sexually assaulted," Evelyn warned her.

To their surprise, Gillian had said she hadn't been, but rape was one of the most underreported crimes. She'd originally refused the exam, but after Sophia had insisted it was important, she'd reluctantly told doctors she'd have one. They were still waiting to hear the results.

"You think she didn't want to admit it?" Sophia asked, not sounding surprised, just sad.

"I'm not sure. I would have expected it, with this kind of abduction and prolonged captivity. If there was none, we may be looking at someone who can't perform sexually for some reason. Either that or his motivation isn't sexual. And if that's the case, we'll want further details on his behavior to be able to narrow down motivation, which is going to be key to finding him."

"Okay," Sophia said. "What do you think so far? Show me some of that profiling magic."

Evelyn nodded, feeling the pressure ratchet up. She looked at the incomplete profiles she'd written, wishing she'd been able to provide more when all they'd had was Haley's disappearance to go on. Wishing that profiling really was magic and not a combination of psychology, criminal behavior knowledge and the gut instincts that developed further with every case she worked.

"Here's what I can tell you with pretty high certainty about the offender," Evelyn said. "He's unmarried. Probably never been married, in fact. He's socially insecure and socially isolated. Those two things are partly why he resorts to abductions, and partly why he chooses much younger women."

"Much younger?" Sophia asked. "How old is he?"

Evelyn frowned. Gillian had described him as "an older guy," but when asked for more specifics, all she'd been able to say with certainty was older than her, maybe thirties or forties. She'd sounded so uncertain about it Evelyn remembered Sophia shooting her a confused look. "Age is one of the hardest pieces to profile. That's because *actual* age isn't the same as *emotional* age."

"Meaning you get a lot of immature perps?" Sophia guessed. "That doesn't surprise me."

"Well, meaning that when you talk about someone who acts in this way—abducts women and locks them in his basement—he's not what we'd call well-adjusted. And this particular unsub is definitely socially unskilled."

"Okay. So, he goes after high school girls instead of, say, thirty-year-old women who would be more savvy?"

"Right. Although it isn't so much about a fear of approaching them, because he's not talking them into his car. It's that he feels more comfortable with younger women, because it's easier for him to assert control."

"So what's your best guess on age?" Sophia asked.

"Probably thirties. He could be older, but I doubt he's any younger. People in his life would definitely notice his social awkwardness. They'd consider him *weird* or *different* if you were to ask them about him. We're not talking about the kind of guy who's so strange that everyone will say they expected him to end up in jail for this kind of crime, though."

"Okay," Sophia said slowly. "So, how does that help us?"

"When the right suspect comes onto our radar, we should see pretty quickly that the people around him find him odd. Also, because of his social awkwardness, interactions with the opposite sex in particular will have always been a sore spot for this guy. It's possible his abduction of Haley wasn't his first offense of this nature, but he'd have *some kind* of other incidents involving women, either younger women or women who were vulnerable in some way, maybe because of their situation or their profession."

"Like prostitutes?" Sophia guessed.

"That's a definite possibility. I'd say probable if he sexually assaulted Gillian. If not?" Evelyn shrugged. "Then maybe not prostitutes, but an awkward and inappropriate incident with a younger woman or a woman who was vulnerable in some other way, such as a mental disability."

Sophia scowled. "This guy sounds like a real winner."

"Well, there's a spectrum and this perpetrator definitely doesn't fall on the sociopathic, charming end of it. He's on the awkward, insecure end, the guy people sort of feel sorry for and sort of feel uncomfortable around, but can't quite put their finger on why. But he's got at least moderate intelligence, and he's extremely attentive to detail and planning. We're talking about OCD-level fixation on the details, especially when it comes to something important to him, like these abductions."

"Okay," Sophia said slowly. "We do know he put a lot of planning into the abductions."

"Exactly. Both Haley and Gillian were high risk for this guy. And for someone who's as socially awkward as he is, he knew that if he ran into trouble, he wasn't going to be able to talk his way out of it. He's not naturally confident, so he spent a *lot* of time thinking about all the details, all the variables. It also tells us that this guy wanted these specific girls, because he definitely could have grabbed more vulnerable victims."

"They look really different, though."

"I know. Which means what he wants isn't a physical type. It's their personalities that are the draw. My guess would be it's because these girls have reputations as being nice to everyone. This guy hasn't had much of that in his life."

"Great," Sophia muttered. "Teach your kids to be good to people, and this is what happens." She dropped her head back, shaking out her shoulders.

"Yeah, and it also means this guy tried to get close to them. Probably not so close they really noticed him, but my guess is that he talked to them, interacted with them in some way. Had that personal experience about the way they treated people."

"Well, that's creepy. What about work? Because our best guess is that he abducted Haley from her school before cheerleading practice on a weekday. And Haley lived two hours south of Gillian."

"Right. So this guy has a job that's flexible in terms of hours, or maybe he works for himself. His social awkwardness would probably make that a necessity, anyway. He's smart and organized enough to hold down a job, to be a good worker who wouldn't stand out. My guess is that he works the sort of job where he has little to no interaction with others, maybe a night shift position. A job where he's mostly overlooked, invisible."

"What about people who know this guy?" Sophia asked. "Is he going to have family or friends who, if we put out a description, will recognize him from it?"

"You mean if we release a profile?"

Sophia nodded.

"It's an option. He may have a social circle, but it would be pretty limited, primarily relatives and long-term friends. This guy has always been awkward, but it would have gotten more pronounced as he got older, so friendships are going to be from childhood, and probably not a lot of close ones."

"Is that the connection for the guy who helped Gillian get away?" Sophia asked.

"Definitely. Which is why we're seeing such loyalty. He's known this guy a long time. He's either related, or has been a friend since childhood. He knows the kidnapper's personal challenges, his social awkwardness. He's seen the guy struggle to navigate real life, and he's probably seen him get bullied growing up, too."

"So he decides it's okay for his friend to ruin young girls' lives?" Sophia asked incredulously.

"No. There's more. There has to be an extremely strong connection here, a loyalty that goes even deeper. Because this second guy doesn't seem to have *participated* in any way. And that's a really important distinction. So, he feels he owes the perpetrator a pretty huge favor. Or he needs him for a job, a social connection, something."

"But if he owes this guy so much that he's willing to overlook the kidnapping, then why try to help them escape?" Sophia stared at the wall full of Haley's pictures, shaking her head. "I don't get it."

"Well, it's possible he only just found out. He tried to help," Evelyn said. "After that? Possibly the perpetrator caught him doing it and convinced him to stop or maybe even hurt him."

"Or killed him," Sophia said grimly.

"That could be. Honestly, that's a really strong possibility, unless this guy also ran, or their connection and that loyalty goes both ways."

"What's the other possibility?"

"He knew all along, and was trying to help them when he thought the kidnapper wouldn't suspect him, or when the perpetrator wasn't there to stop him. Just because he feels loyalty to the perpetrator doesn't mean he's not also afraid of the guy. We know this second person has at least *some* moral compass, that he feels at least some guilt."

"Not enough," Sophia muttered.

"I think we need to try to find out," Evelyn said. "We need to put out an appeal to this person to turn his friend in."

"Don't we run the risk of the perpetrator killing him—or killing Haley, if he managed to catch her again—if we do that?"

"Yes," Evelyn said honestly. "And I want to talk to Gillian some more before we do anything. But this could be our best option, because since Gillian got away, the kidnapper will be worried about what she knows, how much she can tell us. If he still has Haley, he could be making plans to move her."

"Or eliminate her," Sophia added softly, turning back to Evelyn. "But if this is our best option?" She nodded. "We need to act. We need to try to bring this girl home."

16

"So, these guys who came after Evelyn," Jimmy mused, swiveling his chair from side to side.

"Bastards," Kyle contributed.

"Right. These bastards who came after Evelyn. They have to be connected to Jordan, since you said she and Sophia had just interviewed him?"

"Yep," Kyle agreed. "But Haley Cooke's abduction doesn't seem to have anything to do with Jordan. Evelyn and Sophia showed the victim at Augusta Heath Hospital Jordan's picture and nothing. Same with Nate. So, unless we have a third partner in the human trafficking business—"

"Which is looking a lot less likely, since Nate had the book," Jimmy said. "No way some older, more savvy guy is in charge of this, and he just let one of his college student recruiters hold all the customer and finance information. That means Nate is at the top of the food chain, and if he has a partner, I'm betting on Jordan."

"Right. Jordan must have sent those guys after Evelyn because he was worried she was closing in on his trafficking business, not because of Haley." And Kyle damn well planned to prove it. And then make him pay for it.

"So that would mean Haley's note was because she'd found out, was scared Jordan was going to hurt her, and ironically someone else grabbed her?" Jimmy made a face. "I don't know, Mac. That seems really coincidental."

"Except what if she ran?" Kyle suggested. "What if she found out what Jordan was up to, got scared and made a run for it? She was trying to hide from him, and someone else grabbed her? It would explain how she ended up kidnapped with another girl who lives two hours north of her. Because maybe he didn't actually take her from the school. Maybe he took her from the same town where Gillian Murray lives."

Jimmy nodded slowly. "If Haley did run, then she'd be alone in a city she didn't know. She's young, probably pretty naive, so I doubt she's street savvy. This guy spots her and realizes she's an easy target. Yeah, that would explain why the cases seemed to be connected. They were—just not in the way we expected."

"Another possibility?" Kyle stood and paced back and forth in the small interagency coordination room they'd snagged for a few hours, to lay out all the papers they'd amassed in this case. For an investigation that had been dragging, in the last twenty-four hours, they'd added a ton of paperwork. Nate Stokes's financials, the infamous book, what they could piece together of Jordan's movements in the past month, plus all the standard background details for every player in the case. They were slowly working their way through all of it.

"Yeah?" Jimmy prompted when Kyle went silent.

"Evelyn said there were rumors that Haley and Nate were secretly involved. She thought they were created by a jealous best friend, but what if the rumors weren't totally false? It might not have even been romantic, at least not on Haley's end. But what if we go back to the idea that Nate and Haley planned to run off together?"

Jimmy nodded. "Nate was interested in Haley. Maybe she used that to her advantage to get his help. Or maybe she just thought he was going to help her, not knowing he was part of the trafficking ring, too, and he wanted to get her out of town before she blew their cover."

Kyle picked up the narrative, his gut telling him Haley's and Nate's disappearances had to be connected. "So, Nate goes first, to divert suspicion, since he's got a history of taking off without informing anyone. Then Haley runs. They're supposed to meet up somewhere, but Haley never shows, because someone else grabs her first."

"And Nate stays hidden because he's afraid he'll become the obvious suspect if he comes forward." Jimmy nodded. "If that's the case, then we have a logical reason for Nate to just take off, without his business partner knowing where he went."

"One more option," Kyle said, because they had to toss every possible theory out there and see what they could make stick. "What if, again, there's no connection between Nate and Haley? Haley's grabbed by the same person as Gillian, and it's a stranger. Before this happens, Nate and Jordan had a falling out over business. They get into it and Jordan kills Nate. Then Jordan goes after Evelyn once she brings him into the station and starts asking about Nate's whereabouts, thinking she's on to him for Nate's murder."

"It would explain why we found that book at all," Jimmy agreed.

"Right. Because Nate hid it from Jordan. It would explain why Jordan didn't go into Nate's house and get it after Nate went missing. Because if he honestly thought Nate had just gone surfing, then why didn't he get that book? Especially when he realized the police were suspicious about Nate being missing? He had to assume that eventually we'd get permission to go into Nate's house and look around."

"Because he didn't know where it was," Jimmy said. "The book was well hidden. We almost missed it."

"That was a great find."

Jimmy beamed. "Hidden compartments have become kind of a hobby for me. I researched them for another case, and it's really cool."

Kyle tossed him a picture from the morning's autopsy, of Rick Cooper. The kid who'd come after Evelyn with a baseball bat last night. They'd finally identified him from his prints, which had been in their system. "We need to find his partner. See if the other guy will turn on Jordan."

"Before Jordan turns on him," Jimmy said. "Agreed." He pushed an open laptop toward Kyle and dragged another one in front of himself. "All right. Let's get background and associates for this guy. Last one to find a connection to Jordan has to buy the coffee?"

"I'll see that bet and raise you," Kyle agreed. "First one to find a connection gets to slap the cuffs on Jordan Biltmore and drag that bastard in for questioning."

Back at the hospital.

Evelyn held in a sigh as she and Sophia headed down the long, sterile white hallway. Sophia led the way, her strides long and purposeful as always, probably boosted by the phone call they'd received two hours ago.

Gillian was ready to talk to them again. And doctors had confirmed she hadn't been sexually assaulted.

It gave them hope, both for Gillian's emotional recovery, and for Haley's condition. But the entire drive to the hospital, Evelyn had been letting this new certainty roll around in her mind. No sexual assault was unusual for this kind of case. And it made the perpetrator's motivation more complicated. Which meant they needed everything Gillian could remember to help them narrow down what he'd wanted with her and Haley.

At the door to Gillian's room, Sophia glanced back at Evelyn. "You ready?"

Evelyn nodded, already mentally preparing the questions she wanted to ask, all the details she wanted to go through about Gillian's time locked in some awful man's basement.

Sophia pushed the door open and Evelyn followed, discovering that Gillian already looked stronger. The young woman they'd seen yesterday had been terrified and traumatized, her skin an unnatural bluish-gray color from being out in the cold for so long. Today, she looked healthier, and instead of fear on her face, Evelyn recognized determination.

Evelyn had to admire Gillian Murray. At seventeen years old, after the trauma she'd been through, she was showing remarkable strength.

"Did you find her?" Gillian asked, glancing from Evelyn to Sophia and back again, hope on her face. "Did you find Haley?"

"Not yet," Sophia said. "Which is why we need to go through what happened to you both, to help us bring her home."

"I shouldn't have left her. I should have made sure she was still with me when I got out of the house. Instead, I ran and didn't look back. I was desperate to get out. I just assumed she was right behind me." She cringed. "If something happens to her, it's my fault."

"That's not true," Evelyn said firmly. "And we're going to do our very best to make sure Haley's just fine."

"But what if she's not?" Gillian asked. "What if he caught her and because I got away—"

"If she's not okay," Sophia interrupted, "it will be our fault. It's our job to find Haley and put the person who grabbed you both behind bars. You did exactly what you needed to do. And because you're here, it means we have a *better* chance of bringing Haley home to her family, too."

"Really?" Gillian asked, her posture relaxing.

"Really," Sophia promised, reminding Evelyn that Sophia had her own children.

Maybe that was why Sophia was better at connecting with victims. Or maybe it was because Sophia was just better with people. Ironic, really, since Evelyn's job was to understand people—often in ways they didn't even understand themselves.

Every good detective knew that getting too emotionally connected to the victim could be a disaster for the case, blinding you to what you needed to see. But a profiler had to be able to do both: keep that analytic distance and climb inside the victims'—and the perpetrators'—heads and try to feel every emotion, vicariously experience everything they did. Often, that sort of intimacy made it even harder for Evelyn to connect with the victims in person, as though they'd know she'd been trying to reach inside their heads and use their experience to profile the person who'd chosen to victimize them.

"Mind if we sit down and go through everything with you?" Sophia asked.

"Yes. Let's do this," Gillian said.

Sophia dragged one of the chairs over to Gillian's

bedside and Evelyn took the seat already pulled up on the other side, a blanket draped over the top of it. She suspected one—or both—of Gillian's parents had spent the night in her hospital room.

"The doctors say I can go home today," Gillian said. "But—"

"A pair of police officers will go with you," Sophia said before she could finish. "It's already been arranged with the police department in your hometown."

"Okay." Gillian nodded quickly. "Thanks. I know he's not going to come back for me or anything, right? But that makes me feel better."

Sophia nodded. Evelyn knew they really had no way to be sure Gillian's abductor wouldn't make another grab for her. That would be high risk for him, even without the police presence. But if he'd fixated on Gillian for some very specific reason—if he felt no one else would do—he might try, anyway. He'd definitely gone to a great deal of trouble to grab Haley the way he had.

If they could figure out his motivation, it would give Evelyn a much better idea if they needed to worry about him returning for Gillian. But she had to start out slow, chronologically, to help Gillian ease into the questions.

"Can you tell us about the day you were kidnapped?" Evelyn asked. "Whatever you can remember. Start at the beginning of the day."

"Okay." Gillian twisted the blanket in her hands until they were wrapped tight, then started. "My school isn't that far. I can take the bus, but I prefer to walk. I'm fast, so it only takes about ten minutes."

"Did you notice anything unusual on your walk that morning? Anyone following you? Any cars that seemed to linger?"

Gillian frowned, staring at the wall a long moment,

then shook her head. "I don't think so. It's busy by the school, lots of cars at that time, but my neighborhood is quiet, and I always cut through this empty lot." She shivered, as if she suddenly realized that might not be a good idea. "I never saw anyone. Why? You think he was following me?"

"We're just trying to cover our bases," Sophia said.

"Okay. Well, school was normal. It was after school that day when it happened. I stayed late for orchestra practice with one of the violin players—we were entering a competition, so we'd been doing that for about a week." She frowned suddenly. "The competition was two days ago."

Sophia made sympathetic noises while Evelyn cataloged all the little things talking to Gillian had already given her. Clearly, her abductor had known her schedule, had realized she'd be staying late at school. He'd chosen then to grab her, instead of on her way to school, when he would have had an opportunity. Maybe because he figured he'd have more time before anyone confirmed her missing—perhaps he assumed parents would spend time checking with friends first, whereas an absence at school might have sent out an alarm immediately.

Evelyn had also learned details of Gillian's personality, both from watching Gillian and from her parents downstairs in the cafeteria before coming up to talk to their daughter. Gillian was soft-spoken, a little shy, but not without friends. She loved playing the cello, running track and did well in school, even tutoring those who struggled. Different activities than Haley, and different personality. Very different appearance, too. But her parents said her fellow students had voted her as Nicest Girl at the end of her freshman year. It fit into

Evelyn's theory that they'd been grabbed for the way they treated others.

"I went out the rear door at school," Gillian said. "It's quiet there after classes are over for the day. And it takes me to my shortcut back to my neighborhood. After school, I usually run it, especially in winter, because it keeps me in shape for when track starts up. I made it to the edge of the parking lot and that's when he grabbed me."

"Did he talk to you first?" Evelyn asked. "Did he approach you?"

Gillian shook her head, clutching the blanket so tight her fingers went bloodless. "No. He must have been in the bushes, because I didn't even see him. Just all of a sudden, I felt someone grab me real hard. He put something over my mouth so I couldn't breathe, and the next thing I knew, I was in the dark, in the basement."

"Did you smell anything when he blocked your mouth?" Sophia asked.

"Chloroform, maybe? Whatever it is people use in the movies," Gillian said. "It was gross when I breathed it in. And then I just don't remember anything. I woke up and I was somewhere else."

"Did you ever see a car? Maybe parked in the school lot that you noticed as you were running through it?" Evelyn asked.

Gillian bit her lip, stared down at her lap for a minute, then shook her head. "I don't remember."

"That's okay. Let's move to when you woke up. You said you were already in the basement. What did you see when you opened your eyes?"

"Just darkness. At first, I thought he'd blindfolded me, but then I adjusted and I realized it was just really dark down there."

"Because a lot of time had passed and it was night, or because there were no windows in the basement?" Sophia asked.

"Well, there were some little windows, up high, but he had them covered over with wood. Nailed down. And there was this thick foam stuff on all the walls."

Sophia glanced meaningfully at Evelyn and she nodded. Soundproofing. He'd either done it after grabbing Haley and realizing she might scream for help, or he'd planned ahead. Set up a place to hide Haley beforehand. The question was, had he always intended to grab both girls? Or had kidnapping Haley made him realize he wanted another girl? And what about now that Gillian was gone? Would he be frantically trying to cover his tracks, or plotting yet another abduction?

"Can you describe the basement? Was it the only area you were ever kept in, or did he move you around?"

Gillian shook her head. "I was in the basement the whole time. The days were okay, because he'd flip on the light for us. It wasn't much, just this dim old bulb. Night was the worst—my eyes could never adjust to it."

"And he never let you go anywhere else?"

"No. I don't know about Haley—I didn't ask where she was before I got there. But there wasn't much to it. There was a bathroom set up in the corner, but no door or anything. Just a toilet and a sink and washcloths, so we could sort of sponge bathe if we wanted." She shuddered. "I didn't do it. I was afraid to even go to the bathroom, because I didn't know when he'd come downstairs."

"What else was down there?" Sophia prompted.

"Not much. He brought us food every morning, on trays. And there was a mattress on the floor for us to share, with a blanket. Haley had extra clothes and she said I could wear some if I wanted."

Evelyn frowned. "Do you know where the clothes came from? Were they hers? Or did he buy them for her?"

"I don't know. They fit her okay, but I don't know where they came from."

"What kind of clothes?" Sophia asked, surely because she planned to check with Haley's mom whether those clothes were hers.

"Just sweatshirts and jeans. Nothing special."

"What about pom-poms?" Sophia asked.

Gillian nodded. "Yeah. Which was a little weird."

So, he hadn't just dumped Haley's bag somewhere, taken it simply to make it appear as though Haley planned to run off. He'd brought it with them, which meant one more thing he had to carry when he brought Haley through the school and out to his vehicle. It suggested he wanted her to have her own things, that in his own odd way, he cared about her comfort.

"Okay. Let's talk about what happened when you saw this guy," Evelyn said, glad she already knew he hadn't sexually assaulted Gillian—and hopefully not Haley, either. "How often did you see him?"

Gillian wrapped her arms around herself. "A couple of times a day. He'd bring us food in the morning, ask how we were doing." She let out a short, pained laugh. "How we were doing! Can you believe it? And sometimes he'd give us things to do, tell us we needed to learn."

Sophia frowned, leaning closer. "Can you give me an example?"

"One time it was a cookbook. He'd marked the pages of things he liked. I don't know what he wanted us to do with it. It's not as if we had anything to cook with. Another time it was this weird novel, about a family who lived in the middle of nowhere, off the land."

"What did he say when he gave you the book?" Evelyn asked.

"That we needed to learn to be self-sufficient, to care for family. It made no sense, since he took us away from our families!"

"Did he ever talk about the future?"

Gillian shrugged, a shaky little twitch of her shoulders. "He said we were special and that we'd learn our roles, but it would take some time. After he left, I asked Haley what he meant, and she got real mad and said it didn't matter, because whatever he had planned wasn't ever going to happen. And then she wouldn't talk to me for the rest of the night. The next day, the door opened and, at first, I thought it was him, but it wasn't. It was the other guy, the one who told us to run."

"I know we went through this a little bit before, but can you describe them for us again?" Sophia asked. "Both of them?"

"The one who grabbed me, he was—I don't know, normal? Normal looking, anyway. He was as tall as my dad—five-ten—and kind of skinny. But strong. Brownish hair, real thin. I don't know about his eyes. Brown, maybe? Or gray? It was always so dark, so it's hard to say for sure. And he kept his distance, like he was worried one of us would try to run past him. He always stayed between us and the door. Haley once said that he'd told her she'd get to go upstairs once she'd proven herself. She didn't know what that meant, but she said she was gonna prove herself so she could get upstairs, and then she was gonna run away."

Gillian fell silent, and it hung heavy in the air that

Haley hadn't managed to run when she'd finally gotten the chance.

"Okay," Sophia said. "What about the other guy? The one who told you to run?"

Gillian squinted, staring intently at the wall, then shook her head. "I just remember the door opened, and I thought it was the guy who took us. And then I heard a different voice, a man's voice, but someone new. And he said to hurry, to run now. At first, we both froze, in case it was some kind of trick, but then Haley jumped up. She grabbed my arm and told me we had to go. We ran as fast as we could up the stairs and it was so bright at the top I could barely see. It felt like staring at the sun, maybe because I'd been downstairs in the dark so long."

"And then what happened?" Sophia prompted when she fell silent.

"We got to the top and we heard *him*. The other guy was braced against the doorway of the basement, kind of leaning on it, telling us to go. We ran for the door, and *he* was there, and the guy who let us out was screaming at him to let us go, and I ran past and got out the door. I thought Haley was next to me, but maybe she wasn't." Gillian frowned. "Maybe she didn't get outside."

"Then what?"

"I ran and—no wait, Haley was there, because I could hear her. She was outside, too. I think she ran the other way. And then I heard him behind me and I just tried to go as fast as I could, the way I do for a track race. And I didn't stop until I got to that truck stop."

Gillian looked back and forth between her and Sophia. "I know he was behind me. He almost got me once, but I ran faster. So, if he was chasing me, Haley must have gotten away, right? He couldn't be chasing both of us. So, where is she?"

Sophia frowned, staring at Evelyn across Gillian's hospital bed. The expression on her face said she wondered the exact same thing.

What had happened to Haley Cooke?

17

"They've got a body on the outskirts of Neville," Jimmy announced.

Kyle looked up from the laptop he'd been staring at all day. "Who?"

Jimmy glanced at the notepad in his hand. "Name of Ted Meyers. Neville police just found it. They gave us a call because of our case being connected to the university."

"Ted Meyers," Kyle muttered. "I know that name."

"You do?"

Kyle flipped through the multiple documents he had open, searching for the name. "Here it is. Ted Meyers. Shit."

"What?" Jimmy asked, leaning over his shoulder in the small cubicle.

Kyle tapped the screen, then spun his chair to face Jimmy. "Ted Meyers grew up with Rick Cooper."

"What do you want to bet he's the second person who came after Evelyn last night?"

"No question," Kyle said with a sigh. "Which means someone is tying up loose ends. We need to work faster."

"Two guys who like to wear ski masks and beat on women," Jimmy said. "They're probably the same ones who went after Tonya."

"They're the operation's muscle," Kyle said. "This has to be a small operation, so they might be the *only* muscle. With Nate in the wind, it's possible we're only looking at Jordan Biltmore now. That's assuming he's the one running it with Nate, but I don't see any other promising options. We need to get a tail on him. Make sure he can't silence anyone else. Especially since the kid's lawyered up. There's no point in trying to talk to him until we have stronger evidence."

"What about Rick and Ted?" Jimmy asked. "Did you find a connection to Jordan?"

Kyle frowned, spinning back to his computer. "Nothing. Ted and Rick grew up together, both went to Neville High, but they graduated before Haley got there. They're in their midtwenties, never attended college. Jordan and Nate went to private school, so they didn't know these guys from school. Best guess is that Nate met Rick when Rick worked at the marina where Nate's parents docked their boat before they died. But I can't find any evidence they were ever friends."

"And Ted?"

"No connection that I can see, except through Rick. But I didn't dig all that deep on him before, since I just had him on my list as a known associate of Rick's."

"Rick had some legal trouble," Jimmy said. "What about Ted?"

Kyle accessed the database, looking for criminal history. "What do you know? Similar problems as his buddy. Both of them have been charged with assault and sexual assault. We have a few nights in jail here and there for each on the assault charges, usually bar fights, a few times together. The sexual assault charge didn't stick, but that one was on both of them, too. They attacked the girl together. Jeez."

"So, not really a surprise if they jumped at the chance to be bodyguards for a human trafficking ring," Jimmy concluded.

"Son of a bitch," Kyle said, scrolling down for more information on the sexual assault charge that Rick and Tim had been cleared of—which had happened because the girl had suddenly recanted.

"What?" Jimmy asked.

"The girl who accused them of sexual assault said it happened at Warehouse 53."

"So?"

"Does that sound familiar?" Kyle glanced back at Jimmy, who was peering over Kyle's shoulder at his computer again, looking confused.

"No. Do you know it?"

"No. But Tonya said she paid the blackmailer for the sex tape at a warehouse on the outskirts of Neville. I assumed she meant an actual warehouse. But this place is also on the outskirts of Neville. When Tim and Rick had the charge pending against them, it was a dance club. Since then, it's been shut down." Kyle pulled up information about it on his laptop. "Seems there's a private owner, some company that sure as hell looks like a shell corporation."

"You think it could be the location of the human trafficking ring?"

"I think we need to get to the bottom of this shell corporation and see who really owns it. Hopefully, it's in Nate's name, because then it will be easy to get a warrant and take a look inside."

"Hopefully," Jimmy agreed. "Because if it's in Jordan's name, we're going to have a hell of a time getting anywhere near the place. His lawyer's never going to go for that."

"Not to mention that we have a legitimate reason to be digging into Nate, to try to locate the kid. No judge is going to give us a warrant on Jordan's property, not unless we find a lot more," Kyle said.

"What we really need," Jimmy said, "is to find one of the women who was being trafficked. Someone willing to go on the record."

"I agree," Kyle said. "We need to make an appeal on the Neville campus, see if we can get anyone else to step forward. Let's talk to the head of Administration in the morning, see if we can get the names of other students who were struggling financially and then suddenly paid their tuition in full."

"See if we can get someone to turn on Jordan," Jimmy said. "Good idea, Mac."

"Hopefully with Rick and Ted gone, it will eliminate some of the fear for these women. But it's no wonder no one has stepped forward yet. You saw how Tonya was beaten in that alley."

"A hell of a warning to everyone else. Keep your mouth shut or you'll be next."

Kyle scowled, thinking of the two guys who had come after Evelyn with baseball bats. "Even if you're a federal agent."

"Kyle." Evelyn heard the surprise in her voice as she opened her front door and found him on her porch. They'd both worked late and they hadn't had plans tonight. Had they?

She'd come straight home and settled on her couch. She'd taken off her suit jacket, rolled up the sleeves on her blouse and stuck her gun and handcuffs on top of the armoire she'd finally bought for her TV. But that's as far as she'd gotten. She'd been debating dinner versus sleep.

Kyle palmed her cheek with a hand that was less work-roughened now that he wasn't sliding down ropes out of helicopters on a regular basis. Then he smiled, one of those big grins that brought out his dimples, and made his ocean-blue eyes glint. "I missed you."

She flushed, still not used to actually *dating* him, not used to anything more than his flirty banter and her pretending not to notice. Even though it had been a few months now, and even though they'd formally informed the FBI, it still felt forbidden.

But as his lips came down on hers, she pushed up on her tiptoes and decided maybe forbidden was just fine. Suddenly, she didn't feel tired at all, and frustrations with the case fled. His hands slid around to the small of her back, and then he practically lifted her as they moved backward into her house and he kicked the door shut behind him.

"Mmm…hang on," she mumbled, and strained out of his grasp just far enough to throw the lock. It didn't matter that Kyle was literally armed, and her own weapon was a few feet away in the living room. With the cases she profiled, and the things she'd seen, it was second nature.

Kyle lifted his head just far enough for her to see the laughter in his eyes, but it faded fast and his tone was serious. "Are you jumpy from last night?"

The reminder of being in that gas station with two men suddenly leaping out of the shadows with baseball bats made her body tense up. But she'd been in much worse situations, and she wasn't really worried anyone would come after her at home tonight. "No. I'm just a safety fanatic."

She grabbed a fistful of his dress shirt and pulled his face back down to hers. She tugged him into her living room, happy she'd actually spent some time furnishing it in the past few months. With a few clumsy steps, she dropped backward onto the couch, taking him with her.

Somehow, he managed to flip them over so she was lying on top of him without toppling them both off the couch. He pressed his lips to the pulse point on her neck and was slowly working his way downward when the doorbell rang.

"You expecting someone?"

"No," she panted. "Aren't you glad I locked the door?"

She felt rather than heard his laughter, but then the doorbell rang again, and Evelyn dropped her forehead against the top of Kyle's head. "I better see what's happening."

Disentangling herself from him, she got to her feet and straightened her blouse. Kyle followed close behind as she grabbed her weapon—because even though she *wasn't* still shaky from the gas station incident, someone *had* sent two men after her. She might not have been scared, but she wasn't stupid.

Before she made it to the front door, the bell rang a third time.

"Someone's desperate to see you," Kyle said, nudging her out of the way as he peered through her peephole. Then he looked down at her and shrugged.

But he didn't immediately reach for his weapon, so Evelyn leaned forward and looked out, too. "Shit," she swore loudly enough that the person on the other side of the door probably heard her.

Kyle gave her a questioning look, but instead of explaining, she flipped the lock and ripped the door open just as the woman standing on her stoop was reaching for the bell again.

"How did you get this address?" Evelyn demanded.

Lillian Baine glanced from her to Kyle and back again, then tried for a smile. Her lips trembled and the nerves were clear in her eyes. Her joking tone sounded forced as she asked, "Is that any way to greet your mother?"

She could sense Kyle's surprise, and knew he was probably reevaluating Lily. He'd notice her eyes for sure, the one thing that unquestionably marked them as family. She wondered if he'd see any other similarities.

Evelyn gritted her teeth, wishing Kyle wasn't here to witness this, and holding in the response that desperately wanted to escape. Lillian Baine wasn't her mother. She hadn't been in twenty-five years, not since Evelyn's father had died. In all the ways that mattered, her grandma Mabel was her mother.

Kyle slid a hand around her waist and leaned close to her ear. "Do you want me to go?"

"No." She kept her eyes on her mother, and one hand braced on the door so Lily didn't try to walk inside. "What are you doing here? I told you to leave us alone."

"Evie," Lily said, and Evelyn cringed at the nickname. "I want you to understand. I need a chance to apologize."

"Why? Is it part of your program?" Evelyn heard the nastiness in her voice, but she couldn't stop it. Apart from her mother's visit to Mabel's nursing home, it had been thirteen years since she'd seen Lily. And it had been close to ten years since her mother had given up all contact, including those unwanted phone calls. Or so she'd thought. She'd never expected to see or hear from her again.

"No," Lily said, strained patience in her tone. She flinched a little as she looked over at Kyle, then squared her shoulders and said, "I've been clean almost a year. I waited until I knew I'd really kicked it before I searched for you. I understand that you're mad at me—"

"*Mad* at you?" Evelyn demanded. She took a breath, because she sounded more than just mad. She sounded furious. And she didn't want to be furious. Truth was, she didn't want to care at all. She hadn't thought she did, hadn't realized her mother still had the power to hurt her.

But she wasn't a kid anymore, and this time she had a choice. "It's too late. I'm glad if you're clean—good for you. But there's no going back. I made a life without you. I made a life *in spite* of you. And I'm sorry, but you're not going to be a part of it."

Lily stared at her, eyes wide, mouth open a little, and Evelyn could tell she was trying to regroup, trying to find the words to convince her.

Regret threatened to overwhelm her, but she didn't want to feel that, either, so she repeated, "I'm sorry," and closed the door. Then she locked it.

Kyle followed her silently, his hand tucked in hers as she walked back to the living room and sank onto the couch. She felt sick to her stomach, and she wasn't sure why. She wasn't wrong. The things her mother had done to her were unforgiveable.

In her job, her profiles of perpetrators almost always included abuse in their childhoods. Hers had it, too, but she'd used it as fuel to do good with her life. Now that her mom was back, though, the ground seemed to be slipping out from underneath her.

She wasn't sure how long she was silent, when finally Kyle said, "What if you gave her a chance? She sounded sincere."

A small part of her was angry Kyle would think that, let alone suggest it. But the anger was far outweighed by a sadness she couldn't explain, as though she'd lost something all over again.

Or maybe it was just the longing for something she'd never had at all.

"We lucked out," Jimmy said when Kyle walked into work the next morning.

He was stiff from falling asleep the night before on Evelyn's couch. After her mom had appeared, Evelyn had gone silent for a long time. He knew she'd been angry when he suggested she give her mom a second chance, but he'd had to try. Evelyn didn't have much family left, and although he knew enough of the story with her mom to know it would be a challenge, he wanted to encourage her to consider reconnecting.

Maybe he should have kept silent. But her bond with her grandma was so strong, and her grandma's health was failing more and more. He hated the idea of Evelyn alone with no family left.

Maybe because he was so close to his own family. His parents were still married after forty years, and he talked to his brother and sister pretty regularly. He'd come from a small town, and he didn't regret leaving it, even when it meant living thousands of miles from them. But the idea of not having them in his life at all was painful.

He'd thought maybe Evelyn could have another chance with her mother. But she hadn't even wanted to talk about it.

When he'd woken early in the morning, Evelyn had

just been stirring herself, looking confused when she'd found herself on the couch. He'd considered carrying her upstairs after she'd fallen asleep where they sat, but she was a light sleeper. So he'd decided to curl up next to her instead.

Today, as he stretched out his sore shoulder, he was regretting it. And he was sure as hell ready for a little luck.

"Lay it on me," he told Jimmy, not bothering to get settled in his cubicle, since his partner looked ready to head right out the door. "Did we hear back from Neville Administration about students who could suddenly pay their tuition after having trouble?"

"Uh, well, sort of. We did hear from them, but they don't have anything that clear-cut. They said they can give us a list of students who were late on tuition payments and a list of scholarship students, but they want a warrant. The dean did tell me there was no one obvious who was a low-income student who'd had trouble before and suddenly it wasn't a problem."

"Okay, so what's the news?"

"Warehouse 53? I went for a run this morning and it made me all hyped up. So, I got into the office early and did some digging." He waved around a piece of paper, snatching it back just before Kyle grabbed it. "You were right about the company that owns it being a shell company. Couple of layers in, and guess who I found?"

"Please say Nate Stokes."

"You got it."

"Really?" This was the break they needed—he could feel it—but along with the surprise was a little unease. The book with what seemed to be coded customer information was in Nate's house. The warehouse that *might* be the location for their business was owned by Nate.

If he and Jordan both ran the business, why did everything point straight to Nate?

They'd considered that Nate was hiding things from Jordan, and that's why they'd found the book. But what if Jordan knew about Nate's hiding spots? What if it *hadn't* been there until recently? Until Tonya had gotten an FBI audience and Evelyn had called Jordan in for questioning? What if Jordan was trying to frame Nate?

"This is good news, right?" Jimmy said, rubbing the beard that covered his scar as if he, too, had a bad feeling.

"Let's go find out," Kyle said, snatching the keys off Jimmy's desk.

"Hey!" Jimmy hurried after him as Kyle headed for the WFO's parking structure at a jog.

Considering that morning rush hour was in full swing, they made the drive out past Neville quickly, in just an hour. Jimmy spent most of the time typing away on his laptop, digging up as much history as he could on the building between the time it had gone belly-up as a dance club and when Nate Stokes purchased it.

"Nate might have originally planned to open it back up as a nightclub," Jimmy told Kyle as they left behind the bustle of the campus area.

"Why didn't he?"

"I don't know. He did all of the legwork, even applied for a liquor license, and then just canceled work on the place. He had contractors hired and everything. They'd even started putting up new drywall for some kind of VIP rooms, and then he called the whole thing off."

"Really?" Kyle glanced over at Jimmy as he turned onto a long, single-lane road that led to the building they wanted. "Maybe it was a front all along. I'd be curious to know what work the contractors did before he let them go, and get a look at these 'VIP rooms.'"

"That's a good point." Jimmy leaned forward to stare around Kyle and out his window. "Are you sure this is the right way?"

They were surrounded by nothing but empty space and a few sparse trees. Kyle rolled down his window and was greeted by the sound of the wind rushing past, and a few birds.

"According to GPS. Weird place for a club. Do we know why it shut down?"

"A variety of problems. Serving to minors, sexual assault and physical assault on the premises, et cetera, et cetera. Eventually, the legal problems overtook the income stream and the constant police visits discouraged the customer base. The original owners advertised it as a good place to—and I quote—'get wild.' I think the location, away from campus and everything else, was intentional."

"Maybe Nate and Jordan came here and saw potential for a whole different business," Kyle suggested.

"Or Rick and Ted told them about it," Jimmy said. "We know they've been here. Or it could be another possibility for where they all met."

Kyle pulled to a stop at the end of the lane, in front of a big block building with few windows. Architecturally, it was boring, but someone had made an effort once, because the sign that had advertised Warehouse 53 was still hanging, a huge laser-cut metal design mounted high above the structure.

"This place is creepy," Jimmy said.

Kyle glanced around, taking in the extreme silence, even more noticeable here than on the drive. They weren't really that far from the university—about a ten-minute drive—but compared to the bustle of campus, this place might as well have been a hundred miles from anything. No one was keeping up the landscaping, and hadn't been in a while, so grass was overgrown all around the building. The few windows were boarded up with wood from the inside, even though the glass was still intact.

"Check out the parking lot," Kyle said, pointing to the area to the left of the building. For a spot that had supposedly closed down a while ago, some of the litter and oil spots didn't look that old.

Jimmy's arm went to ninety degrees, his hand hovering near his holster.

"I don't think anyone's here now," Kyle said, trying to keep the amusement out of his voice.

"Probably not," Jimmy said, a red flush creeping up his face. "But you can never be too careful."

"Can't argue with you there," Kyle said as they approached the building together.

Jimmy was probably overcautious because of his experience with a serial killer nine months ago, but Kyle certainly knew what it was like to be injured on the job. They'd gotten the bullet out of his shoulder, even given him small odds at a total recovery. He'd believed he would get back to his normal strength and mobility, because his motto had always been mind over matter. But this injury was proving that sometimes wanting it wasn't enough.

Pushing the doctors' most recent warnings out of his mind, Kyle tested the door handle, expecting to need to grab the drill to take out the lock. But the handle turned, and then Kyle felt his own hand drifting toward the Glock resting at his hip.

He eased the door open, peering inside, but he didn't

need to go far to know something was wrong. His eyes instantly watered and he fought the urge to gag as a rotten smell rushed toward him. There was no mistaking that odor.

"Shit," Jimmy said, backing up a step and pulling his suit jacket up over his nose.

"Damn it," Kyle said, stepping back. He hurried to the car, grabbing him and Jimmy booties to put over their shoes. "We better not screw with the scene. Let's see what we've got and then call it in." Locard's Exchange Principle said that any time you came into contact with a place, you both took something with you and left something behind. He didn't want to leave anything behind if this was about to become a crime scene.

Once they'd yanked on the booties, they entered. Inside, the smell was worse. At least it was cold out, and the heat was off in the building, because there was no question there was a dead body inside. The question was whether or not the body was human.

"This isn't how I wanted to start my day," Jimmy muttered.

He followed on Kyle's heels as they stepped into a dark, relatively open area that must have once been the entrance of Warehouse 53. Maybe coat check and bouncers checking IDs before kids got into the dancing and drinking area.

"Let's hope whatever died in here isn't human," Jimmy said. More quietly, he added, "I hope we didn't just find Haley Cooke."

"ERT is going to hate us," Kyle said, trying not to imagine pictures of young, vibrant Haley Cooke.

Evidence Response Team agents would be the ones who'd come through looking for forensics. And they were going to have a hell of a time, because for a place that was presumably closed down, there was junk everywhere. The floors were concrete, but they were so covered over with plastic cups and condom wrappers, the actual floor was barely visible.

"You think kids came out here to party once it was abandoned?" Jimmy suggested, sounding hopeful, but dubious.

"I think we've just found our human trafficking base," Kyle said, nodding up to a dark corner before he pushed open a second door. There was a camera mounted there, the plug dangling uselessly, as though someone had stopped filming at some point but hadn't bothered to remove the camera.

Jimmy made a gagging sound behind him as Kyle's eyes stung and watered. Didn't matter how many times he'd encountered it, he never got used to the smell of death.

In the middle of a large room sectioned off with curtains on a winding track was a body, positioned dead center on one of the filthy mattresses. It was already decomposed enough that Kyle could tell he'd been here awhile. But not so decomposed he didn't recognize the kid from the pictures he'd been looking at over the past few days.

"Is that…?" Jimmy asked.

"I think we just found Nate Stokes."

18

"We've got a problem," Sophia said as she came back into the Haley Cooke war room, closing the door behind her.

Evelyn glanced up from the message she'd been preparing to put out to the media about Gillian's abductor, hoping someone would recognize the description and come forward. Or better yet, that their "Good Samaritan" would step up and identify the perpetrator.

They'd sent a sketch artist out to see Gillian, but between the darkness of the basement and her overwhelming fear, the images were pretty generic. The one of her abductor was at least finished, but the one of the guy who'd helped was practically nonexistent, since she'd barely seen him. They were actually so vague that the sketch artist had suggested they not be released at all, fearing it would do more harm than good.

In both cases, the behavioral evidence was far stronger than the images. If someone was going to recognize this guy and turn him in, it would be from the description of who he was. And that was Evelyn's job.

But she'd been distracted all morning by her mother's visit late last night. This morning, after Kyle had left for work, she'd discovered a slip of paper in her mailbox. Her mom had scrawled the name of a hotel and her room number, claiming she was sticking around, and would wait for Evelyn to change her mind, no matter how long it took.

Suddenly realizing Sophia was staring expectantly, Evelyn tried to remember what she'd said. "What's the problem?" Evelyn finally asked, her mind snapping back into work mode as she realized how pale Sophia looked.

Evelyn vaguely remembered another officer stepping into the room and talking quietly to Sophia, and Sophia heading out into the bullpen, leaving Evelyn alone with her thoughts. But she didn't know if it had been five minutes ago or fifty.

"I asked one of our officers to go over all the footage she could find from around the school the day Haley went missing. Traffic cams, social media posts, everything and anything she could think of. We've done it already, but I'm getting desperate for a new break, since Haley didn't reappear like Gillian. And…"

"What?" Evelyn shifted in her uncomfortable folding chair, turning to fully face Sophia.

"I think you'd better take a look." Sophia moved her laptop in front of Evelyn and loaded a flash drive, pulling a video up to fill the screen. "This is a traffic camera about ten minutes away from the school. This footage was taken twenty minutes after Jordan claimed to have dropped Haley off at school."

"Okay," Evelyn said, leaning close to the grainy footage. There were quite a few cars going by on the busy road, and Evelyn squinted, trying to figure out what she was supposed to see, when Sophia hit Pause.

"There! You see him? In the black Hummer?"

"Jordan Biltmore," Evelyn realized. "You said this

was twenty minutes later, and it should have been a ten-minute drive?" She leaned even closer to the screen, as if that would let her see farther into the car. "It's a tight time frame, but it's possible it gave him enough time to grab her. She could be in the back, down below the seat." As an afterthought, she added, "How many cars does this kid own?"

"Two," Sophia said. "I already knew he'd used this one to drop her off. But that's not the problem." She hit Play again, let it run for a few seconds, then jabbed at the pause button.

Jordan's SUV was out of the frame, but a few vehicles back was another black vehicle, this one a dirty truck. And in the driver's seat…was that…?

"It's Quincy," Sophia said so quietly Evelyn barely heard her.

"Is there any reason for him to be in this area at that time of day? Could it be coincidence?"

"I don't think so. He was off that day. I know because it was all hands on deck when Haley's mom reported her missing."

"And he seems to be following Jordan," Evelyn said.

"Yeah," Sophia agreed. "I can't believe it. He's been working here for *twenty years*. Hell, he could probably retire if he wanted, get his pension and say buh-bye to the whole thing. Why would he have been following Jordan right when Haley disappeared? And why would he keep it secret?"

"He's involved," Evelyn stated the obvious. "Or someone is paying him."

"He'd never take a bribe," Sophia said instantly, then swore. "I say that, but what the hell do I know? Obviously he's not the person I thought he was."

"Maybe it's a threat," Evelyn suggested.

"But if Quincy is following Jordan, and he saw Jordan kidnap Haley, would he keep that quiet? Trade that information for what? Jordan to shut up about something he has on Quincy? What the hell could Jordan be holding over him to make him sacrifice a young girl's life?" Sophia looked as horrified as she sounded.

Evelyn knew from experience that it didn't matter how much you saw on the job, when someone close to you was doing the betraying, it always came as a shock. She'd sealed her offer to join the BAU when she'd been a regular Special Agent at the Houston field office and she'd picked a serial rapist out of the local police force. To this day, she remembered the look on his partner's face when he'd heard the news, the complete shock and disbelief.

"I don't know," Evelyn said grimly. "But I don't want to confront him with this yet. If he's willing to go that far, he's not going to come clean just because we have a tape of him driving near Jordan. We need to look into his life, and we need to do it very carefully and quickly, and very quietly."

Six hours later, Sophia's voice startled Evelyn out of her research into Quincy Palmer's life.

"Son of a bitch." Sophia was staring down at the display on her ringing phone, then she looked at her laptop and swore again. "News of Gillian's escape just broke. It's all over the news."

They'd been trying—and miraculously succeeding—in keeping Gillian's identity and what had happened to her under wraps. Evelyn had advised it for two reasons. First, so they could give the media the information the FBI and police wanted released, and in the way that would do the most good. And second, to make the perpetrator doubt Gillian had made it to help, hopefully keeping him calmer and increasing Haley's odds if he had caught her. And if he hadn't, local police and first responders were still on the ground searching the area where Haley could have been.

The plan had been to make the announcement tonight, along with the details of Evelyn's behavioral analysis. "Shit," Evelyn agreed.

Sophia squeezed her eyes shut and her hand tightened around her phone. "And this is Haley's mom. We should have told her."

Evelyn shook her head. "After the media stunt she pulled before, we couldn't risk it."

Sophia took a breath, then answered, "Mrs. Varner, I was going to give you a call tonight." A pause. "Yes, it's true…No, we don't know—" Another pause, then Sophia cringed. "I'm sorry you found out this way. I promise, we're doing everything we can. Please don't cry."

Sophia looked over at Evelyn, a pained expression on her face. Then her eyes widened and she said, "Hang on, Linda, okay? Let me put you on speaker with Evelyn— uh, Special Agent Baine."

"Agent Baine?" Linda Varner sniffed.

"Yes, I'm here," Evelyn said, lifting her attention completely off her computer search.

"Is it true? A girl was abducted with Haley?"

"We think so," Evelyn said, shooting Sophia a perplexed glance, wondering why she'd put her on the call. "We're going to go over everything with you tonight. We have a strategy in place to use this to help us get to Haley."

"Mrs. Varner, tell—" Sophia started, but Linda spoke at the same time.

"So this had nothing to do with my husband?"

"Your husband?" Evelyn asked as Sophia nodded meaningfully at her.

A forced laugh rang out through the speaker. "I know it's ridiculous. I never thought he had anything to do with it, but the other day, my girlfriends insisted we all go out for lunch, get my mind off things. When I was coming back from the bathroom, I overheard Marissa's mom. She was saying… Well, it wasn't true."

"What did she say?" Evelyn asked.

"Well, I didn't believe her. Marissa is always telling stories. But she said…" Linda's voice dropped to a near whisper. "She said Pete looked at Haley in a bad way, that Haley was afraid of him, and afraid to tell me."

Evelyn's gaze locked meaningfully with Sophia's. If that was true, why hadn't Marissa told them?

"But it's not right, is it?" Linda pressed. "I mean, if you found this other girl and…" She trailed off, then asked with a catch in her voice, "Could Haley be out there somewhere, trying to get home?"

"At the moment, all we know is that this second girl was kidnapped and she claims Haley was there, too."

There was a loud sob on the line, and Sophia told her quickly, "This girl is doing well now. He hadn't hurt her, so we have every reason to hope Haley is also unhurt. We're going to release an official statement in a few hours, and then I'll call you back and tell you everything, okay?"

"Okay," Linda said, her voice soft and near broken, so different from what Evelyn was used to hearing on the news interviews.

As soon as Sophia hung up with Linda, she dialed a new number, and Evelyn listened to one side of a conversation which could have only been with Marissa Anderson.

When Sophia set down her phone again, she told Evelyn, "She didn't think it was relevant! Can you believe that? Says Haley claimed Pete never touched her, just made her uneasy the way he stared at her. She also says Haley never told her mom because she didn't think her mom would believe her, and that she didn't tell Jordan because she was afraid Jordan would go after him."

"So, she only told Marissa?" Evelyn summarized.

"Yeah. You think she's saying this now to get attention?"

"Maybe. Either way, it's probably not relevant. You showed Pete's picture to Gillian, and she didn't identify him."

Sophia sank into the chair next to Evelyn. "I didn't want Linda to find out about Gillian this way."

"We couldn't risk her leaking it."

"It leaked, anyway," Sophia reminded her.

"Yeah, and speaking of potential leaks…" Evelyn spun her laptop toward Sophia, showing her what she'd dug up in her hunt into Quincy Palmer's life.

The detective frowned at the image for a minute—the screen showing Liam Palmer's arrest record—then looked up at Evelyn. "I don't get it. What does Quincy's son's arrest record have to do with anything?"

"You know him?"

"Not really. Met him once or twice at Quincy's place. He barbecues for everyone sometimes. Anyway, I got the impression they were sort of estranged and the barbecues were a way to have him over in a low-pressure environment."

Evelyn gestured back to the screen. "His son's got a record."

"Yeah, I already knew that. Drugs, right? I think he's done a stint in jail. If he did his time, what does that have to do with anything?"

"He's done two stints," Evelyn corrected her. "A third would put him away for serious time."

Sophia still looked perplexed. "You think someone is threatening Quincy about his son? Maybe has information on Liam using again?"

Before Evelyn could comment, Sophia said, "Because yeah, I mean, I can see that being blackmail material. But honestly, I can't see Quincy watching Jordan kidnap Haley and not doing anything about it just to keep his son out of trouble."

"He didn't do time for using," Evelyn said. "He did time for dealing. Small-time stuff, but maybe he's gone bigger. But actually, here's what I'm worried about." She flipped to a new screen, this one on Facebook.

"Liam Palmer's profile is public?"

"Yeah. People leave this stuff accessible more often than you'd think. Take a look at this picture." Evelyn tapped the screen, an image of Liam at a party, holding a red plastic cup up in the air. Above him was a huge crystal chandelier, with underwear dangling from it.

"That's in Jordan's frat house," Sophia said. "Isn't he a little old to be at a college party? He's got to be midtwenties at least."

"Yeah, and a teenager might have thought he was closer to thirty. Liam fits the basic description we got from Gillian."

Horror washed over Sophia's features. "You think Quincy was keeping up with the case because he knew his *son* abducted Haley and he's trying to keep him out of prison?"

Something about this case stank. And it wasn't just Nate Stokes.

Kyle tipped his head back, letting the spray of the

shower flow over him. It was his second shower today, but he swore he could still smell the stench from the autopsy department this morning, like death was stuffed in his nostrils.

That was one thing he sure as hell didn't miss from his days as a regular Special Agent. Attending autopsies. Nate Stokes's autopsy hadn't been any better or worse than others he'd watched. The decomposition was bad, but Kyle had once worked counterterror, so he'd been there for autopsies of body pieces, blown apart by bombs.

But he needed to move past the autopsy and focus. Because the scene from this morning's crime scene had stuck in his head and refused to leave.

There was DNA all over that building where they found Nate. Yes, it would take their labs a hell of a long time to collect and process all the evidence, but it was there. They had it now, and eventually they'd have names to match to a lot of people. Leaving semen in an old dance club wasn't a crime, but with names and the clear trafficking setup, they'd build a case. It would be slow, but it would happen.

And yet, someone had left Nate Stokes's body right in the middle of that mess, almost on display. As if not only were they not afraid of being caught, but they were sending the FBI a big "fuck you."

It was a double "fuck you" to Nate Stokes. Had that message been delivered by his best friend?

The kid was certainly cocky enough. But he was still only nineteen, and he couldn't have been involved in the trafficking ring for long. Did he really have that much confidence, to leave the body displayed, instead of trying to get rid of it? Not to mention the callousness of doing it to someone he'd called his closest friend, someone he'd known most of his life.

The autopsy had determined that Nate Stokes had died from being struck by a blunt object, right in the face. The fatal blow had been hard enough to smash in one side of his face. So whoever had done it hadn't waited for him to turn his back; he'd literally struck the most identifiable part of him, as if he'd truly hated Nate, wanted not only to kill him but to destroy him.

Kyle scrubbed until his skin felt raw, but every breath still seemed to bring the scent of death in. Giving up, he turned off the shower and stepped out, straining to hear.

"Shit!" His phone was ringing, and the ringtone told him it was work. He'd finally left an hour ago, but he'd pulled every string he could think of to get one piece of DNA evidence rushed.

The medical examiner had noted a foreign substance underneath Nate's fingernails, possibly skin cells. How he could tell anything about what was under Nate's nails was beyond Kyle, but it suggested that Nate had fought with his killer.

If that killer *was* Jordan Biltmore, who could very well be the same person who'd gone after Evelyn twice now, Kyle wanted him behind bars. And he didn't want to wait.

Grabbing a towel, he did a half-ass job of drying off, then slid across his bathroom floor and into his bedroom to grab the phone. "McKenzie," he answered just before it would have gone to voice mail.

"Hey Mac, it's Jimmy."

Kyle's shoulders came down. "What's up?"

"I'm still at the office. We just got a call from the lab."

"Did they get anything?" Kyle asked, his pulse picking up once more. What were the chances there would actually be usable DNA and it would match someone in their system?

"Yep. Get this. The ME was right. There *were* skin cells under Nate's nails. And you won't believe who they belonged to."

"Jordan Biltmore?" Kyle asked hopefully.

"Nope. Haley Cooke."

19

Linda Varner sat in the darkness of her living room, the TV on low, her hand pressed over her mouth as images of Haley flashed across the screen. Her daughter as a toddler, stumbling across the grass, her little legs unsteady. Then Haley as a young girl, her eyes bright with happiness, a huge smile on her face as she threw back her head and laughed. Finally Haley as a teenager, looking so much like the last time Linda had seen her. So much like the woman she was becoming.

She'd watched the footage three times since Ginger Tippens had dropped it off. The reporter had done an amazing job of capturing Haley's spirit, of sharing the details of what had happened to her without going too far into conjecture. And most importantly, she'd been true to her word. Ginger hadn't aired it without her permission.

Linda watched as the film cut to her, sitting stiffly on Haley's bed. Pete was beside her, his arm tucked around her shoulders, worry clear on his face. Seeing him that way, she felt guilty for ever doubting him, for listening to those ridiculous rumors for even a second.

She listened to herself talk about Haley's volunteer work, her plans for college, her infectious smile. Then she tuned her own voice out and just stared as the camera panned around Haley's room.

Somehow, the cameraman had known just what to focus on. A set of Haley's pom-poms, looking forlorn on the chair in the corner, as if they were waiting for her return. The stuffed bear she'd slept with since she was little, missing half its stuffing and one eye. The framed picture Haley kept on her dresser, of the pretty little cabin they'd all gone to in the summers, back before Linda and Bill's marriage had fallen apart.

The three of them looked so happy in that picture. The camera had caught her daughter midlaugh as she and Bill stood on either side of her, smiling. They hadn't been back since the divorce, but Linda vowed that as soon as Haley came home, they'd go out there again.

"Honey."

Pete's voice startled her and Linda jerked, clicking off the TV as he pressed a kiss to the top of her head.

"Come on." He pulled her to her feet. "Let's go to bed."

She let him tug her toward the stairs, but couldn't help herself from turning back toward the TV. Even though it was off, she could still see Haley there, the way the image of the sun imprinted on your eyelids after you stared at it too long.

Was this the only way she'd see Haley now? In pictures and images? Memories that would slowly lose their sharpness over time?

She sobbed and started to fall, but Pete caught her. She closed her eyes and let him carry her upstairs, toward the pills she kept at her bedside table. Toward the blackness she craved more and more with every day Detective Lopez didn't call, telling her there was news about Haley.

"Where are you, Haley?" she whispered.

But of course there was still no answer.

"What the hell is going on?" Sophia gaped at Evelyn ten minutes after Evelyn had arrived at the Neville police station that morning. "How would Haley's DNA have gotten underneath Nate's fingernails?"

Evelyn had gotten the call from Kyle late last night and she'd been mulling over that question herself ever since. "They probably fought." Murder victims always had their nails trimmed and checked for DNA in case they'd tried to fight off their killers.

"You're suggesting that *Haley* killed Nate," Sophia said, disbelief in her voice.

"It's the most likely possibility. Or maybe they fought and then someone else killed him, possibly to protect her. Or it could be that he's…uh, rough in bed, and they really were seeing each other."

Sophia crossed her arms. She was wearing another one of her bright blazers—this one emerald green. "I don't buy it. This girl is not a killer, and she's not a cheater."

"She's seventeen," Evelyn stressed. "Maybe she went with Nate somewhere, then panicked and fought him. Maybe she was trying to protect herself and didn't mean to kill him."

"What about Gillian's story?" Sophia asked the obvious question.

"Honestly, I don't know. Her information about Haley seemed legitimate, and I don't see a reason for her to lie. But…"

"But Gillian's doctors found no obvious signs of injury besides what she got running through the woods," Sophia finished. "And, of course, we got the typical loony-tune calls on the tip line. But no one has come forward with anything promising since we released the profiles yesterday evening."

"Right. I don't think Gillian's lying about her experience. At least not intentionally. But we considered it before, and we need to consider it again. What if she just *wanted* to believe Haley was there? She said he sometimes let her watch TV. Maybe she watched news stories, and latched on to the connection."

"So some asshole locked her in the basement, but let her watch news about another girl getting kidnapped? Why? To show her how little airtime she was getting?"

"It sounds horrible, but I've seen it before. Girls locked up for almost two decades who watched news about the investigations into their disappearances on TV. Just one more way to torment them, exercise control."

Sophia scowled, but it quickly turned into a frown. "You think that's what this setup with Gillian was? Some freak who planned to keep her for decades, locked in that basement?"

"It's possible. We need to talk to her again, obviously, but her details about her captor and the man who released her are vague. Maybe because she's still scared, or she doesn't want to talk about it. Either way, I need more specifics on the things this guy said and did. And we need to determine for sure if Haley was ever in that basement. Because Gillian didn't identify Nate as her kidnapper."

"Maybe Haley hit Nate over the head, accidentally killed him because he was trying to hurt her," Sophia suggested. "Then she ran and was grabbed, and that same person took Gillian, too."

Evelyn nodded. "That would explain both the DNA

and Gillian's story. But if Nate tried to hurt Haley and she accidentally killed him while fighting back, why'd she run? Why didn't she just come forward?"

Sophia shrugged. "She was afraid. You said it yourself. She's seventeen."

"But she didn't disappear for a *week* after Nate died."

"Nate died the same day he disappeared?" Sophia asked. "Are we sure?"

"Yeah, the autopsy confirmed that. So, if it was panic, it took a while to set in. And no one seemed to notice Haley acting differently in that time."

"And Nate had no other defensive wounds?" Sophia asked. "That kid was a lot bigger than Haley. How'd she kill him that easily? You said he took a blow to the face, right? I mean, he clearly saw that coming. Why didn't he fend her off? He's got, what? Half a foot and forty pounds on her? And all he did was scratch her?"

"Well, he was decomposing for a month," Evelyn reminded Sophia. "There were no other major injuries, but there could have been smaller defensive wounds we missed."

"Okay, but if he had her skin under his nails, why didn't anyone notice her being injured? Could someone have planted her DNA?"

"I doubt it. But it's winter. She could have easily hidden scratches on her arms or even her hands."

"This is crazy!" Sophia studied the massive wall of Haley's pictures, all so innocent-looking. "Well, even if she did kill Nate—and I'm not convinced—she's still missing. And we still need to find her."

"I agree. And I think there are two things we need to consider."

"All right." Sophia sounded suddenly exhausted. "Tell me."

"It seems pretty clear Nate was involved in a human trafficking ring. The location where he was found has been sealed off, and the FBI's Evidence Response Team is going over it carefully, but it will take a while. Still, no question Nate was involved, probably at the top. Most likely with Jordan, but the evidence on Jordan is sketchy at best. Haley's note could have been about their criminal business. Her fight with Nate—if she killed Nate—could have been because he wanted to involve her."

"*Sell* her?" Sophia asked.

"Since she's publicly Jordan's girlfriend, I doubt it. But Nate could have suspected she knew, and wanted to cut her in on the action, to keep her quiet. She said no, they fought, she killed him."

Sophia sighed. "Yeah, maybe. But that still doesn't explain where Haley is now. Or why it took her a week to run."

"If Jordan's involved, after Haley killed Nate, he still had a mess to clean up. Maybe he hoped he could keep Haley silent, or he wasn't sure how much she really knew, which is why there was a week in between. But then he realized she might go to the police, and so he grabbed her."

"Then let's go chat with Jordan again."

"The way he's lawyered up, it won't get us anywhere."

Sophia stared back at that wall, all the images she'd compiled before Evelyn had even arrived, plus the new pictures of Tonya and Gillian on the edges. "Okay, then what's the second thing we need to consider? Besides how the hell Quincy is involved?"

Evelyn nodded, conceding the point. They'd shown Gillian a picture of Quincy's son, Liam, and she'd said he wasn't the person who'd abducted her, or the person who'd helped her get free. So, Quincy's involvement was still a big question mark.

But considering the new development with Nate, Evelyn had a more pressing question. Because there was still a chance the video of Quincy could be explained away as coincidence. But Haley's DNA under Nate's fingernails was definite. "Remember the rumor Linda mentioned about Pete the other day?"

"About him looking at Haley in an inappropriate way? Yeah, I remember."

"What if Haley did kill Nate? She comes home, doesn't know what to do. But her mom was out of town the week before Haley went missing, remember?"

"That work conference." Sophia nodded slowly, obviously catching on to where Evelyn was going. "So, she talks to Pete. Asks him what she should do."

"And he blackmails her. Says he'll protect her if she does something for him. Then he starts thinking she's going to tell her mom, so he makes her disappear."

Sophia cringed. "God, really? You think he's that horrible?"

"I don't know. But he gave us both a bad feeling right from the start. I want to go have another chat with him, just in case."

Sophia pushed herself away from the wall, determination all over her face. "Let's go."

"Is it true? Is Nate really dead?"

The moment Evelyn and Sophia stepped outside the station, they found Jordan Biltmore pacing out front, as if he'd been getting up the courage to go inside. He was in his typical jeans and sweatshirt, no coat or gloves despite the light dusting of snow on the ground. His normally calm hazel eyes were red-rimmed, filled with a mixture of panic and fear.

"Is it?" he demanded, taking an aggressive step closer when neither of them immediately responded.

She and Sophia took wary steps backward, and Jordan rolled his eyes. "Jeez! What's with you two? If you're really that scared of me, should you be cops at all?" He glanced at Evelyn, then amended, "FBI. Whatever."

"Where did you hear that about Nate?" Sophia asked carefully, little puffs of white escaping with every word into the icy air.

"Is it true?" Jordan snapped.

"Yes," Evelyn said, watching closely for a reaction. It would hit the news soon, anyway, and rumors about the swarm of investigators at the old dance club were sure to follow. As hard as they tried, that wasn't staying under wraps for long, not with all the official traffic going out to that secluded location.

For once, Jordan wasn't accompanied by his lawyer. Chances were he was at the police station now for one of three reasons. He genuinely didn't know his best friend was dead and wanted answers. He knew Nate was dead, but either didn't know who'd killed him, or wanted to see if he was a suspect. Or he'd been there when Nate was killed, and his real purpose was to see if the police had connected Nate's death to Haley's disappearance.

Gillian had seen pictures of all the players in the Haley Cooke case and she hadn't identified any of them as her abductor. Sometimes, victims of captivity would be too afraid—or sometimes brainwashed—to identify their abductor, even if they could. But Evelyn had watched Gillian closely for signs of recognition when she reviewed the images. She'd looked pensive at Pete

Varner's picture, but it hadn't sparked fear in her eyes. And Pete's job took him all over the state, and definitely into high school cafeterias, installing vending machines, so Gillian might have simply seen him before.

Chances were Haley had never been in that basement at all. Or somehow, Nate's death had landed Haley in the clutches of an unknown monster.

If there was anyone who could have stomached handing his girlfriend off to a dangerous man, it would be the head of a human trafficking ring. It would be a guy who could lie straight-faced to a federal agent and a police detective without a twitch.

But right now, Jordan stared openmouthed at her, shaking his head slightly. "No," he said quietly. "It's not true. Nate's fine. He's off somewhere just…being Nate."

"I'm sorry," Evelyn added.

Jordan looked from her to Sophia, a strange half smile forming. "You're lying. This is some bullshit move to get me to turn myself in about Haley, right? I don't know why you're so fixated on me." His voice picked up until he was almost yelling. "I had nothing to do with it! Stop harassing me and find her! Find Haley!"

"What the hell's going on?"

Evelyn spun around to discover Quincy stepping out of the police station. She and Sophia had managed to avoid him since they'd discovered the traffic-camera footage.

"What the fuck's it to you?" Jordan snapped. "These bitches are claiming my best friend is dead, all because they have some crazy idea about me and Haley."

"Your best friend *is* dead," Quincy bit back. "And he died doing some damn unsavory things."

Jordan blanched, his eyes wide as he glanced between them. Then he doubled over and gagged.

Sophia reached out to help him and he pushed her off, his face red as he headed for his car. "I don't know what you're talking about," he muttered. "Nate wasn't involved in anything."

His car burned rubber as he raced out of the lot.

"He's lying," Quincy said quietly.

Evelyn eyed him speculatively as Sophia nodded. Jordan's outburst—insisting Nate wasn't dead and even his insistence he didn't know what had happened to Haley—sounded genuine. Compared to his denial of Nate being involved in anything unsavory, which definitely didn't. But Evelyn had learned early that nothing about this kid was easy to read.

She didn't know if Jordan had recognized Quincy, but Quincy definitely radiated animosity toward Jordan. If the kid had something on him, it was surprising Quincy had confronted him that way. But maybe Quincy saw that Jordan's world was falling apart, and was hoping to get the kid behind bars before Jordan used whatever leverage he had on Quincy.

"What exactly is going on here?" Quincy asked. "Where is this investigation headed? And why do I feel like you've been avoiding me?"

"The investigation has become very fluid." Evelyn dodged the questions before Sophia could confront Quincy. She wanted to dig deeper, see if they could uncover anything, before she accused a twenty-year veteran of the police force of being an accomplice in a kidnapping. "And we've got to run out and follow another lead."

"I'll talk to you when I get back," Sophia said, her tone odd enough that Quincy's features hardened in response.

Then she followed Evelyn to her sedan and Evelyn drove the short route toward Linda and Pete's house.

"Nate's death is the key," Evelyn said as they pulled up to the house. Her certainty in those words came through in her voice, and she could tell Sophia heard it. "Whether or not Haley killed him, she was there. Whatever happened that day led to her going missing. Now, we just have to figure out how the rest of the day—and that week—played out."

Sophia stared up at the big white colonial in front of them, dusted with a tiny bit of snow over the dark roof. "If this theory about Pete pans out—she told him about her fight with Nate, and he used that information against her—it explains Haley's note." There was sadness in her eyes as she looked over at Evelyn. "And it means she probably *is* dead. And I'm going to have to watch her mom's face as she's reminded that the first man she married turned out to be a real asshole and now the second one killed her only child."

Her words hung in the air as Evelyn turned off the ignition. "We can't change the past," Evelyn reminded her. "All we can do is the job. Find out what happened to Haley, bring her home if we can and make sure the person who did it pays."

"And that's enough for you?" Not giving her a chance to answer, Sophia said, "Neville is quiet. Pretty safe. We've got a low crime rate. I worked another kidnapping once, soon after I started. Worked it with Quincy actually. He was a hell of a partner."

When she went silent, Evelyn asked, "What happened?"

"We found the guy. He'd been worked over pretty good by then, lost his hearing, had some permanent disfigurement. But he went home alive. And I mean,

obviously no one deserves it—to be kidnapped, hurt—
but this guy…we could see it coming. He'd gotten himself involved with some bad people, logged a bunch of
debts he couldn't pay. I did my job, I did my best to find
him, but I didn't lose sleep over that case. But I'm losing sleep over Haley."

Evelyn could see it, now that she really looked. Sophia's suit jacket was loose on her, as if she'd lost weight
suddenly, and the dark circles under her eyes that Evelyn had noticed early on resembled bruises now. For Sophia, this was probably a once-in-a-career kind of case.
For Evelyn, it was the kind of thing she saw every day.

"How do you do it?" Sophia asked. "Case after case,
and not let it get to you?"

"It does get to me. But it's…it's what I'm good at,"
Evelyn tried to explain. "I know I can make a difference, so I learn to manage the sleepless nights and the
nightmares. I know I can help find these people, bring
them to justice."

"Because you can think like them," Sophia concluded.

Evelyn resisted the urge to squirm, because it sounded
horrible, to be able to really get deep in the mind of a
person who would kidnap a seventeen-year-old girl. To
understand their motivations, when those motivations
were sick or depraved. "Yes, I can. But it's not just the
perpetrators. I have to think like the victims, too."

Sophia shook her head, reaching for her door handle. "All I can say is, you might not ever want to have
kids. Every day I look for Haley, I get more panicked
about my two boys being out of my sight, at school, at
home, wherever. There's too much bad in this world."

She was out of the car before Evelyn could reply, but
Sophia's words replayed in her head on repeat. Kids.
The very idea filled her with a vague dread.

She'd always thought about her life in terms of her job. But things were changing. Her future had started to take on a very different image, one that had room for *both* the job and a real personal life, maybe even a family of her own. She wasn't sure she was cut out for that kind of normal.

The tap on her window startled her. She spun her head to find Sophia standing there, mouthing, "You coming?"

Pushing her personal worries out of her head for now, Evelyn got out and followed Sophia up the drive.

The door was open before they made it up the front steps. Linda stood on the porch, still in her bathrobe at noon. She had one hand pressed against her heart. "Is there news?"

"Not about Haley," Sophia was quick to reassure her. "We just want to go over a few things."

Linda's shoulders fell, and her whole face seemed to crumple. "Okay," she managed, gesturing for them to follow her inside.

As Evelyn moved closer, she saw that the glassiness in Linda's eyes had gotten worse. There was an unsteadiness to her walk that said she was medicated, enough that it might explain why she hadn't been on the news the past few days.

Evelyn felt a familiar anger bubble up, this time tempered by sadness. Everything she'd seen about Linda Varner suggested she'd tried hard to protect Haley. But had she allowed herself to miss what was happening right under her roof?

Before they even made it to the living room, Pete was hurrying toward them, some kind of game controller in one hand and a mix of worry and anxiety on his face. Next to Linda, who was beginning to fall apart under the pressure, he looked somehow bigger, sterner.

Eight days ago, when Evelyn had arrived on the case, he'd seemed to be enjoying the spotlight. Now, she was beginning to see cracks in his protective persona. Mostly around the eyes, in the new creases and darting gaze, as though he was on guard against more than just the media.

"What now?" Pete demanded, looping an arm around his wife and pulling her close, using enough force that she stumbled into him.

"Let's sit down," Sophia said. "We need to talk about what happened a week before Haley's disappearance."

"A week?" Confusion was on Linda's face. "I was at a conference." She looked up at Pete, and swayed a little, even jammed up against him. "You said everything went fine." She turned back to Sophia and added, "It was the first time I'd gone away and left just the two of them at home." She seemed to be pulling away from Pete slightly. "I'd been to a few other conferences, but since Pete and I got married, Pete usually came with me, and Haley stayed with Marissa and her family."

"Let's sit down," Sophia suggested as Pete muttered, "Everything *did* go fine."

Linda stumbled along tucked inside Pete's grasp, with Evelyn and Sophia close behind, until they were all seated in the very floral living room. Evelyn remembered that it had been Linda's house before Pete married her and moved in.

"The day Linda left for her conference, did Haley act any differently?" Sophia asked as Evelyn watched Pete carefully for nonverbal responses, little unintentional motions that would indicate lies.

Pete's lips turned down, into an exaggerated frown. "No. I mean, she's a teenager. Teenagers are moody."

"What do you mean? Was she particularly moody that day?"

"Why are you suddenly asking about this?" Linda cut in, her mind obviously still keen enough to see something wasn't right despite whatever she was taking. "What's going on?"

"We have reason to believe that day could be connected. This is important."

Linda instantly tensed, shifting toward her husband. "Tell them every detail. What was wrong with Haley the day I left? Why didn't you call me?"

Pete's mouth drooped and his shoulders bunched up. "Nothing happened. I told you, she was pulling typical teenager crap. She stayed out past curfew and I wasn't having it. She got on my case about not really being her dad and went to her room. Slammed her door." A bit of a blush crept up his overly tanned face. "It's not really out of character. She's a kid. It's hard for her, her dad being such an a-hole, and then me marrying her mom. I get it."

"Did she say where she'd been, why she was late that night?" Sophia asked. "And did she seem injured in any way?"

"Injured?" Linda screeched, her fingernails digging into her husband's arm so hard they looked close to piercing the skin.

"No," Pete said. "She was fine. There…" He paused, squinting up at the ceiling. "Wait. You know what? She had some scratches on her arm. I asked about them, and she said a tree branch hit her when she was running."

"Is Haley a runner?" Evelyn asked, remembering Gillian's story about liking to run home from school.

"Not really," Pete said. "So it was kind of weird. But it didn't look too bad. Some hydrogen peroxide and a couple of Band-Aids, and she was fine."

"And she didn't say where she'd been?" Sophia pressed. "Did you have any idea where she might have gone? Who she was with? How late was it?"

"After curfew," Pete said. "So—"

He never finished his sentence, because there was a loud *bang, bang* and then something big crashed in the front hall.

Evelyn jerked in her seat, panic jolting through her body. She reached for her gun, but before it was free of the holster, a cylindrical object came bouncing into the room.

"Down, get down!" Evelyn screamed, diving for a terrified-looking Linda and Pete as the room exploded in light and a massive *boom* rocked the air.

20

Evelyn crashed onto the couch, hitting hard enough to shoot pain down her legs. But it was too late to cover Pete or Linda, who were screaming at the pain in their ears and surely blinded from the light.

Evelyn flipped over, her adrenaline pumping too hard, her gun clutched in her hand. "Stop!" she screamed, even though all she could see were big black blobs moving toward her through flashes of intense white light.

Her pulse skyrocketed at the number of dark shapes. Too many to take down without being shot herself, and probably killed. And they had the weaponry of an army. What the hell was happening?

"Drop your gun!" someone screamed back at her, the sounds penetrating through her throbbing eardrums.

On the floor nearby, Evelyn could just make out Sophia struggling to grab her own weapon as someone wearing all black tackled her, pinning her to the ground.

Then the barrel of a submachine gun was inches from her face as a deep voice warned her, "Last chance. Put down the weapon or I'll put you down."

Evelyn drew in a few heavy breaths, squinting as she tried to see more than just the barrel of a gun. Firing her weapon was a death sentence, but was dropping it any better?

Through the high-pitched ringing in her ears, she heard someone close to her say, "Shit! It's Detective Lopez from the Neville station."

Beside her, she saw the guy who'd tackled Lopez jump off her, even as the submachine gun jammed even closer to her face, making her press her head back into the thick carpeting.

"I'm FBI!" she shouted.

Then the gun was out of her face and someone pulled her to her feet. Evelyn kept blinking, her hand so tight on her gun that her arm was shaking. She swayed a little on her feet, the aftereffects of being so close to an exploding flash bang grenade. Finally her vision cleared enough to see the word *SWAT* emblazoned on the chest of the man closest to her.

She looked around the room as her vision cleared, and realized she was surrounded by a police SWAT team. Her pulse still pounded. "What's happening?"

"What the *hell* are you doing?" Sophia chimed in, visibly shaking as she got to her feet and someone handed her weapon back to her.

The guy closest to them tucked his MP-5 under his arm and straightened his spine. "We got a 911 call that there was a hostage situation here."

"And you didn't call to check it out? You just broke down the door and tossed in a flash bang?" Sophia snapped. "Who the hell called it in?"

"We did call the house first, ma'am," he replied. "We got a busy signal."

"We took the phone off the hook today," Linda said, then hiccupped a sob. "Too many reporters calling."

"You didn't recognize this address?" Sophia pressed.

"We did, which is why we came in hard and fast," the SWAT leader replied. "We didn't know if it was connected to the girl's abduction. Neville took the call, and they informed us, since you don't have your own SWAT."

"I know the process," Sophia barked, then let out a heavy breath. "Who made the call to 911?"

"It came from this house."

"What?" Evelyn glanced back at Pete and Linda.

Linda was shaking, but she looked more dazed than scared, as though the pills had slowed down her reaction rate. Pete, on the other hand, still looked terrified, breathing so heavily his massive chest was heaving up and down. One hand clutched the couch arm and the other was wrapped around his wife, his grip hard.

"We didn't call the police," Pete said, his voice barely above a whisper. "We were right here with you."

"What's that you're holding?" the SWAT officer asked, striding over and taking a video game controller that was squashed between Pete's hand and the couch.

"I was playing a video game earlier. I can't make a phone call on a game controller. *Shit*." He visibly tried to relax, loosening his shoulders and easing his death grip on Linda, but it just made him look more afraid.

The officer looked back at Sophia and Evelyn and let out a stream of curses. "You've just been swatted."

"What?" Sophia asked.

"A spoofed call to police, claiming an emergency, to get a SWAT response," Evelyn said. Realizing why the SWAT officer had noticed the controller, she guessed, "The call came in through a computer, didn't it?"

"Yeah, and the caller gave this address. IP came back here, too."

"Hey, I didn't do that! I've been right here with you!"

Pete said, jumping to his feet, then immediately swaying hard enough that he sat right back down.

"You were online in a game?" the SWAT officer asked. When Pete nodded, he said, "It was probably still spoofed. Called through the game connection, to mimic the IP address here. We've seen this shit before. Not our station, but a couple of towns over."

"We're going to need all the details on this," Evelyn told him. "This is the third time someone has come after me since this case opened."

"The third time?" Linda gasped. "Because of Haley?" Over a sob, she asked, "What happened to my girl?"

"You know whose father owns a gaming company?" Sophia asked quietly, practically into Evelyn's ear.

Evelyn nodded silently at her, not wanting to give Linda or Pete a name, if they hadn't already made the connection.

All roads led to Jordan Biltmore.

"You just missed Jordan Biltmore," Quincy announced when Sophia and Evelyn walked back into the police station. Then he did a double take. "What happened to you two?"

"You didn't hear about it?" Sophia asked, rubbing her ear. "The chief approved a tactical operation on the Varner house, and we were inside when SWAT breached."

"What?" Quincy glanced back and forth between them. "Are you kidding me?"

"Jordan Biltmore was here again?" Evelyn asked. "For how long?"

"He showed up ten minutes after you left. Looked like he'd been crying—probably for our benefit, the little bastard—but he was marginally calmer. Wanted more details on what happened to Nate, which of course

I refused to give him. But he was making such a spectacle, Chief asked me to walk him down to the coffee shop and have a chat with him. I just got back fifteen minutes ago."

Sophia scowled, surely not happy that Quincy and Jordan had had a private conversation.

Before she could remark on it, Evelyn asked, "Did he use a laptop while he was with you?" Ten minutes meant he might have been able to follow them to the Varner house, target them there. But would he have had time to also make the spoofed phone call?

"No. I'm not even sure that kid had a wallet on him. He probably has millions at his disposal, but I bought coffee. He fiddled on his phone a little, but that's it."

Could he spoof a 911 call from a cell phone? And that fast? Evelyn had no idea. Cyber wasn't her specialty.

Then again, it had been Pete Varner on the game. What if he'd set it up himself? Set some kind of timer? Of course, he hadn't been expecting them, unless he'd done it after they'd arrived and before he joined them. Or what if someone had been targeting *Pete*, instead of them? If Jordan wasn't involved in Haley's disappearance, but he thought Pete was, Evelyn could see him trying to take action. She remembered the first day she'd spoken to him, and his big words about how he would have protected Haley if he'd seen her in any danger.

"What did you and Jordan discuss?" Sophia demanded at the same time Quincy asked, "Why did a SWAT call go out? Does this have to do with Haley's case? Are you all right?"

He looked genuinely worried, and honestly ignorant of what they'd been through an hour ago.

"Yeah, we're fine." Sophia sighed. "I feel like my freaking eardrums were punctured, but I've been told they'll feel normal soon. But someone sure is intent on scaring us off this case, and the attempts are getting bold."

Quincy's lips bunched up, his jaw working furiously. "That damn kid. You're telling me he used me as an alibi, aren't you?"

"I don't know," Sophia said, glancing at Evelyn. "Whenever we talk to Jordan, bad shit happens. But is he smart enough to pull off that kind of hack? And from a cell phone?"

"Hell if I know," Quincy replied, as if she'd been asking him. "But the kid is behind it, no doubt. Oh, and the other thing that happened right before you got back? Marissa Anderson called. Apparently Haley's mom called her once you left their house, asking about some scratch on Haley's arm?"

"Yeah?" Sophia asked.

"She said it happened at lunchtime. Haley left school for lunch—kids who have a pass can do that. Anyway, according to Marissa, Haley told her that she had a fight with someone. Wouldn't say who, apparently, but Marissa wanted you to call her."

"Thanks." Sophia grabbed the sleeve of Evelyn's jacket, tugging her toward the war room. "Let's regroup. I want to talk to Marissa in person."

"I want to pay a visit to Jordan Biltmore," Evelyn countered.

"I thought we were leaving him alone for now because of the lawyer?"

"Yeah, well, I'm getting tired of people trying to hurt me."

"This was a little more sophisticated than the nail in the tire and the thugs with baseball bats," Sophia said as they walked into the war room and she closed the door behind them.

"That's true," Evelyn mused, then added, "Don't you think Quincy is going to find it a little weird that we just ran away from him?"

"I can't fake trusting him for long. Every time I look at him, I want to scream. Maybe he's innocent, but I can't get that tape out of my head. I know you want to dig deeper, but I can't hold this in much longer."

"All right," Evelyn said, glancing at her watch. Mid-afternoon. "How about you go see Marissa, then do a little digging into Quincy's son? If Quincy is connected, it's got to be because of Liam Palmer."

"All right," Sophia agreed. "What are you going to do?"

"I'm going to give Kyle and Jimmy a call, see if they can get their supervisor to okay paying Jordan a visit with me. Since our cases are looking connected, we should make use of the extra federal resources. We may not have enough to bring him in for Haley's abduction, but I think they're getting close on the trafficking. I talked to Kyle this morning and he and Jimmy think Nate was the recruiter and Jordan was the money and the management."

"But wasn't everything in Nate's name?"

"Yep. I think if it all went south, Jordan was going to wrap the whole thing around Nate."

"What if Nate realized it, confronted Jordan while Haley was there? They fight—Haley ends up in the fray—and Nate ends up dead. Jordan leaves him at the warehouse, and tries to get Haley to keep her mouth shut. He thinks she will, but after a week, he starts to worry she can't hold it together, so he grabs her. Or after a week, she knows he's going to kill her, too, so she runs. And Gillian's abductor grabs her."

"Yeah, well, Jordan is guilty. I'm just not a hundred percent sure of *what* he's guilty."

"Well, let's find out," Sophia suggested.

Evelyn nodded. "These attacks are escalating. One way or another, I want this kid behind bars quickly. Let's get to work."

"Does she know about the rumors?" Jimmy asked as soon as Evelyn hopped into the back of his and Kyle's SUV.

"What rumors?" she replied, buckling in as Kyle glanced back at her and gave her one of those dimpled smiles.

As Kyle pulled out of the parking lot, Jimmy twisted in his seat to face her. "We've been talking to kids on Neville's campus. There were rumors that if you wanted to pay for it, you could have your pick of women, and all you had to do was visit Jordan's frat house."

Evelyn leaned forward. "Did these people visit Jordan specifically?"

"No one would admit to actually doing it," Jimmy answered. "And no one mentioned Jordan by name. Just the frat. Apparently there was some kind of system, a box where you left money and a name and you'd be contacted with details about how to proceed."

"If it's true, someone has dismantled the box, or we couldn't find it," Kyle added.

"It's smart," Evelyn conceded. "Easy access for Jordan, but plausible deniability in a frat house where, what? Twenty guys live?"

"Thirty-two," Jimmy said.

"Where are we going?" Evelyn asked as Kyle headed

in the wrong direction, away from the Neville campus. "I thought we were going to talk to Jordan."

"We are," Kyle answered. "But I called ahead, because there's no sense in getting there just to be told we need to make an appointment with his lawyer. We don't have enough to arrest this kid yet, so he doesn't have to talk to us. I said we needed some information about Nate. Apparently he went to his dad's house this afternoon. We're meeting them there. No lawyer this time."

"Interesting," Evelyn said, wondering how much Jordan's billionaire father had taught him about coding and hacking gaming systems like the ones he built. Ironically, they'd discovered Pete Varner had been playing one of Biltmore Gaming's programs when the 911 call came in. And when Evelyn had looked at it after SWAT finally left, she'd discovered the game was just as disgustingly misogynistic as Sophia had told her. For a game supposedly about going on a quest, there sure seemed to be a lot of scantily dressed women on the sidelines, and half of them in Pete's game appeared to be dead.

"Extra points," he'd told her meekly when she'd raised her eyebrows at the scene on the screen. "It's just a little decompression after a hard day."

If this was his idea of decompression, she couldn't totally rule out the idea that he was connected to Haley's disappearance, or her note. But Jordan was still her top suspect, and angry anticipation lit her nerve endings as she thought about questioning him today. Would he be surprised to see her unshaken after the latest attempt to scare her off the case? Smirk at her questions about the SWAT ambush?

"…theory."

"What?" Evelyn asked, realizing Jimmy had been talking.

"I said, Mac has a theory about Haley."

"Oh, yeah?"

"You've probably already considered this," Kyle said. "But potential customers came to the frat house. What if one of them spotted Haley there and started following her around? If it was one of Jordan's customers that grabbed her, it could explain why Gillian didn't identify Jordan."

"Everyone said Haley rarely went to campus. But it might explain the note. Maybe she saw something she wasn't supposed to at the frat house. She realized what Jordan was doing, and was scared. Honestly, I'm also considering the possibility that Jordan sold her to one of his customers to get her out of the way."

"Jeez," Jimmy said. "You really think so? He's an asshole, but the kid honestly seems worried about her."

Evelyn nodded, not able to disagree. The only things Jordan seemed to not be completely blasé about were Haley and Nate. Then again, he'd lied to her and Sophia about being faithful to Haley while a woman was literally in his bed. "Either way," Evelyn said. "We need to get Jordan to give us his customer list."

"How the hell are we going to manage that?" Jimmy asked. "If he provides it, he's practically handing himself a prison sentence."

"If he sold Haley to the person who has her, there's almost no chance," Evelyn said. "But if he didn't—if it was Nate's doing—and we can convince him his business is going to get Haley killed if he doesn't help us? I think he might."

Kyle punched on the gas. "Then it's time to find out if he really cares about Haley, or if it's all for show."

21

The trees lining the long entrance to the Biltmore mansion had all lost their leaves for the winter. Now they were nothing but long skeletal branches forming a canopy overhead, a foreboding welcome.

The house in the distance was enormous, a massive colonial with big columns, and a fountain in the center of a drive that circled up near the house. The fountain was shut off, covered in a light dusting of snow. Everything about the place looked big and cold.

Driving up the long entryway seemed to take forever, but finally Kyle parked, and Evelyn asked, "Do they know I'm coming?"

"Nope, I didn't mention that part," Kyle said, hopping out and opening her door. "Figured you might want it to be a surprise."

"That's one way to put it." She followed him and Jimmy to the door, which was opened before they knocked by a man she knew immediately was Jordan's father.

Sophia's case files gave a brief background on anyone connected to the suspects, so Evelyn knew Franklin Biltmore was in his midfifties. But he looked a decade younger, with the same lean frame as his son and the same good looks.

The same hazel eyes, too, she discovered as his gaze locked on hers, a flash of surprise there. Then his eyes narrowed and he held out a hand, reaching between Kyle and Jimmy. The scent of whiskey floated on the air as he spoke. "I'm Franklin Biltmore. And you are?"

"Special Agent Evelyn Baine, FBI."

He shook her hand in the typical CEO fashion—a little too hard, to project power, and lingering a little too long, for extra emphasis.

Then he pulled back his hand, and glanced from Kyle to Jimmy. "That makes you two Agents McKenzie and Drescott, I assume?" When Kyle nodded and stuck out his hand, Franklin ignored it and spun around. "Come on in. Let's get this farce over with."

He led them through a huge entryway with marble floors and a massive crystal chandelier and not much else, while Kyle gave Evelyn an amused smirk.

She glanced into the formal living room they passed. She figured an interior designer had put it together, and from its untouched perfection, she guessed it was only used for entertaining.

She got the impression he did a lot of entertaining, for business and otherwise. Despite owning a company that was constantly being boycotted for its products' portrayal of violence against women, Sophia's notes also mentioned his popularity as a bachelor. His wife had died when Jordan was five, and Franklin had never remarried.

"Here," Franklin said, ushering them into an office, complete with a big antique desk and oversize leather chairs. "Let's chat."

Jordan was already waiting for them in the office, sprawled on one of those four chairs. When he spotted her, he let out a noisy snort of disbelief. "Seriously?

You're back? I thought the case was finally getting turned over to someone a little more competent."

"Why?" Evelyn asked. "Because you got the call from a male agent, or because you expected me to be too shaken up to go anywhere today?"

"What?" He made an exaggerated face of disbelief at her, then rolled his eyes. "You're seriously crazy. Why would I expect you to be shaken up?" He turned away from her, but not before Evelyn saw him fidget.

Still, his reaction was odd. Unless he hadn't really expected the SWAT call to scare them off, just to harass them?

Evelyn took the seat at the far end of the room, leaving two chairs between Jordan for Kyle and Jimmy. Probably Jordan would assume she was afraid of him, but really she wanted to be able to keep both father and son in her eye line without turning her head.

She glanced speculatively at Franklin as he took a seat behind the massive desk, in a chair that put him higher than everyone else in the room. It told her instantly where Jordan had learned his power plays.

Did Franklin think his son was guilty of Haley's abduction? Did he suspect what Jordan was doing at the college, out of his old frat house? Or was he completely oblivious?

Kyle and Jimmy took their time getting settled in their seats, and Evelyn watched Franklin's expression grow more and more annoyed.

"We just have a few questions," Kyle finally said. "To help us determine what happened to Nate and put together a timeline."

They already knew when Nate had died—the medical examiner had been able to narrow it down to a single day—but Kyle was setting the stage to get details on Jordan's whereabouts.

"Poor boy," Franklin said. "We've known the Stokes family forever. His parents died when he was just fifteen and the uncle who took him in was never around. It's not an excuse for his behavior, of course, but sometimes boys act out when there's no strong parental figure."

"You've known Nate a long time, then?" Jimmy asked.

"Since he was a little boy. I can't believe someone hurt him. And the rumors going around about what he was doing…"

"What's that?" Evelyn asked.

"Well, I don't want to speak ill of the dead," Franklin said with a sad smile that looked fake. "He and Jordan have known each other for years. The boy has always been a little…flighty…but I certainly never saw a criminal side to him."

Across the desk, Jordan's jaw was clenched tightly, like he was trying not to comment. But the rest of his posture looked relaxed.

"What was he like with women? How did he treat the women in his life?" Kyle asked, still addressing Franklin.

"He was fine," Franklin said, folding his hands on top of one another on his desk. "Respectful."

"Did he play the video games your company put out?" Evelyn asked, wondering if Franklin had any clue what being respectful to women meant.

The muscle underneath his eye twitched. "Are you trying to make some kind of snide statement, Agent Baine? Those games are just that—games. Innocent fun. Obviously whatever Nate was into that got him killed wasn't."

"Obviously not," she replied calmly, then turned

to look at his son, peering past Jimmy and Kyle, who were both leaning back in their chairs. "But what about Haley?"

"What about Haley?" Jordan snapped, then he jerked upright in his seat. "Are you telling me she's dead, too?" He glanced at his father, then back to her. "How do you know? Did you find her body?"

"I'm not telling you that," Evelyn said softly. "But I have a theory about what happened to her. Do you want to hear it?"

Franklin leaned forward, too, lifting partway out of his seat as he stretched toward her. "Where are you going with this, Agent Baine? I thought this was about what happened to Nate. If my son is a suspect—"

"This *is* about Nate," Evelyn said. "Haley and Nate fought before Nate died. Before Haley disappeared."

Jordan frowned, then adamantly shook his head. "They never talked. What would they argue about?"

"It was a physical fight. Nate tried to sell her to a customer and Haley tried to get away."

"What?" Jordan bellowed, leaping to his feet.

He either believed her—which suggested he really didn't know what had happened to Haley or Nate—or he was a hell of an actor. Evelyn figured the odds were about even on which it was.

"The only way we have any chance of finding Haley is by figuring out how to read Nate's customer list," Kyle said.

Jordan's expression froze and then he glanced slowly down at Kyle. "You found a customer list?"

Behind the desk, Franklin jumped to his feet, as well. "I want you out of here! This obviously isn't about Nate. This is about some misguided attempt to frame my son—"

"We have DNA evidence from Haley on Nate at the

crime scene," Kyle interrupted. "We're running a hell
of a lot more DNA now. It might be best to get in front
of this. And even if your son has nothing to do with
what Nate was into, they were best friends." He turned
his attention to Jordan. "Maybe Nate mentioned something to you that could help us. Maybe you didn't even
know what it meant at the time."

Evelyn kept her own face impassive as Jordan glanced
back at her. Kyle was trying to give the kid plausible deniability. Risking that whatever he told them now might
not make it into a courtroom on the chance that it could
help them save Haley.

As Jordan's eyebrows came down and his chin trembled, she could sense it. He was going to bite.

"Get out!" Franklin bellowed before his son could
say anything. He jabbed a finger toward his son. "Jordan, you keep your mouth shut. The rest of you, out of
my house before I think about exactly what charges I
plan to lodge against the FBI."

"He was going to go for it," Evelyn fumed as she
hopped into the passenger seat of their SUV, frustration making her hot despite the cold January wind. "I
could feel it."

"Maybe we would have been better off with the
overly intense lawyer instead of the overprotective father," Jimmy said, climbing into the backseat. "And am
I the only one who noticed the older Biltmore drank his
lunch today?"

"Kind of an odd thing to do before you okay a visit
from the FBI," Kyle said. "But I smelled it, too. Maybe
it's why he didn't call his lawyer when we set up the
visit."

"More likely he just thinks he's smarter than everyone else and that's why there was no lawyer," Evelyn replied. She'd dealt with people like him before—in positions of power who thought no one could ever take them down.

"How much do you think he knows?"

"I'm not sure," Evelyn said. "His concern might just be about shielding his kid from getting into trouble with the law, or doing anything that could hurt his future."

"I understand the need to protect your child," Kyle said, starting up the ignition. "But at what cost? Someone else's daughter is out there enduring God knows what, and Jordan may be our best chance to stop it."

"I hear you," Evelyn said, her mind on Quincy Palmer, a man who'd devoted his life to justice. What threat against his son had it taken to turn his back on an innocent teenager? Or were they way off base there?

Almost as though thinking about the case's connection to the station caused it, Evelyn's phone rang and Sophia's number appeared on her cell. As Kyle swung around the circular drive, Evelyn picked up.

"I confronted Quincy," the detective said, sounding out of breath and speaking so fast Evelyn didn't have time to say hello. "I know we were going to wait, but I couldn't help it. It's been eating away at me, the idea that he could be involved, and he came in here and wanted to talk about the case, and I just blurted it out."

Sophia finally paused for air and Evelyn tried to keep the frustration out of her tone as she replied, "What did he say?"

"He admitted it."

"He…*what*?" She sounded as surprised as she felt.

"Apparently he got a package at his house three months ago. No return address. Just a flash drive inside, and when he played it, he found a video of his son, Liam. It was a sex tape, Evelyn. Well, 'sex tape' is a nice way to put it. This was clearly rape. Even worse, although you can't see anyone else in the tape, the setup—mattress on the floor, nothing but curtains in the space, money passed through the curtain to a hand that's out of frame—it sure as hell sounds like human trafficking. Quincy didn't realize it then, but given what we know now…"

"Of course," Evelyn realized, mad at herself for not realizing earlier. They knew Liam had been to the university, and they knew he had a history of drug use, so they'd considered he could have grabbed Haley and they'd considered blackmail against Quincy based on dealing. But a rape charge? Even if it wasn't connected to human trafficking, if he was convicted, Liam's name would forever be on the sex offenders list. If Quincy was hoping to get Liam back on his feet after two strikes, this would probably be the one to send him spiraling again.

And if Quincy was lying and he did suspect trafficking, and that charge stuck? Liam Palmer would be going away again, probably for life.

Plus, the setup sounded like the old dance club Kyle had described. The one where Nate Stokes had been found, dead.

"There's more," Sophia said as Kyle pulled out of the Biltmore drive and onto the street. "Quincy says he didn't know who was blackmailing him. He assumed it was Jordan because he was asked to keep an eye on Haley, make sure she didn't go to the police, and squash a report if she did. He said the concern was particularly about any visits she made to the university. Everything was on the flash drive, just a document with instructions."

"So, Quincy was following Haley the day she was grabbed? That's why we saw him on the traffic cam?"

"Yeah, but he didn't stick with Haley. After Jordan dropped her off, he followed Jordan instead."

"Which means Jordan Biltmore isn't our abductor."

"What?" Kyle asked, braking the SUV and turning to look at her. "So our theory that a customer of the trafficking ring grabbed Haley *is* a real possibility?"

Evelyn nodded at him as Sophia continued, "Quincy says he was following Jordan because he didn't know what Haley might make a report about. But he claims that as far as he could tell, Haley had no clue what her boyfriend was up to, either."

"Then what about Haley's note under her mattress?"

"I don't know. I asked him. Quincy's best guess is that she started to suspect shortly before she was grabbed."

"Did he ever see Haley with Nate?"

"No. Obviously he wasn't following her 24/7. This was more of a 'keep general tabs on her' sort of thing. But here's the best part. After he talked to Jordan today, he says he stopped thinking it was Jordan who was blackmailing him. Jordan didn't seem to have any particular idea who he was, beyond just a Neville cop."

"Maybe he was faking."

"Maybe, but Quincy seemed pretty certain."

"Then who?" Evelyn asked. "Nate? Kyle and Jimmy think they were the only two involved at the top. The enforcers are both dead. Out of all of them, only Jordan is still alive."

"Nope, not Nate, either. Quincy tells me he took another look at the flash drive this afternoon. A last-ditch effort, because it looked clean, but we all know a good computer forensics expert can dig up things you think are completely erased. So he had someone with cyber specialty take a closer look. And what was on there before the sex tape? Corporate information for Biltmore Gaming."

"*Franklin* Biltmore?" Evelyn asked. "Son of a bitch. That explains the weird look he gave me when I arrived. *He* expected me to be traumatized by the swatting, not Jordan. He spoofed the SWAT call. It makes sense, in a weird way. He wants to protect his son and he certainly has the technical know-how. Jordan probably called him after he came to the station, his dad told him to see where we went and he took care of it from there. Sophia, I've got to go."

She hung up and turned to Kyle, who'd been waiting, his foot on the brake, while she finished the conversation. "Let's go back. Franklin Biltmore knows what his son was doing. He blackmailed a Neville detective to keep Haley from ratting out Jordan."

"What if he also eliminated Haley when he thought she was getting too close?" Jimmy asked.

"Maybe," Evelyn said. "Gillian's description of her abductor was younger than Franklin, but it was dark in that basement, and Franklin doesn't look his age."

Kyle backed the vehicle up and then swung into the driveway again. "Then let's have another chat with Franklin Biltmore," Kyle said. "We have a strategy or are we winging this?"

"Well, I don't want to give away our evidence about the flash drive, because that's going to get us a warrant."

"We do know how customers were making 'appointments,'" Kyle said as he made his way back to the circle at the front of the house. "And it happened at the frat house where Franklin was a legacy. Maybe we can lead with that."

"Yeah," Jimmy agreed. "And—"

His words were cut off by a loud, unmistakable *crack* Evelyn recognized from years of firearms practice at Quantico. A shotgun blast.

It hit the front of the SUV, and then a sudden *whoosh* sucked the oxygen away from her as fire burst out of the engine. It billowed up in front of the windshield, seeming to reach for them through the glass.

Panic burst as Evelyn sank low in her seat, fumbling with her seat belt. She tucked her feet in close, trying to get as far away from the front of the SUV as possible. Intense heat filled the vehicle and every breath seemed to singe her lungs.

Beside her, Kyle dove low, too, screaming at her and Jimmy to stay down as he tried to shift the burning vehicle into reverse. But it just made a high-pitched squeal and died, and the fire jumped higher.

"Shit, shit, shit!" Jimmy exclaimed as smoke surrounded them. She heard him open his door seconds before another shotgun blast rang out.

Her eyes burning from the smoke, Evelyn peered between the seats, her relief at seeing Jimmy still crouched inside the SUV short-lived. The fire was spreading. They weren't going to last long in here.

"Wait until I shoot," Kyle said, his voice ringing clear and calm in the car, sounding wrong amid her growing terror. "He's shooting from the side window. I'm going to hold him off while you two get out. Once you're under cover, aim for the second window from the far right, first level, and I'll join you. Got it? Now, duck!"

He didn't give her time to argue, just rose above the steering wheel, squinting through the smoke, and fired right through the windshield.

She flung her arms over her head as glass burst all

around her. It peppered her arms as new, even more intense flickers of heat reached for her. Gasping in a breath that was more smoke than air, Evelyn leaped for the door handle. It burned her skin, but she ignored it, wrenching open the door, and diving outside.

She landed hard on the cold pavers, then rolled, getting to her feet and running in a crouch to the poor cover of the closest tree. Better cover was twenty feet away, but the vehicle was going up soon, Evelyn could sense it. So, she spun and aimed at the window Kyle had indicated, firing until she emptied her weapon, praying Kyle would get out.

The shotgun fired again, and then the SUV was engulfed in flames. An anguished scream rose up and then Kyle and Jimmy's SUV exploded, raining bits of steel and fluid all around.

Consumed with dread, Evelyn fought the need to rush for Kyle, to find him, because she knew that would get her killed. Instead, she pressed hard against the tree, praying they'd all avoid the debris, praying she hadn't imagined Kyle's form streaking away from the SUV seconds before the explosion.

"I'm okay," Kyle called before she could yell for him. "Evelyn?"

"I'm good," she yelled back, gagging on the smoke still burning in her lungs. "Jimmy?"

"Okay," he said weakly. "I think that last shot was inside the house, though, not aimed at us."

Then the same agonized scream she'd heard before filled the air, and she saw someone emerge from the house, running into the smoke. "Help!" Franklin Biltmore screamed, tears streaming down his face as he tossed a shotgun aside and threw his hands in the air.

"Help me! Jordan is hit! Don't let him die! Please help him!"

All three of them rushed for Franklin at the same time. Kyle reached him first, knocking him to the ground and yanking his hands behind his back as he screamed and thrashed.

"I've got him," Jimmy said, snapping on handcuffs as Franklin's screams turned to sobs. "Go get the son."

Evelyn raced up next to Kyle and whispered, "I'm out of ammo."

"Stick behind me." Kyle's voice cracked from the smoke inhalation, but his tone was still firm.

She did, following him through the living room she'd noticed before, and into a second study, this one lined with gorgeous bookshelves. Lying on the edge of the intricate Oriental rug was Jordan Biltmore.

Blood spread out from underneath him, and a shotgun-sized bullet hole had torn open his stomach. His mouth and eyes hung open, a glaze over his pupils.

"He's dead," Kyle said, bending over to check his pulse even though it was obvious he was gone.

"And he's the only one who can give us customer information. If a customer grabbed her, Jordan's the only one who can lead us to Haley."

22

Franklin Biltmore slouched in a flimsy metal chair in an interview room at the FBI's Washington Field Office. His khakis and sweater were smeared with dried blood, and his eyes were bloodshot and glassy. His mouth hung slightly open as he stared blankly at his hands, which, once they'd tested for gunshot residue, he'd scrubbed until they were a bright pink. Periodically, a sob would rip out of him, and then he'd go back to the dazed silence.

"Is this the right time to question him about Jordan's business? A half-decent lawyer is going to make the argument that he's in shock from his son's death and doesn't know what he's admitting," Jimmy said.

"And the prosecution will counter that he just tried to kill three federal agents," Kyle argued. "And that in the process he killed his own son. Everyone we suspected to be involved in the human trafficking ring is dead, and no one from our Cryptoanalysis squad has been able to make any headway deciphering that customer list. There are too many variables. But if Franklin sent the tape to blackmail Quincy, he's got some kind of access to the trafficking ring. If one of their customers grabbed Haley, Biltmore Senior is our last chance at getting a name. Besides, we offered him a lawyer and he refused. Now is probably our best shot for information."

Evelyn tore her attention away from the one-way glass and the shell-shocked Franklin to look at Kyle and Jimmy. Like her, they still stank of burning fuel and smoke eight hours after they'd left the Biltmore mansion.

She'd hit the FBI's bathroom to try to clean up a little, and one look in the mirror had told her it was hopeless. She was covered in soot, her suit pants and jacket both had multiple tears, the edges of her bun had gotten singed and she had bruises and cuts all over her exposed skin. The hand she'd used to grab the door handle throbbed, the top few layers of skin gone from the intense heat on the metal. Jimmy didn't look much better, and Kyle, having been inside the vehicle longest, looked worse.

But at least they were all still alive, all still moving under their own power. The EMTs on the scene hadn't seen any evidence of damage to their windpipes or heard anything rattling in their lungs, so they'd been allowed to come back here without stopping at the hospital. They'd loaded her hand up with ointment and wrapped it, and done the same for Kyle. Jimmy's door hadn't been as hot, so he'd avoided any serious burns.

"This guy just killed his own son," Jimmy said. "Do we really think we can get him to betray the kid on top of it?"

Evelyn shifted her attention back to Franklin, whose transformation from cocky CEO to devastated father was harrowing. "Now is our best chance. Later, he might regroup and start thinking about his business, about his own life, about a defense strategy to salvage what he has left. But at the moment, he's only thinking about his son. He's got nothing left to protect."

"And given the fact that he was just shooting at us, maybe he's involved in the trafficking, too," Kyle contributed.

"Maybe," Evelyn replied. "But if so, he gave Nate and Jordan a lot of control. Given his personality, my guess is he's not directly involved, but just trying to protect Jordan."

"You want to take the lead here, Evelyn?" Jimmy asked, stroking the beard that didn't quite look natural on him.

She shook her head. "This guy is a misogynist. He lost his wife when Jordan was young, and he's been bitter about it ever since, using women and tossing them aside. He's made a ton of money depicting them as disposable in his games. He'll respond better to you two. Especially since his swatting stunt led to us being there in the first place. He'll connect it to Jordan's death, and he might flip it so he blames me instead of himself. I'm going to stay out here."

She hated to say it, because she wanted to be in there, wanted to be up close to Franklin Biltmore, to demand he hand over whatever he knew that could help them save Haley, if they still could. But this was where she was best—profiling the players and advising the right approach.

Kyle shifted, giving her his full attention. "What strategy are you thinking?"

"Identify with him, father to father. Every father wants to protect his child. You understand why he wanted Haley followed."

Looking amused, Kyle grinned. "I have a kid?"

"Today you do. A son, much younger than Jordan.

Five years old. It's the age Jordan was when his mom died. It's when Franklin got full responsibility for raising him, for protecting him."

"So I'm guessing Mac's a single father?" Jimmy asked, gesturing to Kyle's empty ring finger.

"Yeah, but you don't need to mention that unless he asks. See if you can lead with how he's tried to take care of Jordan. Hopefully he'll talk about some of his own actions to help Jordan and it'll slowly spill over to *why* Haley needed to be followed. Keep him talking, try not to let him think about it too long, and let's see what slips out."

"Works for me," Kyle agreed.

"So, what's my story?" Jimmy asked with his usual toothy grin, which she hadn't seen a hint of since they'd been shot at. "How many kids do I have? I'm thinking maybe six. And a girlfriend who lives with me, but is marriage-shy because of a previous relationship that ended badly."

Evelyn felt her lips twitch and tried not to laugh. "Let's keep it simple, and keep Biltmore focused. One connection. Jimmy, you don't need to volunteer personal details. Just be sympathetic and if he gets offtrack, you be the one to move him back with the business questions."

"I'm the kind-of bad cop," Jimmy said. "I can do that."

She nodded, liking it because Kyle naturally appeared to be more of a threat than Jimmy. He was older, and bigger, and after years in the HRT screamed *alpha*. Jimmy was probably in his late twenties, but he looked younger, and the beard, instead of adding years, just made him seem to be trying too hard. Going against expectations would help them with Franklin, she hoped, because he was used to having the most control in any room.

"All right." Kyle looked at Jimmy. "You ready?"

"Let's find Haley," Jimmy said, heading for the door.

Kyle gave her a quick kiss on the lips and squeezed her uninjured hand, then followed.

A minute later, they emerged on the other side of the glass, pulling up chairs across from Franklin, their backs to her. Franklin didn't even look up at their entrance, just continued staring, dazed, at his hands.

Apparently he'd thought one of them—or other FBI agents they'd called in—had crept up behind him when he heard a noise in the study. He'd swung away from taking shots out the window and fired. But it had been Jordan coming in, wondering what was happening.

The shotgun blast to his midsection had killed him almost immediately. When she and Kyle had gone back outside to meet the arriving backup, Franklin had taken one look at them and burst into tears.

At this moment, knowing he'd have to live with the fact that he'd killed his only son, he was most vulnerable. Some part of her wondered what it said about her that she was willing to take advantage of his pain, but she pushed it aside. He'd made his choices, and they included hiding knowledge of girls being forced into prostitution, of a teenager being kidnapped and firing on federal agents.

"Franklin," Kyle said softly, bringing Evelyn's focus back on the scene in front of her. He stretched a hand toward the man. "We're so sorry for your loss."

Franklin raised his head, no comprehension in his red-rimmed eyes.

"It's hard raising a son alone. It's hard wanting to protect them no matter what. I understand. You just wanted to keep him safe."

Grooves lined Franklin's forehead and he finally seemed to focus as Kyle kept going.

"We love them even when they make bad choices. We do our best, but it's hard to always know the right way to look after them, right?"

"You have kids?" Franklin croaked, slowly, like he was still one step behind the conversation.

"One. A boy. He's five. And he's a handful, let me tell you. Sometimes, I don't know what I'm doing. His mother would've…" He shrugged, a quick jerk of his shoulders. "But I do the best I can."

Franklin's eyes narrowed a little as he glanced at Jimmy. "You have kids?"

"Nah. I have enough problems with a girlfriend."

Franklin gave an anemic, forced laugh, then looked back at Kyle. "Jordan's still just a kid, really," Franklin said, his voice so soft Evelyn could barely hear it.

But his words made her pulse jump. It was working. And he was still using present tense, still stuck in that transition where the reality of Jordan's death hadn't fully sunk in yet.

"It doesn't matter how old they get, does it?" Kyle asked. "You just want to take care of them, make all of their worries go away."

Franklin tilted his head sideways. "I knew he'd picked a dangerous business. High risk, high reward, the way I always taught him. A lucrative area, lots of growth. But lots of risk. Too much risk."

She couldn't see the expressions on Kyle's or Jimmy's faces, but they must have been holding in their disgust.

"You wanted to reduce that risk," Jimmy said. "So you had a Neville officer keep an eye on Haley? Just to make sure she wasn't going to turn on Jordan. Am I right?"

Franklin turned his head awkwardly, still propped on his hands, to glance at Jimmy. "That's it. I just wanted an early warning if a report came in. Just to make it go away, and then I'd handle Jordan. I'd make him shut it all down, keep him safe. But he was good. No one knew. He was worried about Haley, but the cop followed her all over, and we had a system. He sent emails to an anonymous email account. Every week, a report. Every week, nothing. And we had serious goods on his son. He wasn't lying."

When Franklin fell silent, Kyle asked, "What changed?"

"What do you mean? Nothing changed! Nothing changed until Haley went missing. Then that crazy FBI woman and her detective friend kept coming after Jordan as though he was guilty."

"Are you sure he wasn't?" Jimmy asked.

"Damn right!" Franklin snapped, his head jerking up, some of the glassiness leaving his eyes.

"But he was guilty of trafficking women," Jimmy said.

Fury filled Franklin's face and his eyes started to come further into focus. "His business was his business."

"What if Haley found out?" Kyle started. "And Jordan decided to take care of it on his—"

"No," Franklin cut him off. "My boy was devastated when she went missing. He loves that girl, stupid as it is. She was just a naive little high school kid. He could have done better, could have aimed higher. But he's crazy about her. He would never have hurt her. Besides, she didn't know anything."

"But one of his customers saw her," Jimmy said. "And decided he wanted Haley for himself."

"What?" Franklin asked, then he straightened in his chair. "That's what you were throwing around in my office, trying to trick Jordan. I'm not going to let you…"

He trailed off, as if he suddenly realized Jordan couldn't be tricked anymore.

"No," he said, his voice returning to its normal tenor. "That's not possible. Haley was never around Jordan's business. That I know for sure. He'd never expose her to it, for her sake and for his. He was smarter than that."

"He didn't do it on purpose," Kyle said, still in the same calm tone he'd used for the whole interview. "Did you know Nate had a crush on Haley? Nate wanted to be around her. *He* brought her too close to the business, and someone saw her. That person took her. And you know your son would want us to find her. You know Jordan would want us to do everything we could to bring her home."

Franklin stared back at him for a long moment, then finally shook his head.

Evelyn thought they'd lost him, that he'd come out of his grief-ridden stupor enough to realize that he was giving them a legal case against *him*.

But then he said, "I can't help you. I figured out what Jordan was up to, sure, and I tried to look after him the best way a father could. But I didn't have anything to do with the actual business. I don't have any access to his client lists, or any idea how to read the crazy code he and Nate used. Those two had their own special language."

He looked back and forth between them. "I'm sorry." Then he looked directly at the one-way glass, which to him would appear to be a mirror, and added, "I want a lawyer."

Evelyn rolled over and opened her eyes, finding Kyle staring back at her, already awake. She gave him a sleepy smile and rubbed her eyes. "Have you been up long?"

"Not long," he said, although he sounded wide awake.

Then again, this was Kyle, who bolted instantly to alertness no matter how little sleep he'd had, no matter where he was. It was that HRT training.

Thinking about it made her long to ask about his PT, to find out how his plan to get back onto the team was going. But staring into his deep blue eyes, she couldn't bring herself to say the words. Being a Special Agent wasn't exactly a safe desk job, but it was far less dangerous than the HRT. And she'd had a nagging feeling lately, a fear that he was hiding something about his efforts to get back on the team.

So, instead, she snuggled a little closer to him, wishing she didn't have to get up and go to work today. It may have been Saturday, but the search for Haley was reaching a critical point. She couldn't lose momentum, or she might lose any chance of finding Haley.

After the initial interview with Franklin had ended, they'd waited for his lawyer to arrive. And then they'd started again, trying to dig out any additional details. But all they'd really been able to determine was that he'd known nothing about Evelyn's flat tire or the thugs who'd come after her with baseball bats. But she'd already suspected those were Jordan's low-tech attacks.

The swatting was a different matter. She'd come to believe that was Franklin. He wasn't admitting it, especially not with his lawyer beside him, but hopefully their forensic lab would be able to pull up the proof on his computer. The Biltmore house was a crime scene, sealed off for evidence collection, and it had been easy to get a warrant for Franklin's computers based on the day's events.

Franklin was still in a holding cell. Bail would be determined this morning.

To her frustration, although he'd admitted to knowing about Jordan's business, he'd never been specific enough during the interview to implicate Jordan specifically in human trafficking. So, while they had access to Jordan's bedroom at the Biltmore mansion, they still didn't have the legal grounds to go through his frat house bedroom. And she somehow doubted any of his frat brothers would invite her in for a look around.

Kyle trailed his fingers over her bare arm, making her shiver. "Penny for your thoughts."

She propped her head on her hand. "I'm trying to figure out how to identify Jordan's customers."

He grinned at her. "You and your pillow talk. Always work."

"Not always," she replied, wiping a smudge of soot that was somehow still on his forehead, even after the shower they'd shared once they'd finally returned from the WFO.

"I guess not." He leaned in and gave her a quick kiss, then propped himself up, facing her. "Honestly, I'm surprised Dan's even letting you stay on this case with how many requests your office gets every day."

"Yeah, well, he's been really distracted. I'm not sure how long it's going to last, though. I need to identify those customers."

"Go from another direction. Since we can't figure out how to decipher the customer list, go back to Gillian. Try to get more from her."

Evelyn nodded slowly. "It's still possible we're wrong about it being a customer who grabbed Haley, but if it was, maybe Gillian has some kind of peripheral connection, too."

"You think she was trafficked?"

"I doubt it. She's got a pretty solid support system.

No sign of prior victimization. But maybe she's similar to Haley, someone on the edges of a dangerous scheme and she didn't even realize it."

"She lives pretty far from Neville," Kyle said.

"Two hours. Yeah, it's also possible we've got someone who was purchasing women from Jordan for sex, and then got a taste for it. He got tired of paying, so he started grabbing women. He happens to spot Haley near the campus and that's the start."

"But you said there was no sign of sexual assault with Gillian, right?"

Evelyn sighed. "Right. Which makes the customer theory less likely, from a behavioral standpoint." She ran her fingers along the wrist of his injured hand, careful not to touch the burned skin. "What about other victims? Has anyone else come forward since Jordan died?"

"No, but that news probably just hit campus. Jimmy and I are going back there today, to see what else we can find. We're hoping now that all the threats have been eliminated, someone else will come forward."

"Good. Keep me updated, will you?"

"Of course," Kyle replied. "But what about your investigation? If our customer theory is off base, who have you got?"

"The father. The stepfather. And honestly, we can't one hundred percent rule out Jordan himself."

"You think maybe he killed her?"

"Or what if he *didn't* kill her? His dad seemed convinced he'd never turn on her. But what if she found out what he was doing, so he kidnapped her to prevent her from turning him in?"

"I thought Quincy Palmer had eyes on Jordan the whole time?"

"That's true," Evelyn conceded. "But Jordan had two enforcers who were willing to beat a federal agent to death with baseball bats at his say-so. They probably wouldn't blink at kidnapping a high school girl."

"And now they're all dead."

"Yeah. And if Jordan *did* kidnap her, there's no one left to go wherever she is and bring her food or water."

Kyle stared back at her grimly. "So either the investigation needs to dig hard into any property Jordan or his father owned, or it needs to go hard at the customer angle."

Evelyn rolled toward her nightstand, grabbing her cell phone. "I'm going to call Sophia. Find out if there's anything else Quincy gave us that could help. Otherwise, I want to have her set up another visit with Gillian. She hasn't been able to give us a good description of her attackers, but she sure was specific about Haley. That's odd. Could be just the mix of fear and stress and adrenaline from running. Or it could be that she made up Haley being there, and she's created all these details to avoid focusing on what happened to her. Either way, we know Gillian was kidnapped. Maybe if I can get more on her kidnapper's actions, I can fine-tune the profile we released and go back to the media, put out another request for information."

"Jimmy and I will follow up with the Cryptoanalysis specialists, see if they can give us anything from that customer list. Initials, anything that might be useful. I know they've been swamped with a terror case and haven't been able to spend a ton of time on it."

"Thanks," she mouthed at Kyle as she hit Sophia's number and the detective picked up on the first ring. "Sophia, hi, it's Evelyn. I want—"

"Evelyn, I was just about to call you. Haley's mom

just called me, totally hysterical. It had to do with pictures she found, but that's all I could make out. We need to get over to the Varner house."

Sophia hung up before Evelyn could get more details, and she jumped out of bed, grabbing the first suit she spotted in her closet.

"What happened?" Kyle asked, looking a little less anxious to move as he climbed out of her bed.

"I don't know," Evelyn replied, tossing aside the T-shirt she'd worn to bed and yanking on her suit pants. "But whatever it is, I've got a bad feeling."

"So you're telling me the pillow talk is over?"

Evelyn nodded. "Back to work."

23

They found Pete Varner standing on the front lawn in a pair of boxers and a T-shirt. He had his arms wrapped tightly around himself, and he was shivering violently and stomping his bare feet as he yelled toward the house. "After everything I did for you, this is what I get? This is bullshit, Linda, and you know it!" When there was no answer, he screamed, "I took care of you, damn it! Let me back in the house!"

When Sophia and Evelyn got out of their car, slamming the doors, he spun around and his face turned an angry red. "She called you? This is completely ridiculous. She's overreacting. Can you tell her to let me back in the house? Or at least throw me some pants and a pair of shoes? It's freezing out here."

Sophia glared at him. "We'll see," she answered, striding up to the door at her typical pace. She was wearing her standard brightly colored blazer, jeans and high-heeled boots, but with every day that passed, her game face was slipping a little more.

Linda wrenched open the door before they knocked, her face streaked with tears that made a mess of her mascara, but her eyes clearer than Evelyn had seen them. She was also visibly shaking, either from whatever she'd discovered or because she'd stopped medicating without easing off it. "That bastard has pictures of Haley!"

She looked ready to run outside after him, so Sophia pushed her way inside, forcing Linda backward as Evelyn followed, shutting the door behind her.

"Try to calm down," Sophia told Linda. "Take a breath, and tell me what happened."

The words came pouring out so fast it was hard to keep up. "I was cleaning. I just—I needed to stay occupied, so I guess I've gotten a bit compulsive about it. Pete keeps telling me to stop, to try to stay calm, and just let the anxiety medicine my doctor prescribed kick in, but I have to keep busy or I go crazy. And I had to stop taking those pills—they're making me feel numb, and I can't find Haley if I can't even think! And if we're really going to go forward with that news special Pete suggested… Well, so today, I decided to clean the garage. I guess he didn't expect me to do that, it being winter and all, but I'd already been through the house so many times. I found a shoebox, which didn't seem like it belonged, so I opened it and I found this!"

Linda thrust out a stack of images toward Evelyn, who took them and began flipping through, holding them up for Sophia to see. She could tell by the resolution they'd been taken digitally, likely with Pete's phone, and then printed out on low-quality printer paper. Probably he'd been printing them at home when no one was around, rather than risking having someone else print the images. They all featured Haley, in her cheerleading uniform, in her pajamas, even some while she was sleeping. There were close-ups on body parts, but no nudity.

"I married a pervert!" Linda sobbed. "And this whole

time she's been gone, I thought he was the best husband in the world, how he's taken care of me and been so supportive. Meanwhile, he had *this* hidden away. Do you think he's been looking at these, getting off on them, while I sit here, praying my baby's not dead?"

"Linda," Sophia said softly. "I'm sorry this is happening. Let's try to calm down and talk about what it means, okay?"

She nodded, but the determination on her face was partly ruined by a wrenching sob.

"Did Haley ever try to talk to you about anything Pete said or did that bothered her, or scared her?" Evelyn asked.

"No! I mean, she didn't want me to marry him. She said he was creepy, but I just thought she didn't want me to get married again! You know, her dad was no prize, and Pete came to her school a few times, because of his job, and I think she was embarrassed by that. I thought she was just being obstinate. But she never said anything about—" Linda gestured to the images and then finished in a defeated voice "—this."

"Well," Evelyn said carefully, "there's nothing pornographic here." Talking over Linda's whimper, she continued, "But it's disturbing."

"That bastard!" Linda fumed, hanging on to Sophia as though having the detective beside her was the only thing keeping her from racing out of the house and attacking her husband. "He married me to get to her, didn't he? All this time, I thought I'd finally gotten lucky, finally found a good man, after Bill, and it was all just a show, wasn't it? What was he doing to her?" She sucked in a sob. "God, was he…?"

"I don't think he touched Haley," Evelyn said, knowing what Linda was too scared to say out loud. "These photos were taken by someone who was watching from a distance. Some people never get beyond that stage, but for others it's just a first step. You do have reason to be concerned about where it was headed."

"Son of a bitch!" Linda erupted, bolting for the door.

Sophia grabbed her before she could go outside, almost tripping as she tugged Linda backward. "That's not the way to handle this. Let's focus on finding Haley, not on defending you from an assault charge."

"I want him out of my house," Linda said, her whole body tense.

"We can stay here while he gets some things and then we'll make sure he leaves," Sophia said.

Technically, he had a legal right to be in the house. But Evelyn doubted Pete would try to stay after what his wife had discovered.

"Can you handle staying here while he gets his things?" Sophia asked. "I really don't want to have to arrest you for assault today, okay?"

Linda gave a curt nod, but before Sophia could go outside and get Pete, she asked in a broken voice, "Did Pete hurt Haley? Do you think while I was away, he tried to do more than just take her picture?"

"We don't know," Evelyn said when Sophia looked like she was struggling to come up with a response. Memories of her own past, with a man her mother had brought into their apartment when she was too young to fight him off, filtered through her brain. "But we're going to find out. And if he's guilty, we'll make him pay."

When they'd pulled him into the station for questioning, Pete Varner had squirmed and muttered a lot of nonsense about the pictures being "no big deal" and "a misunderstanding." He'd fidgeted in his chair like a kid in desperate need of the bathroom, but no matter how hard she and Sophia pushed, he'd denied having anything to do with Haley's disappearance. And he'd claimed she'd never confronted him about anything.

Evelyn didn't know what to believe. But she was praying Gillian Murray could give them more to go on. As Sophia punched the car up to ninety on the freeway, Evelyn's phone rang.

She glanced at the readout and then picked up, barely daring to hope there would be good news on the case. "Kyle? What's happening?"

"Two women just came forward at Neville University. They said they were blackmailed. It happened close to the same time as Tonya. The details are legit. Both said they went home with Nate and then had sex tapes delivered along with threats."

"Nate was the recruiter," Evelyn said.

"Yep. A hell of a recruitment method, but I guess it's a variation on the boyfriend scenario. I can't confirm it yet, but I suspect all three were targeted during a special orientation the university sponsored for their scholarship students. And although these women didn't have direct contact with Jordan, when they showed up for their 'appointments,' they saw Nate handing Jordan the money to count at the end of the night."

"Wow." She was glad they had answers, but she wished there was someone left to prosecute.

"And one other thing we weaseled out of Franklin this morning? Jordan knew Quincy was following him. So he'd temporarily shut down the business since right before Nate went missing. Which in my mind gives some credibility to the idea that he had nothing to do with Nate's death. He figured they'd put the business on hold, so Nate took a vacation."

"That does explain how Jordan didn't happen to find him at the warehouse, even if he didn't kill Nate. And why he didn't try to clean the whole place up when we started poking around. He was scared he'd lead Quincy right to it."

"Probably. But we've finally got it, Evelyn. It's going to take me a few more hours to finish up their statements and get a warrant, but we'll be heading to Jordan's frat house later today. You want to get in on this?"

"Maybe. We're on our way to talk to Gillian. I'm not sure how long that's going to take. But keep me updated."

"I will. Talk to you soon."

"Bye." She hung up and relayed the information to Sophia, whose lip curled.

"You think Nate sold Haley to one of these assholes who came to pay for women who didn't want to sleep with them?"

"I don't know. That's the line I gave Jordan, but honestly, it was partly to piss him off, get him talking. Kyle's theory is that they chose women for the trafficking because of a combination of specific factors—including lack of a support system and an opening for blackmail. Haley doesn't fit that. If Nate sold her to a customer, wouldn't he worry the customer would let her go at some point, and she'd go straight to the authorities?"

"This was your theory," Sophia reminded her.

"I know, and it could still have happened, if Nate thought Haley had found out about the operation and might turn them in. It could have been Nate's way of getting rid of her. But Nate had a crush on Haley. Maybe he made a play for her, she turned him down, and so he retaliated by offering her to a customer. It would explain the DNA under Nate's nails, but not the timing. But the week in between Nate's death and Haley's disappearance is bothering me."

"Yeah, me, too. Honestly, maybe Haley and Nate's fight had nothing to do with his death. Haley and Nate could have fought at lunchtime and Nate was killed that night. It could have been simply bad luck and bad timing that they ended up dead and missing a week apart."

Sophia got off the freeway and navigated through the small town where Gillian lived until she reached a little red ranch. Reporters had set up camp on the front lawn and a police car stood guard on the street. "Let's see what Gillian can tell us."

"Maybe if we can get a better description from Gillian, we can pass it on to Kyle. See if one of the women who came forward can match it to a customer, give us a name."

"I'm all for that." Sophia walked up to the house, straightening her bright blue blazer over her gun. She knocked a few times before there was a scraping sound from behind the door and then someone answered, just a sliver of her face in the doorway.

Gillian, looking physically stronger and healthier than she had in the hospital four days ago, but fear plain in her eyes.

Behind her, Evelyn spotted her father, sticking close until she told him, "It's fine," a heaviness to her voice. When he went silently back into the house, she turned back to them.

"Detective…sorry, I don't remember…"

"Lopez," Sophia said. "And this is Special Agent Baine."

"Right. The profiler. Did you catch him?"

"Not yet. But we want to ask you a few more questions, to help us do that," Evelyn said.

Gillian peered past them, at the news crews angling their cameras to get a shot of her. "Come on in," she said, opening the door but staying behind it.

Once they were inside, she closed the door, throwing the dead bolt and pushing a chair up underneath the handle. "Let's go to the den."

Gillian led them into a small family room with dark paneling on the walls. All the curtains were shut, and a heavy blanket was draped across the couch. The room was dreary and dim, as though Gillian was recreating the atmosphere she'd been forced into over the past week, as if she didn't know how to go back into the sunlight.

She huddled under the blanket and nodded at the two recliners. After Evelyn and Sophia were seated, she asked, "What else can I tell you? I gave you everything I know."

"Are you familiar with how profiling works, Gillian?" Evelyn asked.

Gillian looked at Evelyn, her eyes wide and wary. "You figure out who did a crime by looking at the evidence."

"Sort of. What I do is analyze behavior in particular, and it helps me pinpoint noticeable attributes about someone that would help him be identified. So, for example, learning more about the things this guy said and did while you were in his basement will help me figure out why he did it."

"And from that, she can tell us what direction to go to find Haley," Sophia chimed in.

"Okay," Gillian said, burrowing deeper under the

blanket. "What exactly do you need that I didn't already tell you?"

"What did he say to you about the future?"

She chewed on her lip, then said, "He told us he knew we were going to be perfect, that we just needed to learn. He said he'd gone to so much trouble, searching a long time for us. And he said we were malleable, like clay, and that we hadn't known our intended path before, but they would show us."

"They?" Evelyn jumped in.

"Yeah," Gillian said, looking surprised. "I wasn't thinking about it when he said it, because I only ever saw the guy who kidnapped me until I escaped, but it was definitely *them*. Well, he said *we*." She sounded horrified as she asked, "You think he was going to pass us around some group?"

"Probably not," Evelyn replied. The man who'd helped them escape clearly had access to the house. So maybe the kidnapper had grabbed one girl for himself and one for his friend. Only his friend hadn't known about it beforehand, and when he'd found out, he'd wanted nothing to do with it.

The idea bloomed, gaining strength in her mind. It would explain why the girls he'd picked were so different physically. They weren't both for him.

And if he'd risk a second kidnapping for another person, then their loyalty *did* go both ways. So, stronger than just a friendship. Family. It had to be. A brother, maybe, or a son.

Realizing Sophia and Gillian were both staring at her, Evelyn asked, "Can you think of anything else he said where he mentioned another person? Or talked about himself as part of a plural?"

Gillian's lips pursed. "I don't think so."

"What else did he say about the future? Anything at all that you remember."

Gillian heaved out a sigh, hunching into herself, almost disappearing into the couch. "He didn't talk a lot about the future, but I got the impression he was planning…something. I barely remember the upstairs. I only saw a bit of it when I ran, so I don't know what he might have been working on. Or maybe it had nothing to do with the house. But he was preparing something, and I think it was for us, because I heard him tell Haley once he knew how happy she'd be when she saw it. That it was her favorite spot."

"Haley said he was going to bring you upstairs once he could trust you, right?" Sophia asked. "Had she been upstairs before?"

"I don't think he'd ever taken her up there. But she said he was going to, and so I kind of figured he was getting a room ready for us. Putting in that foam stuff he had on the walls in the basement or covering the windows. But mostly when he came downstairs, he would ask us these random questions, or he'd tell us weird things."

"Can you give us some examples?" Evelyn asked, watching Gillian carefully, both for signs of extreme stress from the questions and for twitches of discomfort.

"Yeah, okay. So, one day he asked me if I enjoyed running on a treadmill as much as on a track or through the neighborhood. And he asked Haley if she wanted to learn to cook his mom's stew. Really weird stuff like that."

"How did you answer?"

"I said I hated treadmills, that nothing beat running outside. He looked kind of mad, so then I said maybe I hadn't given treadmills a fair chance. He smiled and said I was a good girl." She shuddered. "I didn't want to be his good girl."

"How did Haley answer?" Sophia asked.

"She said she thought she could learn to be a good cook. That she loved stew."

Haley had learned from her month in captivity. She'd learned how to make him happy. She'd been setting the stage to get him to trust her, to give her more freedom. Trying to give herself an opportunity to escape.

"And what about the other man? I know you never saw him until the day he opened that door, but think carefully," Evelyn said. "Could you hear anyone upstairs? Did you ever think there was more than one person moving around above you?"

Gillian shrugged. "I couldn't hear anything from upstairs or outside. It's why I never wanted to go in the bathroom, because you never knew he was coming until the door opened and there he was."

"And what about when this other guy opened the door? He told you to run. Did he say anything else to you? Anything about not being afraid of him, or to go while the first guy was gone? Anything at all?"

"He told us to go now. To hurry. But that's it."

"What about when you were out the door and you heard them arguing behind you?" Evelyn asked. "Did either of them say a name? Think back to when you got through that door and try to replay the memory in slow motion, just focusing on their words."

Gillian stared at her lap, her forehead furrowed in concentration, her teeth digging into her bottom lip. Finally she said, "The guy who helped us was screaming for the other one to just let us go. He said it wasn't right, and that they'd be fine, just the two of them. And…"

"What else?" Sophia asked when Gillian fell silent.

Gillian's gaze darted to Sophia's, her chest suddenly heaving up and down. "He said they didn't need wives."

"That's it," Evelyn said quietly. That was his motivation. He wasn't looking for sex slaves. He was looking for companions, for him and someone he cared about a lot. He was looking to create his own perverse version of what he saw people around him doing, but he could never figure out how to have it for himself.

"I glanced back when I heard that," Gillian said, her whole face pinched with the memory. "And I almost tripped. But I remember..."

"What?" Sophia leaned close.

"The guy who helped us get away? He'd been leaning against the door frame, almost like...almost like he needed it to hold on to. The kidnapper shoved him, really hard, and you could see the basement steps from the door, and I saw him go down."

"He fell down the steps to the basement?" Sophia asked.

"Yeah, and I kept running. I only looked for a second, but I think he was hurt bad. And I think..."

"What?" Sophia prompted.

"I think maybe there was a wheelchair on the other side of the door, off to the side, as though maybe he'd pulled himself out of it to open the basement door."

Evelyn's pulse jumped and she couldn't stop herself from lurching to her feet, even as Sophia and Gillian stared back at her questioningly. But this was the detail. She could feel it. This was the detail that was going to get them a name for their Good Samaritan, and then their kidnapper.

This was what they needed to find Haley.

24

"This is it," Evelyn announced, hearing the excitement in her voice. "This is the key."

They'd just left Gillian's house and Sophia was behind the wheel, driving much slower than she had on the way there. She looked distracted, as though her mind was still back in Gillian's house.

"The fact that this guy wanted to kidnap himself and his friend a pair of *spouses*? Yeah, that's truly fucked up. Does that give you enough, though? I mean, I get that it gives you new insight into his plans, but does that tell you where he is? Or *who* he is?"

"Not that," Evelyn clarified. "I mean, yes, knowing his intent does get me deeper into his head. And it solidifies his relationship with the Good Samaritan. The second guy is family, has to be. There's a history that isolates these two, so they rely mostly on each other. My first guess would be brothers, but the other possibility is that the Good Samaritan is the kidnapper's son."

"His son?" Sophia asked, glancing at Evelyn and then back at the road. "Why?"

"Think about it. You have a socially awkward, isolated guy. He has trouble relating to the opposite sex. But he gets a girl pregnant—my guess would be early

on in his sexual experience, or possibly his only one—
and he ends up with the baby."

"Who in their right mind leaves a *kid* with that kind
of jerk?"

"Well, if the boy's in a wheelchair, maybe the mom
was struggling with his care. Or maybe as he got older,
she saw more of his father in him and couldn't deal with
it. The kidnapper is *not* someone who could sustain a
romantic relationship, so this was not a child that came
out of a long-term relationship. If this is the right scenario, the child was from a one-night stand, probably
a really awkward experience. The woman might have
immediately regretted it. The kidnapper saw it as his
opportunity for normalcy."

"But it wasn't," Sophia said.

"No. But he got a child from it, and he wanted that
child to give his life a sense of normalcy. Somehow, he
ended up with the boy and raised him in relative isola-
tion. Now the child is older, probably nearing twenty,
which would make the father closer to forty. And the
father decides they should both have that feeling of normalcy. Since he's never been able to achieve that the
way other people do, he convinced himself he could
take it. He convinced himself he could train young girls,
the way he'd trained his son."

"Okay, but you said they were more likely to be
brothers, right?"

"Yes. And if it's two brothers, then the Good Samaritan feels this loyalty because the kidnapper—his brother,
probably his older brother—looked after him. The parents would have been out of the picture early. The Good
Samaritan knows his brother isn't quite right, but this is
his brother. He loves the guy and he thinks he owes him,
too. And they probably live together."

"But from Gillian's story, it sounded as though he didn't know she and Haley were in the basement that whole time," Sophia argued.

"No. Probably his brother snuck them in the house. My guess is the kidnapper knew deep down that his younger brother wouldn't approve, but he decided he could convince him. But the Good Samaritan suspected something was going on, even if he didn't know what, before the kidnapper was ready to tell him. If he's in a wheelchair and the brother put them in the basement, the Good Samaritan couldn't go down there. He couldn't go see what was happening. And if it was soundproofed as well as Gillian's describing, he didn't hear the girls, either."

"So what changed?"

"Probably the kidnapper told him. Expected his brother to be excited, to be grateful. But he wasn't. My guess would be that he argued for their release before he tried to help them escape."

"Okay," Sophia said slowly. "So are you still thinking the kidnapper is a customer of Jordan and Nate's human trafficking ring?"

"I do. I think it's also possible the kidnapper saw Nate and Haley argue, saw Haley hurt Nate. Maybe he decided he was doing Haley a favor. Honestly, it's even possible he's the one who killed Nate, and then began stalking Haley, learning her routines before he grabbed her."

"But didn't you say his sexual experiences would be limited?"

"Yes, but human trafficking is different. These women couldn't say no, and they may have been forced to pretend to enjoy it."

"Then why grab Haley and *not* do that to her?"

"Because, deep down, it was never about sex. He was

searching for companionship. He wanted a regular life, or at least what he perceived to be normal."

"Haley," Sophia said, nodding. "She's about as all-American as they come. And then after he had Haley settled, he started hunting for someone for his brother or his son?"

"Yes. But he was smart enough not to troll where he'd been before."

"Well, this is interesting, in a disturbing kind of way. But how exactly does it help us?"

"Think about it," Evelyn said. "Gillian told us the kidnapper pushed his brother. She thought he fell down the stairs."

"She also thought Haley escaped, but we're assuming this guy still has her."

"Probably he caught Haley pretty quickly after she got out the door, then chased Gillian."

"Okay, so I'm confused. How does this help us?"

"We now have two crucial facts. One—the Good Samaritan is disabled in some way, and he uses a wheelchair. Two—he's now injured, possibly seriously, from falling down the stairs."

The car slowed and then Sophia seemed to realize and punched down on the gas. "Hospitals," she muttered.

"Yes. Even though the Good Samaritan betrayed him, the kidnapper still cares for him. He'll try to get him help. We need to contact all the local hospitals and see if anyone showed up four days ago, either a father and son or two brothers. Give them the description."

Sophia nodded, smiling for the first time all day. "And get some names."

"And get some names," Evelyn confirmed.

* * *

Evelyn kept her head down, trying to focus on the list of Virginia hospitals in front of her on the folding table and not the commotion coming from the Neville police station's bullpen.

Quincy Palmer had officially been put on suspension today, pending an investigation into his actions. A whole slew of charges were coming down, too, from hindering an investigation to concealing evidence of a crime to destroying evidence. The last charge was because he claimed the flash drive of his son—which showed what was definitely rape, and probably also human trafficking—had been destroyed while in his possession.

"I'm sorry I failed you all," Quincy said, his voice soft but still carrying all the way to Evelyn because the station had gone so quiet around him.

She glanced over and saw him standing, shoulders back, in the center of the bullpen. He held a cardboard box that looked sadly light after more than twenty years serving the city of Neville.

Without the detective's shield she'd grown accustomed to seeing him wear around his neck, his heavy tan blazer and jeans looked strange. His already craggy face seemed to have acquired dozens of new grooves overnight, like a map of his mistakes. Even his beard was suddenly more salt than pepper.

Across the bullpen, near the chief's office, Sophia had her arms crossed over her chest, a furious expression on her face. When Quincy glanced at her, a glimmer of hope on his face, Sophia dropped her arms to her sides and disappeared into the war room. She kicked the door shut behind her.

"What?" Sophia demanded as Evelyn stared at her.

"He endangered this investigation, and by doing it, he endangered Haley's life. He deserves whatever he gets. You can't tell me you feel sorry for him."

Evelyn sighed, staring at the closed door. "From what you've told me, Quincy and his son were estranged most of the time the boy was growing up because Quincy was always here, always working. He probably feels guilty, thinking if he'd been around more, his son would have chosen a better path."

Sophia sank heavily into the chair beside her, fury radiating off her so strongly it was almost palpable. "You're kidding, right? I mean, what he did is sort of tantamount to the kidnapper's brother or son or whoever he is keeping that secret about Haley being locked in his basement! It's not okay, no matter what spin you put on it. Family loyalty be damned, I'd never do that."

"Not even for one of your boys?"

Sophia glared. "I'm raising them to respect women. I enjoy my job, don't get me wrong. But it's not my whole life. And what Quincy's turned into? That's not my future."

"I'm not saying it is. And I don't condone what Quincy did. I just feel a little bad for him."

Sophia snorted. "Well, I don't," she said, grabbing the list Evelyn had been writing. "You start at the bottom and I'll start at the top."

"Okay," Evelyn said, knowing that no matter what Sophia said, she was only this angry because she cared. Quincy had been her friend, her mentor. He'd let her down and she wasn't ready to forgive that.

The thought made Evelyn stop in the process of reaching for her phone. Was she feeling the same way about her mom? If it was anyone else, would she suggest they give Lily a chance to prove she'd changed?

The thought made tension lock all her muscles, and she forced it aside. She wasn't sure why Quincy's story made her feel sympathy. Normally she'd be taking the same stand as Sophia. Wrong was wrong, no matter what the motivation.

She'd always felt that way. She could get deep into the minds of predators, and understand exactly why they did the things they did, but she never sympathized with their choices.

Life had thrown a lot of challenges her way, especially when she was young, and she'd never used any of them as an excuse. But along the way, she'd become so obsessed with the idea of justice that she spent too much time working. Even now, with a new commitment not to be at work until ten at night every weekday and all her weekends, she still couldn't remember the last time she'd seen her friends. And she owed her grandma another visit.

That wasn't a thought she wanted to dwell on, either, not with her grandma still asking about her mother when they spoke on the phone. Mabel had a vague feeling Lillian had visited, but couldn't remember if it had been this week or many years ago. Evelyn had tried to dodge the question, because she'd told Lillian never to return. And she couldn't bring herself to regret that. But neither could she stand lying to her grandma.

And she couldn't be sure what her grandma would say if the dementia *didn't* have her in its grasp. Her grandma had always been more forgiving than her, but Mabel had been the one to tell Lillian she wouldn't be raising Evelyn anymore and she wasn't to come around again. Evelyn had no doubt that her grandparents' actions when she was ten had saved her from a horrible fate.

But now? They'd both seen Lillian thirteen years

ago, but Mabel had been in no condition to make decisions right after her debilitating stroke. If she had the chance now, especially knowing dementia was taking a stronger hold of her every day, would she decide differently? Want to see Lily while she could? Want to forgive and forget?

"Evelyn!"

"What? Sorry. What did you say?"

"I *said*, I'm not having any luck with the hospitals. No one seems to know anything about either a father and son or two brothers who came in four nights ago meeting the description I'm giving them. I'm running into a little bit of trouble with privacy, but when I explain it's about a missing kid and tell them I'm with the Neville station, I get more cooperation. Still, nothing. Are you planning to call some with me or are you fine-tuning that profile in your head?"

"No, sorry. I'm going to start calling," Evelyn said, picking up her cell phone and dialing the first number from the bottom of the list.

But when she asked about a man in a wheelchair visiting the emergency department with another man, the first place she called said no one matching her description had come in that night, or the day afterward. The same was true of all the other hospitals on her list. When she finished, she looked at Sophia hopefully.

Sophia shook her head. "Nothing. Do you think the brother died from the fall? Or he wasn't hurt? Or maybe the kidnapper just decided not to get him medical care?"

"All of those are possible." She was frustrated, but her profiler instinct was still screaming, telling her if the kidnapper cared enough about his brother or son to steal him a wife, he cared enough to get him help. Even if the only reason the man needed help was for trying to let the kidnapper's victims go.

"Maybe he was wary of hospitals, worried about attracting attention. He couldn't be sure how much Gillian had seen. If he was worried we'd know to look for him there—"

"He might have left without being treated. Or gone to some kind of urgent care clinic instead," Sophia finished her thought.

"Exactly."

Sophia hunched down in her chair. "We can call all the hospitals and try again, but what are the chances they'll remember someone who didn't stay to be treated? And do you know how many urgent care places there are? It's going to be hard to cover them all. That'll take forever."

"Then we'd better get started."

"I think I found him," Evelyn announced, hanging up her most recent call, to an urgent care center up in Highland County.

Sophia instantly stopped rubbing her bloodshot eyes and asked, "Really?"

"It's not one hundred percent. But what I have is two men who showed up in urgent care, one of them in a wheelchair. The woman I spoke to said the man in the wheelchair was pretty badly injured. She actually thought he fell down the stairs. When she asked what had happened, the guy who brought him in got very closemouthed and it made her suspicious. She worried about abuse and was planning to call the cops. I think the kidnapper knew it, and he was scared off. They left without being treated. But she did say they looked close in age, within ten years."

"Brothers."

"Looks like it."

Sophia leaned toward her, looking hopeful. "Did they give a name before they took off? And can this woman describe them for us? Work with a sketch artist, maybe?"

"We can try on the sketch artist. Her description matches Gillian's. She said they were both pretty average. White men, average weight. She thought our kidnapper—assuming it was him—was about five-ten and probably in his thirties or forties. I tried to get more detail, but she just kept repeating how average they were. It was cold outside, and they were both in big coats and hats."

"What about names?" Sophia pressed.

"They filled out a form for treatment, and although the guy grabbed it when he left, she said she saw the name. Samuel Davids."

"Let's go!" Sophia jumped to her feet. "We need to get an address and go see what's in their basement!"

Evelyn just stared up at her until Sophia dropped back into her chair with a sigh.

"Okay, you're right. We don't have enough for a warrant. And if it is him, I don't want to tip him off. We need to get close and see what's going on."

"Gillian said all the basement windows were boarded up and there was nothing surrounding the house for quite a ways," Evelyn reminded her. "We're not going to be able to get a peek. What we need to do is dig into this guy's life. If we can match him to the profile, find some dirt on any past problems, we can push for a warrant. And if we don't have enough, then we plan the best approach and go from there."

"Okay," Sophia said, looking suddenly revitalized. She glanced at her watch and pursed her lips. "Let me call my babysitter and beg him to stay another couple of hours again tonight."

"Sure," Evelyn said. While Sophia stepped out of the room to make her call, Evelyn dialed Kyle.

When he answered, she asked, "Did you find anything at Jordan's frat house?"

"Hi to you, too, honey," Kyle joked.

"Sorry," Evelyn said, flushing.

"It's okay," he said, and she knew he was trying not to laugh at her. "Well, the visit was useful. I wouldn't say we got our smoking gun, but then again, we're pretty sure all the players are dead. At this point, we're basically going after the customers and Franklin Biltmore. And we'll attempt to provide resources for the victims."

"And make sure there's no opening for someone else to take over where they left off," Evelyn added.

"Yeah, definitely. But from what we found in Jordan's room, that's unlikely. We did find a stack of papers relating to the operation. Copies of the ownership information on their location, dirt on their two enforcers, even dirt on Nate. All locked up in a nice little box, along with another blackmail flash drive. There was the original of the one used to hook Quincy—I think Jordan made the video, then spilled the trouble he was in to his dad, who took a copy and used it. Unfortunately, I don't see any other videos with customers, though I think there must be some, because we found a disconnected camera at the site."

"Unless that was just for show," Evelyn suggested.

"Maybe, but they taped Quincy's son. So, either they taped everyone, or they taped him because they already knew who he was when he came into the place."

"We saw a picture of Liam Palmer taken in the frat

house, so it's definitely possible they knew who he was from the start, and saw an opportunity there."

"Well, I'm still pushing forward."

"Any more insight into how they got into this or where it was going?"

"Yeah, we suspect they'd planned to turn that old dance club not only into a place for business, but ultimately to have women actually living there. There was a spreadsheet of a cost/benefit analysis related to paying tuition and profits made on each woman. What's scary is that they were still making a hell of a profit. Once I can really line these numbers up with each person, we'll have a stronger case."

"What about when Franklin mentioned them taking a hiatus around the time Nate went missing? Any more on that?"

"Sort of. It seems that Nate usually handled the actual transactions. Jordan managed things from the customer side—getting out advertisements and how to pay for services through the frat house—and managing the books. When they closed things down, these women got a reprieve, a break from the constant control and threats."

"That does explain the timing. Tonya goes to the police, and Jordan gets his enforcers to handle it because he doesn't want to go anywhere near her with Quincy on his tail."

"I think so, too," Kyle agreed. "And I think Jordan and Nate had a vision for what they considered a business, put it into play and discovered the problems along the way. This is why trafficking victims are usually kept close by, under tight control."

As Sophia came back into the room, giving her the thumbs-up, Evelyn told Kyle, "Good luck with it. I have to go back to my case. We're looking at a possible break. I'll give you a call if it pans out. If you come up with anything related to customers, let me know."

"I will. We're working on it."

"Thanks."

After saying goodbye to Kyle, Evelyn turned back to Sophia. "Let's find Samuel Davids."

"Yes," Sophia agreed. "And let's find the bastard's brother, too."

25

"He's dead," Sophia greeted her outside the Neville police station before 6:00 a.m. the next morning.

"Who's dead?" Evelyn asked, but before she finished the question, she knew the answer.

It was written in Sophia's red-rimmed eyes, and the splotchiness on her face. She'd been crying—a lot— before she arrived at work.

"Quincy," Sophia said. "He went home from the station yesterday with that pathetic cardboard box full of all his stuff, and you know what he did?"

"I'm so sorry," Evelyn said, knowing exactly what was coming next.

"He left messages on his ex-wife's machine and his son's voice mail. He apologized for not being there for them when they needed him. And then he had a couple of beers, sat down in his favorite recliner, stuck his pistol in his mouth and pulled the trigger."

"Damn it," Evelyn said. "Sophia, I'm sor—"

"Yesterday, when he was in the bullpen and everyone was staring at him like he was a common criminal, as though he'd never been one of us, I knew he needed someone to understand. Someone to at least tell him they'd be there if he needed them, even if they couldn't approve of his actions. He looked at me, Evelyn. I was his friend. I let him down and he went home and—"

"You can't think that way," Evelyn said. "This isn't your fault."

"Yeah," Sophia snorted. "It wasn't anyone's fault." She pushed past, going into the station and leaving Evelyn standing outside in the cold.

Sophia hadn't seen Quincy's suicide coming, but Evelyn should have. It was her job to profile people. She'd watched him in the bullpen, seen his desperation as everyone in the station stared at him with disgust. He'd traded his personal life for the job. When that was gone, she should have realized this could happen. She should have told his chief, gotten someone to go home with him.

But it hadn't even occurred to her, because she'd been too busy worrying about Haley, too busy worrying about her own personal life. Evelyn hurried inside after Sophia, where the mood was somber. The few officers in the station shared similar expressions, a mixture of disbelief, guilt and sadness.

"Come on," Sophia said, keeping her head down as she barreled through the station toward their little war room. Once they were inside, she shut the door behind her and released a long breath.

She tossed her wool coat aside and sat hunched over in the chair, in a pair of wrinkled jeans and a too-big sweatshirt. "I can't deal with anyone from the station. I woke up to the call about Quincy and my boys both wanted to know why Mommy was crying and what was I going to tell them? They know Quincy. He's taken them to ball games. He came to their birthday parties, did guy stuff with them." She choked on a sob, then slammed a fist on the table. "Shit! Why'd he do it?"

"It's—"

Sophia held up a hand. "I know you're trying to help. I appreciate it, but that was my one outburst for today. What I want to do now is put Quincy out of my head for the rest of the day and focus on bringing Haley home."

"Okay. Good plan."

They'd dug for details on a Samuel Davids for hours last night, until Evelyn had finally called back and asked if the woman at the clinic was certain about the name. She'd had a brief burst of panic thinking he'd used a fake name, but the woman had been certain that's what they'd written. They had nothing else to go on. If it was a fake, Evelyn prayed he'd used a name connected to his life, anyway.

At around two in the morning, Sophia had finally stumbled on a Samuel Davids who was a possible match. He was born in Ohio, and he'd suddenly appeared on the grid when family services had made a call to the house because of trespassing complaints from the neighbors. They'd found two boys inside, and estimated their ages at six and fourteen. There had been no sign of parents or a guardian, and the six-year-old had been using an old, barely working wheelchair.

When pressed, the older boy had provided two pieces of information. Their names: Eric and Samuel Davids. And the status of their parents: they'd decided to live on a special commune and kids weren't allowed.

Family services had tried and failed to locate extended family for the boys. Apparently the family had been squatting in a foreclosed house for years, so they couldn't even trace them through mortgage or deed information.

The parents had taken off months before, and the older boy had been looking after the younger one ever since. When the state had tried to put the boys into the foster system, they'd disappeared.

Evelyn and Sophia had tried to pick up where family services had left off, but had gotten nowhere. It was as though Samuel and Eric Davids had never existed. Or if they did, they weren't living anywhere in Virginia.

Finally Sophia had suggested they catch a few hours of sleep and come back refreshed. Evelyn hoped they'd have better luck with the hunt today.

But before they could start, one of the other officers poked his head into the room and said softly, "You've got a visitor."

"Who is it?" Sophia snapped.

"Linda Varner."

"Shit," Sophia muttered. "Okay." When the officer disappeared again, Sophia said, "I hoped I was going to get a reprieve from this today."

Evelyn got up. "I'll go with you."

For a second, Sophia looked like she was going to tell her it wasn't necessary, but then she just nodded. "Thanks."

Evelyn followed Sophia back through the eerily silent station and out front, where Linda Varner waited.

Instead of her usual business clothes and carefully applied makeup, Linda was wearing baggy sweats and her blotchy face had been scrubbed hard, erasing any trace of makeup. But her eyes were clear, and her hands shook less than they had yesterday. The barely hidden pain and fear that had been lingering just below the surface were now doused with fury.

"Why isn't he in jail?" Linda demanded as soon as they appeared.

Sophia closed her eyes briefly and let out a heavy breath.

"It's not that easy," Evelyn spoke up. "We can't prove he took those pictures—"

"Who the hell else would have taken them?" Linda demanded.

"Both of your fingerprints are going to be on all of them, since you went through everything when you found them," Evelyn said, keeping her voice calm and even. "I know it seems obvious to you, but that will plant reasonable doubt in a court case. And although the pictures are a concern, there's nothing overtly pornographic. We might be able to make a case on it, but it would be sketchy. We need more."

"I want—"

"He's on the backburner," Sophia said. "That doesn't mean we've forgotten about it. That doesn't mean we won't pursue it. But right now, Haley is our concern. We'll worry about Pete once we find her, okay?"

Linda seemed to deflate, her shoulders slumping and her chin dropping almost to her chest. "Where is she?" Linda asked, her voice near a whisper. "After everything with Jordan... I can't believe what he was doing. He seemed to really care about Haley."

"I think he did care about her, in his own way," Evelyn said, even as Sophia's lips curled up with distaste.

"But you think Haley's disappearance was connected to what Jordan was doing?"

The way she said it, as though it wasn't a question but a confirmation, made Evelyn shoot Sophia a sideways glance. Sophia looked at her feet as Evelyn answered, "Maybe in a roundabout way. We're running a lead, and we want to get back to it, okay?"

"You think you've found her?" Linda demanded.

"Not yet. But we're working on it. I promise, the second we find Haley, we'll call you."

A tiny smile, projecting hope and relief and nerves, lit Linda's face, then disappeared. "Okay. I'll let you go and work. Just find her. Please. Bring my girl home."

"We'll do our best," Sophia said, and Linda nodded, heading back to her car.

Evelyn followed Sophia back inside and Sophia kept her head down again, not making eye contact with anyone as she hurried back to the war room.

Five hours later, after numerous false leads and Sophia drinking more coffee than should have been humanly possible, she shouted, "I've got it!"

Evelyn jerked in her seat, taking her eyes off the screen she'd been staring at all day. She tried not to get too excited, because they thought they'd found Eric and Samuel's trail before, only to land at a dead end. "What did you find?"

"Check this out," Sophia said, sounding triumphant and looking a little glassy-eyed. She turned her laptop screen toward Evelyn. "Name-change document. Two of them actually. For Eric and Samuel Davids."

"They became Eric and Samuel DuPaine," Evelyn read, her excitement starting to build. "No wonder we couldn't track them. I bet Eric was panicked and didn't have a plan when he drove his brother to the hospital. Then staff asked for his brother's name, and Eric's instant response is his real first name."

"He tries to fix his mistake by adding on their old last name. That makes sense," Sophia said. "And it gets better." Sophia leaned over and minimized the name-change information, then jabbed at the information that came up her screen. "This is where they live. It's in Highland County."

It was in the same area where Gillian had been picked up after her escape. Evelyn peered at the address, and the map Sophia had dragged up next to it. The house was in the middle of nowhere, surrounded by lots of country land and almost no other population for miles. "You're right. It's got to be them."

"Now, do we want to keep digging, see if we can find a reason for a warrant? Or do we want to go out there on a pretext? Because I've got to tell you, I'm worried about how long it's already been since Gillian escaped. Every day that goes by…" Sophia lifted her hands.

Evelyn frowned, feeling as anxious as Sophia to rush to the house. "This guy is smart enough to abduct Haley out of her own school without anyone spotting him. He stalked Gillian and grabbed her, leaving behind a town convinced that someone else in her life had taken her. A pretext isn't going to work. Eric DuPaine may be socially inept, but he's intelligent. And he's always been an outsider, so he spends a lot of time *watching* people. He'll recognize the signs that we're lying to him and refuse to let us in the door. Then where will we be?"

Sophia nodded slowly, slumping down in her chair.

"Besides, we don't want to let him know we're on to him or he might kill Haley and run. We need a warrant, so when we show up, we can take him by surprise and he has no option. We go in hard and get her out of there."

"Well, I can get on board with that plan." Sophia dragged her laptop back to her. "Let's keep digging."

"You know what we haven't figured out?" Kyle asked at the same time Jimmy muttered, "We should have enough now, if Evelyn is right."

"Enough for what?" Kyle asked as Jimmy said, "What haven't we figured out?"

Jimmy made a snort of amusement. "What time is it? I think I forgot lunch."

"Lunch has come and gone, man. We worked through it. It's past four."

It had been almost five hours since Evelyn had called and let them know she and Detective Lopez were feeling confident that a man named Eric DuPaine was their kidnapper. Apparently he used the name Eric Davids sometimes, so Kyle had immediately talked to their Cryptoanalysis experts, asking them to dive back into the customer lists. With two names to try plugging into the code—Liam Palmer and Eric Davids—the odds of figuring out how Jordan and Nate had been coding the customer list increased.

"How the hell did two rich kids skating along on trust funds and exploiting women for extra cash figure out how to code this list so damn well?" Jimmy asked, stretching his arms over his head and leaning so far back in the conference room chair he almost tipped it.

"Did you look at Jordan's major?" Kyle asked, trying to keep a straight face as Jimmy frantically jerked himself upright.

"What?"

"Dual major, I should have said. Math and business management. This kid was smart. And you know his dad is a whiz at computer code. It's not really a surprise he was in charge of this end of it and Nate just handled recruitment and the actual…transactions, for lack of a better word."

"Yeah, I guess," Jimmy said. "So, what haven't we figured out? Besides how to crack this stupid code."

"Where's Nate's car?"

"Shit. You're right. There was no vehicle at the scene. So, either someone drove him there and left him, or someone dumped his vehicle."

"I'm thinking it's the second one. I can't imagine

Haley driving Nate out there unless he forced her to do it, and then, honestly, I don't see him making her drive. Jordan was analytical, looking at this as a business venture. Nate wanted to be there when it happened. He got off on the power and control, and the manipulation of talking these women into going home with him and then blackmailing them with it. He would have forced her into his car."

Jimmy shrugged. "Maybe he did. Maybe she drove his car somewhere remote and then…hmm. She didn't call Jordan to pick her up, I assume. Maybe she called her stepdad? She could have claimed to be out there for some other reason."

"But neither Jordan nor Pete mentioned anything like that to Evelyn or Sophia, and neither did Haley's best friend. What if Haley went there with Nate, not knowing where he was taking her? When they get there, either he tries to hit on her, or he tries to sell her to a customer who's waiting. She freaks out and fights him, and the customer is already there, and Haley is stuck with Nate's car. Either Haley's attack kills Nate, or the customer—Eric—finishes him off and decides since he's already been promised Haley, he'll go back and grab her."

"Then what happened to his car?" Jimmy asked.

"Maybe he parked somewhere and walked? I don't know. Neither scenario is perfect, but Haley is a high school kid with no sign of violent behavior in her history. Even if she killed Nate, it was because she was afraid, not because she wanted him dead. I just don't see her having the presence of mind to hide the car but leave the body that way, almost displayed."

Jimmy nodded slowly. "But someone who'd kidnap two girls definitely would. Shit. I can't believe we didn't think of this sooner."

Neither could Kyle. It was a major oversight. But their discovery at the old dance club had come at a time when they were desperately looking for a way to connect it to Jordan Biltmore. He'd been focused on getting the kid in a jail cell, so he couldn't keep going after Evelyn.

"It could explain the week in between Nate's death and Haley's disappearance, if Haley got out of there after Nate died. Then the customer had to track her down. All right. Let's get the license and description and get a BOLO out on the car. But warn anyone who spots it not to approach, just to follow and report back immediately. You want to do that? Because I want to call Evelyn and run this by her, see if it resonates. She might have an idea of what Eric would have done with the car—hide it or take it home."

"Sure," Jimmy said, but before either of them could dial, Jimmy suddenly dropped his phone and swore.

"What is it?"

"Eric Davids. I know that name." Jimmy started digging through the huge stacks of paper, until he waved one at Kyle. "Damn it! He's not a customer. He's a videographer. That shell company Nate owned that bought Warehouse 53? Before they shut down the nightclub, they hired someone to put in a video security system."

"Or a video spy system," Kyle said, thinking of the unhooked camera near where they'd found Nate's body. He was still pondering that when his cell phone rang.

"McKenzie," he answered.

"We got it!"

"What?" It took Kyle a second to place the just-graduated-high-school voice, but then he realized. "Cryptoanalysis," he mouthed to Jimmy.

"This was what we needed. Two names to go on, and

more letters than we had with just Liam Palmer," the agent said excitedly. "Which, you know, has duplicates, so we had fewer letters to try to pair overall. With some codes, it would actually be *helpful*, but not the way this kid did it. Smart as hell, I'm telling you. Anyway, we used a combination of—"

"Sorry," Kyle interrupted. "But can you give me the quick and simple version?"

"Sure," the agent said, his enthusiasm replaced with resentment. "We've decoded the customer list. We've got over fifty names on here, and almost all of them are repeat customers. Some are regulars, as in everyday kind of regulars. Until about a month and a half ago, that is, at which point, nothing. And from what I can tell, just three women were used in the operation."

"The three we know about," Kyle said. "Okay. I want to know about this particular customer. What can you tell me about Davids?"

"He shows up on the date book part just over two months ago. Handful of visits."

So, Eric had found the business because he'd been hired to set up a camera system, and he'd stayed for the girls.

The agent added, "The book says that Eric, uh, never got what he paid for, if you catch my drift."

"Performance problems?"

"Yeah. There's also a notation here about preferences. You want to hear that?"

"Not really, but tell me."

"Ponytails and knee socks. Then the last visit also said pom-poms. I don't know if that's some kind of euphemism—"

"No," Kyle said. "It's actual cheerleading pom-poms. Probably after he spotted Haley."

"This is Haley Cooke, right? It's connected to that missing teenager case?"

"Yeah."

"Then I have one more name that might be of interest."

"Lay it on me."

"Isn't the stepfather's name Pete Varner?"

Kyle held in the slew of swear words that wanted to burst out. "Yeah. He's on the list?"

"Yep. And he's got some weird proclivities, too."

"Okay. Send the whole thing over. It's time to start getting arrest warrants."

26

"There it is," Sophia whispered.

Evelyn crouched next to her, sticking close to the cold ground, making certain to stay below the ridge-line as she peered through the darkness. In the distance was a plain brick ranch, surrounded by a handful of fir trees, swaying in the wind. A few hundred yards to the right was another building, an old red barn in the process of crumbling.

Evelyn glanced back at the weathered ranch, which looked forlorn through her binoculars. Shades were drawn over all the windows, no lights visible. But the house was ominous, all by itself in the middle of no-where. Even if she didn't know the house was owned by a man who locked teenage girls in his basement, it would fill her with unease.

"Eric DuPaine's house," Kyle said softly.

He was hunched beside her, wearing Kevlar and car-rying not just his standard Glock pistol on his hip, but also a battering ram in his hand and a shotgun slung over his shoulder. Jimmy fidgeted next to him, dressed similarly, one hand reflexively stroking his beard and the other hovering near his weapon.

Kyle had called in a ton of favors to get a warrant

immediately, so they could go out to Eric DuPaine's house and make entry. The minute the approval had come through, they'd gotten in Kyle's SUV and driven out to Highland County, watching the sun sink lower and lower in the sky as the houses became fewer and farther apart.

Now they were finally here and Evelyn hoped they weren't already too late. "No sign of movement," she reported as she stared at the house, hoping to see some evidence Haley was still in there, still alive.

"I don't see any obvious signs of a security system, either," Kyle replied as he peered through his own set of binoculars. Then he glanced down at his watch, glowing green in the dark night. "It's midnight. All the lights are off in the house. Let's hope both brothers are asleep."

"What's this guy going to do when we breach?" Jimmy asked, looking at Evelyn. "Try to get out, try to protect the brother, try to get to Haley?"

"He'll want to protect both of them. If Samuel hadn't attempted to help Haley and Gillian escape, I'd say his brother would be his first priority, then Haley. But since he did? We can't be sure. Still, he'll either run or fight. Unless we get him off guard, he's not going to simply surrender. He's planned too long for this to just give up because we come in there."

"And the brother?" Jimmy asked.

"Don't underestimate him. He's got a hell of a lot of loyalty to his older brother. If Eric tries to fight back, Samuel might join in to try to keep him safe."

"Well, let's get in there fast and take them down before they have a chance to do anything," Kyle said. "Stick to the tree line until we get close. And then stick with the plan. Let's move."

He got to his feet, running in a low crouch as he

darted from the cover of one fir tree to the next along the border of the property. Jimmy followed close behind, then Sophia, and Evelyn brought up the rear.

She was in the suit she'd been wearing all day, but she'd traded her low heels for a pair of gym shoes she kept in the trunk of her car. Without a coat over everything, the frigid night air chilled her as she raced for the end of the tree line.

Then the four of them huddled together, assessing again. "House still looks dark," Kyle said, shifting the battering ram. "Everyone ready?"

He glanced back, and Jimmy gave a quick, curt nod, looking jumpy. Sophia had her weapon gripped tightly in both hands, finger lined up alongside the trigger guard.

"Let's do this," she said.

Evelyn took her SIG out of its holster, the grip both familiar and foreign. She'd used the same gun during her entire tenure as an agent, but her nearly two years at the BAU required more brain than brawn. Rarely did she pull her weapon outside of target practice. She looked over at Kyle and gave a curt nod.

Then they were off, running in a staggered formation toward the front door. She and Jimmy kept their weapons leveled on the windows, even though there was no sign of movement, and Sophia covered Kyle as he raced up to the door, lifted the battering ram and slammed it into the door. It splintered, but didn't break.

From her peripheral vision, she saw him flinch and then hit it again, this time sending the door into the house in two large pieces. "FBI!" Kyle boomed as he raced inside.

Anticipation and nerves blended as the rest of them followed. In the back of her mind, Evelyn registered that

Kyle's shoulder was giving him problems, that he wasn't almost back to 100 percent like he'd told her. *Worry about it later*, she reminded herself as she glanced left and right.

Inside, the front of the house was exactly as Gillian had described. Her pulse picked up, the certainty that they were in the right place. They'd come into a small, bland entryway. There was a closed door ahead of her, with a dead bolt on the outside, up high. It had to lead to the basement.

As planned, Kyle and Jimmy continued into the depths of the dark house as Sophia slid the lock open quietly and nodded at Evelyn. She yanked the door open, flipped the lights on and off three times to disorient whoever was down there, then moved out of the way so Evelyn could go in first.

The steps were the most dangerous place, because she couldn't tell who was at the bottom, or where they might be hiding. So, she raced down as quickly as possible, staying close to one side to try to reduce the target she'd make. She was wearing a bulletproof vest, but that wouldn't help her if Eric DuPaine could make a head shot.

"Now," Evelyn said when she reached the bottom, and Sophia flipped the lights on again.

Evelyn spun from one side to the other, cataloging the space, searching for hiding places, hoping to see just Haley. But she saw no one. It looked empty, but she knew that didn't mean it was.

Directly in front of her was a bathroom, no door, just as Gillian had described. A stack of washcloths on the floor, a simple toilet and sink and nowhere to hide.

Were the washcloths bloody? She peered a little

closer, her heart thudding an affirmative, even as she kept moving, kept assessing.

Behind her, Sophia pounded down the stairs. To her right was a sagging mattress, lying on the concrete floor, a thick blanket on top. Beyond it, she saw a furnace and water heater. And at her feet, a dark red stain that could only be blood, hastily cleaned.

But where was Haley?

Evelyn glanced left, taking in the bare, empty space, just concrete floors and walls, and lots of spiderwebs. Then she swiveled back to the right, hope and nerves jumping as she approached the furnace and spotted a piece of red fabric sticking out. Could it be Haley, hiding when she heard the crash of the battering ram?

Evelyn glanced quickly at Sophia, nodding at the furnace, and keeping her weapon level as they approached. They split left and right, so if it wasn't Haley, they wouldn't make one big easy target.

But when Evelyn darted into the space beside the equipment, she discovered nothing but a duffel bag, a red sweatshirt spilling out of it. A sweatshirt she recognized from pictures at the Neville police station walls. Haley's sweatshirt.

"Where's Haley?" Sophia asked as they glanced around the empty basement, just as Kyle's voice called down to her from upstairs.

"The house is empty."

Evelyn's tensed shoulders came down and she holstered her weapon, meeting Sophia's troubled gaze.

There was no question Haley Cooke had been here. But where was she now?

"I think I just found all of the tapes from the human trafficking operation," Kyle announced, holding up a big green duffel bag in what had to be Eric DuPaine's bedroom.

The other bedroom was clearly Samuel's, fitted with extra-large doorways and an accessible bathroom. Most of the brothers' personal documents had been cleared out of both rooms. They'd packed light, though, probably leaving fast, because they'd left behind what had to be most of their clothes, books and other belongings.

And apparently they'd left so fast they hadn't even remembered to grab the tapes.

Or at least Evelyn assumed they'd gone together, taking Haley with them. The bloodstain on the basement concrete was the only one they'd found. She hoped it was from Samuel's fall down the stairs, but there was no way to know for sure. It was big enough to suggest a serious injury but not so bad that it meant certain death.

Still, if the blood was Samuel's, and he'd left urgent care before being treated, what if it had been so serious he'd died since then? After learning why Eric wanted Haley, she didn't think he'd kill her for trying to escape. He'd just think she needed more training. But if that attempt led to his brother's death? Then Haley's time was limited.

They needed to find her fast.

Evelyn pulled her attention away from a framed picture on the nightstand that was nagging at her memory and glanced over at Kyle. "How do you know it's from the trafficking business?"

"They're labeled with names I recognize from the customer book we found. And Nate Stokes had some pretty distinctive handwriting—this is definitely it."

"Too bad we don't have anyone left to prosecute in that case, since they're all dead," Jimmy muttered.

"Well, the owners might be dead," Kyle replied. "But the customers aren't."

Sophia looked up from digging through Eric's drawers. "Any updates on those arrests? Pete Varner in particular? I want to see that bastard behind bars."

They'd gotten a handful of other warrants at the same time as Eric's, customers they could easily pinpoint. Most they were waiting to execute, but since Linda had kicked Pete out of the house, they wanted to pick him up now, while they knew where he was staying—a cheap hotel on the outskirts of Neville.

Jimmy pulled out his cell phone, tapped the screen, then shook his head. "No word yet from the agents we sent to make the arrest."

"What the hell do you think Eric was doing with the trafficking tapes?" Sophia asked.

Kyle shook his head. "My best guess is that he stole them. It's possible he's the one who killed Nate, and that was on tape. Or he was worried they'd taped him when he'd come in. Just because he couldn't perform doesn't mean his actions were legal."

"Maybe he only left behind the ones he wasn't on," Sophia suggested.

"Maybe," Kyle said. "We'll find out when we go through them."

"Why was he paying for sex, anyway?" Sophia looked at Evelyn. "I thought you said he'd be sexually inexperienced, awkward. And he took Haley and Gillian because they were nice to him, innocent."

"It's a progression," Evelyn said absently, still looking around the room. "His search for normalcy begins by trying to create a sexual experience. But even if they pretend to enjoy it, he's not fooled, and it's not what he wants. He wants a real girlfriend. But he doesn't know how to get one. Then he sees Haley and he decides to try something different."

"Okay, I get why the motivation matters," Jimmy jumped in. "But can we go back to the tapes? How'd he get them? Seems a little weird that they'd keep them at the old club, although Eric set up their system, so he might have known where they hid the tapes. Guy had a freelance business and he set up video monitoring systems for Nate on the property."

"Where the *hell* did they go?" Sophia spoke over Kyle. "If the DuPaines have any other property, I couldn't find it. This is the only thing that came up in either name. You think they took off right after visiting that urgent care center?"

"Probably," Evelyn said. Which meant they were already five days behind. Five days for Eric to come up with a new location, maybe even a new state. Five days for Samuel's injury to get worse. Five more days that Haley was alone with them, while Eric's whole plan unraveled—and, Evelyn suspected, his mental state along with it.

The four of them had been going through the DuPaine household for the past three hours, trying to find any clue as to where the brothers could have taken Haley. So far, they'd come up with a lot of books on living off the land, and even a handful on raising children and homeschooling. But nothing that gave them any clue where Eric might run to if he needed to disappear again.

But if he could make himself and his six-year-old brother completely fall off the map when he was just fourteen, what could he do now, at thirty-six?

"Hey," Jimmy said, spinning around from his spot near the nightstand, an empty key chain dangling from one gloved finger. "Does Eric own a BMW?"

"Not that we know of," Sophia said.

Kyle set the duffel bag down and reached across the bed for the empty key chain. "Nate Stokes did."

"I bet that's where Eric got the tapes," Jimmy suggested. "Nate probably had them in his car. We know he hid the customer book, possibly from Jordan. Maybe he was moving these, too, and Eric found them when he took the car."

"Let's get his license plate number," Sophia said, excitement in her voice.

"On it," Jimmy said, texting away on his phone. "We already have a BOLO out on the car, but I'll pull the info."

Evelyn looked around Eric's bedroom, cataloging all the things that weren't right. "This house is all wrong. It bothers me."

"No kidding," Jimmy agreed, not looking up as he continued to text. "Everything in this place is dark and dingy and depressing. I felt claustrophobic in here after five minutes."

"That's not what I mean. Gillian said Eric was getting ready for the future. But nothing about this house is prepped for her or Haley. It's barely functional for Eric and Samuel. I mean, it has the basics, but look at this room. There's hardly any personality. If they'd planned to bring wives up here, what were they going to do with them? There's no soundproof room with a lock, and this room certainly hasn't been prepped for a woman."

"Good point," Kyle agreed. "But getting ready for the future could mean anything. It could just be about brainwashing them enough to make them want to live here."

"Gillian thought he was literally getting the house ready for them," Evelyn argued. "But what if it wasn't *this* house?" She picked up the framed picture of a little white cabin on a small lake that had been nagging at her since the second she'd seen it. "What if it's this one?"

Sophia straightened from digging through Eric's drawers, her forehead creasing. "I recognize that place."

Jimmy and Kyle peered closer, but both of them shook their heads.

"How would you possibly recognize something Eric DuPaine owns?" Kyle asked, just as Jimmy swore, "No fucking way."

"What?" Evelyn asked.

"I just heard back from the agents we sent to get Pete Varner. He checked himself out of the hotel. The guy's in the wind."

Evelyn reached a hand out to grab Sophia, who suddenly swayed backward, looking unnaturally pale.

Before she could ask what was wrong, Sophia said, "That's why I recognize the cabin."

"This is Pete's place?" Evelyn glanced down at the image again, and this time, a new image imposed itself over the top in her mind. A different image of the same house. A picture that had three people in it. A picture she'd seen in Haley's bedroom.

"No," Sophia said. "It belongs to Linda Varner."

27

"That's Linda's cabin," Sophia said.

"And that's Nate's BMW," Jimmy added.

Their words came through over Evelyn's headset and she craned forward to peer out the tiny window of the helicopter Kyle had taken from the FBI's fleet. Down below, in the driveway of a small white cabin she recognized from the picture in the DuPaine house, was a bright blue BMW.

"They're here." Sophia's determined voice, fueled with half a pot of coffee she'd downed at the hangar, came through.

"I think so," Evelyn agreed, nerves settling in her stomach as Kyle continued past without slowing or circling.

With the sheer number of military bases in Virginia and the surrounding area, the sound of a helicopter shouldn't spook anyone, as long as it didn't linger. And it was the quickest way to get to Haley. She hoped.

They'd sent a pair of officers to Linda Varner's house as soon as Sophia had identified the cabin. Evelyn didn't think she was involved, but how the hell had Eric DuPaine known about Linda's cabin? If Linda was connected in some way, she wanted eyes on her. And if she wasn't, Evelyn wanted someone protecting her, because they still had no idea where Pete had gone, or if he was gunning for Linda after she'd kicked him out of her house.

They'd also sent officers to sit with Bill Cooke, because once upon a time, it had been his cabin, too. From what Sophia remembered from her brief discussion with Linda after she'd seen the picture on Haley's dresser, Haley had loved the place. They'd spent summers there when she was little, but hadn't gone in many years, not since the family dynamic had started to sour. Linda had gotten the cabin in the divorce, and apparently it had pissed Bill off, especially since she and Haley hadn't used the place since.

Evelyn glanced around as they started to descend, lowering almost straight down, shooting up bits of grass and dirt and snow. The sun was rising in the sky, sending streaks of pinks and purple over the world.

"This is it," Sophia said as Kyle set the helicopter down in an empty field near the cabin.

She looked nervous as she tossed her headset on the seat and jumped out. The little vacation community was popular in the summer, with a handful of cabins situated on a big man-made lake. In the winter, when the lake partially froze over and the community center was closed, they'd been told it tended to be empty. A good place to hide away from the world.

"I sure as hell hope they brought Haley with them and didn't kill her and dump her somewhere along the way," Sophia said.

"Let's just be ready for anything," Kyle said, a little slower to get out, a wary expression on his face that told her his thoughts were traveling the same direction as hers: this whole scenario was wrong.

Jimmy climbed out of the helicopter last, one hand stroking his beard and the other tightening the sides of his bulletproof vest. He checked his cell phone one last time before tucking it away, and told them, "Police are with Bill now. He's flipping out, since they're not telling him anything. No one's answering at Linda's house."

"Well, we don't have time to wait," Sophia said, her weapon already in hand and anxiety on her face as she stared into the distance toward the cabin, just out of sight behind a line of trees. "Tell the agents to get in Linda's house. Kick the door in if they have to, and I'll take the heat for the decision. Let's go. I know it's still early, but with our luck, Eric or Samuel is an early riser or a light sleeper and they're wondering about that helicopter that flew past. I want to get in there now."

She took off at a careful, crouched run, and the rest of them fell in behind her.

The grass was damp and only half frozen, sucking at Evelyn's gym shoes as she ran through the long field toward the cabin beyond a line of trees and a second, bigger house that would block the helicopter from view if Eric or Samuel glanced out the window.

And then, before Evelyn had really prepared, they were there, racing up the side of the cabin toward the front door. Just like in Virginia, Kyle went first. This time, instead of hauling a ram with him, he used his foot, and one powerful kick sent the door crashing into the house.

Then they all raced inside, weapons ready. She and Sophia split left, while Kyle and Jimmy went right, but they all darted around a little wall at the front that opened into a bigger room in back. There was a huge picture window, and an open sliding glass door that led out onto a huge deck.

And right in front of them—Eric DuPaine. He was bigger than she'd expected, with thinning brown hair, frenzied brown eyes and a muscled hand locked around Haley's neck as he held her in front of him as a terrified human shield.

"Don't move! Drop your weapons, or I kill her!" Eric shouted, his voice unsteady, his eyes darting everywhere at once.

Kyle didn't blink, didn't twitch, didn't move his weapon an inch from where he had it sighted on the top of Eric's head. But he didn't dare pull the trigger. Because Eric might not be able to snap Haley's neck before a bullet took him out, but the knife he had pressed so hard against her side that tears ran down her face was a real problem.

Evelyn's words from right before they'd breached the house in Virginia ran through his mind. This was Eric DuPaine's fairy-tale ending, and they were destroying it. If he couldn't run, he would fight. And although she hadn't said it, he could see it in Eric's eyes. If he couldn't have Haley, no one would.

Off to his right, he could see Jimmy's weapon lowering a little, but not dropping. To his left, Sophia holstered hers and put her hands in the air. Evelyn started moving away from all of them, farther left.

"Stop right there! Now! Or I'm going to hurt her! Don't make me hurt her!"

"Eric," Evelyn said softly, very slowly holstering her own weapon. "You don't want to hurt Haley. I know you love her."

Eric's hand trembled, the knife dancing along Haley's side, slicing little cuts in her thin T-shirt and making blood dot the fabric. In front of him, Haley's blond hair hung in limp clumps, and her eyes looked enormous in her gaunt face. But even as tears dripped down her face, she locked her eyes on his, silently begging Kyle to help her.

In that instant, all the footage he'd seen of her on those damn news features ran through his mind. Haley standing on top of a cheerleading pyramid, grinning, looking so proud and so young. Haley's mom, pain in her eyes but strength in her voice as she begged whoever had stolen her daughter to bring her home. Haley's friends and classmates and teachers, all talking about how nice Haley was to everyone she met, how they all expected her to go on to make a difference in the world.

Kyle wanted to reassure her with his eyes that they would get her out of this, that she would still get that amazing future, but he had to keep most of his focus on Eric and the relevant surroundings—to read the situation perfectly. He glanced out into the space beyond the house. A big pond, surrounded by weeping willow trees with huge tree trunks, a few other houses in the distance. Where was Samuel DuPaine?

He tried to will the thought to one of the others, but they all seemed laser-focused on Eric. And he didn't dare move his weapon, not when he was the only one with a clear shot. Jimmy had a better angle, but he'd lowered his own weapon so far that it would take him too long to lift it again if Eric suddenly decided to use that knife against Haley. And Kyle was the only one with significant training in this sort of hostage situation, from his time on the HRT.

"You cared for her over this past month," Evelyn continued, still in that same soft, soothing tone she might use with a small, frightened child. "Please, do what's right for her now, Eric."

He shook his head, a frantic double-jerk movement that made Kyle cringe and Haley yelp as the knife slipped and drew a little more blood.

"Please," Haley sobbed. "Let me go."

"No!" he shouted, stepping backward, toward the open sliding glass door, pulling her with him.

Kyle took a step forward, too, keeping his gun level on Eric's face, but Eric shifted a little more, making Kyle's shot infinitely harder. And since leaving the HRT, his weapons practice had gone from many hours every day to once a week at most.

He could feel the sweat beading on his temples, and he suddenly felt hot in the too-cold house. Could he make this shot, hit Eric without taking Haley with him, before Eric could hurt her? Kyle's bad shoulder twitched, an unexpected spasm, probably from tweaking it when he'd used that battering ram.

"Jimmy," he muttered quietly, hoping his partner would know he might need to be the one to fire.

"No!" a new voice rang out, making Jimmy whip his attention—and his weapon—toward the man emerging from a long, dark hallway to the left.

Samuel DuPaine rolled closer, moving fast in a lightweight wheelchair, clearly unarmed as he insisted to his brother, "Let her go!"

Before Eric could even consider it, Sophia's gaze darted from Samuel to Eric and back again. Kyle started to give a warning, but it was too late.

Sophia pulled her Glock from its holster and darted behind Samuel, locking him in a choke hold and putting her gun to his head. She slid her finger under the trigger guard, a furious and untamed glint in her eyes as she screamed at Eric, "Let Haley go, or your brother is dead."

* * *

"Sophia," Evelyn said, her pulse leaping as she looked from Sophia to Eric and back again. "What the hell are you doing?"

She said the words quietly, hoping they wouldn't carry to Eric. If Sophia shot Samuel, Evelyn knew Eric would kill Haley.

Sophia's lips turned up in a near snarl. "I'm not letting him kill anyone else."

"Eric hasn't hurt anyone," she said calmly, a little louder, so Eric could hear her, even though they suspected Eric might have killed Nate. "Let's keep it that way, okay? Everyone drop the weapons. No one needs to get hurt today."

"He did hurt someone," Sophia snapped. "If you think he's not responsible for Gillian, locking herself in the dark like she's afraid of the whole world, you're wrong. If you think him and everyone else even remotely connected to that damn trafficking ring weren't responsible for Quincy, you're wrong. If assholes like him didn't want to *purchase women*, those stupid kids wouldn't have had a business to protect. Quincy wouldn't have lied, and he'd still be here." Her lips curled, trembling with disgust. "Samuel sat by and let it happen. He's just as guilty. And I'm not letting Eric hurt anyone else."

Evelyn looked over at Kyle and Jimmy. Kyle hadn't moved. His arms were locked, his weapon steady on Eric, but the tension in his arms told her the shot was no guarantee. Jimmy's weapon swiveled back and forth, until finally he settled on Eric, too.

"You can't let her do that!" Eric barked.

Evelyn wished she believed Sophia wouldn't pull the trigger, that it was a mistaken ploy to get Eric to lower his weapon. But she couldn't be sure. Evelyn knew Sophia carried guilt over the way things had gone with Quincy, over not finding Haley earlier, too, that she was redirecting at Eric. But would she be willing to throw away her own career by killing Samuel?

Eric's brother had gone deadly still in front of her, just his hands moving as they opened and closed reflexively over Sophia's choke hold. He looked younger than she'd expected, even though she'd known his age.

"Samuel," Evelyn said, making him turn his head a tiny bit toward her. "Your brother always looked after you." She hoped she was taking the right track as she continued, "He looked after you your entire life, right?"

He gave a tiny nod, the only movement he could manage with Sophia's arm locked around him.

Hope flared, but she didn't dare look up at Eric. This was a risk, but maybe her only move if Sophia was as close to the edge as she appeared. "But he doesn't need to do that anymore, does he? You can both move forward."

Another small nod, and Evelyn peeked up at Sophia and then over at Eric. They'd both gone very still, listening.

Evelyn made her tone a little stronger, a little firmer. "You can choose to let Haley go. You know she needs to go back to her life, to her family."

"Yes," Samuel agreed softly as Sophia's hand loosened just a little from his neck.

"She'd be better off dead than back with that family!" Eric shouted.

Then a bullet blasted through the glass door behind him, raining shards of glass all around them. Another one followed as Evelyn dove for the ground, wondering who the hell was shooting.

28

"What's happening?" Sophia shouted, then more bullets blasted around her as Evelyn rolled, pulling her SIG from its holster.

Sophia dropped to the floor, too, and Evelyn gripped Samuel's chair, tipping him over so he slammed down with them. Across from her, Kyle screamed something she couldn't make out over the bullets, then Jimmy dropped to his knees and fired a bunch of shots through the open doorway beside Eric.

Instead of letting Haley go and heading for cover, a feverish glaze came over Eric's eyes and he dropped his arm from her neck to her waist, dragging her outside with him, toward the gunfire instead of away from it.

Then Evelyn was up, running toward them, too, firing her weapon in the direction of the gunshots. Kyle was beside her as she pounded onto the deck toward Eric, yelling at him to stop, yelling at whoever was shooting to stop firing, too.

But Eric kept moving backward, getting closer and closer to the edge of the deck, with no railing between him and the water. He dragged Haley with him, even as she scrambled to get away from him. "You can't have her!" Eric yelled.

"She shouldn't be yours, either!" a voice shouted from much closer than Evelyn had expected.

The shooter. It had to be. And she recognized that voice.

"Pete Varner," she whispered to Kyle. But where the hell was he? And what was he doing here?

Eric swiveled toward the sound of the voice, giving Evelyn an angle to shoot him. But he still had that knife along Haley's side. Could she hit him without giving him time to kill Haley? Could she hit him without sending them both over the edge into the water?

"You ruined my life, you bastard!" Pete shouted, then Evelyn saw a flash from beside a tree off to the side of the pond. Another gunshot rang out and Haley let out a shrill, panicked scream.

Then Eric's whole body jerked backward, his eyes wide. He seemed suspended that way for a minute, his body in a backward arc, and then he fell, Haley still flailing in his grasp as he splashed into the frigid water.

From behind a tree, Pete darted away, trying to make an escape.

Rather than leave it on the deck, Evelyn slapped her weapon into Kyle's hand, screamed at him not to let Pete get away, then dove into the water.

Her fingertips slammed into the broken layer of ice at the top, shooting pain and cold through her body before the rest of her followed. Then she was surrounded by it, the cold instantaneous and so much worse than she'd expected.

It made pinpricks of pain burst all over her body, and her lungs seemed to seize, desperate for air even though she shouldn't need it yet. Panic hit, the memory of having her air cut off during a different case racing through her.

She flailed, fighting the urge to gasp for breath, knowing she'd only take in water. Black spots danced under her eyelids and as hard as she tried to shoot back to the surface, she just kept sinking deeper into the icy water.

Kyle leaped off the deck, bypassing the short set of steps leading down into the grass. He kept his own Glock in his hand and put Evelyn's SIG in his holster. His legs pumped, reminding him of his days in the HRT, as he chased down Pete Varner, who was a lot faster than he looked.

The man was weaving between the willow trees along the pond, probably trying to deny Kyle a good shot. But unless he was forced to do it, Kyle wanted the bastard alive.

What the hell was Haley's stepfather doing here? Had he simply been trying to hide out at his wife's rarely used cabin, or had he known Haley would be here? His goal had obviously been to take Eric out, but what if the rest of them hadn't been there? What had his plan been for Haley? And what had he meant when he'd screamed at Eric about ruining his life?

"Stop now!" Kyle yelled, jumping over the protruding roots of a huge willow tree as he gained ground on Pete.

Pete glanced back, looking panicked, and almost went down. He threw his arms wide for balance and kept going.

But it didn't matter. Kyle was close enough.

He took one more step, then launched himself forward, slamming into Pete the way he'd done back in his high school football days. Most men would have stayed down after that kind of hit. But Pete jerked his elbow back, catching Kyle just below his bad shoulder.

Something crunched in his shoulder and pain danced down his arm all the way to his fingertips, and then bounced back the other way, into his chest.

Then Pete tried again, and Kyle rolled away, not sure he could absorb another hit. It gave Pete space to slide out of his grasp.

"I'm not letting that asshole ruin my life!" Pete screamed, sounding unhinged.

He twisted his gun toward Kyle, who forced his bad arm out, grabbing Pete's hand and slamming it into the ground before he could fire. Kyle's shoulder felt like it was on fire, but he ignored it and hit Pete again, this time under the chin.

While Pete tried to recover, Kyle rolled, using his good arm to deliver another hit to Pete's wrist. When the gun slid out of his grasp, Kyle got to his knees and flipped Pete over.

He tried to cuff Pete, but the man was thrashing violently, and Kyle struggled to hold him down with his good hand as Pete continued to yell.

"He took everything away from me. He deserves to die! My wife, my house, my girl, everything I worked for, everything! And he played me, cornering me outside the news station, convincing me to do a special feature on Haley. Convincing me I'd be helping her. I let him in my house, let him film her room! That bastard deserves to suffer!"

Kyle slammed him back to the ground, practically sitting on him. He didn't have time for the man's insane rants, not when it had been a good five minutes since he'd watched Evelyn dive through a layer of ice to get to Haley.

A lot could happen in five minutes.

He wrestled a pair of handcuffs on Pete and dragged

him back toward the cabin as fast as he could, looking everywhere for Evelyn.

He didn't see her.

Evelyn pumped her arms and legs, desperately seeking the surface. Desperately seeking air.

Then her panic receded just long enough for her to remember. She had to get Haley.

She opened her eyes, but the cold rushed in, making her feel like she was moving in slow motion, her vision too blurry. A cloud of red bloomed around her. Blood. But she couldn't see Haley or Eric. Where had they gone?

She looked around, knowing her time was limited in this temperature before she was in serious danger. Her air was limited, too. She'd spent too long fighting panic. She needed to find Haley and get out fast.

Then a flash of gold floated past her and Evelyn snagged it. Hair! She reached down farther, realizing the pond wasn't actually that deep here, and scooped Haley up, trying to pull her to the surface.

The girl was limp, and heavy in the freezing water. Evelyn kicked off the ground, trying to propel them both up, but they didn't go far enough, and no matter how she kicked her feet, they started to sink back down.

Her lungs burned for a breath, and Haley felt heavier and heavier on her arm. Panic threatened, the desperate need to draw in air sending warning signals through her brain. Would she have to leave Haley in order to save herself?

She tried kicking them both up again, and this time, when she got near the surface and started to sink again, a hand locked around her wrist and pulled, dragging until her arm was awkwardly over the top of the deck and Evelyn could suck in air.

She kept her shaking grip on Haley as she looked up into Sophia's face. Leaving Evelyn gripping the edge of the deck, Sophia reached down and pulled Haley out first.

Then footsteps pounded toward them, and Kyle grabbed Evelyn, yanking her out of the water so fast she lost her balance. She might have fallen over, except he pulled her to him, wrapping one arm around her tight, the other dangling at his side.

She registered that it wasn't quite right that she could barely feel his warmth, but then she looked over his shoulder and saw Pete Varner, bleeding and cuffed as Jimmy forced him against the cabin wall before he could make a run for it again.

Her ears were waterlogged, but she could hear Pete muttering about how he'd let Eric into his home, and Eric had stolen what was his. She tried to make sense of his words, but her attention was drawn in the other direction.

Through the ruined door, she spotted Samuel, pulling himself forward on his belly through the broken glass, tears on his cheeks as he looked up at her. He must have seen the answer on her face, that his brother hadn't come up with her, because he stopped moving toward them, buried his face in his hands and wept.

Evelyn turned her head a little, and saw Sophia giving Haley mouth-to-mouth. The girl was unnaturally pale and chalky, like a corpse. A violent shiver passed through Evelyn at the sight, and then Haley suddenly spasmed, too, spitting water and sucking in air.

She was alive.

She was going home.

Haley Cooke would have her bright, beautiful future.

Epilogue

Nerves beat a frantic tempo in Evelyn's chest as she stood in front of the plain wood door with the faded gold numbers on the front. The hallway lights were dim, but that didn't disguise how dingy the hotel was. It was freezing, too, but Evelyn wasn't sure if that was because they were stingy with the heat or because she was still cold from her dive into the lake that morning.

She'd spent the afternoon at the hospital, being evaluated for hypothermia and cleared for any other issues, until finally they'd agreed to release her. They'd suggested she go home and rest, but instead, she'd met Kyle and Jimmy at the Neville police station.

There had been tons of paperwork to fill out, from the death of Eric DuPaine to the booking of Samuel DuPaine and Pete Varner, who'd come to the cabin to hide from the police only to discover Eric had taken Haley there. At Sophia's intense, angry interrogation and the threat of Linda's fury, Pete had finally broken down and admitted he knew Eric.

Pete hadn't had any idea Eric knew where the cabin was, or that Eric had been the one to grab Haley until that moment. He'd only gone there to lie low after Linda had found his pictures of Haley. But when he'd seen them at the cabin, he'd become enraged. He'd realized Eric had found the cabin because of him, because Eric had convinced him to talk to his wife about letting Ginger Tippens get an exclusive feature on Haley. They'd filmed in Haley's room, and Eric had spotted the picture of the cabin on Haley's dresser. Eric had asked about the cabin, and Linda had innocently told him all about it.

The one thing Pete hadn't been able to tell them was how Eric had come across Haley in the first place. It had been Samuel who'd confirmed that Pete had unintentionally led Eric to not just the cabin, but Haley, too.

Eric had finally told Samuel the full story once Samuel had tried to set Gillian and Haley free. He'd been ashamed of his brother's actions, but Eric had cared for him his entire life. Although Samuel hadn't admitted this part, Evelyn could tell that he'd also been afraid of Eric—afraid of what he'd seen his brother becoming.

Bit by bit, Samuel had given them the story he'd heard from Eric. He and Pete had been at Warehouse 53 at the same time one day. Eric had been there to work on a video cable problem and he'd seen Pete drive up and show Nate pictures of Haley, requesting someone who resembled her. Apparently he'd gone on and on about what a great girl Haley was, how sweet and kind. Eric had snooped, watching Nate slap Pete, telling him to put the pictures away, and threatening to kick him out, warning him what would happen if Jordan saw them.

Eric had assumed Haley was one of the trafficked women and that Pete was trying to find another one similar to her. Pete's words about Haley had stuck with Eric. Eventually, he'd gone to Nate, asking to buy her, planning to take her away from that life. He'd figured Pete couldn't have her because he didn't have the money, so he'd offered to pay any rate. Nate had still refused.

At first, that was going to be the end of it, but then Eric had seen her on the Neville campus, arguing with Nate. He'd been too far away to hear what was being said, but he'd seen Nate's anger, had seen him grab Haley and watched Haley yank free. Nate's second attempt to grab her had left deep gouges in Haley's arm, but she'd run off even as Nate screamed that she was going to get herself killed.

So, Eric had followed Nate back to the warehouse, asked again to buy Haley. Nate had been furious, told him he was finished and couldn't come back, and Eric had hit him with a fire extinguisher nearby. He'd told Samuel he hadn't intended to kill Nate, but he hadn't been sorry it happened.

Then he'd begun following Haley, learning her routines, and realized that she wasn't connected to the trafficking business at all. He'd become more and more infatuated with her until he'd decided to make her his wife. And after he'd gotten away with having Haley under his control for a while, the rest of his plan had come together. He wanted a wife for Samuel, too.

Samuel had broken down in tears as he'd told them, "All Eric ever wanted was to be normal. For people to stop looking at him as though he was weird or scary or different. Not to be constantly invisible, just the camera guy in the background no one ever really saw. Just to be happy the way other people are. He wanted it for me, too, wanted me to have someone who cared about me as much as he did. He wanted it so badly that he left me all alone."

He hadn't been able to go on after that, and finally they'd left him with the doctors. He'd be in the hospital at least one more night, because he'd gotten an untreated concussion when he'd fallen down the stairs, so they wanted to take a closer look. He'd face charges related to Haley's and Gillian's abductions as an accessory, but somehow Evelyn doubted any punishment the court gave him would be harsher than the torment he'd feel for not doing more to save the girls and prevent his brother's death.

The only thing he'd asked her before she'd left him to the doctors' care, besides how Haley and Gillian were doing, was what would happen to the man who'd shot Eric. Pete Varner had gotten treatment for superficial injuries when Kyle had tackled him outside the cabin, but he was spending the night in jail. And she suspected soon a judge would tell him he'd be spending all of his nights there.

Somehow, she and Kyle had managed to avoid getting shot. Jimmy had two bullets nick him, but he'd only needed a few stitches.

Kyle's shoulder recovery had faced a setback after he'd reinjured it, but he was telling her it wouldn't keep him down for long. And although she knew the pain was worse than he was saying, she believed he'd overcome it.

Sophia had suffered the worst injuries of any of them, from the flying glass shards. But physically, she'd be fine. Her career was less certain. Her actions from the evening would eventually face review, and a lot was probably going to depend on the interpretation of her motives. Were her threats against Samuel real, or had they been all for show, an attempt to get Eric to let Haley go?

Evelyn hadn't known what to say when Sophia had told her she never would have done it. Evelyn had seen the look in Sophia's eyes, seen all the emotions there. And she honestly didn't know. It could have been the truth. But she didn't think even Sophia really knew what she would have done if Eric had killed Haley.

She'd still been debating what she'd eventually tell Internal Affairs as she'd walked down the hall to Haley's hospital room, her limbs oddly stiff. Kyle had been with her the whole way, with Jimmy trailing close behind as soon as he'd gotten stitched up.

Haley had told them the rest as she'd lain in her hospital bed down the hall from Samuel, with her mom and Marissa by her side. She'd never suspected Eric was stalking her, but the week before he'd grabbed her out of her school, Nate had approached her.

He'd wanted Haley to leave Jordan for him, claimed that Jordan was going to hurt her one day. She'd already started to suspect what Jordan was doing, but Nate's words had made her fear for her life. She'd refused Nate, and when she tried to walk away, he'd grabbed her arm, leaving a deep scratch behind. She'd gone home that evening and written the sentence in her notebook, then hidden it in her bed frame.

She'd debated the rest of the week what else to write, second-guessing her fear, but not sure where to turn. Her mom had been away, her dad wasn't someone she'd ever been able to go to for help and Pete Varner had always made her uncomfortable. When she'd said she was afraid of him, but afraid to tell her mom why, Linda had broken down.

Then Evelyn had watched as Haley had reached over, her hands still tinged with purple, and pulled her mom close. They'd both been telling the other that everything would be okay when Evelyn had silently slipped out and left them alone to reunite.

And now here she was, standing in a dirty hotel hallway at almost midnight, freezing despite the ridiculous number of layers she was wearing, and afraid to knock on the door. She glanced down at the number scrawled in her mother's block handwriting, the promise she'd left in Evelyn's mailbox six days ago.

Kyle was waiting in the car downstairs, and was probably going to start wondering if everything was okay soon. She'd been frozen here for too long, debating whether she was making the right decision.

She wasn't sure if she could forgive. She knew she'd never forget. But maybe she needed to give her mother a chance, if nothing else, and let her grandma make up her own mind. Give them all an opportunity to see if they could make a different, better future.

Squeezing her eyes shut, Evelyn lifted her hand and knocked hard, before she could change her mind. Her pulse thudded, faster and faster, until she had to open her eyes because she wouldn't be able to hear if the door opened over the rapid beating of her heart.

The door opened slowly, the chain still on, and Evelyn remembered it was very late, and this wasn't the safest area. "It's me, Evelyn," she croaked.

"Who?" an unfamiliar voice snapped.

Evelyn blinked in the poor lighting, and realized the face in the crack of the doorway wasn't her mother. She glanced down at the number written on the paper, then back at the number on the door, and mumbled an apology.

On autopilot, she trudged back down the stairs, bypassing the elevator she'd discovered on the way up was broken. She stopped by the front desk and asked whether her mother was still checked in, just to be certain, then went outside and got back into the passenger seat of Kyle's car.

She opened her mouth to tell him, but the words wouldn't come, and he didn't seem to need them to know. He just pulled her into his arms. Tucking her head closer, Evelyn closed her eyes and tried not to care that her mother had disappeared again. "Checked out two days ago, didn't say where she was going," the clerk at the front desk had told her.

Evelyn had a brief burst of regret that she'd let herself care again, that she'd tried to make things right with someone who'd never done right by her.

Then Kyle's deep baritone rumbled in her ear. "I'm sorry. But you've got family all around. Your grandma, me. I'm glad you gave it a chance."

And suddenly she realized so was she. Maybe she hadn't gotten her mother back. Maybe she'd never really expected to, not deep down. Maybe what she'd really needed was a little bit of closure.

She'd spent the past two weeks chasing a girl surrounded by secrets that had nearly ended her life. And the moment came back to her, as vivid as if she were ten years old again, when she'd climbed out of that bathroom window in her mom's first-floor apartment. When she'd ran down that dark, empty street in bare feet and torn pajamas. When she'd made the choice not to keep her own secret.

When she'd called her grandma Mabel and put into motion all the things to come in her life. Her journey to become an FBI agent. Her journey to Kyle. Her journey to a life of her own, not so burdened by the secrets and lies from her past.

She lifted her head from Kyle's chest and said, "I'm glad I gave it a chance, too. Now, let's go home."

* * * * *

Acknowledgments

As my *Profiler* series hits the fourth story, I want to send a special thank-you to the team at MIRA and Harlequin, for believing in me. My deepest gratitude to Paula Eykelhof, whom I met at an RWA conference and who, a year later, bought five books from me; it has been an honor to work with you these past few years. To Margaret Marbury and Nicole Brebner, for your support and encouragement. And to everyone in the Sales, Marketing and Art departments, for your passion for books!

Thank you to my agent extraordinaire, Kevan Lyon, for taking a chance on me long before the books were on shelves, and for helping me chase the career path I wanted.

To the FBI special agents and police officers who gave me insight into the job, the cases and the life of a law enforcement officer, thank you for your assistance, and for all you do.

To my first readers—Robbie Terman, Andrew Gulli and, of course, my mom—thank you for the quick turnarounds, the on-point suggestions and the never-ending support. To my sisters, Kathryn and Caroline, and my sister of the heart, Kristen Kobet, thank you for your belief in me!

To my mystery group—Ann Forsaith, Charles Shipps, Sasha Orr and Nora Smith—it's been amazing to share early drafts with you and to laugh and work and climb together. To the fellow writers—Dana Corbit, Heather Novak, Barb Han, Janie Crouch and Tyler Anne Snell— who meet me, virtually or in person, to get "all the words," here's to many more! To Mark Nalbach, thank you for always saying, "I can do that," whenever I have a crazy website or book trailer idea.

To Lee Child, my humble thanks for taking the time to read my last *Profiler* story and offer an endorsement! I can't adequately express how much I appreciate your support.

Thank you to the booksellers and librarians who invited me into their worlds, and invited readers into mine. And finally, thank you to the readers who have picked up my stories, written to me and chatted on social media. I hope to entertain you for years to come!

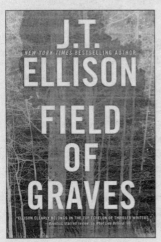

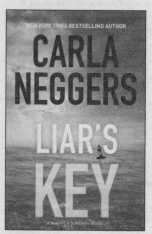

REQUEST YOUR FREE BOOKS!

2 FREE NOVELS
FROM THE SUSPENSE COLLECTION,
PLUS 2 FREE GIFTS!

YES! Please send me 2 FREE novels from the Suspense Collection and my 2 FREE gifts (gifts are worth about $10). After receiving them, if I don't wish to receive any more books, I can return the shipping statement marked "cancel." If I don't cancel, I will receive 4 brand-new novels every month and be billed just $6.49 per book in the U.S. or $6.99 per book in Canada. That's a savings of at least 18% off the cover price. It's quite a bargain! Shipping and handling is just 50¢ per book in the U.S. and 75¢ per book in Canada.* I understand that accepting the 2 free books and gifts places me under no obligation to buy anything. I can always return a shipment and cancel at any time. Even if I never buy another book, the two free books and gifts are mine to keep forever.

191/391 MDN GH4Z

Name _____ (PLEASE PRINT) _____

Address _____ Apt. # _____

City _____ State/Prov. _____ Zip/Postal Code _____

Signature (if under 18, a parent or guardian must sign)

Mail to the **Reader Service:**
IN U.S.A.: P.O. Box 1867, Buffalo, NY 14240-1867
IN CANADA: P.O. Box 609, Fort Erie, Ontario L2A 5X3

Want to try 2 free books from another line?
Call 1-800-873-8635 or visit www.ReaderService.com.

* Terms and prices subject to change without notice. Prices do not include applicable taxes. Sales tax applicable in NY. Canadian residents will be charged applicable taxes. Offer not valid in Quebec. This offer is limited to one order per household. Not valid for current subscribers to the Suspense Collection or the Romance/Suspense Collection. All orders subject to credit approval. Credit or debit balances in a customer's account(s) may be offset by any other outstanding balance owed by or to the customer. Please allow 4 to 6 weeks for delivery. Offer available while quantities last.

Your Privacy—The Reader Service is committed to protecting your privacy. Our Privacy Policy is available online at www.ReaderService.com or upon request from the Reader Service.

We make a portion of our mailing list available to reputable third parties that offer products we believe may interest you. If you prefer that we not exchange your name with third parties, or if you wish to clarify or modify your communication preferences, please visit us at www.ReaderService.com/consumerschoice or write to us at Reader Service Preference Service, P.O. Box 9062, Buffalo, NY 14240-9062. Include your complete name and address.

SUS15R

Turn your love of reading into rewards you'll love with
Harlequin My Rewards

Join for FREE today at
www.HarlequinMyRewards.com

Earn **FREE BOOKS** of your choice.

Experience **EXCLUSIVE OFFERS** and contests.

Enjoy **BOOK RECOMMENDATIONS** selected just for you.

PLUS! Sign up now and get **500** points right away!

Earn **FREE** REWARDS! Join Today!
HarlequinMyRewards.com

MYR16R